THE ABYSSAL DESCENT

THE ABYSSAL DESCENT

ELYSIUM'S MULTIVERSE | BOOK 6

Ranyhin1

Podium

Cover design by Art of Neight

ISBN: 978-1-0394-9297-4

Published in 2025 by Podium Publishing
www.podiumentertainment.com

THE ABYSSAL
DESCENT

CHAPTER 1

"Gentry," the man said, slowly taking Riven's outstretched hand and warily eyeing the other demons stepping out of their portals. "You're . . . a warlock? A summoner? It isn't often you see true battlemages before the C-grades, but after watching your brief fight I'm not sure whether your strength and speed are your focus—or whether it is your magic."

Riven chuckled at the uncomfortable dark elf in gold-trimmed blue robes and shrugged. "Does it matter? The better question is, what do you know about this 'Abyssal Descent' we're about to enter? There are only minutes left, and I'm rather curious about the details."

Gentry's purple eyes flitted to the corpses of the other two drow warriors nearby on the floating, mile-wide platform, or what was left of them, as Athela and Azmoth went to pick up the spatial bags and whatever materials they could salvage from the dead. "You really don't know?"

"I'm in the integration phase, remember?" Riven winked good-naturedly despite the man's discomfort. "My planet hasn't even entered the true multiverse yet. It's still shrouded by Elysium's protections."

The dark elf scowled, looking down at Riven's armor, the ancient unreadable tattoos of Unholy make visible across his face where the helmet had been removed, and then to the large sin-afflicted weapon that had actively flowing streams of blood running along the dark metal. "For an integration-labeled planet, you sure do have quite the set of equipment . . . Equipment that would bankrupt any F-, E-, or D-grade faction should they attempt to buy it at a fair price. And I don't even know how it's possible to acquire the Mythic title—I can't remember there ever being one in our sector of the galaxy."

"Which galaxy?"

"Narwali sector of the Cheshish galaxy in Universe 16. Not that it means anything to you, but your universe is labeled seventy-eight, if you're in the integration phase right now. Integration is mostly complete, and within the next ten thousand years, Elysium should be moving on to Universe 79, wherever it may be." Gentry's free hand hesitantly settled into a pocket as he curiously studied Riven through squinted eyes. "Just who are you?"

Riven's eyebrow raised, and he put a hand around Gen-Fay's waist to pull her close, which is what he was calling the combined bodies of Genua and Fay until they decided to unmerge. "What's that supposed to mean?"

"What do you MEAN, what's that supposed to mean?" Gentry asked, exasperated. "Are you a plant?"

"I don't think I grow leaves, no."

Gentry snapped his fingers in irritation. "You certainly know that's not what I meant!"

"I definitely meant, 'What is that supposed to mean,' and I sure don't know that's not what you meant."

"Stop it!"

Riven chuckled as the amusement from Gluttony rose in turn. "Fine. But in all seriousness, I don't know what you meant by am I a 'plant.'"

"It's a term some people use to describe older factions who breed younglings and place them on pre-integrated worlds in anticipation of Elysium integrating the planet soon. An easy way to conquer worlds," Athela called out, hooded and cloaked and walking toward him in her rogue outfit of black and red leathers made in part from her own bloodsilk. Her red eyes scoured the drow before she handed Riven a spatial sack. "Very rarely does it work, because Elysium usually punishes the faction attempting to cheat the rules—and executes the plant as well."

Riven hummed thoughtfully at the idea, then shook his head and thanked Azmoth when the large demon came over to hand him the other drow's sack in turn. Putting them both in his own, he closed it and flicked his gaze to where the portal arch was starting to rotate. "I'm no plant. Not an intentional one, anyway."

Gentry's frown deepened. "Not intentional? That's . . . an odd way to answer. So you ARE affiliated with another force, then?"

Riven shrugged. "Perhaps. Why does it matter?"

Gentry gestured to the two drow bodies nearby. "Because despite how much I genuinely hated those two self-centered idiots, they were my ticket into an ally enclave. Without them, I'm devoid of any real connections."

He glared back at Riven, and then to Nora, who was flippantly waving around the other token Riven had acquired for her. "And they were also my teammates for descending into the lower levels."

Azmoth snickered, folding all four of his large, clawed arms over his chest. "Bad teammate, let Riven kill all without help fight."

"He makes a good point," Gen-Fay said, the two feminine voices overlapping with one another.

Sighing and glaring, Gentry lifted his hand and facepalmed before dragging that hand over his face with a defeated look. "All right, how about this. I'll tell you all I know about the event, and in turn you'll escort me to my sister's complex on the third floor down. She and I aren't close—in fact, I haven't ever even met her—but she's been there for the past six hundred years and last two cycles. She'll know who I am after I take the bloodborn test. I'm sure she'll have some advice on how to go about this."

Riven, who'd been listening intently up until this point, blinked rapidly in confusion and scratched the back of his head with a clawed gauntlet. "Um . . . did I hear you right? Your sister has been there for six hundred years? Two cycles of three hundred years each?"

Gentry raised his own eyebrow, unamused. "Yes. That's what I said. Some cultivators stay in this place far into the E-grade, even after their soul lattice is completed. Why?"

Pausing and not knowing how to proceed with that information, Riven clicked his tongue a couple times and stared up at the sky. "Well, . . . how old are you, exactly?"

"Me? I'm 192 years old."

Riven nearly choked. "You don't look like you're more than thirty."

Gentry did not reply, only continuing to stare.

Clearing his throat, Riven continued. "And you're just now hitting level 200?"

Gentry's face darkened, and his hand reached for his blade before he took a quick hiss of air into his lungs, letting the anger go. "Are you insulting me, vampire? Unlike some races, the drow do not go around butchering others for their meat. Nor am I on a planet that is full of the opportunities an integration could provide, with wars between our clans only seldom coming. That may be a foreign concept to you, but that is the reality of it."

"But don't you have beasts or animals to fight for leveling?" Riven pressed, still curious.

Gentry's mouth opened, closed, opened, closed, and then opened again before he spoke in quick, irritated clips. "My mother was sick and my father was gone for quite some time. I was needed to rule over our house in his absence and prioritized my mother's care over my own success. Laugh at me like all the others do, if you wish, but my family comes before my personal gain."

It was almost a challenge, and the man's purple eyes flared angrily while glaring Riven down. However, Riven's response was not one the drow elf could have guessed.

"That's very admirable," Riven said calmly, even giving the other man a smile and a small bow. "It speaks well of your character. I did not mean offense. I would be more than happy to escort you to your sister's estate, wherever it may be. Now, could you tell me more about this event? We'd all be very appreciative of any help you can give us."

The backstory of the Abyssal Descent was wrapped in layers of folklore and legend, according to Gentry, and Riven's demons knew a little bit about it—though not nearly as much as the drow did.

The general consensus was that Elysium itself had sequestered a piece of the abyss, which was the deepest and darkest part of the void, and utilized the rich, naturally Unholy environment for cultivation purposes. It handed out tickets as prizes for various other events or accomplishments and prioritized people who showed the most promise for growth in the future. The abyss was the same place where Gluttony itself had been imprisoned, along with all the other sins and even the commandments, and was in most cases incredibly hard to reach or leave. But under the controlled hand of Elysium's own insights, it was also an incredible experience to undertake for any potential Unholy foundation user.

Which was why Gentry's sister had opted to stay for a couple extra centuries, sculpting her soul skeleton for the D-grade in secluded cultivation before leaving— even though she'd already created her soul lattice and ascended into the E-grade long ago. Grudgingly, Gentry had admitted his family wasn't the most talented set of cultivators out there and that in many circumstances people wouldn't take that long to ascend. His own highest affinity was 24 percent, and his noble house had been founded on maneuvering through financial markets rather than by the martial paths. However, he'd been very adamant in explaining that although his clan wasn't considered a cultivation powerhouse, many of them had still been scored as ELITE by system standards due to their skills with a blade and utilization of techniques in various wars, and that the vast majority of the multiverse had affinities below 30 percent.

It was obviously a touchy subject for the drow man.

Aside from this, Gentry had also gone on to explain what they should expect. The first three floors were habitable going down, with the first floor being the largest and cheapest to stay in. The second floor was more expensive and full of entire younger generations from various factions across the multiverse. The third floor, his sister's floor and the last that did not experience frequent abyssal monster spawns, was far richer than the other two habitable floors in ambient Unholy energies that expedited a cultivator's formation of soul constructs. How his sister had even set up a compound on the third floor was a complete mystery to both Gentry and the others of his noble house, but none of them had complained when she'd informed them of this by waystone—at a massive cost to her own coffers—about a century ago. Many of the factions even warred with one another over such spots, leading Gentry to believe that his sister had gained some powerful allies from undisclosed factions in her time spent in this isolated abyssal zone. People could travel together through portals between floors in groups of five, not including minions, and not moving in a group often meant you'd be picked out as a potential mugging or murder victim—where they'd strip you of your gear to sell on the internal markets here.

"Your two friends may attract unwanted attention to our group considering their levels," Gentry stated, head-bobbing to Gen-Fay and Nora in turn as the portal finally flashed to life, revealing a spinning disc of green that began to suck in like a wormhole. "I'd say the same about the brutalisk, but everyone who knows what he is will stay far away, as their physical strength is absurd regardless of the significantly lower level. Even with myself in the picture, I am without a system affiliated title—without the normal Elite tag that so many of the others here will have."

Azmoth had gained a good number of levels after fighting the monster wave that was meant for Outpost Number 84 and had leaped to level 129. However, it was still far below the norm in the descent, which Gentry claimed to be anywhere between level 180 and 250, with most people averaging level 200 or so. Anyone above level 250 was automatically kicked from the area, as were people who'd progressed past the halfway stage of creating a true soul skeleton in the E-grade—the step beyond a soul lattice.

Gentry then glanced at Athela, who was juggling her two red katanas alongside two balls of red webbing like an acrobat, and then looked to Riven. "Athela, however, is quite the opposite. No one would want to take on a Legendary except for other Legendaries. Most people here are Elite ranked, as I stated, but you . . ."

He rubbed his chin thoughtfully, looking Riven up and down with a frown. "Your Mythic tag will no doubt draw a lot of attention, and probably in a bad way. I've heard stories about it but have never seen it for myself, and I'm sure it'll create quite a ruckus. To the point that it might even be dangerous. Here, take these—we'll all use them, with the exception of your minion Athela. It'll help hide our identification information from most."

He took out a series of star-shaped amulets and passed them around to Azmoth, Gen-Fay, and Riven in turn before putting one on himself. Immediately the ability to identify him became fuzzy when Riven tried, and the same could be said for the two minions who donned them next. Even trying to identify the amulets themselves was a no-go, and Riven was happy to see that the effect worked on him just as well. It even obscured the information of other items he and his allies were wearing.

"Good shit," Riven said, eyeing the pendant with a smile. "Thanks. I owe you one."

"Damn right you do," Gentry spat with mixed humor and irritation in his voice. He folded his arms. "You killed the two men who were supposed to be my way down into the fifth, sixth, and seventh levels. I'm going to need to hire an entirely new team thanks to you. But they did genuinely suck to be around, so I'll forgive it. Come on, I've never been there before, but I have a map. If you don't mind, I'll lead the way—at least until we get to my sister's compound."

The portal winked out, and Riven found himself among a crowd of tens of thousands that was rapidly growing by the minute. Large, flat mountaintops numbering in the many dozens surrounded a sprawling city far beneath, each of them having a huge green portal overhead just like his own. The city itself was speckled with lights all down the mountain slopes and in the valley against the absolute-black abyssal hole in the center that took up a solid third of the city's entire volume between mountains. The dark sky overhead was flecked with crackles of what could only be purple sin lightning, stone skyscrapers crawled toward the heavens above, and the air was thick with ambient energies that permeated Riven's very being.

The environment was a cultivation paradise that radiated power related to Unholy, Shadow, Blood, Chaos, Depravity, Infernal, Void—which was not technically part of the Unholy branches—and lastly, Sin. It was like being hooked up to a battery, and Riven could see why Gentry's sister had chosen to stay for so long.

"Keep a lookout for that naga bitch who attacked us earlier," Riven whispered to Athela as she glanced around at the growing crowd. "Kill him immediately if you see him. It won't perma-kill him because of the world quest parameters, but it'll at least knock him out of this event if he's here."

"I don't think he'd be here, because he was a glacial-water specialist," Athela replied evenly, considering Riven's words. "He's most likely to be a threat only in the altars' realm, but then again, Greed is likely the one that utilized him if Gluttony's guess is correct. I'll remain vigilant, don't worry."

She gave him a peck on the cheek and a spank before giggling at his eye roll.

"This event will be open for a year's time, and stragglers will continue to come in," Gentry said as he motioned for them to quickly follow him toward the large stone walkways leading down the mountain's slope. "But the faster we get out of here, the better, or so I'm told. Fights often break out when the scions of rival factions find one another, and we don't want to be caught in the middle of one."

As if on cue, explosions from an opposite mountain peak roared to life in a series of violent and thunderous booms. The energies were quite potent even from here, and it quickly humbled Riven to realize that there were other people in this place capable of such destructive force.

Looking back over his shoulder and then down to his side as they continued to walk, he noted how the back ends of the mountains not facing the internal city faded away into a deep black landscape where light did not penetrate even to his eyes—and he wondered whether anything was surviving out there in the dark.

Another flash of sin lightning crashed against a suddenly visible dome overhead, illuminating the sky to a greater degree than what was normal for just a split second and eliciting screams from the crowd around him. Riven's own heart sank at what that light had shown. For in the briefest glimpse of that purple lightning flash, there'd been a giant, eel-like creature with milky-white eyes, a coiled body, and flashing black scales staring down at them beyond the barrier. It was so large, in fact, that it could have swallowed the entire city and all the mountains surrounding it in a single bite.

"A void titan," Gentry said reverently, urging Riven to continue moving. "It won't be able to break through Elysium's barrier—ignore it. Keep your amulets on to conceal your identity and don't get trampled in the crowd. If you stop now, you'll just get run over. Come on, we can find an information broker farther down. Ignore the people on the sidelines; they're usually scammers if my family's information is correct."

Keeping Gen-Fay and Nora in front of him to make sure the weakest members of their group were guarded, and having Athela and Azmoth on either side, Riven took up the rear as they all followed Gentry down the giant stone steps that traveled for miles into the valley. It was like watching a mass exodus from the portals, and life-and-death battles continued to erupt all across the dozens of peaks.

Riven could see why Gentry had wanted an escort. This place was dangerous, and as he identified one person after another, Riven saw that roughly 60 percent of the crowd bore an ELITE tag. Scattered among the crowd were rare LEGENDARY tags, just a handful of them that he saw, and then the rest were predominantly untagged, just like Gentry was. Most of the LEGENDARY-tagged participants were followed by entire groups of other cultivators, while some had clan squads of people who'd already been here for the last three hundred years waiting to escort them.

Riven also noticed that there were significantly fewer people here of certain races, while other races were in abundance. This was likely due to how Charisma worked, and how certain races leaned toward the Unholy foundational pillar while others did not.

Drow—or dark elves—were in abundance, their chief features being silky white hair, dark skin, and fair features. As were chaos dwarves like the berserker cultist he'd recently killed in battle, with inherent runic sigils of gray and black light carved into their very bodies at birth. There were enormous numbers of undead from dozens of varying races—including vampires like himself, a significant number of demonic races in equal varieties, and a paltry population of scattered humans, too. Then there were the less common races, or the ones that didn't fit the mold. A few fallen angels on black wings, though rare in number, were seen flying overhead along with some of the winged demons like imps or devils. There were some humanoid, rock-based golem creatures with red eyes that lumbered down the walkways and trampled people who were too slow to get out of their way. Wingless draconic races of humanoid sorts were seen in small numbers, too, and the occasional gnome or pixie was also noted.

"Fascinating . . ." Riven muttered to himself, appreciating the variety of species coming to intermingle here in the abyssal depths. "I've never seen so many races at one time in one place."

An abrupt shove from behind nearly caused Riven to fall, and he heard a gruff voice bark out a shout. "Move faster, bloodsucker! You're in—"

CRASH

Riven asserted dominance by whipping around and smashing whoever or whatever had shoved him with a spiked fist. Body parts exploded under the charged strike with a resounding crash. Not wanting to be seen as weak in front of so many other elites of the multiverse, he wasn't taking any chances of making himself a mark.

What he left behind was a smoldering wreckage of blood and gore, flickering with Black Lightning that sparked out of the crater he'd created; numerous people nearby had either dodged out of the way or managed to erect shields in time to stop from being thrown back. Other people HAD been thrown back, being blasted into others on the ground or off the ledge to roll down the slope into one of the buildings on the mountain, but nobody besides the creature who'd shoved him had taken the direct hit. Riven had been careful to keep his power isolated to a single point as best he could, but he honestly couldn't even tell what or who had shoved him after the devastating attack had landed.

Perhaps he was just on edge.

The others stared wordlessly, some sneering, some expressionless, and others giving him impressed looks.

"Keep moving," a horned draconic man in flowing silver robes hissed from between bronze scales, notably with a LEGENDARY tag and at level 200 when Riven identified him. "You are holding up the line."

Riven blinked, then nodded after making sure no one else was coming to bother him—and he steadied himself before turning around and following the others in his group who'd stopped to watch.

"You heard the man, let's move." Riven began to head out, but stopped as Gluttony pierced his mind with a mental message.

"There is a hot springs farther down in the city. Travel with the others to the location I've marked, and you may find that it is more than what it appears."

There was a pause.

Riven's brows furrowed at the information being laid out in his head after Gluttony's words, before his brows rose with mixed emotion. "Hey . . . Maybe let's find something to eat? Or a place to relax? Maybe a hot spring. Do they have hot springs here?"

Gentry chuckled nervously as the others in the crowd occasionally shifted their gazes his way amid the descent. "I'm not sure, but we could find out. Regardless of where, it would certainly be wise to get off the main path near the base of the mountain before getting our bearings. We can then get insider information from people who've lived here for the last few centuries, and we can compare it to the information my house has acquired to assure ourselves of its validity. Does that sound okay to you?"

Nora nodded vigorously. "Sounds good to me."

"Me, too," Azmoth grunted, growling at a passerby who got too close. "I not like these crowds. Need larger space, more room."

The first level of the Abyssal Descent did indeed have a hot springs, though it was quite pricey. As was everything here in this alternate realm, as Riven quickly found out. His sum of twenty-two million that he'd thought so outlandish back on Panu was pennies and pocket change here in the abyss, where the young elites of the Unholy-oriented multiverse congregated by the millions. A basic meal for one person cost thousands of Elysium coins, and most of the people either dealt in platinum or in coins that Riven had never seen before such as Etherium—which was the equivalent of one hundred thousand platinum, or Basdum, which was the equivalent of ten Etherium.

One platinum Elysium coin was equivalent to a thousand bronze coins. Thus a single Etherium coin was worth one hundred million bronze Elysium coins, and a Basdum coin was worth one billion bronze Elysium coins.

Meaning that Riven's total wealth of twenty-two million coins—even after all he'd done—only attributed to about one-fifth of the wealth of a single Etherium coin, and he wasn't anywhere even close to an equivalent Basdum coin.

Yet he saw many people exchange these coins with one another, somewhat flippantly, for various items or services around the city as they went. The amount of money some of these people had was just mind-boggling, and he wondered what kind of stuff he could buy from the Elysium store back home with that kind of money. He honestly hadn't explored the store much, but what he had seen from it—before even upgrading the altar at all—had led him to believe that the utmost of what he could afford was basics and necessities.

Then again, he was on an integrating planet that was only starting to reach the one-year mark.

"You will have your meals delivered to you in the springs, and your time is reserved for two hours," said a pretty but stern-looking succubus with red hair, eyeing Gen-Fay warily before handing each member of Riven's party a set of keys. "Storage containers with basic alarms and wards are in the hall but are not guaranteed for safekeeping. Any theft that occurs here is not our responsibility, so keep that in mind."

Gentry's eyes lingered on the woman's bosom for a short time before he snapped out of it and gave her a nod. "Thank you."

"It is appreciated," Riven stated with a smile, laughing underneath his ivory helmet as his girlfriends tugged at his hands excitedly. "I suppose I'll be going now. Make sure you bring the scones!"

With a final tug, Athela dragged Riven off into the changing rooms, with Azmoth coming in last.

Behind them and out of sight, the redheaded succubus rubbed at one of her horns under the stone ceiling of her hot springs abode. Hesitantly picking up a communication orb, her eyes lingered on the presence of sin left in the vampire's wake—and the image of the maw across his chest was prominently burned into her retinas.

She waited for the click, then the light flashed in the stone she held and she began to whisper into it with concerned glances in the direction of the springs she'd just rented out. "Amano? Yes, it's me. Please contact the church—I think I may have some information that they'd be very interested in learning about regarding a certain individual who just entered my establishment. Yes, yes, I think so. Well, that's why I'm calling. Of course. No. All right, I'll do my best to keep him here. I'll see you soon."

There was another click, and the stone faded away.

Taking in a deep breath, the succubus looked at herself in the mirror across the room and turned around to make sure she was showing a lot of skin. Hastily getting out a brush and combing her long red hair, she scurried into the kitchen, where she began yelling at the cooks to prepare a special meal for the newcomers who'd just arrived.

CHAPTER 2

The symbols of a scythe, a red teardrop, and a black sun were joined by the visage of the maw. The related pillars of his soul continued to form branching spires each time the symbols flared.

Riven hovered three feet up off the water's surface, bare-backed and only wearing pants. He gently let his mana swim around him and created a galaxy of teal, black, red, and deep purple in the underground hot springs room where the others were relaxing—wondering just what to expect if Gluttony was correct.

"Are you sure this is the right place?" Riven whispered, just loud enough for Gentry to turn his head with a confused look his way.

"Did you say something?" Gentry asked from where he sat beside Azmoth in the water, shooting the three women nearby a glance as they ate along the water's edge and had drinks served to them courtesy of the house. Fay and Genua had decided to unmerge upon arrival, now that they were in a relatively safe haven outside the crowds.

Riven shook his head absentmindedly, keeping his eyes closed, feeling Gluttony pulse inside him with affirmation to his question. "I was just . . . muttering to myself. Don't mind me. How's getting ahold of your contacts going? Any luck?"

Gentry frowned, sighed, looked down at his crystalline artifact, and shook it rapidly again before giving up. Putting it back into his spatial sack and slapping a wet hand across his face, he let himself sink into the dark waters of the spring and groaned. "No. Not a single contact has pinged me back."

The drow elf made no move to continue the conversation, only looking downtrodden.

Riven continued to watch the symbols flare in his mind, watching their energies intertwine like a network of neurons or intricate webs. Occasionally when he didn't like the look of it, or when Gluttony pointed out a flaw in the matrix, he'd shift one connection to another spot to reinforce the bridgework he was currently working on. He hadn't known it then, but his lattice had been taking form ever since the Path of Red and Black had been created back when he'd fought the Azag hive. When those two pillars had started interlocking with one another, branching to connect, it'd been the start to his very foundation for the E-grade—and that lattice was only continuing to build. Spontaneous connections were replaced with ones made from intent, adding organization to the chaos that would better prepare his soul for ascension.

Though even while bonded to Gluttony, the specifics of what needed to be done were not there—rather, they were just impressions from Gluttony's past life. Impressions were, however, better than nothing—and the two of them worked tirelessly over the hours spent here in this exquisite abyssal environment.

Oddly enough, it almost reminded Riven of graphics—the same ones that Gragle the gnome used and was using to replicate some totems for him in the Altars event.

Why was that?

His eyes opened, and the pulsing flow of mana froze in place when he made eye contact with Genua. She and the two women on either side of her were all submerged up to their collarbones, but she was the only one who seemed reserved while the other two were drunk off their asses.

She avoided his gaze instantly, looking down into the dark waters of their underground spring with a mixed expression, and then turned around to pretend to grab at some of the food the establishment had left them.

Riven's black-and-red eyes followed her movement, and he closed them one more time before creating a rift in space and stepping onto semidry rock next to Genua's hand. Bending down and pulling the woman up, much to her surprise, he wrapped a towel around her and motioned for her to follow.

"We'll be back in a minute," Riven said with a wave of his hand when Athela scowled his way. "I need to have a private conversation with Genua."

"What about OUR private conversations!" Fay laughed loudly, slapping the water and getting a grin from Athela. "WE WANT ONE, TOO!"

Rolling his eyes and ignoring her, he brought Genua around a corner and into an adjacent changing room where the storage lockers were kept. Sitting down on a bench and letting the control on his mana go, he rested his chin in his hands and gave the elf thrall a sad smile.

"I'm sorry," Riven eventually said after a long pause as they just stared at one another, and his shoulders straightened as he went to stretch. "I probably should have said that earlier."

Genua raised both eyebrows slightly, but avoided his gaze again and shrugged. "Sorry for what?"

"Recently? Sorry for what happened with the assassination attempt. I was too weak and too oblivious to do anything about it, and that's on me." Riven gave her a sad smile as her gaze returned to meet his. "I'm sorry for your husband, Farrod. For your daughter Ethel. For turning you into a thrall out of my hate and spite for what your family did to me. It's . . . not something I'm proud of. I wish I could turn back time, but I can't. I know I've said it before, if not in so many words, and I don't expect complete forgiveness. But I do want you to know that I'll try to make the best for you out of the life you now have. When all this is over, I'll make sure to cut your tie to me so that you can spend more time with Len. And I want you to know that I'll keep . . . our baby safe. I'm sorry I failed you this time. It won't happen again."

Genua studied him intensely for a time, her hands clasped together in front of her as she stared wordlessly. Then she let out a soft breath of air, blowing a long strand of blond hair from her face. "I don't know how much of it is the vampirism and the thrall's pact that make me want to not hate you, but I don't, if that's what you think. As I've said before, what my family did was unforgivable. But I was just as complicit and knew what we were doing back then. In many ways, I wish I had been the one to die—and that Ethel had lived. She had been brainwashed into hating you, if nothing else. The elder, and my husband . . . eh. Regardless, that is in the past now, and we can only look forward. I do not wish to talk about it again—it will only make me cry."

Hearing some commotion from farther down the hall and up the stairs to where thousands of people were migrating from the portals onto the streets of this abyssal city, Genua watched a burly set of incubus men walk by and give her a side-eye before traveling to their own hot springs. She turned her head. "Do you really intend to let me go?"

Riven furrowed his brows when he saw the doubt, guilt, and regret in her expression. "Is that not what you want?"

She opened her mouth, hesitated, then continued to speak while nervously wringing her fingers together like one would wring water out of a wet cloth. "Is it because I'm weak?"

He blinked, then laughed. "Absolutely not. Even now I'm having Gluttony's forces train Hakim and the others back on Panu so that, one day, they'll be able to join me despite being what most powerhouses on Panu call weak. 'Weak' is a relative term and has nothing to do with my decision. I was going to leave you behind because of your daughter."

Genua shook her head, then took his hand and pushed it onto her slightly swollen belly. "Do you feel it?"

There was a pause, and he blinked rapidly when he felt something inside gently kick.

Smiling, Riven nodded. "I do."

She let his hand go, ran her fingers through her hair, and huffed. "That child is going to need its father. So is Len. I was hoping that, perhaps, you'd consider adopting Len, too. I don't want you to cut me from your life, and if you feel guilty, you can make it up to me by being there for my little girl. And for the new child on its way."

Riven was stunned, visibly so, and the ancient Unholy tattoos along his body even did a quick rearranging of themselves due to his emotional backlash at the words. "Len doesn't want me as a dad. You remember how she reacted to the news when we told her."

"Do not make me beg, Riven," Genua snapped, an unusual spunk to her words, given her position and usual submissive tone. "I will not allow my first daughter to lose herself to despair when she feels herself an outcast after this child in my womb is born. Just try to imagine, just for a moment, how she would feel if she was not included. To be the child left behind, when a younger sibling born of a lineage akin to that of a demonic elder god overshadows your every step. When I play mother to this child with you as a father, what will Len see? It would be devastating. Despite what you did and how I sometimes even now hate you for what you did, you are a good man at your core. Despite all your flaws, Riven, you would make a good father—and I already know you've tried to make amends on Len's behalf."

Genua was now glaring at him from across the room, and she got up to walk over, sitting next to him so that her shoulder was touching his. She gave him a suddenly anxious glance, avoided eye contact, and cleared her throat. "Well? Are you just going to sit there? Or are you going to take responsibility for what you did and adopt her as your own—so that she can have a family again?"

Riven remained slack-jawed until she gave him a fiery snort.

"Don't be a coward," she hissed, almost pleadingly—but with venom, too.

Guilt, embarrassment, and sadness reared their ugly heads—but he put on a forced smile and nodded, reaching out to touch her stomach with a nod. It was a big decision to make, not one that he took lightly, but he owed it to that little girl to at least try. "I'll adopt Len, too, or at least I promise I'll do my best . . . but I'm not sure she'll accept me."

Genua's shoulders immediately slumped in relief, and she let out a long breath that she'd been holding in during her glare. "Thank you. And she will, she just . . . she just needs time. She knows that you were not the one to choose the fight that led to Ethel's death, or Farrod's death, and she is already excited about the prospect about a little brother or sister. Even if she had other concerns when we first broke the news to her."

The laughter of his two girlfriends splashing in the hot springs was masked by the slapping of bare feet on the stone walkway coming from the stairs. Riven looked up and down the hall, noting the redheaded succubus and owner of this establishment walking his way with her black dress flowing out behind her.

She stopped just in front of him, bowing slightly and sweeping back her hair behind her two short, thick horns. "Sir. I was hoping to have a word with you." The succubus shot Genua a quick look. "In private."

Genua exchanged a glance with Riven, but he put a hand on her shoulder and gave a reaffirming squeeze.

"Go have fun," Riven said, ushering her out of the room and closing a sheet curtain behind her. Turning, he put his hands behind his back and gave the succubus the lackadaisical gaze of one who was assessing a cheap car salesman selling a poor pitch. "It took you long enough. I was beginning to wonder whether or not this was the right spot."

The succubus, who'd now straightened, raised an eyebrow curiously and withdrew her wings into her back, leaving her long black tail to flounder out behind her. "I'm not quite sure what you mean by that. Are you saying that you know why I've come?"

Riven raised an eyebrow, then snapped his fingers.

A sigil flared to life on the woman's neck where there'd been none before, one of the Great Maw within a pentagram, and she gave him a wicked grin.

"Clever boy." She tilted her head to the side with a wide, brilliant smile, then withdrew a pendant of similar design and took a step forward. Her blue eyes tracked down to the jewelry in her hand, then back to him. "I thought I'd hidden my identity as a contact rather well, but then again—if you do know without my introduction . . . that must mean you're of one of the blooded families. Who are you working for? Are you a scion of one of the greater houses?"

Riven smirked, then shook his head. "No. I was just told to come here on good faith by a friend who—more or less—is part of the higher rungs of the church himself. Personally? I'm a nobody."

"Well, I wouldn't say that, based on all the markings you've gained . . ." the succubus muttered, head-nodding to the numerous Unholy scripts laced across his skin. "You don't just get those by being a nobody. Very well, keep your secrets. As long as you're one of the touched, I am able to offer you information and services paid for by our church. Fencing stolen items, contracts, guides into the deeper realms, arena matches, hard-to-get resources for cultivating your lattice—you name it and I'm here for it."

She smugly stuffed the pendant between her large breasts with a wink. "And for you, love, I'd do more. You've got a real sense of . . . *umph* about you. If you know what I mean. So, how about it? Want to ditch your three enslaved minions and let a real woman ride you for once?"

Riven didn't even twitch. "I'm going to pretend like you didn't say that last part, regardless of how pretty you might be. And for the record, I'm doing you a favor. The archdemon back there, Athela, already has a jealousy problem, even with Fay. If I added another succubus to the picture, she'd probably castrate me and would no doubt kill you, too."

The woman chuckled, and held out a hand. "Lavini, Church of Gluttony representative, at your service. I've been here a few thousand years now and know all the dirty secrets of what goes on here."

"Riven," he replied, taking her hand to shake.

She eyed him curiously. "You don't happen to be an ex–shard holder, do you?"

"Shard holder?"

"Did you hold a shard of Gluttony before he reincarnated? You have a very distinct and potent smell to you. Maybe even two shards? Were you a harbinger?"

Riven grinned and withdrew his hand to fold his arms in front of him, pausing to let a couple of drow elves accompanied by a slave pass by. "Yes, I was. Is it normal for people to have slaves here?"

Lavini looked over her shoulder to where an elf woman was being led up the stairs by the two other drow men. "No. They must come from a very wealthy family to afford buying a ticket for a mere slave. Some people just have too much money to know what to do with it."

"You don't say. Do you think they have the money on their person?" Riven asked curiously, thinking back to the new types and tiers of Elysium coins that easily outstripped his relatively pathetic display of wealth from an integration world. "Do you think I could mug them and get away with it?"

Lavini again shook her head and even pressed a hand to Riven's chest when he went to take a step forward. "Not here, and not them. We don't want to blow up a perfectly situated rest spot for the church. And even if you were a harbinger, and are one of the touched, those two men are particularly powerful drow hailing from the Yerus Dynasty. If you didn't notice, they're both LEGENDARY tagged, and they'd kill you before you knew what happened. Meanwhile, I don't see a tag on you at all. Or is that just the necklace you have on, masking it from my sight?"

Riven had to repress a snort but backed off as the elves and their slave left the establishment. "I see. Well, I was hoping that you may know a man by the name of . . ."

Riven paused, waiting for Gluttony to give him the identity of the man they were looking for. "Amano is the name. Half minotaur, half gargoyle. Ever seen him around these parts?"

Lavini arched an eyebrow and folded her arms, scrutinizing him. "You really do have contacts in high places, don't you? Yes, he's currently assigned as master of the church sanctuaries here in the Abyssal Descent. I'm afraid that if you're looking for him, he's already on his way. I am obligated to report the sigils that I see and recognize, and he seemed a bit put off when I mentioned this one . . ."

Her finger drifted to Riven's chest and pointed out a seven-pointed star being devoured by the Great Maw with Unholy markings in languages Riven didn't entirely understand. "I hadn't seen it before."

"I was wearing armor," Riven pointed out, confused.

"And just as you were able to sense mine, I was able to sense . . . yours." She shrugged.

Riven hadn't necessarily sensed her marking him but rather had acted on Gluttony's own instincts and had infused Sin energy into his finger snap from earlier to elicit the glow on Lavini's patch of skin. Not being able to sense such things caused a minor amount of irritation to rise up in Riven's chest, but he knew he'd probably have such things come to him as he cultivated a greater grasp on the Sin energy that permeated his new soul pillar.

A buzzing sound came from Lavini's pocket, and she picked up a black orb—holding up a finger Riven's way before nodding and turning around with a swish of her tail. "Looks like he's already here. Come on and follow me."

He nodded, and the two of them left the hot springs behind.

However, instead of going back up the stairs, she went left. Winding and twisting, then coming into a closet after deactivating numerous enchantments, she pressed a concealed panel in the stone wall and let the hidden door swing open. "I have one of my coworkers currently running the place, but I don't like leaving her by herself with all the new bloods walking around. It's dangerous, so let's hurry so I can get back."

"Are you implying you're a fighter?" Riven asked, skeptically eyeing the scantily clad succubus.

She gave him an amused smirk over her shoulder while pushing into the dimly lit hallway when the door clicked shut behind them. "Of course, Mr. Vampire! I'm one of the instructors here. Maybe I'll fight you for an opportunity to hold you down!"

Instructors?

She gave him a flirtatious wink and didn't bother expanding on the subject, but as the tunnel curved into a spiral descent through the ground, Riven soon found himself looking upon a very large rectangular room. It was big enough to fit a few thousand people inside, and there were dozens currently there. Some were meditating on prayer mats with Sin-affiliated energy crystals in their hands, others were sparring in semitranslucent barrier cages, and some were eating at one of two long tables set at the far wall. To his right, there was even an altar to Gluttony—where a horned priest garbed in black was reading scripture from a book to three other hooded demons.

"Pass," a muscular red devil standing twice Riven's height said, stepping in front of the path into the room and folding his burly red arms while glaring toothily down at the duo.

Lavini rolled her eyes with a huff, then presented a medallion. "Jevis, you know me well enough by now to stop asking me every time I come in. You're doing it just to annoy me at this point, aren't you? This man is a new blood who just came from the portal openings. Let us through."

The devil snickered, then head-bobbed over to a set of large, sturdy couches. "Amano is waiting for you. Get movin'."

Grumbling and glaring at the devil, Lavini started for the couches Jevis had nodded to. There, on the middle one, was Amano.

Just as Gluttony had said, he was a gargoyle-minotaur mix. He had large black wings, obsidian skin, and the face of a bull. His legs were also bull-like instead of the claws gargoyles usually had, and a large patch of brown fur ran down his back and along his tail. All he wore was a large loincloth and a red sigil of Gluttony tattooed into his chest, and he had two wicked-looking obsidian horns curving out from his skull.

"Amano, master of sanctuaries." Lavini addressed him with a low bow, motioning for Riven to do the same.

Riven didn't bother, instead eyeing the level-248 demon with moderate amounts of curiosity. When the demon's brow furrowed in annoyance at the lack of respect, and Lavini shot him a piercing look that could kill, Riven bowed.

He followed Lavini's lead when she straightened with a huff.

"We answer your summons," Lavini said, awaiting the demon's words as others in the underground sanctuary occasionally shot them curious looks.

Amano continued to sit silently, arms folded, while his demonic tail slapped the ground from time to time during the staring contest he was having with Riven. Eventually he grunted and stood to his full height, towering over Riven by almost four feet and looking down at him with mild amusement. "I can already tell you've got an attitude, boy. But I like people like you. Believe it or not, it takes that kind of arrogance to get to the top—or so my elders tell me. May I see the sigil?"

"Which one?" Riven countered.

Amano smirked. "Show me all of them, if you wish, but I was hoping for the seven-pointed star."

Acknowledging his words, Riven sent Sin energy pulsing through his tattoos as they lit up across his body and glowed through his thin clothes. They covered his arms, feet, legs, torso, back, and face—and as the seconds ticked by, he brought out more that'd been hiding just underneath the surface.

Stacked layers of the sigils poured out as the eyes of Amano and every single demon in the room went wide in shock, until Riven finished and had his colors on full display like a peacock.

Bending down to get a better look at him, Amano studied the runes and circled him with intent—coming to a halt right in front of where Riven stood while scratching his chin. "These are all . . . ascendants."

He tapped the front of his chest. "Like mine. They are not just Gluttonous markings, but they are on a level I haven't seen before. Only high priests of our order, S-ranked or higher, can mark someone like this . . ."

Lavini seemed surprised, then confused, then ended with a mixture of lust and fear as she settled her gaze on Riven—only to tear it away when he met her eyes.

Amano's words trailed off, as if asking a question, and when Riven didn't respond—he let out a long sigh. "Which elder sent you here? I do not play in the political games of our church, I swear it on Gluttony's name. I merely need to know so that I can avoid pairing you with others who would intentionally cause friction."

Riven let on a slow grin. "I believe there is a misunderstanding . . . I do not wish to form a group. I already have one heading here now made up of those who aren't already present upstairs."

Amano seemed to be confused by this proclamation, as was Lavini. "You already have a group for the descent? Are they people I know? Usually we have guides, people who've already been down to the deepest levels, so that our scions from the outer realms don't get killed."

Riven waved a hand, sensing a very familiar presence entering his aura from the opposite side of the room. He smiled. "Oh, my guide has already been down. More than anything, I'm here to use your training halls. Recently I've been told that I'm quite lacking in certain areas and am too dependent on overwhelming force rather than skill. I have been told that when deemed ready, I will be able to make the descent with said party. Until then, until I am up to par with a very particular person's standards, I won't be allowed to finish the descent."

Now both Amano and Lavini gave him furrowed brows and tense expressions, exchanging glances with one another while Lavini scratched her head.

"Did your elder send a personal trainer?" Lavini asked with a frown. "What clan do you hail from?"

Before Amano could ask anything else, a silent, ominous shock wave of presence radiated from where the door to the sanctuary had opened across the hall.

Nearly everyone immediately fell to their knees or hit the floor, despite their desperate attempts to stand back up. The sparring ring barriers flickered and died, people started to gasp or gag in shock, and a couple people fainted outright under the sheer weight of the aura afflicting the room. Shadows wreathed around a woman seemingly made from the abyss itself as her lithe, athletic form stepped into the room with one bare foot. The very stone underneath her rippled, and a large crack formed under her position as she walked and pulled back her hood to let her seven black horns materialize across her head like a crown.

Pale white eyes stared out at the demons present, black hair flowed down to her waist like a flag, and the only signs of color on her figure aside from them and the cloak she wore was a small yellow flower clinging to one of the horns on her right-hand side with its roots.

"Ah . . . there you are." She began walking forward, and behind her, two more figures appeared. One was the presence Riven had sensed coming their way, and despite her features having changed, Allie was still unmistakably beautiful with her angelic wings folded behind her.

Though she did look rather put off, sad even, until her eyes met his—and then she beamed as bright as a sun before dashing over to slam into him with a bear hug.

"Riven!" Allie exclaimed, retracting her wings entirely while squeezing him all the tighter. "I have so much to tell you! So much has happened!"

He embraced her back, kissing her on the forehead and feeling a warmth spreading from his chest.

"Allie. Remember our talk about presence and how to carry oneself in public? You are a queen. Act like it," Lillith said, almost scoldingly, and she cleared her throat when Allie stood straighter to step back with a sheepish smile.

"Sorry, Lillith," Allie muttered, which surprised Riven to no end considering how Allie had become something of a lovingly self-assured psychopath ever since the integration had begun.

The third figure was someone Riven didn't recognize. He was no doubt a lich of some sort, and looked pretty bad—he was missing one skeletal arm and had cracks or burns all over his bone body. The odd organs that were visible inside the bone cage of his torso were partially rotten, and clothes that'd once been exquisite robes were now patched and torn with burn marks and bloodstains.

The aura faded when Lillith came to stand in front of Riven, and the audible gasps and deep breaths the demons around the room were taking were mixed in with angry roars and shouts—tempers flaring with auras all around them as they called out.

"WHO IN THE SEVEN HELLS—"

"KILL THAT BITCH!"

"DO YOU KNOW WHO WE ARE?! HOW DARE—"

Above the ruckus and threats, with imposing figures closing on their position, Lillith gave Gluttony a sad smile. "Forgive the younglings. It is not their fault that they don't know who I am."

Riven could literally feel the anger that'd been building up slowly fizzle away as Gluttony considered Lillith's words—and a pulse of thought traveled between them that Riven could only barely make out.

Lillith nodded and then turned to face the only person in the room who seemed to be aware of who she was.

Amano was visibly shaking, and it looked as though he was about to vomit before her eyes fell on him. He immediately hit the floor and prostrated himself on all fours, crashing his horned head into the ground with a shrill, high voice. "ALL HAIL LILLITH! ALL HAIL THE BLACK HAND OF GLUTTONY!"

Abruptly the shouting and threats stopped, and the angry crowd looked at one another in confusion.

"The Black Hand of Gluttony is dead," a large three-eyed, skinny, gray-skinned humanoid said while gesturing with all four of his clawed hands. "What is this nonsense, Amano? Are you playing a trick on us? Is this a joke?"

Some of the people around the room gave nervous laughs, while others continued to stare as if finally making the connection. One incubus had actually taken out an old recording crystal and was watching what was no doubt a history of the church based on Gluttony's memories.

When the images on the crystal stopped on Lillith's figure, and he took in a sharp breath of air, everyone nearby went rigid and stiff.

There was a long pause. Many exchanged looks as if to confirm what they were seeing, and slowly one of the devils nearby knelt with deep, horrified breaths.

"H . . . How . . . ?" The same three-eyed humanoid who'd spoken earlier looked deathly pale as he let out the whisper, and then true horror overtook him as he realized the truth of things when he attempted to identify her and saw the purple flames. One by one the others did the same, and a mixture of fear and awe permeated the room in mere seconds.

[Lillith, Level 119 Archdemon: Unique ???. ???. ???. ???. ???. ???. ???. ???. Commander of the Gluttonous Legions. MYTHIC.]

"Forgive me . . ." the demon said, eyes bulging, and his head hit the floor so fast that blood splattered along the stone. "This one does not deserve your mercy, but I plead for it nonetheless! I did not know you had come back with Gluttony's rebirth!"

The others rapidly followed; all around the room, demons big and small—humanoid or monstrous—all prostrated themselves in an absolute silence while Lillith eyed Amano.

She then turned her attention to Lavini the succubus and smiled widely. "Thank you for escorting Gluttony's reincarnation, Lavini. He gets lost and forgets to keep his guard up quite often. I have no doubt he'd likely have stumbled upon a spike trap or some kind of bomb on the way here at the rate he's going."

There was an absolute silence after she proclaimed Riven the reincarnation, and Riven could almost feel both Amano and Lavini rapidly pale while they remained prostrated. He heard a few hushed whispers of disbelief and further awe from around the room, but that was all.

Riven winced at the mocking jab, despite Lillith's teasing smirk. "Hello, Lillith. It's good to see you."

"Yes, quite," Lillith said with a chuckle. "I'm glad you made it here without getting stabbed or something. Are you ready to begin? I brought your sister and a rather interesting dog that I found begging for scraps on the side of the road in Panu. They'll be your teammates in the descent, along with me as your escort, and that Nora girl you're playing house with upstairs. But only when the three of you aren't so utterly demoralizing in your . . . displays. I would call it 'skills,' or 'spells,' or 'battle readiness,' but you're all so far beneath the standard definition that I gag at the thought of putting them upon even a single one of you."

She held up a finger. "Oh, and bring your minions down here, too. Your contracts need a lot of work, especially that Fay girl and the elf thrall. Truly, without offense being intended, you could do better in your choices."

Allie and the undead lich winced when Lillith's gaze fell on them, but the archdemon was quick to turn her attention back to Riven. "I've heard just how pathetic you were in that recent attempt on your child's life. I've also been told you have no real training under your belt, other than with an old high elf thrall and some very limited attempts at the Blood Moon Requiem's compound. It's time that we kick it into high gear and pit you against some real combatants. It'll be a good opportunity to see just how you stack up against some of the best the Unholy pillar has to offer for your range and league. You have extreme potential and amazing amounts of mana for your grade and level, but to say you are lacking any real skill would be an extreme understatement. You win most of your fights because you're bringing . . . Ah, what was it Gluttony said when comparing it to your world's jargon?"

Lillith paused to think it over, then snapped her fingers with a smile. "Yes! That's it! You win most of your fights because you're bringing a nuclear warhead to a knife fight. But what happens when the other guy brings a warhead to match yours? Perhaps by the end of the descent, and by the time you exit Chalgathi's trial, you'll realize that you're not the only one with large amounts of mana or high affinities to throw around. Hopefully you'll be something of a warrior wielding a sharpened sword—rather than a barbarian baby wielding an unbalanced club. So to speak."

She gestured to Amano, who was still kneeling and shaking in what was either excitement or absolute terror. "You, master of the sanctuaries. You're a LEGENDARY-tagged demon and are almost maxed for this zone at level 248, which is forty-eight levels higher than Riven is now. To begin our training session, I want you to fight this vampire. I want you to beat him so badly that he cries tears of blood by the end of it. I want him to feel humbled, or else none of this will be taken to heart. Do you understand?"

The half-gargoyle, half-minotaur looked up in shock, still visibly shaking while he glanced uncertainly to Riven nearby. "I—I could never! The reincarnation of Gluttony is too sacred to—"

His words were cut off when the visage of Gluttony itself split open in the air, to both gasps and shrieks of delight—along with some shaky sounds of weeping— around the room. "I would ask that you do as Lillith says, Amano. Do not think of it as fighting me. Rather, think of it as helping me. My partner and I are bonded, but he needs to hone his skills if we are going to work fluidly together. Please . . . destroy him in the ring. Go all out—we will make sure he lives."

A twinge of irritation couldn't help but fizzle to the surface in Riven's mind at the needless insults to his pride and the apparent lack of caring concerning bodily harm.

Amano was torn between elation and confusion while staring at Gluttony, but he rapidly nodded his head and continued groveling on the floor. "Yes, oh Great Maw! I will do as you ask! But perhaps it would be better to enter our largest arena in the central sanctuary? I won't be able to utilize my full power here in these practice arenas, but I promise you, I will make it a showing that the entire membership of the church here will remember for the rest of their lives!"

CHAPTER 3

The main arena of the central sanctuary was, in one word, enormous. Numerous platforms, steps, balconies, and seats ranging in size from small to huge were located all around the stadium in a nonuniform manner. A mile high and a mile wide, this place had been carved out of the very bedrock of whatever dark metals were native to this strange abyssal realm, with an enormous statue of Gluttony's maw standing as a monument on one end.

It was under this monument that the largest balcony was located, where Riven's minions and Lillith had taken up residence at the front amid a hesitant but excited swarm of higher-ranking young demons from various clans across the multiverse.

And with word having quickly spread among Gluttony's followers, the crowds of demons from dozens of different species continued to flow in. Teleportation gates flashed, openings in the numerous enormous passages let out the sounds of thundering feet and claws, and Church of Gluttony clergy—dressed in hooded black and purple robes, for the most part—were singing strange hymns while guiding people to their seats.

Watching them come in such numbers and in such a fervor, especially with some kind of scrying orb putting Riven on full display for the masses to focus on with an image overhead, really put into perspective just what his position had become.

Previous to this, he'd thought of Gluttony as more of an abstract . . . eh . . . friend? More or less, anyways. They'd actually gotten along really well, if Riven had to say so himself. Despite what Athela and Fay had told him numerous times over, it hadn't really clicked until now that he was a bonded symbiote and the physical representation of a being that many demonic societies worshipped as a near-godlike figure. Lillith was treated much the same, and by proxy, so were his minions.

Devils, void beasts, succubi, incubi, imps, minotaurs, beholders, Arshakai, driders, fallen satyrs, Jabobs, brutalisks, demonic wyverns, Cthulhu-like humanoids, and dozens of other species he didn't know the names of were all in attendance. And the vast majority were focused on him.

"You seem slightly nervous," Gluttony whispered in amusement through their thoughts, and Riven could only nod.

"This is a lot more than I'd been expecting," Riven said slowly, watching the mulling crowds start to settle down when Lillith and a number of robed clergy stepped forward to the balcony's front underneath the large statue of Gluttony.

Lillith raised a hand, and her aura of shadows lightly pressed against the noise and beings present with a gentle rush all across the mile-wide arena. The people and creatures present all immediately fell reverently silent, some of them even bowing their heads or prostrating themselves in respect.

And when Lillith spoke, her words traveled across the large underground room like a whisper—as if she were actually standing beside Riven and speaking into his ear, rather than standing nearly seven hundred yards away from him.

"Greetings, children of the maw."

It'd become dead silent as her white eyes crossed the crowds of demonic beings. "It pleases me to see that, despite untold eons of banishment to the deepest parts of the abyss, we have not been forgotten. That Gluttony has not been forgotten."

As one, the clergy scattered throughout the room echoed a nonsensical chant.

Riven would really have to learn whatever language they were speaking.

Lillith continued her speech after a short pause. "The younger generations of our great houses stand before me now, scions of the pillars of our monumental societies that have remained to flourish even in the aftermath of Gluttony's passing and the descent of Elysium—when it caught the sins and dragged them down into darkness to almost fade from memory."

At the mention of Elysium's action, the room went into an uproar as the demons cursed the system itself.

But Lillith held up another hand, causing them all to quiet down once again. Her seven black horns seemed to gleam under the firelight of balls of hellfire as they burst into radiance overhead, illuminating the dark colosseum and giving it a warmer ambience. She smiled. "We are not here to dwell upon the past. We are here, as first contact with the greater multiverse since our return, to show you all that Gluttony is back. That he intends to take this era into new heights! To rebuild what we have lost, and to reclaim his place as the greatest of the sins so that all may know his glory!"

The crowd immediately went into another uproar of applause.

"After you leave this place—" Lillith continued to speak over the thundering crowd. "I want you to return home to your families! To your clans and your countries! To your kingdoms in the hells and your ziggurats in the void! To your nether realm homes where the weaker members of your clans remain huddled in fear after millennia of persecution during our absence, just for holding true to our cause, to let them know their time for fear is now past! To your strongest on the battlefields, call them to arms! And finally, I wish you to let our enemies and those who have turned traitor know that it will not be long before their time of reckoning is at hand! Before we enter the eternal war, Gluttony has made it clear to me that we will wipe clean the filth of those who betrayed our trust! Who seized our assets and killed our faithful to obtain our artifacts! Those who took our once-sacred lands and sold them off to the highest bidders, or the demonic tribes who subverted the bedrock of our orders for their own greed! Let them ALL know that it will not be long before the banished regain our former power, and that we are coming for them."

Lillith lifted her arm, and a long, intricate spear made from abyss itself flashed into focus before exploding with her aura, and the entire underground arena shook under her might. Everyone there, even Riven himself, was put to their knees under the pressure she exuded for that brief instant.

"THIS IS MY PROMISE TO YOU!" Lillith shouted as her aura vanished once again, and she slammed her wicked spear into the rock of the balcony with a resounding boom that sent cracks spiraling down the reinforced walls. "WE WILL SEE THEIR BLOOD SPILLED AND OUR GLORY RESTORED!"

The demons all roared in agreement. Wings flared, auras heightened, feet stomped, and fists pounded against the ground as a chant started arising from the crowd—the same chant that some of the priests had been uttering in that strange language earlier. It rose higher and higher, until every time the chant was uttered, the ground underneath Riven's feet shook with the force of it.

A quick snap of power radiated from up above, and the room fell silent once more. Eyes widened and gasps appeared to all as Gluttony's Great Maw opened up across the ceiling—stretching the entire length of the arena as wisps of black tendrils snaked out and slowly down toward the floor beneath.

Some demons began to weep, while others began to cry out to him as others took knees or prostrated themselves once again.

They all watched in awe as those tendrils began to spiral, intertwining with one another and closing in on Riven's position—before they embraced his body like a blanket.

Riven felt the cool tendrils of Sin energy surging through his vessels and soul aperture, felt the soul start to change, and closed his eyes as he activated his demonic form for the very first time while whispering under his breath. His hands clasped together, with his last three fingers on each hand forming a roof while the thumb and pointer finger formed holes. Bringing his hands up to his face, the third eye on his forehead tore open and glowed a deep purple under the roof—while his red eyes looked out through the holes his finger and thumb made.

[Gluttony's Aspect of Demonic Heritage (Sin) (Tier 3): A martial art that enhances you through the power of your fully formed Mark of the Sinner. Your body merges with your soul clone for one minute, allowing you to take on an ultimate demonic form as an aspect of the Great Maw. Very long cooldown, which can be reduced by killing and eating others.]

His body exploded as the tattoos along his skin all lit up from black to violet.

Muscles surged and ripped. A long, huge tail tore out of his tailbone and whipped around in a frenzy. His chest split down the middle to incorporate Gluttony's usual visage in a vertical maw. Huge demonic horns sprouted from his head, and his hair receded to reveal pitch-black skin emblazoned with glowing violet sigils, and his hands and feet exploded with claws. Legs snapped backward and grew larger, inverting like a T. rex, and spikes tore open across his spine while he grew to five times his normal height. Bone gaffs tore out of his kneecaps and elbows, and his teeth grew like knives.

When the four, bat-like black and violet demon wings spread open with a wingspan that could encircle a house, Riven finally opened his eyes again.

He slowly looked down, a little over thirty feet tall, with his tail and wings slowly drifting out behind him. His chest opened up to reveal tongues of dark black licking out at the air in front of him for dozens of feet, tasting the air while his body thundered with power.

He was unstoppable in that moment, a being of pure destruction with no equal that caused the very space around him to flex and bend.

And when he spoke, it was as one with Gluttony. The two of them had temporarily merged in both body and soul, and their consciousness had become linked. The Sin energy was beyond anything that Riven could have ever imagined, being so palpable and so raw, and it felt like Riven could literally tear the world apart if he wished.

"You come here and bring honor to your clans." Riven and Gluttony spoke out in a dual, deep voice that echoed effortlessly across the stands. "It pleases me to see such loyalty in ones as young as you. Lillith has voiced my thoughts well, and we will see it done that our enemies find an early grave. However, today is a day of celebration . . . one that will be celebrated with trials by combat for all our F- and early E-grade prodigies to witness. And perhaps it will even be an opportunity for many of you to participate."

A huge set of double doors on the opposite end of the colosseum creaked open, and through it walked Amano. The half-gargoyle, half-minotaur master of the church sanctuaries in the Abyssal Descent was fully outfitted in sleek silver armor that starkly contrasted against his black skin. He had a huge battle-axe in one hand, and he knelt in reverence when the doors shut behind him.

Riven and Gluttony spread their wings to their fullest extent and raised a clawed hand to point in Amano's direction. "You all should know Amano, master of the sanctuaries, quite well. He will be the first to challenge my symbiotic partner—Riven—in one-on-one combat. Through the coming weeks we will hold trials of combat meant to teach Riven both humility and technique, and those who manage to best him will be greatly rewarded. Anyone who wishes to challenge him may do so, and anyone who is able to take him to the point of death's door where Lillith and the clergy need to personally intervene to save his live— you will even be granted a boon."

Murmurs of both confusion and excitement began to echo throughout the room as Gluttony held up a clawed hand.

"Though you may find this request odd, it is essential that my partner learns that simply wielding a bigger stick isn't always a viable option. This is an opportunity for him both to learn and to correct a personality flaw when subjugated to the reality of what the multiverse can provide as opposition—as opposed to the weaklings on his currently integrating planet. So what boons and rewards do I speak of? To any F- or E-grade church member here who beats Riven into submission, you will be granted a minor blessing. To anyone who does it without being harmed at all, your house will be honored with an artifact from the church coffers."

The murmurs of excitement grew in volume and pitch.

Riven's mind and body twisted, and suddenly he was standing in his own body again. Sweat drenched his skin, and Gluttony's maw was separated from him by a couple feet as it continued to speak.

"Together, we will celebrate our return by clobbering my counterpart to death time and time again. In between, instructors that have already been selected from your ranks will train him for the next round of challenges. During these intermittent periods of time, others will be allowed to fight for the entertainment of the crowds. This will repeat for however long I deem fit, until he is an acceptable vessel to take farther into the Abyssal Descent. Let the games begin. Please feel free to partake of the highest-quality food and drink available as it is brought out over the coming days, provided as a courtesy of the church."

Gentry, the drow man who'd been either unfortunate or fortunate enough to follow Riven to the "special event" hosted by Lavini the succubus, had been expecting some kind of scandalous get-together with Lavini's sisters. Maybe some of her friends. The way that succubus had looked at Riven on their descent while following the strange but very powerful demon Amano had made Gentry scratch his head in jealousy and confusion.

But he'd never expected something like this.

A secret complex full of demons that followed one of the lost sins. Lillith, a figure of myth and legend, stood directly in front of him while he sat back with

Riven's minions. Dozens of some of the most prominent demonic figures of his age and tier group vying for attention with people he'd been having a hot springs bath with only an hour ago, while Riven himself was the reincarnation of some godlike demon?

He felt his throat catch as Lillith came back to sit down beside the Allie girl, who was apparently Riven's sister—and a fallen angel at that. Looking over his shoulder, he recognized two representatives of the Scythe—reapers, if he was correct—who were waiting to speak to Allie but had been told they'd have to wait until the ceremonies were done.

Nobody told reapers they had to wait.

Gentry pushed his fingers up against his temples and got a knowing pat on the shoulder from Azmoth—who was the only one Gentry felt comfortable talking with at the moment, given the three women minions of Riven's retinue hadn't taken much of a liking to him after his gawking stares.

"It okay. You fine," Azmoth consoled the drow man, who was trying not to hyperventilate, but failed when Gentry let out a startled scream at Fimrindle, who flashed to his left and took a seat in an empty chair.

The strange metal scarecrow slowly turned his head to the startled drow, scoffed, and then shook his head before passing Azmoth a large slab of meat he'd confiscated from the refreshments table. It was the size of a fully grown hog, and Azmoth started chomping down noisily without a care in the world to the attempts at getting his attention from ambitious young scions of the more prominent demonic families here.

"This should be a good fight—Amano is very capable, from what my informants tell me," Fimrindle said, uncharacteristically upbeat and talkative. "I heard Lillith say that Riven doesn't stand a chance with his current capabilities after viewing some of Amano's fight records, but it'll be good to see Riven get pushed to his limits. I don't think I've actually seen Riven fight at 100 percent, not truly, and certainly not recently. Even Allie wants to fight him. I'll be interested to see how my own master stacks up to yours . . ."

Fimrindle glanced past Gentry to Azmoth. "Don't you think?"

"Allie get crushed under Riven's might like fly under boot!" Azmoth roared happily, chomping down onto the meat and ripping a piece off to swallow—only to get a glare from Allie, who'd heard his comment. Azmoth raised a hand in his own defense. "I must support Master because he friend. You just sister of friend. Sorry."

Fimrindle chuckled at the innocent comment, and Lillith grinned with a sideways glance before the sound of a booming drum and the rolling thunder of cheers announced the start of the fight—with the announcing high priest shouting, "BEGIN!"

CHAPTER 4

Metal boots and greaves were secured and tight. Messenger snapped on like a second skin, and Jackal flashed into his hand as the crowds roared, and he tossed the spare spatial sack he'd borrowed off to the side just before the high priest called for the fight to start.

Barriers went up all around the arena, and the drums echoed around them.

Even though he was here to improve himself, there was certainly a large part of Riven that wanted to prove all of them wrong. To show them that he wasn't as unskilled as Gluttony and Lillith seemed to think he was, but then again, he knew that line of thought was arrogant. He'd had little to no training and was self-taught in magic, so he pushed his pride aside and assumed one of the few stances that his ex-thrall Luke had taught him. His red eyes narrowed, and he stared out at the demon in front of him.

"I hear you're pretty strong," Riven stated, raising his weapon as his body exploded with Hell's Armor and Blessing of the Crow—the latter of which influenced by his Path of Red and Black. His body roiled with flame and Unholy energies, and rivers of blood flowed across the long blade of his spear-staff. "I won't be using any summons or minions. I hope you have a lot to show me."

Amano, for his part, bowed low at the waist in a sign of respect before swinging his silver battle-axe around with practiced ease in a defensive stance. The thick silver plate armor along his body glinted under the fireballs illuminating the arena, and he smiled. "It is an honor to fight Gluttony's chosen—for the entertainment of the Great Maw and the great general Lillith herself. Please forgive me for what transpires next, and know that I am more than willing to give pointers after it is done—but I will not be holding back. Lillith has informed me that they will not let either of us die, no matter what happens, so I am free to truly try and kill you."

Riven hesitated, then nodded just once. "I wouldn't expect you to hold back. Let's not keep them waiting."

The fight was on.

He tore open a black rift in space, and in the next millisecond Riven's swing blurred in a downward arc into Amano's back. The demon's axe was there in an instant in a shower of sparks as gray and black chaos energy swept up around him to block—sending a blast of energy that threw Riven backward through the air in an uncontrolled spiral before a follow-up slash of Amano's weapon sent an arc of dark lightning like a crescent wave.

Riven managed to discharge a Black Lightning bolt of his own that counteracted the crescent, and the colliding powers tore a fifty-foot crater into the stone ground that sent debris spraying into the air.

Riven finished his uncontrolled spin and landed on his two feet, then got up and dusted his pauldron off, cracking his shoulder.

Amano put his hands on his hips and laughed as the crowd cheered. "Vampire! I am impressed! For a level-200 F-grade to block my attack like that is noteworthy. However, I am aware that you have a warlock class. Is that correct?"

Riven lifted his head and nodded from across the crater as the dust cleared amid still-falling stone rubble. "That's right. Warlock Devastator."

"Ah!" Amano nodded appreciatively. "So that is why your physical strikes hit so hard. I see . . . The passive bonus to physical damage, infused with magic."

[Class: Warlock Devastator, Devastator Class Trait (physical strikes are imbued with Unholy damage equal to 1% of damage being done at full mana capacity).]

Riven smirked. "I'm surprised you—"

The vampire prince didn't get to finish his sentence as Amano slammed a spiked fist into his face. The demon had moved so fast that Riven had barely even seen it coming, and he'd not been able to react in time.

Riven's body crashed into the stone floor beneath them and bounced off the floor from the impact, only for his head to be smashed back into the stone yet again. His vision went black for an instant as Messenger's armor rang loudly in his ears while Amano's attacks picked up speed. Fist strike after fist strike crashed into Riven like a machine gun with the power of cannons behind each hit slamming him square in the face, again creating a crater underneath the two combatants as the back of Riven's helmet dug farther and farther into the ground.

"FIRST LESSON OF YOUR TRAINING, VAMPIRE!" Amano yelled over the crashing stone as Riven went in and out of consciousness, his vampiric healing in overdrive to keep him awake. "EVEN IF YOU HAVE A CLASS PARTIALLY ORIENTED TO CLOSE COMBAT AS A MAGE, YOUR FOCUS IS STILL IN MAGIC AND MANA! YOU SHOULD BE FOCUSING ON YOUR STRENGTHS AND UTILIZING YOUR STATS APPROPRIATELY! YOU'RE ALREADY AT A LEVEL DISADVANTAGE, AND MY CHAOS GUARDIAN

CLASS WHEN PITTED AGAINST YOUR HYBRID WARLOCK CLASS ISN'T A GOOD MATCH TO FIGHT ME IN CLOSE QUARTERS!"

Riven had a moment of clarity amid a forced spray of blood from his mouth when Amano slammed a fist into his chest, then Riven exploded with hellfire as he put more and more of his mana into Hell's Armor.

The demon flipped out of the newest crater they'd created and picked up his axe again with a twirl and a laugh, then activated a martial art that turned his skin into ebony stone just before the entire stadium lit up with flame.

The ground shook with a secondary explosion, and the stone floor underneath Riven melted away before being shredded in a groundbreaking thunderclap of power that blinded the onlookers. The barrier remained firm, however, and the roars of the crowd grew louder as the light faded away to reveal the two still-standing combatants.

Riven was glaring angrily from underneath his helmet, vision spinning, an inferno covered with additional black metal plates from his body modification hovering over a sea of molten rock that bubbled and churned.

Amano's body, on the other hand, was completely untouched while he stood in the lava, not even a scratch on his pristine silver armor, and his skin remained a hard ebony while he called out to Riven with a raised hand, "There it is! This is what I was told I would see! This is the power I was told of!"

He nodded approvingly as Riven floated down, spitting blood and landing two feet deep in the liquid rock while starting to walk toward Amano.

"As a Warlock Devastator, you have the option of close-quarters fighting. But that option should only be used sparingly. In a scenario where you fight an opponent of equal or stronger standing than you who is geared toward classes such as berserkers, paladins, knights, guardians, or warriors—they will have a distinct stat advantage." Amano jabbed a thumb into his silver-covered chest. "I have almost no points in Intelligence, Willpower, or Faith at all. That black lightning you saw was derived from stamina, a martial art, and I'm a purely physical combatant. My race also provides me with more baseline stats than the mortals you are used to back on your home planet, so your pureblood vampire race doesn't give you an advantage there, either. Even with your Hell's Armor and Blessing of the Crow spells, and even with your percentage-based class trait to enhance your physical strikes, it would be in your best interest to keep me at a distance if you can. That way, you are able to capitalize on your strengths while not allowing me to utilize my own. I'll say it one more time: When fighting opponents of greater or equal strength, your close-quarters combat should be as limited as possible to take advantage of your own magic-based stats—that means stop walking toward me."

Riven snapped his head left, eyes wide as a trail of azure-blue light trailed Amano's axe and snapped a horn off his left pauldron with a clean cut. Again, the minotaur-gargoyle hybrid had moved so quickly that Riven could barely tell he'd done it before the attack was already landing.

But it'd been a bait.

Riven's aura soared to an extreme, freezing everything around him, including Amano's feet, as the molten rock quickly cooled and caused him to stick in place. Spires of crimson shot into the sky and turned back before crashing down on Amano's position.

The demon's eyes widened, and an approving smile crept across his face when Riven's arm snapped up—coated in writhing blood mana.

Pouring as much energy as he could into the Snipe-infused Blood Lance, he let the long spear of red loose with a crackle of black sparks.

The attack met just as the spires came down, and—

CRASH

Riven's vision spun, and he found himself embedded into the floor again—leaving a two-hundred-meter line of torn bedrock in his wake as he came to an abrupt stop. Debris and lava had been flung into the air in his passing, and a stinging, painful sensation resonated through his right shoulder. Looking over, he saw that his own armor had been cut completely through—and that he was now missing his entire right arm.

Standing over him, and with Riven's arm in his hand, was a wickedly grinning demon with his wings flared out to either side. Tauntingly, he bent over Riven and showed his teeth. "Come, come, we can't be letting the crowds go without a better show than—UMPH!"

Riven smashed his foot into the cocky demon's crotch so fast that it created a sonic boom—and only barely managed to create a rift underneath his body before the enraged demon cleaved his weapon into the ground where Riven had been a second earlier.

Riven shot up high, blood streaming out of his stump-arm as a spray of Wretched Snares bloomed overhead to entangle the demon far below.

The snares hit nothing but air as Amano blurred, and Riven's eyes barely followed him as he burst from the ground in a spray of lava and smashed Riven so hard into the ceiling that even the barrier surrounding the arena flickered.

Riven gasped, feeling his spine crunch and his lower body go limp. Looking down, he saw the axe had cut through his waist just below where Messenger ended and his steel leggings began. The blade was lodged there, keeping him stuck to the ceiling, but before Amano could land the follow-up punch to his skull, Riven twisted.

Screaming in pain and literally tearing his upper body off the useless set of lower legs, he sent a pulse of power out from his hand to propel him back toward the ground. Simultaneously he summoned a cloud of Storm Razors in a rush of spinning, crackling red and black blades while falling through the air with no legs and only one arm.

The storm of red collided with Amano in a shower of sparks as he somehow glued his feet to the ceiling, moving with a speed that allowed him to deflect each and every one of the hundreds and then thousands of discs that crashed into his position. His axe spun, wove, and blurred—cutting through, smashing and redirecting the Storm Razors for nearly ten seconds before identifying Riven's position again midfall and launching himself toward the vampire.

"NEFAJIA CRECUS BLOOD NOVA!"

BOOM

Riven saw the giant orb of destructive blood crash directly into the demon right before Amano's figure tore out of it. A shit-eating grin was still plastered on Amano's face, wings flared out to either side, and his large axe raised as he let out a shout of his own—though Riven couldn't hear what he said due to the ringing in his ears.

The axe connected, but the vertical maw along Messenger's armor opened to snap down on the attack right upon impact. Deep tendrils of darkness started reaching out from the armor during their flight to wrap around Amano's arm, but the demon yanked back—exploding in green light—then somehow propelled himself out of Messenger's grip to fly skyward.

"METEOR STRIKE!"

The demon's axe flared with hellfire, and with a scream, he flung the weapon in a spinning arc that torpedoed like a homing missile directly into Riven's already-mutilated body.

Despite Riven's resistance to flame given his Hell's Armor, the prowess of the attack was more than enough to crack through his armor and cleave his chest in two—before erupting into flame and embedding Riven over a hundred feet into the ground with another sonic boom.

Riven woke up with a gasp, heart thudding rapidly in his chest as he looked around. He could hear the cheers of the crowd in the distance and the sound of applause, and he could see two of his minions huddled around him while he lay on a soft bed in a small stone room. Two other attendants dressed in black and purple clergy robes were also there, a Cthulhu-like man and a large imp, both of which bowed and left immediately upon seeing him wake.

"Feeling better?" Fay asked with a worried smile, using a wet washcloth to wipe at Riven's forehead. Her pretty features were furrowed in concern, and she shared a glance with Athela, who wore a very similar look on her own face.

He looked down at his body, pulling off a thin sheet of fabric, and was surprised to see that his limbs were all intact. However, he could see new but already fading scars now present where he'd lost his lower body and one arm not too long ago. There was even a pink area down his chest that looked like it'd been hit with a lightning strike by the way the tissue had healed, but those pink lines were very slowly vanishing right before his eyes as well.

"Are Messenger and Jackal all right?" Riven asked, grunting as he tried to sit up—but he quickly fell back to a reclining position when he felt a sharp twinge of pain in his lower spine. Then he abruptly felt Gluttony's presence shift inside his body, working with his vampiric heritage to repair the remaining damage.

"Yes, they're fine!" Athela pushed him back down and held her hand on his chest with a kind and caring smile. "Kicking that guy in the crotch probably wasn't the best idea. He got really mad after that and stopped going easy on you."

Fay saw the scowl of annoyance on Riven's features and started to giggle, raising a hand to her lips. "Yes, that was actually quite funny. I'm not sure if you heard it during your fight, but the entire crowd erupted in laughter—especially when he became so enraged."

Riven rolled his eyes and got as comfortable as he could in the bed, feeling fatigue wash over him. "Well, where ARE Messenger and Jackal?"

"Being looked over by some of the best smiths here for repairs. Messenger got it especially bad," Athela stated promptly. "The back of the helmet is dented after Amano smashed your face into the ground so many times, one of the pauldrons is seriously damaged, and the entire front where that maw is was obliterated. Jackal only had a small dent in the blade."

Fay cleared her throat.

"Amano was using a relic armor, some family heirloom from the fourth-era wars against the heavens that has been passed down for generations in his clan to their rising E- and D-grade prodigies. It's certainly on par with your own equipment," Fay said with a thoughtful glance out the hall where the two clergy had disappeared. "I was surprised that Messenger actually broke, though. Thankfully, as long as the spirit is intact, your armor won't actually die. And we have a lot of the materials needed for repairing sin-afflicted items in the abyss, so it's easy to do here."

The sound of large, pounding feet echoing through the halls over the screams and shouts of the arena caused Riven to turn his head, and he smiled as Azmoth and Genua made an appearance with Lillith in the back.

Genua gave a small bow but otherwise stayed silent and submissive as she stepped to the side to allow Azmoth through.

"You not fight bad," Azmoth said immediately, kneeling down to the bedside to get closer to Riven's eye level. He took a large bite out of a slab of meat in one hand, chewed, then swallowed with a satisfied grunt. "Amano very strong and in E-grade. You get better and beat him eventually."

Riven raised an eyebrow from where he lay, then turned his gaze on Lillith—who was smiling down at him with an amused expression while the yellow flower around one of her horns turned in his direction. "I got my ass thoroughly kicked.

Honestly, I'd thought I'd at least put up a fight . . . but Amano was just toying with me early on. Even though he said he wouldn't go easy on me."

Thinking about it, Riven hadn't been beaten that badly . . . ever? Even when he'd been starting out and very weak, after first learning his basic spells in Chalgathi's trials and had nearly been killed by that bald cultist . . . It had been close, but he'd won. Here, being pitted against one of the best E-grades the Unholy pillar had to offer, it certainly put into perspective that there were far bigger fish out there than himself, even at his own level.

Amano had taken a Blood Nova head-on without even blinking. That was one of Riven's strongest direct strikes.

"He was toying with you—until you kicked him, that is." Lillith winked, then laughed. "He didn't want to make you look too bad, but going for a cheap shot like that—all bets were off."

"I go back and watch other fights now with Gentry, Allie, and Retesh. And Fimrindle—he weird but okay—and they talking to other reapers now. Lillith pitting different clans against each other to entertain crowd, and it interesting to watch. Get better soon." Azmoth rose up, ruffled Genua's hair, to her obvious irritation, and then walked out while chomping down on more of the meat in his hands.

Riven took Athela's hand when she reached for his, intertwining their fingers, and watched the young brutalisk go. "Who's Retesh?"

"Retesh Vorath," Fay said, shooting Athela a slightly jealous glare and reaching for Riven's other hand so she'd be holding one, too. "The lich from Panu. He's the one who came with Lillith and Allie when you were first introduced to Amano not long ago."

"From Panu? The guy from the world quest? What the hell is he doing here?"

Fay gestured to Lillith with her eyes. "I believe it was decided that Retesh has some promise, and Lillith provided him with a ticket. Is that correct, esteemed one?"

"It is," Lillith said, creating a chair from solid shadow and sitting on it cross-legged while folding her arms. "The dog shows a small amount of promise, and he arrived in your lands asking for our help not long after I brought Allie back out of the underdark. It appears that Elysium is giving our opposition many boons and bonuses to increase their chances of survival and success and has given Retesh and his undead empire across the ocean from Umbra quite a bit of trouble. I believe you know the name Judith Marcina?"

"The previous number-one ranker," Riven acknowledged.

Lillith nodded. "She's allied with the seafaring peoples now and has hired off-world mercenaries from various holy orders that are more than happy to send entire generations of their offspring to their deaths in an attempt to get you killed. And to kill as many of the banished as they can. Even if one of us dies, that's a future powerhouse snuffed out early that their elders won't have to deal with later on. To them, killing even one of us is worth the thousands of their young that will perish."

The archdemoness snorted in derision with a shake of her head, her seven crowned horns shimmering unnaturally in the light. "They're desperate to kill as many of the banished as they can before we grow our strength back and are amassing an invasion force to clear out Retesh's undead cities before mounting an attack on Umbra itself. In fact, we almost lost one of the banished to their number already when Nephilim attempted to finish Retesh off just as he made land. The Nephilim were killed by the hundreds, and Judith escaped, but when I say it was close . . ."

Lillith's face darkened even more with a frown. "It was incredibly close. We had to put Namath, the demon in question, into a stasis ritual to save his life. It was a stark reminder to all of us banished that though we may have the skills and knowledge of the ancients, we are still not as infallible or immortal as we once thought. Even we sometimes fall victim to overconfidence, so do not take the lessons of humility that we are trying to impress upon you lightly, Riven. Overconfidence can easily get any of us killed—it is a flimsy shield, and it is where legends go to die."

Riven pondered her words, slowly mulling over what was to be done and the numerous questions he had. "So did Allie finish her world quest in the underdark then?"

"No. She evolved into an angel of death, lost her vampiric heritage, was unable to absorb the currently semidead vampiric elder god, and three of the necromancers who went down there with her were killed in an attempt on her life. It will fall upon you or another pureblood on the planet to finish the quest. She almost died in her attempt and would have if the ritual I stopped had been left alone. It was using siphoned souls of her followers to attack the very structure of her core apparatus."

Riven's breath caught in his throat as he thought about nearly losing Allie, and he had to quickly repress a surge of worry that flooded through him.

"I see. Thank you for saving her, then."

Lillith gave a nod of confirmation. "Of course. I'll be training her as well as you; I don't intend to let either of you die. The vampiric precursors there will be prepared for our second attempt, though, and I don't think it'll be as easy as the first time to make it to the temple where I found the elder god's coffin. I wish I could have taken the coffin with me, but Elysium would not allow it. We'll talk more about it later. Do you have any other pressing questions before I go over what you can improve upon?"

Riven thought for a moment, allowing Athela to get under the covers and snuggle up against him. "Who is running the Thane Necropolis in our absence? Gurth'Rok? Dr. Brass?"

"Tre'Zix of the Purple Claw, and Kathrine Vonsilla Crushada, the vampiric princess," Lillith promptly replied. "Alongside a man named Crendir No-Name, an E-grade champion sent from the Blood Moon Requiem and a man that your General Viku spoke very highly of in our brief communication. The Blood Moon Requiem's forces arrived just before I came to the Abyssal Descent, but Dungeon Negrada—though they are now able to reinforce your lands through Elysium's new event pacts—has held off in sending reinforcements until its own wars in the hells are over with. Tre'Zix is leading the forces in Negrada's hellscapes to secure the dungeon lands quite quickly, while Kathrine remains in Brightsville to run your country with the assistance of Gurth'Rok and Dr. Brass. General Bruner is finishing his own job conquering the populations surrounding Chicago—ones that I am told tried to assassinate you at one point."

Lillith paused, tilting her head to the side to think. "Forty thousand Sarak slave soldiers from Vartesh have been sent, courtesy of House Wraithtide. Fifteen thousand vampiric soldiers from House Wraithtide have arrived as well, with an additional ten thousand vampiric soldiers from the Blood Moon Requiem's most elite factions and noble families that were all approved by the High Queen Nephridi. The man named Jeltuna, the voice of the Sarak, I believe you called him, is currently being trained for command of his kin by Kathrine. She tells me the chosen Sarak are being leveled on feral undead and are being trained regularly in the heartland of your empire. They are also being harvested—nonlethally— for blood to feed some of the native vampires who'd come out of the underdark to beg for rations, as their thralls were all changed into undead variants, too. Humans from Chicago are being paid very well for voluntary blood donations, too, while prisoners of war are being forced to give blood regularly to maintain the vampiric armies you've recently acquired. Meanwhile, Kathrine has sent Crendir No-Name to command a force of F-grade elites from the Blood Moon Requiem northward. They intend to conquer the city-states and countries of Umbra that have not already pledged themselves to the Thane Necropolis as vassals. There are only a couple holdouts that were turned into undead, and they'll likely fall within the month if they cannot be bribed into submission. Unfortunately the forces from the Blood Moon Requiem cannot cross the sea to assist Retesh or his forces beyond Umbra for a year's time, according to system parameters on the event quest, but he hopes that we can spare some of our other forces to aid his people before Judith commits genocide—or so he says. Did I miss anything?"

Lillith turned to Fay and Athela, who both hesitantly shook their heads no.

"Good." Lillith nodded and uncrossed her arms to lean forward. "Further details on what's happening in Panu can wait. For now, let's go over what you can improve on—and what you did wrong in that fight against Amano. Then we'll pit you against a series of assassins to shore up your obviously lacking areas regarding stealthed opponents."

CHAPTER 5

Days passed, and then days turned into weeks.

Riven was thrown into five different types of public events, and he lost a little more than half of them on average. They were one-on-one duels, team battles, survival courses where twenty people endured a free-for-all in an ever-changing and violent environment that was constantly trying to kill them, sensory deprivation fights where sight and sound were removed, and, finally, one versus many. In between fights he'd be set aside while other events took place in what had become a gigantic training regimen sponsored by the church, where Lillith herself would lecture him on what he'd done wrong and right before providing demonstrations. For an untrained, self-taught warlock, Lillith said, he wasn't doing too bad—but he shouldn't let that go to his head, because he was still miles behind where he needed to be.

During this time, he quickly came to realize three things. First, he wasn't anywhere near as talented as he'd previously thought he was. Yes, he had immense amounts of power, but there were many combatants who had lower energy stores than him but still beat him handily. Second, he was very, very wasteful in how he utilized his magic. Much of his energy was lost to the ether simply because he didn't maintain control over it after it was released. This caused problems whenever he faced opponents that were able to fully utilize their power output and successfully used compact attacks. Thirdly, he'd been relying far too much on his regeneration, better gear, and minions to get him out of tight situations. This was less so for Fay and Azmoth lately, as they'd fallen so far behind, but when it truly came down to it, he had won most of his fights after Negrada because he'd had the bigger stick and a very keen sense of mana manipulation—especially when it came to the Blood subpillar.

Not to mention he was still seriously at a disadvantage against stealth-type opponents, which had a disproportionate win rate against him in any of the given scenarios. This was also something that had been pointed out to him, but it wasn't as if he didn't already know it.

His squad-to-be also trained under Lillith. With the archdemoness as their future guide into the Abyssal Descent, and five being the max that could travel between floors, the other four were Riven, Allie, Retesh the lich, and Nora Lang.

Then, at the end of each training session between fights or events, Riven was forced to meditate along with the others as they prepared their soul lattices. Under the guidance of Gluttony, the five of them were shown how to create bridges between or around their pillars. They were akin to scaffolding, and different structural patterns in different amounts created different effects. It could change the way mana left your body, what mana was produced, how mana interacted with the environment, and more—but the process was slow going and small mistakes could lead to failures of the entire internal soul system. There was even one time where Nora couldn't use a single skill after she'd accidentally rewired her scaffolding improperly and had to completely tear it all down to restart from scratch. Nora was also singled out specifically, being sent back to Chalgathi's altar trials whenever easy quests appeared for quick points so she could gain XP—as she hadn't yet grown to level 200 and had a level cap imposed by the system due to the nature of the world quest. The only way she could actually gain levels right now was by completing those event quests, and she needed to reach level 200 in order to fully utilize the teachings of soul scaffolding.

As for Riven's minions, only Athela had been deemed adequate after another in-depth evaluation of their skills. This was in large part due to the level discrepancy Azmoth, Fay, and Genua had when compared to Riven or Athela—but in the end, why didn't matter. Not to the clergy, not to the onlookers in the Abyssal Descent, and not to Lillith. The reincarnation needed to be protected at all costs, and already there'd been floods of prospects asking for Riven's last minion slot— or even group offers that wanted to replace Riven's current minion set and suggesting that he let Fay and Azmoth go. Azmoth didn't seem to care much, as he had absolute faith that Riven wouldn't do that, but it very seriously impacted Fay's mental health, as they were all forced into a training regimen of their own that— in many ways—was far more brutal than Riven's.

The eye of the vortex at the city's center was one of the few places where you could regularly fight F-grade abyssal creatures in a life-or-death struggle before passing into the second layer of the descent. It was a small, alternate realm connecting the first and second floors that had a filter on it imposed by Elysium, and it wasn't entirely unheard-of for those descending to die, even here so early on. But the abyssal creatures ranged in level from 160 to 200 here in this first layer's bridge, so most of these elites from across the multiverse didn't have too much of a problem.

However, most of these F-grade elites were at the apex of their climb and heading into E-grade, or even already E-grade if they'd chosen to remain after completing their soul lattice. As for Azmoth, Fay, and Genua . . . things were not that way. Genua in particular had been taken by Amano and over eight hundred of the most powerful scions Gluttony's church had here to escort her as she leveled up, making sure she was power leveled effectively while keeping Gluttony's child safe, as she lacked a minion contract that'd let her respawn. At the same time, Azmoth, Fay, and even Athela to a lesser extent were pushed into battle after battle with monsters of the deep to either sink or swim.

It was one of these occasions, in the alternate realm between floors, that Fay found herself in now. Beaten, bruised, and with an ugly, festering wound on her side, she gasped and clawed at the strange black dirt as clouds crackled with Sin energy far above them. A squid-like creature lay rotting at her side, and with signs of recent intervention on behalf of Fay's escorts.

Lavini the redheaded succubus looked down at Fay with a frown. She sighed and shook her head slowly as the blue-skinned illusionist and curse specialist panted and coughed up blood on the floor. Glancing sideways to where some of the five other volunteer tutors had gathered to help whip Fay into shape, Lavini threw up her hands in exasperation.

"Fay," Lavini stated with a hint of irritation in her words, and she leaned over the younger succubus to pour a healing potion over the girl, before handing the rest of it off for Fay to drink. "How is it that you came to be one of the reincarnation's minions?"

Lavini poked Fay with her staff, getting a groan from the young woman and sighing when Fay still didn't get up. Lavini then took a cross-legged position and bent lower to whisper in Fay's ear. "Answer me. I wish to know."

Fay, for her part, struggled desperately to raise herself off the black ground where her blood had pooled underneath her. Her wounds were slowly healing, and she coughed up a ball of phlegm before managing to sit upright and stare Lavini in the face. "It was chance. He was not the reincarnation yet."

"But he still chose you. Why?" Lavini asked curiously, allowing Fay to use her arm for support.

Fay coughed again, grimaced at her torn clothes and the bloodstains on the boots Riven had gifted her, then slumped her shoulders. "It was because I had a good set of utility spells, I think. I was a good fit for him because my illusions helped keep him alive."

Lavini blinked. "I see. What kinds of enemies were you fighting back then?"

"Goblins, orcs, and humans mostly. On Panu."

"And do you think that your spells are still able to do that? Against opponents like this?"

Lavini gestured to the single squid creature, one that she'd damaged beforehand to help Fay fight it. The monster was a level-161 Abyssal Prongsnapper, with large spikes coming out of its legs and hundreds of eyes across its upper body.

Fay's grimace grew deeper. "Of course not. A monster like that would give even the other Apex rankers on Panu a hard time. My charm wouldn't work on it. My dreamwalker illusions were dispersed by the creature just by a mere flex of its aura, and my Curse of Rot was too weak to damage it before it repaired its outer layers of skin—until you helped me at the end. Curse Trap was able to do a little bit, but not much. Dark Pact doesn't work to heal myself. The Willpower of the creature was too high for Silvertongue to do anything other than briefly stagger it. If you're trying to point out that I'm weak, I already know that."

Lavini smirked at the venom in Fay's words, and she patted the younger demoness on the back consolingly. "As long as you truly do know, Fay. You see those other five that followed us here?"

Lavini gave a brief gesture in their direction, where they stood a couple dozen meters away with folded arms and scowls on their faces—two incubi and three succubi. All of them were some of the best the descent could offer for their species.

Fay hesitated. "Yes, what about them?"

Lavini gave her a knowing smile. "Each and every one of them is hoping that you fail spectacularly, so they can report to Lillith that you should be replaced. Either by themselves, or by one of their clan. What you have is the opportunity of a lifetime, and they want it."

Fay's face scrunched up in a combined look of embarrassment, rage, and horror. She spat blood, and her fingernails dug into her palms while she glared at the ground. "Riven is mine. He would not so easily cast me away just because they want him to."

Lavini raised an eyebrow, then giggled and put a hand up to her face while spreading her wings. "Of course not. I'm not implying he would—in the way you're implying. But Riven is different from Gluttony, child. You must realize that the reincarnation's safety is of utmost importance for Gluttony's climb. According to Lillith, Riven is a very rare specimen based on intrinsic power and bloodline— one that can greatly help ease Gluttony's rise back to power. If he dies . . . it will be a catastrophic blow to the Great Maw."

Lavini let the silence stretch as Fay continued to look at the dirt. The redhead sighed. "Your position as his mate is no doubt something that many would kill for, but that should not be your immediate concern. From what I am told, that is not what Lillith is concerned about, either. What she is concerned about, however, is your status as a minion. They are not one and the same, and you could remain his mate while not being his minion if need be. May I be frank?"

Fay slowly looked up to the other succubus, then nodded. "Yes."

"Good. You and the other minions Riven has collected are subpar." Lavini paused, waiting for Fay to get angry about the proclamation—but she saw only sadness and resignation in Fay's eyes. "Perhaps Athela would have made it to the

Abyssal Descent on her own, based only on her skill, but even she is incredibly lazy in her duties protecting Riven. As numerous others have pointed out, she is primarily a stealth-type assassin despite her unique ability to swap between forms. She's also an archdemon, and her combat prowess is rather good. However, despite that, Riven has nearly died numerous times due to her inaction and inattentiveness, and Genua nearly died along with Gluttony's child because Athela was choosing to nap instead of keep guard. Do you know how often an archdemon actually needs to sleep?"

Fay didn't reply.

"Not often," Lavini answered her own question. "Very, very rarely, in fact. Do they enjoy it just like anyone else? I'm sure. But when the fate of Gluttony's progeny hangs in the balance, perhaps having someone a little more on edge—one who is able AND WILLING to fulfill the duty of bodyguard—should be selected."

Lavini raised two fingers. "On to his second minion, Azmoth. That child is barely five years old. Did you know that?"

Fay turned her head in surprise. "Really?"

"Really," Lavini confirmed with a nod. "At five years old, that hellscape brutalisk barely knows his right from left. His head is in the right place and he has a fierce loyalty to Riven, but he is still just a child. Thankfully he shows promise, but he's never been to the battlefields in the hellscapes even once. We're hoping that the other brutalisks here can show him how to tank for Riven properly, but that is still to be determined."

Lavini then held up a third finger. "Then there's you. Tied with Genua for the title of being weakest of his minions—tied with an elf thrall, of all things. Do you know what separates you from her, though? And why, out of all his minions, you are the biggest disappointment?"

Fay sniffled, looking back to the ground, and shook her head silently as tears began to build in her eyes.

"It is because you have a contract that makes you nearly unkillable on an F-grade integration planet," Lavini stated flatly, unmoved by Fay's despair and rising emotions. "The three of you demons, all of you, should be utilizing your demonic contracts to their utmost. You die? So what, you can respawn twenty-four hours later. That is why contracts are so popular to begin with. But each attempt enables you to grab more levels, and here you are, still below level 60 and having entered the descent as what is likely one of the weakest participants in the history of the event. Both you and Azmoth should have been grinding enemies, burying them beneath your might to keep up with Riven—but instead you've both fallen so utterly far behind that I'm not sure we can fix it by the time this descent is over with. So here's the thing: You need to prove yourself to Lillith and to everyone else that's watching. Prove that you can fix your bad habits, fix your attitude, and fix this severe level discrepancy in order to keep up with Riven. Because if you can't keep up, you will probably be designated to only being his lover while more competent demons take up the positions of his minion slots."

"You say that, but Athela did die and I almost did, too! And that was back on the F-grade planet you're talking about!" Fay protested. "I'm not intentionally trying to hold him back!"

"Intentionally? No. But your laziness and lack of action are doing so anyways. Riven has his own problems, but you are adding to them." Lavini didn't back down from the glare Fay was throwing her way as the two women sat in the black dirt.

Another woman's call came out from the sidelines where the five other succubi and incubi stood on the ledge. "We will go find another weaker specimen for her to fight, Lavini. Wrap up your lecture so that we can continue the grinding!"

With that, the others began to walk away—looking for another of the relatively weaker abyssal creatures that roamed this ladder between floors.

Lavini watched them go, then turned her gaze back to Fay, who was still clenching her fists in self-hate and frustration. "Fay. I am not saying these things to anger you. I am merely wanting to warn you in case these scenarios play out as expected. I truly do hope that you prove us all wrong, and that you can show not only me, but Lillith and everyone else in the church that you are worthy of remaining a minion. But no matter what happens, know that you will still have the standing and respect of all of us for being one that Riven cares so deeply about."

There was a pause.

With those words, Fay's composure faltered—and she covered her face with her hands. "I . . . I don't want to be separated from him, Lavini. This is unfair, and I . . . I want to be useful. I don't want him to befriend other demons, other women, that could take him away from me."

Lavini drew the other woman into a hug, patting her on the back. "I know this is upsetting you, and I understand. It's a lot to be thrown into, and I doubt Riven would even want to replace you after hearing of how much he cares about all his minions. However, I'm sure that if Lillith speaks to him about having you along being a potential liability—endangering not only himself, but you as well when assassins come for you . . . He'd probably be willing to see the change done. May I ask, do you know the three most common ways that a minion contract can be involuntarily shattered?"

Fay took a while to reply but regained her composure thereafter and let out a shaky breath. "Weapons or skills related to the commandments, invasions of one's soul aperture, and invasion of one's nether realm to kill the demon there while it is unsummoned—though the last one is usually done by trickery, as you can't brute force your way into a nether realm."

"Good. Now considering who you are bonded to, the chances of those things happening will continue to escalate. The moment Riven steps off-planet and into the greater multiverse, assuming that he is able to conquer Panu and uses Elysium to keep it hidden for the next century, he will have a target on his back. So you must understand that not being able to protect him from even other F-grades, when S-grades will be looking to stomp Gluttony flat before his rise to power can gain momentum . . . it is just not something the church can risk."

Fay sniffled again. "Why doesn't Lillith bind herself as a minion, then?"

Lavini opened her mouth, then realized Fay was being serious. She cackled slightly and then calmed herself before waving Fay's ire down. "I do not mean to mock you. I apologize. You see, Lillith doesn't have someone bound to her like Gluttony does. Lillith's rise to power will likely be far faster than Riven's because of this, even if Gluttony himself will end up causing Riven to match or surpass Lillith in the end should Riven not die. These early centuries of cultivation would be stagnated for Lillith if she was kept to a level cap equal to that of Riven's own, and she needs to grow strong fast to make sure she can protect Riven and Gluttony as they continue to rise together. Not only is there a level cap equal to the master's own, but you should already know that minion contracts reduce the amount of XP gained while underneath a master. Contracts add a certain amount of safety, but in return—a minion doesn't grow as fast as an unbound demon would if they both had the same experiences. Now . . . perhaps I can add some positivity to these training sessions by providing you with a gift."

Lavini opened her palm, and over her white skin a ball of green flames rippled into existence. She smiled at Fay's expression before using her other hand to open Fay's clenched fists. "Raise your hands palm up, and I will pass you the flame. Your mission, as the others hunt for prey, is to stabilize this power and keep it there."

Fay blinked, and as Lavini passed the fireball over, it quickly fizzled out and then flared to singe the tips of Fay's fingers. "Ow!"

Lavini chuckled, shaking her head before producing another ball of green flames. "Again. Take your time, hold the spell that I give to you there, and don't let it go."

Fay hesitated, but opened her palms face up to the sky again and nodded. "If you don't mind me asking, what are those? Is that a curse?"

Lavini winked. "Oh yes, even now my insides are screaming in pain as I produce the flame. But we curse users are used to the give-and-take that is required of such spells, for greater power, of course . . . wouldn't you say? You don't happen to be the only curse user here, and these flames not only burn you, but they afflict your enemies with a very specific debuff that you can stack and then activate. We'll talk about details later, but for now, just know that it is your best interest to learn some real, hard-hitting, long-range attacks. Because right now, your offensive power is actually rather pathetic."

CHAPTER 6

"OH GODS!" Athela cried, dramatically flopping onto the floor with a splat—as the blood she was covered in made a woman-size smudge on the floor around her. "I WANT TO DIE! A PRINCESS SHOULD NOT BE SUBJECT TO THIS KIND OF BRUTAL TORTURE! PHYSICAL LABOR IS FOR PEASANTS, NOT A PRINCESS SUCH AS I!"

Lillith stepped over Athela's prone form and quickly joined Riven at the ornate table of food where he was already starting to eat, surrounded by servants of various demonic races.

"For one as melodramatic as her—" Lillith pointed over her shoulder with a hiked thumb in Athela's direction underneath the candlelight of a chandelier. "—I'm surprised at her level of competence. Her family has sent a very humble request to meet with me, and after today's displays—I very well might indulge them to congratulate them on raising such an excellent young woman."

Riven stopped chewing and looked over Lillith to where Athela still lay facedown on the floor. He chuckled, shaking his head—then winced at the wounds he'd acquired from the arena earlier that day. Despite his vampirism, his healing was significantly reduced when dealing with cursed attacks. "Is she doing all right, then?"

"More than all right. She's a real talent." Lillith stretched her right hand over the table and plucked some fruit and freshly chopped meat from a display, putting them on her plate. "She just needs the seriousness of her position impressed upon her. I think she'll do nicely once she actually applies her skills regularly to protecting you. Speaking of which, how is the mana-zone technique coming along? Have you found the items and people I asked you to find yet?"

Riven gave a half smile and shook his head, looking around the dining hall. Inwardly he continued sending out monotonous pulses of mana—interchanging what type of mana he sent to throw off whoever was still hiding from him. "Not exactly. I've found two of the five people and no items."

"Where are the people you've found?"

Riven pointed to the ceiling and then to an empty seat to Lillith's left. "Those two."

The swamp-weaver spider above them cursed loudly, unveiling herself from stealth as a six-legged, horse-size monstrosity before she skittered out of the room, grumbling. Meanwhile the chair next to Lillith saw a blue-haired, red-eyed, robed woman with a single long black horn protruding from her head materialize, holding a cup of tea to her lips.

The horned woman sipped her tea and silently set her cup down on a porcelain saucer, nodding approvingly. "I was worried you weren't going to find me—considering I am the closest to you in proximity I should have been the easiest. Well done nonetheless; it is an honor to help serve the reincarnation."

Politely nodding to both Riven and Lillith, the stranger silently got up and left the room to follow the arachnid out.

Lillith gave him an approving smile, folding her arms over her chest and leaning back in her large, cushioned chair. "You're getting better over these past weeks, and quickly. But tell me . . . you noticed those two because they had Blood affinities, didn't you?"

Riven raised an eyebrow and rested his elbows on the table over the steaming-hot bowl of refined soup that a servant had just set down. "Yes, you're right."

"To be expected, I suppose." Lillith sighed, inspecting her black fingernails one by one. "Your Blood subpillar is of course your highest affinity, so the mana there is more eager to do your bidding. The others in the room are not of the Blood affinities, though, so you'll likely have a harder time finding them. However, you are still not allowed to leave this room until they are found. Understand?"

Riven rolled his eyes. "Yes, Mom."

The archdemon slowly turned her head and raised an eyebrow. "Excuse me, young man?"

Riven chuckled at her barely hidden amusement and then nodded. "I mean, yes, oh dark goddess of shadowy violent ends—I will obey thine orders to the letter!"

"Now, that's better." She crossed her legs and waved a hand at Athela, who was still nearly passed out on the floor behind them. "Athela, dear? Are you all right?"

Only a low groan escaped Athela's mouth as she mumbled something under her breath.

"I do believe she gained from overexerting herself against abyssal creatures. Servants? Please help Athela to Riven's room for a bath and bed. She did well today and deserves some time off." Lillith snapped her fingers, and four humanoid demons quickly moved to carry her away. "Now, Riven, whenever you're switching up your mana pulses, try circulating the mana through your core a few times before actually pushing it through your pillars. Doing that will enable you to concentrate the mana for a quicker and more potent burst, and it makes the mana more sensitive when using it to scan your surroundings."

"Circulate it through my core . . . ?" Riven muttered to himself, confused. He cocked his head to one side. "I've never really tried that before. Like, recycle it and keep it stable internally in my soul realm? What would be the point in that?"

The blank stare he gave Lillith caused her to laugh, and she put one hand over her eyes while shaking her head. It almost looked like she was embarrassed. "Oh my . . . Gluttony is certainly being lazy if he hasn't told you even this much. Just . . . just humor me. And try it."

Closing his eyes and folding his arms, he took time to evaluate his internal soul realm. Cracks still remained along the pillars that'd once been shattered by Elysium's powerful strikes, from when he'd used his bloodline prophecy one too many times and suffered a tribulation. Those cracks radiated with the Sin energy used to repair the pillars, along the pillars and subpillars of Unholy, Shadow, Blood, Infernal, and Death in equal amounts—but above all, the Sin subpillar that'd once been an alternate core shone brilliantly in a deep purple, almost black.

He ignored the sigils representing skills, the bridges of black and red that criss-crossed thousands of times over between his Shadow and Blood subpillars—the beginnings of his soul lattice—to focus on the bright-white core that supported all the pillars in the very center like a brilliant globe.

There, in the center of it all, he began to summon mana to do his bidding.

Like a factory lit aflame, the soul core went to work producing energy. It was a pure, raw energy, which hadn't yet been converted by his pillars into type or function. It was not mana, divinity, or stamina—but rather it was the basic ingredient to all skills.

He built it, and built it, and built it. Over and over again he watched the pure, raw energy circulate like a building vortex until his body began to hum with power yet to be let loose. Not pushing it through his core like he was so used to doing had put him in new territory, and although the act was a simple one, he didn't really understand the point.

Yet he trusted Lillith's words and experience and kept building until that same radiant white energy radiating from his core enveloped his very body and the room began to shake. And then as it continued to make contact with the universe around him, that same radiant white energy began to turn into an ever-changing multitude of colors.

His eyes flicked open, gazing at the swirling, powerful yet simultaneously peaceful cloud of raw power around him.

"Good," Lillith commented, staring at him with an intensity he hadn't seen before. She steepled her fingers and leaned closer. "That multicolored light around you that you're seeing now? Only you can see it; no one else in the room can visualize that power. Remember that. Now, release it . . . and when you're done, immediately cycle to the next pillar. And then the next, and the next, until you've returned to the original."

Riven kept eye contact and continued under her instruction. This time, when he pushed energy into his pillars for another pulse of mana, the energy kept some of that raw, wild nature that sent tingles down his spine.

The first pillar he sent it down was the Death subpillar, and with an invisible pulse of mana, he swept his senses across the room.

Still nothing in terms of the three remaining hidden people, but he did pick up on one of the items Lillith had hidden.

Curiously reaching over the table and fumbling for a bit, he grasped a cold metal object. Upon contact, the object materialized, and Riven brought it over the table to inspect it with interest. It wasn't anything special, just a fork, but this fork had been imbued with some kind of Death aspect that'd allowed it to go unseen for the entire time he'd been sitting here.

"An aspect similar to how phantoms innately blend in with their surroundings," Lillith commented smugly while Riven set the fork down. "A personal favorite of mine. Do you see how much more the mana reacted to your probing task when you circulated it beforehand?"

Riven nodded, lost in thought.

"That kind of thing can apply not only to simple tasks such as this, but you can actually empower skills the same way. I'm more than certain you've intentionally charged skills to build up their power before, to make them hit harder or fly faster. Perhaps go farther. But . . ." Lillith held up a finger. "Circulating your energy before pushing it through your pillars allows it to become . . . eh . . . how should I say this? Adaptable? Yes, adaptable. It is more adaptable to your will and retains some of the wild flair that it would otherwise lose out on if you pushed it through a pillar too early. Because of this, charging spells—or any type of ability, really—can be made better by the very basic and simple concept of circulating your energy before pushing and converting it through pillars. When you push it in too fast, it becomes somewhat rigid in its nature. Now, can you think of any reason why this couldn't be used in a real battle? Any specific scenarios?"

Riven's jaw had dropped, and he barely caught the end of her sentence. How had he not discovered this already? It wasn't as if it'd been some kind of elusive secret—he'd just thought it natural to create the spell and then build it up afterward. But doing that in reverse, building it up prior to release, made mana manipulation all that much more potent.

He'd have to try this out on the battlefield.

"Riven?" Lillith prodded, amused.

He snapped out of it. "I—I'm sorry, Lillith. I did not mean to ignore you, I just . . . I just can't believe I overlooked something so simple. To answer your question . . . I assume that in a very fast-paced battle, I wouldn't be able to keep circulating the mana. I'd need to buy time to do something like this, because the process is far slower than building a spell externally."

She nodded sagely. "You are directly on the mark. Creating a spell and then firing it, even if you take time to charge it on the outside, is far faster than building it internally by rotating it in your soul core. You wouldn't be able to do this rapidly, and releasing any kind of skill will automatically expel the energy you've been rotating—so this is yet another downside. If you are forced into switching abilities, you could inadvertently release the wrong spell at an amplified level and deplete your energy reserves on something you'd rather not, while needing to start over on the spell you'd initially wanted to cast. So tell me, what does this imply when fighting enemy combatants?"

"It means that if I am able to determine that they're rotating their mana, I can force them into acting in a way that dispels their energy gathering on something useless."

"Precisely. But how do you tell whether they're actually acquiring power internally, when most can only sense external power buildup?"

He paused. "Wait, does this mean I can unleash high-power attacks out of nowhere with little to no warning against enemies? Like a surprise attack, without them realizing I'm building power?"

"Yes and no," Lillith stated flatly. "Yes for people who don't realize what to look for, and no to people who do. Now, that being said, I will repeat myself—how do you tell whether or not they're actually acquiring that power buildup within their soul core?"

The room went silent, and Riven frowned as he glared at the soup bowl in front of him with furrowed brows. "I have no fucking idea."

Lillith responded with a cackling laugh. "Well, at least you can admit when you're lacking! Perhaps you should ask Gluttony. He'd be better at describing it than I am."

Gentry glanced nervously at the two ELITE-class devils walking on either side of him. Huge, hulking, winged creatures with red skin and black horns, they each stood between two and three times his height with enormous claws that gripped halberds that made his jade scimitar look like a child's toy. They were also each at the pinnacle of what was allowed to remain in the descent, in terms of power and level, and walking here with him had been something of an obvious irritation for both archdemons.

But hey. At least he got that escort like he'd been promised after weeks of waiting, even if Riven had completely forgotten about it for a time.

Wiping sweat off his forehead and finishing the trek to what he thought was his sister's manor on the third floor of the descent, he approached the gate where two dozen drow cultivators were wordlessly sizing him up—along with his two escorts. In the backdrop was a three-story mansion made of dark-gray and black stone similar to everything else down here, but the sigil on the gate—the same jade green as his weapon—was familiar to him.

Sighing in relief, he glanced at the barren surroundings before turning to his escorts. It was a land of ashen hills, with black skies and minimal life. Certainly not the prettiest place to be.

He bowed low in a sign of respect. "Thank you for the time and patience you have demonstrated to bring me here, great ones. I will not forget the kindness Gluttony's reincarnation has shown me today."

One of the devils didn't even acknowledge him, just turned around to start walking away. The other one snorted in annoyance and replied in a deep, rumbling voice, "Try to survive, dark elf. The dangers are only greater the farther down you go, and not having the strength to proceed even to here makes me question why you came."

Gentry winced, then nodded. He didn't know what to say to that, so he just stood there, embarrassed, until the devil turned to follow the other.

"Gentry," a familiar female voice called out to him, and he turned around to see that none other than his elder sister had come to the forefront of the group of drow elves. She wore immaculate, dark-blue cultivator robes and had her long white hair done up in three ponytails. At her side were two jade scimitars just like his, though hers were chipped and worn. She motioned for him to come closer with a hurried wave of one hand.

He'd never seen his older sister in person. He'd only very briefly communicated with her through waystones—incredibly expensive ones—with his parents from time to time. So the fact that she'd so quickly picked him out by name and knew who he was . . . it was a little bit odd. He'd almost guessed that he'd need to convince her of his identity, but that hadn't been the case.

Still, given the way she was warily looking around at the barren landscape and shooting the two devils glances as they took to the dark skies with large flapping wings, something felt off. He quickly hurried over and was about to greet her when she abruptly grabbed his wrist and pulled him in close.

"Are they the only ones that took you here? Are there any others?"

Gentry's brow furrowed in confusion, irritation, and surprise as he yanked his arm back out of her grasp as the other drow men and women standing nearby gazed at him. "No!"

"No what?!" his sister pressed, hissing under her breath as she watched them begin to go. "Hurry and answer!"

"No, there aren't any others! Why?! Is something the matter, Asha? This is certainly an odd way to greet family for the first time." His frown only deepened when his older sister gave a curt nod to one of the other cultivators standing in front of the manor, and that man quickly took a stone from his pocket and began speaking into it.

Gentry was about to say something else to try and clear up what exactly was going on here, when an explosion echoed across the barren landscape and a scream lodged itself in his ears.

He whipped around, and to his horror and building confusion, he saw what could only be described as an enormous, writhing mass of green slugs, worms, and leeches reach up hundreds of yards into the sky to snatch one of the huge devils in a vise grip.

Blood sprayed.

Muscles tore.

Bones snapped.

He watched in disgusted awe as he saw the swarm of creatures rip and tear the gigantic demon to shreds. It screamed and cried out in agonizing pain as it was eaten alive, until it was swallowed whole by the pillar of flesh that consumed it—only a single red, clawed hand sticking out and trying to drag itself back out before that too disappeared amid the swarm.

The other devil had not been idle during this time and was engaged in a frantic duel with the swarming, sickly green creatures that dug into the demon's red flesh and began burrowing as he created cascades of fire to wipe them away. The devil swooped and dove, dodging chain-lightning strikes from some of the flesh pillars only to be caught by others when they missed and were flung back.

The sky itself seemed to explode with green haze as a multitude of grotesque, gigantic, bloodshot eyeballs snapped open in the clouds—and the very ground all around the devil exploded into motion as a creature of astronomical proportions unveiled itself from where it'd been buried.

Despite the devil's own large size and prowess, it was quickly crushed and contained—dragged screaming into a writhing mass of flesh that clicked and hissed with Sin energy.

The eyeballs then turned to Gentry, and a feeling of overwhelming dread overtook him as his body went rigid with fear.

"Greed . . . the great sin of Greed is moving. I don't know what friends you made or how you know Gluttony's reincarnation, but you need to do everything they tell you to do. Tell them everything they ask of you and don't hold back, or it won't just be us that die here in this forsaken realm of the dark," his sister Asha whispered as if trying not to be overheard even though the monster was so far away. "And that one you see swarming in the earth and sky, the one digesting those two archdemons? That is the one they call the Gambler."

Gentry's face went even paler. His mind was racing, and it was hard to digest what he was being told. Had he really somehow gotten involved in a struggle straight out of bad fairy tales? Ones that involved two of the great sins? Here? Him?

He let out a shuddering breath. "The . . . the one the storybooks talk about?"

Asha's rigid face became grim, but she kept her words to a low hiss. "Yes. Tell them whatever it is you know, and perhaps we will live to tell the tale."

Before there was time for him to respond, another unfamiliar voice called.

"Drow boy . . . Gentry, I believe?" a hissing, reptilian voice shouted out from where the others had gathered, and it took all Gentry's willpower to turn around to the voice that'd addressed him. There, standing in the doorway, was a blue-scaled naga. He was very scarred, had a dorsal fin marked with holes and tears, and had a prosthetic purple eye on one side. He carried a spear of bones with notches all over the weapon and wore a silver hood with blue trimmings depicting a kraken on the top when he bowed his head.

"It is a pleasure to meet you, Gentry," the naga stated slyly, righting himself and letting out an aura of sin that smashed into all the drow there, as a pentagram of deep purple light tore open on his chest with the sigil of two clawed hands closing in on a world. "My name is Netithi Bluskish, and my new patron—Greed—wishes me to hunt down a very particular person here in the descent. I'm hoping that you can help me, and in turn you will be helping yourself . . . I know that the Gambler can be very, very persuasive if he needs to be. So I was hoping that you'd enlighten us on the details of where you've been these past weeks, and just who you got to know."

CHAPTER 7

[Riven's Quest 6 of the Altars of Despair and Hope: This is a minion-based quest. Only Athela can complete this quest as a representative of you. Assisting Athela will result in a loss of twenty points and no reward.

A Race to Steal the Orb: Other participants hailing from both cultist and noncultist groups in the Altars of Despair and Hope event have been tasked with killing the defending lord of a city in Universe 71 and capturing a particular glass orb he keeps in a safe at the center of his fortress. The city is currently under siege from enemy forces, and they are set on destroying this orb at all costs. With the city set to fall within coming days, it is a race between your minion Athela and the eleven other participants to see who can get to the orb first. Once collected, bring it back to the portal and return to the apocalypse beast's pocket realm to acquire an additional one hundred points and an automatic unlocking of all the orb's protected features.

Respawns for this quest have been set at a randomized location within two hundred yards of the quest portal entering this realm, which only participants of the apocalypse beasts can see, and respawn timers for all twelve chosen participants inside Universe 71 have been set to one hour until this quest is done.

Total event points already accumulated: 124

>>> This quest is currently active.]

Leaving the Abyssal Descent was far easier with the system itself helping Athela out, and she'd even been granted a Return to the Abyssal Descent button on her status page, even though she could return to her master with her demonic summoning.

Perhaps there were normally restrictions on such things when concerning pocket realms?

Athela wasn't quite sure. But with Riven, Azmoth, Fay, and Genua all being occupied with Lillith's training regimens, Athela was the one who'd completed the last few quests in Riven's stead. It was one of the perks of having minions, she supposed, and it'd quickly stopped her stagnation when it came to gaining event points. Compared to Nora Lang, who was also getting training from Lillith here and there, Riven had fallen behind by almost eighty points before having Athela go back to the apocalypse beast's pocket realm to keep the flow going.

During her quests, Athela had defeated a small portaled-in dungeon full of serpentine humanoids, collected various herbs in a designated zone defended by god-damn dragons that could eat her whole, of all things, gone through a puzzle labyrinth full of lava pits, and assassinated three enemy cultists who were on their own quests. The smug look she currently wore while remembering how they'd died said it all, and she'd even received notifications letting her know they'd failed to collect the points due to her—netting her even more points for Riven in the process.

Still, after being transported through yet another portal in this odd mix and match of pocket-realm portal networks, she hadn't ever seen anything quite like this. It was the scene out of a sci-fi novel, like so many of Riven's people from Earth used to enjoy.

F-grade and a few scattered E-grade signatures lit up her mana sense as two fleets of starships battled in a sky full of stars and nebulas—and the planet on one side of the backdrop made Athela realize she was now standing on a large, rocky moon of some kind. Boxy metal crafts with green light emanating from their engines made up the offensive fleet supporting a ground force of what she could only assume were some variant of earth golems—they used siege weaponry to shoot magma-based explosive devices at the defenders.

The defenders, for their part, were humans, but rather tall and thin compared to the ones that she was so used to from Panu. Their ships were fewer in number, sharper-looking, and appeared to be made of glass. They were mostly bunkered up behind hundreds of layers of plasma shields that created a patchwork, pseudo-dome defensive array—and used similarly constructed plasma weapons such as rifles and swords to take on the tide of earth golems. The front lines of the fight were an absolute madhouse, with ramps leading up to battlements stacked one behind the other before coming to what appeared to be a small city and then a palace of some kind in the very center. The walls of both the battlements and the palace were created from white stone and engraved all over with purple runes that reinforced their defensive capabilities, as was evident by the way they often stood strong even when explosive detonations made it through the patchwork of independent plasma shields. Many of the city's smaller buildings were not so lucky, however, and numerous fires or craters now littered the landscape.

As for Athela, she remained standing beside multiple blood spots on the lip of the moon's crater she'd personally painted over the past few minutes. Funnily enough, the cultists would—

Ah, there was another one. The portal began to shimmer and flux.

Athela rapidly condensed into a bloody pool underneath where the portal was located, waiting for the next target to arrive so she could set them on cooldown, too, and watched with an internal cackle as a familiar face came into view.

Splashing into the pool of blood that was Athela's body, the drow woman death knight that Riven had fought on his very first quest here stepped onto the moon's rocky terrain and blinked—looking up to stare at the battling fleets.

With her footfalls dead silent, Athela immediately retook her Arshakai form behind the death knight. Her ruby-studded black tiara gleamed in the light of the nebulas and firefights overhead, and her black and red bloodsilk cloak flared about her while a wide, malevolent smile took over her features. Athela flicked her wrists and called the Twin Red Doves out of her heart space with practiced ease. Two red katanas tore out of her chest, forming from spiraling ribbons of red liquid, and she then struck with two Backstab martial arts just as Mark of the Hunter activated.

[Mark of the Hunter (Blood): This martial art highlights potential threats in a large area around you and allows you to focus on one of them. Has a chance to reveal stealthed enemies depending on compared Perception, Willpower, and Luck. All damage done to this target will include a 0.4% additional bleed damage that stacks with each strike, increases your chance of critical strikes against them by 7%, increases any attempts at stealth while stalking them by 5%, and allows you to pull on the mark just once—destroying the mark in their soul and giving a high chance to make your target freeze up in fear for two seconds. Very high cooldown.]

[Backstab (Shadow): Strike at the back of your enemy while remaining stealthed to your target. If you are noticed by your target prior to the strike, this martial art will partially fail and only give the possibility of a minor bonus with critical damage. If you successfully strike while remaining unnoticed, you will gain a much larger and guaranteed bonus to critical damage. Critical strike damage ranges from three to ten times the normal damage done. No cooldown.]

[The Twin Red Doves (Awakened Weapons, Dual-Wielding Set. Blood Artifacts. Twin Katanas): 899 average damage on strike with each physical strike on flesh adding a guaranteed stack of the Bleed debuff for damage over time. Hidden strikes that land before an opponent is aware cause additional guaranteed damage of +5%. If the strike is a critical hit, deal an additional two times critical modifier. These items, when bound to a wielder, may be stored in the heart of the wielder and withdrawn at will. These items are nearly indestructible while the bound wielder is still alive. Requires a Blood affinity of over 51% to wield.

- Whispers of Agony: From time to time, these blades will whisper to you. The stronger your bond, the louder they whisper, and the louder they whisper, the more pain your strikes inflict regardless of damage.
- The Red Tide: Unleash stamina, mana, or divinity into these blades via your Blood subpillar to charge ranged sweeping attacks in the form of a red crescent. Damage and range depends on the amount of energy infused.]

Her red blades crashed into and through the bone armor of the death knight as spiraling ripples of kinetic energy tore it apart in a flash of bone and blood.

[You have landed a critical hit. Max damage x6.]
[You have landed a critical hit. Max damage x9.]
[Additional x2 critical modifier applied.]
[Additional x2 critical modifier applied.]
[You have applied bleeding stacks.]
[You have applied bleeding stacks.]
[You have applied bleeding stacks.]

The death knight's chest ripped open as Athela's blades passed through with the force of her critical energies, and the surprised drow woman screamed in pained horror while activating some kind of ability.

Or at least she tried to. But Athela sensed the pulse of mana before it fully manifested and pulled on Mark of the Hunter, shattering the mark inside the woman's soul and causing her to freeze up.

The death knight fell to her knees with a gasp as Athela violently ripped her katanas out and unleashed her six arachnid legs from her back, the sharp black blades flaring out to either side of her before they slammed down into the warrior's neck at different angles.

With a wrench, Athela decapitated the woman, flinging her head off to the side in a spinning, bloody spiral.

The death knight's body went limp, hit the ground to begin dumping her fluids onto the rocky terrain, and she abruptly vanished as the system claimed her.

[You have defeated an enemy cultist. She will respawn in one hour. You have gained four event points.]
[You have charged your Tiara of Silent Killing by successfully killing a target without being noticed by anyone else. 100% chance to apply an additional two to eight times critical strike damage with your next attack.]

Athela looked down at the newest of her blood spots littering the ground and cackled viciously, shoved her katanas back into her heart, and began walking toward the battle in the distance.

Vanishing into the darkness, she became one with the shadows.

"Spider girl, spider girl, does whatever a spider girl does!"

Athela skittered over the heads of numerous warriors killing one another in the hallway below, humming softly to herself amid the explosive barrage of skills and weapons only twelve feet underneath her current position.

Blood Weaver was the smallest of her three forms and gave her the best chance of sneaking inside, and thus far it'd worked out pretty well.

[+160% bonus to attempts at stealth, +200 Perception, and alters Charisma points to absolute neutral while in Cute Wittle Blood Weaver form.
+400 Agility, +30% bonus to baseline Agility, doubled chance for critical strikes, and +20% bonus to attempts at stealth while in Gluttonous Arshakai Form.
+500 Strength, +1,000 Sturdiness, Intelligence matches Sturdiness, +20% to Strength and Sturdiness baseline stats while in Gluttonous Fae Drider Form.]

"What I need is a princess form," Athela muttered to herself, turning a corner in the damaged hallway along the ceiling and coming to an abrupt halt when a turret spun her way.

"Shit!"

The turret fired, and she vanished in a puff of darkness as a clean edge of plasma annihilated the spot she'd been only a moment before.

Grumbling to herself, she watched the turret turn back around to settle on the hallway beneath in a ready position while she considered her next options.

Currently she was inside her Limited Shroud Storage, a Shadow ability that she'd originally been using in her drider form to store various trinkets, but more recently she'd figured out that—due to her small size in this Blood Weaver form—she could actually hide herself inside her own pocket of shadow as long as she didn't change back into a drider or Arshakai.

It was a nifty trick, and she was proud of herself for figuring it out.

But despite her success at dodging that last attack, she still didn't want to draw any attention by destroying that turret, so she was currently just waiting in what others would see as a cloudy dark patch of ceiling that more or less blended in with the surroundings. It might even look like a scorch mark from the plasma that'd just been fired.

The corner she'd just turned also let her see a large number of humans setting up additional barricades and more turrets in anticipation of the firefight coming their way—and they were right to do so, as hundreds of molten earth golems continued to fight and die in an aggressive attempt to kill the humans guarding the passage.

A distraction was needed.

Or perhaps . . .

Her eyes flicked toward a dead female combatant in a white and gray engineer's uniform—which was a stark contrast to the dark-purple and silver uniforms of the warrior class humans. She was human, too, with a hole blown in her chest, and she'd been discarded as a corpse along with a couple of the men while the defenders desperately tried to hold the onslaught back.

"Le sigh."

It wasn't often that Athela got to use her shapeshifting abilities, but now was as good a time as any to try it.

Pulling herself out of the hallway's corner where she'd been discreetly changing her face and complexion in the dark, her skin felt stretched as she walked back into the light. She had carved a shallow but bloody wound into her chest to match the hole in the uniform she'd stolen and had tossed the corpse underneath other bodies in the discard pile the defenders were currently using here.

Humans of this moon base dragged other dead past her while she oriented herself until one of them stopped and gestured to her with a gawking expression. "You're mortally injured! What in Drya's name are you still doing here??!! Get to the medical bay now! And then come back to your post—that's an order!"

"Yes, Cap!" Athela gave a salute, and she wasn't sure whether or not it was the phrase or the unfamiliar gesture, but the warrior blinked rapidly and shook his head before tossing another of the dead bodies onto the pile she'd just left before turning back to the front line.

Meanwhile, Athela was pretending to limp rapidly through the hallway full of other engineers setting up barricades and turrets. Eyeing the one that'd fired at her earlier as it scanned a badge she'd picked up from the body, the turret let her go without issue. She stuck her tongue out at it when she was all the way through and then considered talking to another man who was quickly typing into a computer embedded into the side of the wall.

She was tempted to ask him where the commander's quarters were, but then stopped herself. She didn't even know if they called their leaders "commanders" here, and asking would be somewhat suspicious. Not only that, but she was supposed to be headed to the medical bay—her sternum was still dripping blood down her chest from the self-inflicted wound.

Sighing again and ignoring the man's strained expression when he turned her way, she continued down the hall and took a left when it came to a three-way fork. Then she began exploring and set off on what could only be described as a wild goose chase.

Hours passed, and the intricate nature of the base quickly became apparent as Athela scouted one room after another while constantly brushing off concerned individuals who insisted on helping her to the medical bay. She told them all to fuck off, in nicer words than that, insisting that she was fine—and she was also losing time being in this slow, shapeshifted human form to boot. But turrets were stationed all over the damn place in this underground bunker part of the defenses, and though she saw some war hounds the size of horses outfitted in plasma-crafted armor, her shapeshifting abilities were limited to arachnid and female-humanoid only. She couldn't change into a dog even if she wanted to, but it certainly would have made things faster in terms of getting around if she'd been able.

Intelligence hubs, ammo depots, armories, and rushing groups of reinforcements were in high supply as the very base itself shook under the barrage from time to time. Now she found herself in one of these intelligence hubs on the outer rim of the base, after she'd attempted to skirt around the room toward another hallway that she thought would lead into the inner city.

Screens lit up with footage of the battle and troop movements from both enemies and allies alike.

"SQUADS TWELVE AND SEVENTY-EIGHT, REINFORCE SECTOR B11! I REPEAT, REINFORCE SECTOR B11!" the commanding officer in this part of the base screamed through the coms while his soldiers on the other side of the communications line died horrible, gruesome deaths. "WE CANNOT ALLOW THEM TO TAKE THE SECTOR, OR THIS ENTIRE WING OF

THE BASE IS LOST! YOU ARE THE LAST LINE BEFORE WE ARE FORCED TO RETREAT DEEPER INTO THE CITY! THE CIVILIANS—"

BOOM

His voice was cut off as an explosion eradicated the wall to Athela's left, sending a cloud of molten rock and metal inward as a titanic figure of an earth golem barreled through. Screams rose up as the humans tried to flee, but there were too many of them, and now there was only one way out—the small hallway Athela had been trying to get to before big-and-bad made an "OH YEAH" Kool-Aid appearance seconds beforehand.

The golem, for his part, was flanked by a few others that'd apparently dug a tunnel through the earth to get here before crashing through the metal wall. Up close and personal, they were a lot more intimidating than they'd been far away. Especially this one in the front, considering he was both bulkier and taller than any of the others Athela had seen so far.

Standing at nearly twenty feet tall, he had no eyes, but veins of magma pulsed at his joints and all along his featureless rock face. A huge, bloodstained axe was held in one hand, also covered in veins of magma, and in the other hand he carried something akin to a bazooka—which was currently aimed at the mass of struggling people that were screaming in terror and attempting to all squeeze into the one hallway leading away.

The few brave souls who were charging the golem were flattened by the stone compatriots flanking him. One of the golems fell to a rifle blast and a plasma sword to the midsection, crumbling into a pile in death, while the humans sustained a dozen casualties almost instantly as they were caught off guard.

"Jorgi the Destroyer . . ." one of the officers in a purple uniform let out a horrified whisper, eyes wide and stepping back from the foremost figure while ignoring the other soldiers who were quickly being killed in an attempt to fight the golems off. The officer fell to his knees, slack-jawed, as the bazooka began to light up with energy in a charged attack. "We . . . we're doomed . . ."

Athela was caught between a rock and a hard place and figured she didn't have much of a choice in the matter. Especially because the bazooka was pointed just to the right of where she currently stood. Despite the creature being in what she felt was likely the low E-grade, she'd have to fight.

So much for the stealth approach.

The bazooka let off a discharge of molten energy, the crowd let out a desperate cry, and the room lit up with a flash.

A cloud of steam exploded between the crowd of humans and the earth golems, but there was no actual impact. Surprised eyes turned back as a new figure loomed in the flickering lights of the underground bunker, and sharp, scythe-like legs smashed into the metal floor of the room between them.

Crystalline Maw Cannon activated, and a torrent of Sin, Glacial, and Storm energies ripped open from Athela's gluttonous vertical mouth across her front—tearing into the golems like a battering ram. The explosion detonated and flung the cloud of steam away, revealing the huge archdemon as frost began to accumulate around the room and her body began to spark with currents of lightning. Four red eyes narrowed over a grinning smile, and crystalline flowers began to bloom along her white skin as spiders began crawling out from the mouth that'd so recently obliterated so many of the earth golems inside the advance tunnel.

Jorgi the Destroyer picked himself out of the crater he'd been lodged in farther down the tunnel and looked at the scattered remnants of his soldiers before turning his gaze upon Athela's form that was even larger than his own. His voice came out as gravel upon cement. "Archdemon . . . Legendary status. I did not realize the humans here dabbled in dark magics and the art of summoning. Perhaps . . . perhaps this will allow for a good fight after all. A diamond in the rough, found among the piles of organic shit your meatbag masters have otherwise thrown at me."

He lifted his axe as it re-formed in his hand from the shards Athela had blasted away, lowered his head, and gestured at her with his free hand—ignoring the still-smoldering line gouged into his front. "Come to me, demon. Let us dance."

CHAPTER 8

Commander Redgar of the human alliance watched in awe as Jorgi the Destroyer and this unknown archdemon laid waste to the underground in Sector B12. Through camera footage, he and a good number of the officers under his leadership were staring at a few screens where the titanic monsters crashed into each other with a speed and ferocity that outmatched anything any of them could ever hope to achieve.

Not only that, but Jorgi was slowly losing. The pompous, arrogant mass murderer was taking blow after blow as the golem was swarmed with spiders created out of frost, electrified snowflakes, razor-sharp red threads, and pointed arachnid limbs that shot out like pistons to throw him back whenever the golem got too close.

In return that axe-wielding barbarian was trying to close the gap over and over again, but whenever he got too close, the demon would shift into one of two other forms and disappear—only to reappear with blinding speed in another part of the room before reemerging in her drider form to launch attacks that were somehow empowered by her larger size.

To counteract this, Jorgi had turned the room into a molten pit of lava and attacked her with earthen spikes that ruptured from the ground at range—but the demon had repeatedly frozen the lava pit over and was doing a good job of dodging most of the incoming earth spikes.

Commander Redgar caught his breath when it looked like Jorgi was about to land a Cataclysmic Swing of his axe, but the Dao-empowered strike only created a crater in the large underground room and was violently counterattacked with a drider foot through the back. The arachnid leg cracked through where a human's spine would be and out the other side of the golem's chest, and as Jorgi roared in rage and whirled his axe around to hit the demon, the drider popped into her Blood Weaver form and cackled maliciously before rapidly gaining a foothold and crawling inside the hole she'd just made.

"What . . . what is she doing?!" one of the officers exclaimed, horrified, as others began to cheer or yell out that she should get away. "The demon knows his body will mend itself, and she'll be trapped in a molten rock body without a way out! WHAT IS SHE THINKING?!"

Commander Redgar didn't disagree, but there wasn't much they could do. Their forces were already retreating away from Sector B12 to consolidate at the junction leading into the city, as adjoining passages had been lost and earth golems were pouring in. "I'm not entirely sure myself . . . I—"

He abruptly stopped speaking as the golem's upper body ruptured in a spray of rock as whirlwinds of red blades and bloody strings carved through the softer bedrock of his inner body. Bursting out of Jorgi, whose lower body crashed to the ground in a heap of oozing magma coming from where his chest used to be, the cloaked humanoid version of the Arshakai stood atop his remains with a gleeful laugh.

As she sheathed her two swords, the room burst into an uproar of applause before she disappeared from the room down an adjacent hallway and vanished from sight of the cameras that still remained.

[Totem of Bloodforged Rift Sparks: The Path of Red and Black has been imbued into this totem, along with three different ability sigils, allowing it to create combination attacks from the following: Black Lightning, Rift, and Crimson Ice. Due to having a high-grade soul imbued into this totem, it is able to move around autonomously and will follow your will to fight or defend. Elite Tier, level-1 totem. Requirements: 90 Willpower, Blood subpillar, Shadow subpillar. Bound to Riven Thane.

Upgrade downloads are completing: Graphic of Dark Learning, Graphic of Dark Empowerment, Graphic of Hive Mind.]

Gragle the gnome had been working tirelessly on recreating the totems Riven had paid him for and was currently on the fourth and last. He'd needed some of Riven's blood to imbue the Path of Red and Black into the totems, which had been hard to replicate, but Gragle had completed this particular task and had even gained insight into that path himself through the straining of his mind.

Not that he'd actually been granted that path, but he had started to understand it and would perhaps be able to grasp it in upcoming years or decades. It was certainly potent, and Gragle couldn't help but wonder how Riven had managed to create such a connection to begin with. The level of comprehension must have been astoundingly good, which brought his mind wandering back to all the Unholy sigils on Riven's skin that Gragle still didn't recognize— nor had he found anything in the local library about such sigils in the Unholy section.

Nevertheless, the gnome was proud with his work. And due to the large sum of money he'd been paid, he'd even done Riven a favor. Lighting a candle in the darkening room of his small workshop, he glanced out the window at the setting sun where brilliant orange and yellow hues lit up the clouds. What a strange sight for Outpost Number 84, after having been on a relatively dead world for so long.

He turned around and walked over to his short desk and double-checked the gift he'd prepared for Riven as a way of thanks. It was a book, a book he'd written himself on how graphics worked and what to look for when creating graphics. Everything Gragle knew about graphics, but dumbed down so Riven could understand it, was summarized here. He'd seen how the young man's eyes lit up whenever Gragle talked about his ability, and for the first time in his life, Gragle had felt truly appreciated. The gangs had even stopped harassing him after Riven had taken care of their top dogs, and now Gragle felt like the weight of the world had finally come off his shoulders—relieving him of a burden he'd been carrying for so, so long.

A tear came to his eye, and he wiped it away with a laugh. Cleaning off the four metal icosahedrons that were Riven's totems, he made sure each rune imbued into the twenty faces were working properly. The Graphic of Dark Learning and the Graphic of Dark Empowerment were boosting each rune as well, though the graphics weren't entirely absorbed yet, but they could still move around and the soul shards had some minor amounts of self-thought. They wouldn't have been bound to Riven yet, either—at least three of the four wouldn't have been—but the Graphic of Hive Mind had changed them into a collective and they'd absorbed the original parent totem's alignment quite well before he'd installed the other two graphics.

Just thinking about it, Gragle was tempted to create ones just like these for himself, if Riven was okay with it. He still had a small vial of Riven's blood, which was abnormally saturated with high-quality mana from numerous affinities related to the Unholy foundational pillar, and it would easily be enough to make two more totems like the ones he'd constructed. Possibly even three.

A knock came at the door, causing Gragle to blink rapidly and furrow his brows in confusion. What was someone doing at his house so late? He didn't really have any affiliates other than Warden Zuk, especially after the gang he'd once been forced to work for now stayed far away from him in fear of his new employer, so it was certainly odd to get visitors right now.

Grabbing at the doorknob at gnome height and swinging the fully human-size door wide-open, Gragle looked up to see an unfamiliar cloaked figure staring back down at him with a toothy grin. He had an odd, light-green complexion that almost looked sick. His eyes were incredibly bloodshot, with one pointed off to Gragle's right and the other focused directly on Gragle.

"May I help . . . you . . . ?" Gragle asked slowly, reaching for the small stun device on his hip due to the strange, creepy way this man was looking at him.

The stranger, for his part, nodded with a quick and jerky motion. He reached out a hand from underneath his cloak, revealing gnarled fingers that—for a split second—looked like they had something crawling underneath the skin by the way it wriggled. "Yes . . . I have come to trade. Perhaps we could speak inside?"

The man's raspy, eager voice was even creepier than his looks, but Gragle didn't like to turn down money. "Hmm. All right, you want to have me build you a totem? Right now it is a bit late. Could you come back tomorrow and discuss prices then?"

The man shook his head and focused both eyes on Gragle this time while pushing his way through the door and past Gragle with a grunt. "I'm afraid not . . . this is most important and I need it now."

"Excuse me, sir?!" Gragle angrily harrumphed. "Listen, I don't need . . ."

His voice trailed off when he realized the totems he'd laid out for Riven were now gone from the countertop, gone before either man had come back inside. Had the totems moved on their own? If so, where and why?

The strange, green-tinted man came to a stop in the middle of the room— and started to sniff. His nostrils widened to abnormal proportions as he took in deep, eager breaths. The act was almost grotesque, and this time Gragle was certain that his green skin was literally crawling.

Absolutely creeped out now, Gragle decided to keep a very firm hold on his stun weapon. "Sir, I told you that now is not a good time. You need to leave."

Something about this stranger just felt . . . wrong.

As if triggered by Gragle's words, the man shifted his weight and moved toward the vial of Riven's blood on a nearby shelf. Popping the cork, the green-tinted man's eyes widened with delight—and his smile grew to literally reach his ears as his teeth briefly sharpened.

"You see, I am a collector . . ." the stranger stated, turning back around to give the gnome a predatory grin. "And the smell coming out of this vial was just too good to pass up. I do believe I'll be buying this. What is your price?"

Gragle raised an eyebrow at the selected item, then glanced at the numerous other totems on display around his workshop that he'd set out for potential buyers in the past. "You smelled that vial of blood from outside? How is that possible?"

"I have a very good nose!" the man replied, bopping his nose with a finger and chuckling to himself.

"All right, well . . . I'm afraid that vial isn't for sale," Gragle said, folding his arms in irritation. "I am planning to use that for a totem for myself."

The strange man blinked, then began to laugh. "You?! For yourself?! How interesting! Well, let's just say that I won't be taking no for an answer. So, with that in mind, I'll ask you just one more time."

In the blink of an eye, the man had blurred forward to stand in front of Gragle, towering over him with a looming aura of dread seeping from his soul core.

Gragle yelped and fell backward, scrambling for his weapon and pulling out a small iron rod that crackled with electricity as he flipped the switch.

The man didn't even seem to notice Gragle's weapon as he bent over him, looking like a shark about to eat its next meal while holding up the vial. "How . . . much . . . for this?"

Gragle stuttered something unintelligible before the man sighed and rolled his eyes.

Dropping a small sack of what could only be money, he gestured at the gnome to open it. "Despite my appearances, little gnome, I am truthfully a fair person in all my dealings . . . Perhaps this amount would suffice?"

As he gaped up at the hostile intruder, Gragle's fingers slowly inched toward the bag, and he opened it to see what was inside. His eyes widened in shock, and he looked up in obvious surprise, his fear having fled his body in a single instant. "All this? Just for a vial of blood?"

From where one of Gragle's own soul-based graphics was located, he could feel a karmic tie latching onto his core—connecting him and this strange man in a cord that became stronger by the second as he truly considered the man's offer.

The bloodshot eyes of the stranger narrowed approvingly. "Yes, of course . . . Just take the money . . . and we can part ways here. What say you, Gragle?"

Gragle looked down at the extreme wealth in his hands and picked one coin up just to make sure it was real. Putting the money back down and shuddering, he considered what Riven would think about it. Surely the vampire would be fine with Gragle selling some of Riven's blood to this stranger if Gragle split the profits, right? Riven would get rich, too! So . . . why not . . . right?

Gragle nodded his head, and he felt the karmic tie connect him with the stranger that very next instant. Though he honestly couldn't care, because now he was going to be absolutely rich. He wouldn't have to work a day in his life, even if he did give Riven half.

"I can accept that. You may have the vial of blood in exchange for this money." Clutching the bag close to his chest as if trying to protect the massive sum of wealth from leaving him should the stranger refuse, Gragle got back to his feet and dusted himself off with a wide smile of his own. "Nice to do business with you, mister . . . uh . . . what's your name?"

Laughing and letting the hostility drain away completely, the green-tinted man held out a hand to shake. "How greedy you look with that little sack of money! I love it . . . As for my name? You can call me Gambler."

"Gambler?" Gragle repeated, grasping the man's hand to shake. "That's an odd name."

"The Gambler, to be precise," the taller man replied with another laugh. "But it is time for me to go. I have plans and need to get back to them. Perhaps I'll meet you again, but for now—good day to you."

With that, the Gambler stepped around Gragle and began walking down the dark alleys leading away from Gragle's workshop and home.

Looking after him, Gragle only shook his head—but greedily opened the bag to gawk at his newfound wealth with soaring excitement. Perhaps he'd go get drunk tonight and celebrate with some of the other gnomes in this city. He could certainly use a drink, and now that he didn't have the vial of blood anymore, his previous plan to work on his own totems had come to an abrupt halt. Hopefully that man would come back sometime after Riven did, so that Gragle could obtain another vial for the man to buy if it really was as precious as the offered sum Gragle had been given this night.

"Your stance is wrong." Lillith kicked Riven's knee and sent him sprawling to the floor.

Getting up and feeling the joint snap back into place, Riven didn't complain as he came back to stand in front of the living legend he'd been sparring with all night. He dived forward again, only dressed in a thin sparring outfit made of cloth, and slammed his mana-charged elbow into Lillith's side.

Or at least he tried to, but he was sent spinning backward with another kick to the side of his knee.

"It's still wrong," Lillith said with a shake of her head, ignoring the spectators in the stands who often came to watch training sessions. "You bend the joint too early—it signals what you're about to do. When you do move, you need to snap into motion instead of leaning into it first."

Riven nodded. "Got it."

"Have you, though?" Lillith raised an eyebrow and snapped another kick in his direction but began to clap when the act had been a fake-out. Riven hadn't actually moved but had drawn her into a rebuttal despite this when she'd read his projected path. "Oh! Very good. You also canceled out your mana pulse at the last second to stop your body from accelerating. I'm impressed."

Smiling at the compliment, Riven bowed. "Thank you, Teacher. I appreciate your guidance."

"Indeed. Now, perhaps you can try to utilize the things you've learned over these past weeks in another duel?" Lillith asked, gesturing to the stands where one of the contenders to try and take Riven down was seated. "Jerakie! You're up!"

Lillith vanished and the roar of approval from a distant spectator filled Riven's ears as a large draconic man smashed into the arena's floor. He had no wings, but his scales were as tough as armor and glinted a dark burgundy in the fireballs illuminating the arena from above. He had vibrant green eyes, clawed hands, and was about Azmoth's size in terms of both height and muscle. He didn't wear anything at all, nor did he carry a weapon, but he nevertheless had an imposing F-grade aura in the LEGENDARY category.

"I, Jerakie, challenge Riven Thane to a duel of supremacy!" the draconic man roared, letting his hands and arms explode with green fire as he entered a martial artist's stance.

It was a little weird, seeing such a huge, monstrous dragon man enter a sophisticated stance Riven had come to recognize among many of the humanoids here in the descent. But that was all the more reason for worry, in Riven's opinion, and he nodded to the challenger as he adopted a stance of his own.

The stance Riven was learning was called Mage Fist and utilized mana in many of the martial arts with up-close combat. The Mage Fist stances also called for hit-and-run tactics, or retreating to use spells at range while utilizing these martial tactics to put distance between himself and the enemy—thus it was mostly a defensive stance that hinged on the idea of a mage using most of his offensive might through magic.

Riven felt his mana gather within his core and waited for the announcer to start the fight as his heart began to thud. He was getting better, and though he was still getting a lot of beatdowns, his pride allowed it as long as he continued to grow.

When the announcer rang a large bell next to Gluttony's statue overlooking the platform where Lillith was now seated, the fight had begun. Riven launched himself backward to keep himself away from the melee fighter and unleashed a torrent of Storm Razors that ripped out of the air around him like an avalanche and then blocked an incoming tail strike as the dragon man's tail elongated like a whip to lash out at him.

Before he knew it, Riven was in full swing—trying to kite his enemy and fending off blows while sending magical projectiles like a madman as a small smile began to creep across his face. Yes . . . he was definitely improving.

CHAPTER 9

Riven moved through the steps that'd been drilled into him over the past month, shifting his body while simultaneously using his mana to enhance his reflexes even outside the realm of his speed buff Blessing of the Crow.

When the draconic man Jerakie slashed out at him with his flaming green claws and tried to enter close combat, Riven would kite him with a ceaseless barrage of roaring black and red. When he wasn't able to riftwalk or dodge effectively, he'd deflect with his spear-staff and utilize barriers of ice, only truly engaging full-on with physical attacks if he saw an obvious opening. Jerakie was a melee fighter with some midrange abilities involving the green flames of his heritage, unleashing depictions of fiery green drakes at Riven that could wipe out entire swaths of the stone floor for thirty yards out—but those attacks were far shorter than Riven's own abilities, which gave him an advantage as long as he kept his distance.

Thus, he fought like a true mage as much as possible. Ever since he'd truly taken this fighting style to heart, he'd started winning at an increased rate. No longer did he lose more of these duels against the elites of Gluttony's following than he won, although it was close. Nevertheless it was a big step forward for such a small amount of time and very much underlined the truly obvious flaws he'd had and now acknowledged—easy fixes finally coming to rest.

Flame, blood, shadow and sin—with the occasional flicker of death mana that he still wasn't entirely used to—swirled around him in a roaring cyclone by the end of the fight as he hovered twenty yards off the ground with his spear-staff channeling the mana into a point.

His opponent was still pulling himself out of the crater, one arm hanging loosely by charred tendons and his scales ravaged by the onslaught, before acknowledging Riven's win with a grunt.

The mana subsided, the drums sounded, and the crowd cheered as the next contenders for the fights that'd been going on for weeks now started making moves to enter the arena.

As the draconic man shuffled out toward the healers, Riven turned his attention to Lillith, who'd appeared to float alongside him with a stern expression.

"How'd I do?" Riven asked, winking with a laugh when she shook her head and folded her arms.

"Better, but still lots of improvements to make," she stated with a nod in the draconic man's direction. "You let him inside your guard all too often, and your close-combat technique still needs work. Have you been working on your mana pulses?"

"Yes."

"Did you do it during the fight?"

"Yes, Lillith. And if you're about to ask me where you hid them—" Riven pointed toward the left wall and up above. "Those two spots."

A smile crept onto her lips as the two assassins reappeared from thin air. "Very good."

Riven chuckled and was about to ask whether or not that was all of them when a strange sense of pulling overcame him. It was like someone was poking at his soul, and Gluttony noticed it, too, with an abrupt shift in their combined attention to a tiny fluctuation in their shared soul aperture.

In an instant Riven was dragged in alongside Gluttony to meet the odd change and found himself in the equivalent of a nether realm—though he could tell it was more of a mirage rather than a true nether realm.

Swamp lay all about him, a flat marshland that stretched out for miles on end, and a strange, green-tinted man with bloodshot eyes glared daggers at him from across a distance of perhaps twenty feet.

Riven felt Gluttony's disgust and irritation grow simultaneously, and as Riven watched, the strange man's body slowly unfurled. His belly bulged, exploding outward in a swarm of leeches, worms, and insects with a sickly, viscous layer of gunk connecting them like a membrane. The limbs went next, and then the head, and the man's body continued to grow. It grew to the size of a house, then a school, then grew even far beyond that until the abomination cast a shadow over the land from the clouds and beyond.

The writhing mass of creatures grew enormous eyes that flashed open like fleshy orbs, and mouths began to open from within the body and writhing limbs of the creature from a thousand different places at once.

"Gluttony . . ." the creature hissed, glowering down at Riven's position with obvious distaste. "My master greets you from the beyond."

A rumble sounded out from Riven's soul aperture, but otherwise Gluttony didn't bother replying.

This in turn made the abomination in front of Riven laugh sardonically. "Not even willing to acknowledge my presence? After so many untold eons? Come now, Gluttony, I thought we'd—"

A snap of power erupted from Riven's soul core where Gluttony had embedded himself into the very fabric of Riven's internal realm. It felt like someone had just kicked Riven in the nut sack while simultaneously giving him a large dose of cocaine, and his body seized in a rigid spasm.

At the same time, a dose of pure Sin energy shattered the fabric of the false world they found themselves in and crashed into the unknown creature. The monster screamed in agony and reeled backward, and malice poured out of Riven as Gluttony temporarily took hold of his body.

"You are not worthy of my acknowledgment, worm. But since you insist, perhaps I can show Greed's lapdog a little more face after all." Gluttony's third eye opened on Riven's head, and his mouth split open along the corners all the way back to his ears as numerous sharp teeth sprouted. The air thundered, and Gluttony lifted one of Riven's hands to beckon to the creature. "Now tell me, king of worms, what poorly concocted scheme made you think it was a good idea to come and speak to the Great Maw this time?"

The world pulsed around them again, the remaining fabric of reality completely disintegrating until the swamp was no more and they found themselves in a black abyss of nothingness.

The screeching of the monstrous creature abruptly stopped when it flared with a pulse of its own power, and its numerous eyes narrowed into slits as it let out a deafening roar of rage from its thousands of jaws.

Riven and Gluttony just sat and watched, a deep sense of calm malice embedded into Riven's soul, as the monster in front of them quieted down. They pointed a finger in the monster's direction, and Gluttony spoke once more. "Do what you have come to do. Say what you have come to say. I will tolerate your presence for only a small amount of time, Gambler. If this were another era, I would have already flayed you open and devoured you whole—be glad that this is not that era."

Gambler?

Oh.

The Gambler?

Riven had been hearing a little bit about this person over the past weeks. He knew this creature to be something akin to a general in Greed's army, and he was likely responsible or partially responsible for the attack on Genua. The attack on Riven's child.

Cold hate slowly filtered in, adding to Gluttony's own.

He tried to pull on his mana, but none came, and anger turned into confusion. "Gluttony, if you were able to hurt him here—why can't I?"

Gluttony laughed inwardly. "I directly attacked his soul. It's something I'm quite good at, and though I do approve of your aggression, it is impossible to kill him here. Let the worm speak . . . Let us see what verbal vomit he has to offer us . . ."

"He tried to kill our child."

"But he didn't. He failed."

Riven blinked, tightening his fists, and retook control of his body as he restrained himself from giving Gluttony a rude response. However, he couldn't fault Gluttony, because Gluttony had been the one to save their child, while Riven had been an utter failure of a father in that instant. Instead, he turned his ire on the monster ahead with an obvious sneer. "Gambler. I've got to ask . . . Was it you that tried to kill my unborn child? Did you take any part in concocting that plan?"

The monster, which had been seething in the background, suddenly stilled—and then it slowly began to laugh. The laughter built, and built some more, until it echoed across the plane of this strange, false world. "Yes, and I was oh so disappointed that I did not splatter the child's brains onto the pavement as anticipated. Nor did my agent even kill the mother . . . It is a true tragedy, but expected of one with such inexperience. It is a tragedy that will be corrected when I drag them into the depths of hell in days to come. But that is not why I came to speak with the Maw. I came for . . . other things."

Riven's fists tightened further. He opened his mouth to speak but found that he could not put into words the description of just what he was feeling. If he couldn't kill the beast, then there was no point in making himself out to be a hotheaded fool. "Very well. Tell me, how did you contact me? Is it the vial of my blood I sense inside your spatial pocket?"

The Gambler seemed surprised by Riven's deduction and eventually pulled out that same vial Riven had described. It looked down, then up, then down and up again until it settled on Riven once more. "I'm surprised you noticed, hatchling. I—"

Riven formed a fist, and the vial of blood shattered. His essence on the other side of this strangely constructed communication line shuddered to the same extent that Gluttony's pulse had done. The blood was without a doubt the pillar holding up this "phone call," so to speak, but he kept the communication line intact and grinned viciously at the image of the Gambler's body on the other end of the string that connected them. Somewhere out there, he'd created a crater inside the demon that pulsed with remnant blood energy. He perhaps had a few minutes left to talk at most, and he might not be able to kill this creature in this realm, as he couldn't truly summon mana here—but the mana in Riven's blood was still connected to him while in such concentrated form. And the bloody scar it'd left in the monster's side was very satisfying, even if it was in the end insignificant.

"YOU BARBARIC, UNEVOLVED APE! I WOULD BE CURSED TO INTERACT WITH NOTHING MORE THAN BABOONS, IT SEEMS!" the Gambler screamed, irritation flecking his words like a potent venom. "We have not even discussed terms and you already wish to end our talks?! You are a shortsighted fool!"

"Not so foolish as to use the blood of a vampire as a means of communication AFTER trying to kill my kid," Riven shot back, a content grin on his face. He wanted to ask if Gragle was all right but assumed the gnome was dead if the Gambler was here with that vial. "Tell us why you have come. The means by which you contacted us are disappearing and will be gone within minutes. Speak."

Snarling, the Gambler cursed at him in a language he didn't understand—but that elicited chuckles from Gluttony. Frothing at the mouth and writhing his numerous appendages, the bestial creature rippled in irritation. "I have come to set terms."

"Terms?" Riven repeated dryly. "You can fuck right off. How do those terms sound?"

"I do not speak with you, child. I speak to the Great Maw," the monster replied with a hiss, appendages swarming. "Greed has not left the prison that held us yet, because he is waiting and watching. Watching . . . the commandments. Their echoes of hatred still linger in the dark, and they scheme to gain a foothold over demonkind before our rise has even truly begun. Greed has sent me here as a messenger, that we agree to a ceasefire, and work together on a temporary basis."

There was a pause as Gluttony's curiosity was piqued.

Then, seeing that neither Riven nor Gluttony had anything else to say, the Gambler smiled across all its many mouths. "I am glad you can listen to reason. Good. Greed has found the location of an inheritor . . . a reincarnation-to-be. His time in the prison has borne fruit, and he has overheard them talking of treachery. The commandments of Purity, Piety, Judgment, Selflessness, Truth, Humility, and Patience scheme to move soon. Perhaps it would interest us both if we strike together with the combined might of our churches, when the Seventh Wing sends down her blessing and incorporates herself into a reincarnation. What says the Great Maw?"

Gluttony seemed to tense, and he spat the words out like venom. "The Seventh Wing? Purity has chosen a vessel?"

The Gambler growled out his acknowledgment. "Yes. And as much as I'd like to see the both of you kill each other, and as much as Greed holds a deep-seated hate for you, we both know where our priorities lie when it comes to the endless war against the heavens. I can prove to you that I do not lie, and if you wish it, we may work together to send Purity back into the abyss to recuperate. Perhaps, if we are lucky, we may even capture her reincarnation and hold her for an eternity that she shan't break from."

Was it a trap?

Probably.

Was there some truth to what the Gambler had said?

Apparently so.

Did Riven really want to go kill or abduct Purity's reincarnation?

Not really.

But Gluttony did.

And yet . . . would Riven even be involved? He wasn't entirely sure. Rather, it might completely exclude him, as B-, A-, and S-grade players from the churches of Gluttony and Greed—players that were currently far more powerful than Riven—were on the chessboard in attempting the mission should it be enacted.

A lot was on Riven's mind as he looked in the mirror, turning and evaluating his suit. It was a deep burgundy with spikes along the shoulders and came out with a flare in the back like a tuxedo, but had numerous bright-red trimmings and a large black sigil of Gluttony on the inner vest. The style had been picked out by his two girlfriends only a few days ago, and though Athela was still on a mission—she'd no doubt appreciate that he wore it to this event despite her absence.

No doubt she'd make him wear it again when he had the same kind of event with her family.

"You look startlingly good! I'm such a lucky woman!" Fay said when she turned the corner, putting on a wide grin and stepping into the room in a sparkling black dress that fit her slender, athletic body like a glove. She stepped up to Riven in the mirror, put an elbow on his shoulder as they stared at one another, and then leaned in for a kiss. Meeting his lips and then playfully rubbing her horns against his cheek, she reached down for his hand and gently intertwined their fingers. "I, um, I want to say thanks for coming. Thank you for asking to do this in the first place— they're all so excited to meet you. You have no idea how much this means to my clan, to my family. To me."

Riven raised an eyebrow and thought about ruffling her hair, but seeing how much time she'd taken in making it look absolutely perfect, he decided not to. Instead, he just pulled her in for another kiss and wrapped his arms around her waist. "Of course, silly. I wouldn't miss it for the world. I love you, remember?"

Fay's blue cheeks flushed a bright pink, and she looked away but kept her grip on his back firm as she pressed up against him. "Thanks. I love you, too, and I needed to hear that. You've been so busy lately that we haven't had a chance to talk much. You've been distant."

"And I apologize for that, but it's also why I decided to push this forward." Riven brought a hand up to her chin and lifted her face to meet his own. "I wanted to show both you and Athela that you're important to me."

"And Genua?"

The question caught Riven off guard, and he shifted his head from side to side before shrugging. "I'm not sure where that's going. We had a one-night stand and now it's . . . complicated. But right now, I only have eyes for you and Athela."

Fay grinned. "Kathrine is going to be very angry if she hears that."

"Kathrine is in a forced marriage situation due to the Blood Moon Requiem, for political gains, and we all know it. Stop teasing me." Riven shot Fay an irritated glare, only to soften his frown when she giggled up at him and put a hand on his cheek.

"I know," Fay stated softly. "Are you ready to go?"

Riven's frown completely evaporated, and he let out a chuckle with a nod. "Yes. I'm ready. Let's go meet your family, shall we?"

Five minutes later, Riven, holding Fay's hand, was let into the Sojavi clan's combined nether realm. Stepping through the portal, he entered a sprawling complex of stone architecture akin to Mayan designs built into a mountainous jungle landscape. Unlike most of the other nether realms he'd been in, this one had a very real sense of physicality to it. His senses all worked here, and if he remembered correctly it was because the number of demons residing here all gave a portion of themselves into creating the world they shared. Individual realms had an absolute safety to them, which was why they were often used, but combined nether realms like this one made things more . . . communal. Social.

And the sight before him left him somewhat staggered.

Well over a thousand succubi and incubi all knelt in submission on the stone panels leading toward the centermost building of the complex. They were dressed in their finest outfits in a variety of styles and had blue skin and small black horns or tails just like Fay. The complex had been decorated with blooming yellow and red flowers, and incense burned along multiple flat, waist-high pillars in a thick cloud of intoxicatingly good aromas. The very air he breathed was refreshing despite the smoke, and he quickly noticed four people at the very front of the crowd—one of whom he recognized.

"Hello, Tupper. It's nice to see you here," Riven said with a friendly wave, and Fay's brother shot the people beside him a nervous glance before standing to his full height and nodding.

"I greet the Great Maw's reincarnation with utmost respect!" Tupper announced, bowing deeply at the waist and causing Riven to raise an eyebrow.

Fay giggled, whispering into Riven's ear, and he scratched the back of his head.

"No need for that, man, we know each other well enough by now. Just call me Riven."

Tupper abruptly shook his head. "That would be disrespectful of your esteemed position, my lord! Please, allow—"

"That's an order, Tupper," Riven replied with a sigh. "I appreciate the respect, but you're a friend—and you're Fay's brother. Please stand straight."

Hesitating once again, Tupper shot the people beside him another look—getting an unsaid message from one of the women beside him—and did as Riven asked. He cleared his throat nervously and slumped his shoulders before sticking out a hand. "Nice to see you again, Riven. How's the Abyssal Descent going?"

"That's more like it." Riven laughed, clasping hands with the incubus and gesturing to the others. "I assume these are the rest of your family?"

"They are," Fay cut in, quickly walking over to pull the two women and one man to their feet. One of the women was slightly older than Fay—this was likely Fay's mom, whom he'd heard so much about. He could certainly see where Fay got her genetics, and if she was anything to go by, Riven would not be disappointed if he and Fay ever got married and lasted another few thousand years together.

The second woman was Fay's sister, if Riven had to guess. Nithidi? Nitidi? Niridi? He couldn't remember. Fuck. She was taller than Fay and certainly more confident—she held his gaze almost teasingly as his eyes swept over her bright-yellow dress that matched Fay's.

Then, lastly, there was a slightly older and very handsome man that Riven could only assume was Fay's father. He wore a cool, calculating look and—though he showed respect in the formal gestures—he did not have the same aim to please about him that the two women did. Or at least that's what Riven got out of it based on expressions between the three.

Fay gestured to each of them in turn. "This is my mother, Saemi. This is my sister, Nitidi. And this is my father, Artirus. Obviously you know Tupper already, so that's . . . That's my family! Um . . . Thanks for coming again, Riven."

She gave him a sheepish smile, and her mother, Saemi, was already stepping forward with a warm handshake and an extraordinarily wide, brilliant smile.

"It is such a pleasure to meet my daughter's future husband!" Saemi exclaimed loudly, oozing with giddiness as her handshake almost became violent by how excited she was. "A prince of the Blood Moon Requiem and, more importantly, Gluttony's reincarnation! I am so, SO excited to host you this evening in our estate! I hear you have another minion slot open? Is that true? Perhaps you'd consider our other daughter to add to your—"

"Mother!" Fay exclaimed, a blush overcoming her face as her fists clenched with embarrassment—and she dropped her voice into a low hiss. "We've been over this! Stop it immediately!"

"Nitidi," Fay's sister said politely, pushing her mother out of the way and taking Riven's hand next. "I must say, the things Fay tells me about you and your intimacy are rather interesting. Perhaps I'll get to see them for myself one of these days."

Fay's jaw dropped, and Riven's pale face blushed to the next degree as he gave his girlfriend the side-eye.

"I . . . Well, it's nice to meet you," Riven said, taking a step back and wondering just what kind of impression he gave off to these people. As it was, Athela and Fay were more than enough. It was certainly flattering, but already having such a busy life, he was not sure he'd be able to handle another woman even if he wanted to—and he certainly didn't want to invest emotionally in anyone else. "And, uh, you're Fay's father, Artirus? It's a pleasure. Truly, it is."

Artirus, for his part, gave a stiff bow and politely extended his hand to shake with a smile. "I apologize for appearing nervous, if that is how I come off. I was just caught off guard when I heard you'd be attending one of our banquets, and haven't really wrapped my head around the fact that my beloved daughter is marrying into royalty. Please, allow me to escort you into our home. Fay told me that you liked to keep things informal, so it will be more or less without ceremony. I am hoping she told me correctly . . ."

"She did. And yes, please lead on. I'm excited to finally catch a glimpse of Fay's home and the wonderful people who raised her," Riven stated immediately, glad to get an out and avoid the stares of Fay's sister and mother as Artirus began leading him through the crowd while other succubi and incubi began to stand and cheer—creating a roar of approval and chanting Gluttony's name as he went.

Halfway through the crowd, though, he noticed that Fay had fallen behind. Turning and walking back to grasp Fay's hand, he saw her eyes widen and begin to water before she wiped her tears away and laughed loudly amid the happy rise in mood around them.

"You really are quite a sob story a lot of the time," Riven said. "Quit crying and be happy! This is going to be fun! I'm assuming there's alcohol?"

"Oh, we have lots of alcohol—count on it!" Saemi chimed in with a giddy skip to her step. "One benefit of being information brokers is that we know where all the best wineries are!"

Fay just let Riven lead her forward until she locked arms with him and pressed against him. Together, both smiling, they made their way through the crowd toward the inner sanctum of Fay's family home—where many of the incubus and succubus children waited to greet them with a shower of flowers and laughing cheers.

As for Riven—he very much wondered what their children would turn out to look like should they have them. Would they be something like these kids? If so, they were going to make adorable babies.

He should probably start looking for engagement rings after the whole "conquer Panu" thing was over.

CHAPTER 10

The open-air dining area was in the very center of the Sojavi clan's Mayan-style compound on the uppermost floor, surrounded by vine-covered pillars and a golden roof that only covered the outer perimeter where the food tables were. The inner square had many dozens of large circular stone tables covered in white silk, along with vibrant flowers of numerous colors for decoration. Instead of chairs they had soft decorative pillows to sit on, and it gave him a very Oriental vibe.

Riven was positioned at the central seat of honor at the very backmost platform, at the only rectangular table present—one that was raised above all the other tables so he and the others sitting there could look forward and down at everyone else eating below. A band softly played string and flutelike instruments in the background, too, but it was only barely audible—intentionally so.

Everything was very colorful, filled with beautiful people who laughed and joked with one another while shooting him a mixture of curious, awestruck, flirtatious, and even reverent glances more often than he was comfortable with. He didn't know how to take being idolized like he was someone great, and in his opinion he wasn't—he was just a somewhat normal guy who'd been thrust into abnormal circumstances. A guy that did his best, but the lack of ceremony Fay had insisted on did ease his nerves as people went to and from the buffets lined up along the outer perimeter in the shade of the roof.

For his part, he was enjoying the warm, vibrant sunlight on his skin—and due to this being a nether realm, it didn't bother him to the point that he had to bring out Messenger. It was nice, because in a normal world without Messenger, he'd have been rather uncomfortable given his vampiric heritage. Instead he kept on his burgundy, red, and black demon-styled suit and sat cross-legged while holding Fay's hand.

"As you all know—" Saemi called out, with mana infusing her voice "—we have a special guest of honor today! Fay has told me that he doesn't like the spotlight too much, so I'll keep it brief!"

A chuckle rippled across the crowd of smiling, enthusiastic listeners, all wearing their best attire, and their voices settled down to better hear her with many of their eyes turning to Riven.

"As amazing and overwhelming as it is to have the reincarnation of Gluttony himself in our midst, we—" Her voice caught in her throat when Gluttony's visage slowly opened up across Riven's suit—along with the purple third eye on Riven's forehead. But Saemi, despite her surprise, quickly recovered and bowed low, a little more stiffly than she'd done before.

"Please continue," Riven and Gluttony said at once before Saemi straightened her posture and took in a sharp, nervous breath.

"Eh . . . ahem." She cleared her throat and nervously brushed her hair back as many of the succubi and incubi gawked, not knowing whether or not to prostrate themselves—but took the cue from Riven's casual attitude that they should keep standing. "I—It is an amazing thing, as I s-said, to have someone as important as the reincarnation in our midst. I just wanted to take a very brief moment to acknowledge him as our guest of honor, the man who not only saved my daughter's life, but who I hope one day will be married into our clan as an official member!"

When her mother shot them a dazzling smile, Fay turned bright red from embarrassment and squeezed Riven's hand all the more tightly as she simultaneously looked away.

"Perhaps to even bring us children!" Saemi declared, to the laughter, applause, and cheers of the audience while Fay's face flushed even more. "But I'll not dwell too long on the wishes of an old woman concerning her daughter's fate. For today, we will drink and be merry. Per his request, any or all of you are more than welcome to come speak to the reincarnation if you wish to do so, without consequence. He wishes to convey that you should treat him like any other in our clan, and he hopes that we all have a good time. Cheers to that, and that is all I have to say!"

There was an uproar of applause and shouts as the brief speech ended, and Saemi came to sit back down next to Riven on his other side opposite Fay. She quickly shot the maw and the extra eye on Riven's forehead a reverent bow yet again when she seated herself, fumbled with her rather revealing dress a bit, and settled in. "Today, Riven, it is only my children and their father up here to eat with you. But the other elders of the clan would like to speak in private before you head out—with your permission, of course."

"Of course," Riven said with a smile, taking his eyes off the mulling crowds of hungry and invigorated blue-skinned people to look Saemi up and down. "No need to be nervous, Saemi. I'm very excited to be here to meet my future in-laws."

He gave her a wink and heard Fay take in a sharp breath—before he began to laugh at Saemi's excited expression.

"That's not funny!" Fay hissed in his ear, jabbing him in the side and letting out a high-pitched yelp that got Tupper to cackle a few seats down. "Don't tease me like that!"

"Ow, stop that!" Riven insisted, swatting her hand away and then pulling her in for a kiss on the forehead before ruffling up her hair—much to her disgruntlement. But he could tell there was a barely hidden smile tugging at the corners of her lips, and she kept shooting him doe-eyed stares from time to time over the next couple seconds.

Fay's father, Artirus, on the opposite side of Saemi and two seats down on Riven's left, waved down some of the servants who were standing ready along the sidelines. "Bring in the first course!"

Unlike the rest of the Sojavi clan, who were having a free-for-all in the line at the buffets, Riven and the others sitting at this table had been prepared a five-course feast with the best that the Sojavis could afford. Fay had told him not to let the others know, but apparently Saemi had gone well out of their way to spend nearly six times the entire clan's yearly income on the food and drink he'd be eating today. Some kind of spiritual ingredients that cost immense amounts of money, but when Riven had told her to let them know that was not needed, Fay had insisted it'd only bring shame to her family if he didn't at least allow them this show of respect, and that they'd likely have their pride hurt if he rejected it.

So he let the servants come in and fill the space in front of him with the first of five courses, one of them even visibly shaking with the nervousness.

"Esta-Vil-Kwa, a dish from the outer reaches of the Mogin Crus Dynasty, where they raise spirit beasts to slaughter and consume once every thousand years," the main server, an older incubus with a ponytail stated, very much like how a butler would do. The guy even had the same mannerisms as he gestured to the dish after the youngest succubus girl there had shakily placed it in the center of Riven's display. "The first course. The chef hopes it is up to someone of your standing, sire, and apologizes that we could not do more."

It smelled . . . delicious.

The aroma was like a millennia of youthfulness had been injected straight into his brain. It carried scents of nature and fruit, mixed in with cooked meat. The aroma matched the appearance, with strange orange meats sliced in a decorative fashion and slathered in a rich, sugary glaze. Berries surrounded it, with a dipping sauce to his left, followed by freshly baked rolls on his right and three golden cups of different wines to drink from.

"The beverages are Canyiel Brust, Marinarci from Jaghai, and Vampiric Court Ale from none other than your homeland of the Blood Moon Requiem." The head servant smiled, obviously proud of the selection—and he gestured for two more succubi to wheel in a large cart of bottles before bowing and dipping out. "If you would like, we have also brought a number of different blood samples from your homeland that you may mix into your wines at your leisure. We have the blood of elves, dwarves, humans, gnomes, merpeople, demihumans, dragons, demons, and even the blood of angels if you wish to try it. The blood of angels has, of course, been stripped of any afflictions that may harm you. Anything that you don't wish to use today will be iced for any future visits, and if you decide you want to drink all of it, we will simply buy more. Just know that we'll always have a supply here should you wish to sample different flavors."

Riven's eyebrows raised at the mention of angels. Despite how some people might see it, he'd grown very fond of drinking blood since becoming a vampire. He'd tried Athela's blood, Luke's blood, Fay's blood, lots of Genua's blood, and he'd eaten a few humans and goblins to boot. Maybe an orc? He couldn't remember for sure, though, because during the time in question, he'd been crazed with bloodlust.

But he hadn't ever thought he'd get the chance to try angel blood.

"Let's try the angelic blood, if you don't mind," Riven said eagerly and nodded in appreciation when the man pulled out a small crystal bottle filled with golden liquid. The incubus popped the cork and set it down next to the three glasses of overly expensive wine.

"Enjoy, and I'll be on standby if you need anything," the man stated with a happy grin, then walked off with perfect posture to stand beside the other handpicked servants nearby.

The scent of angelic blood hit him like a train when he leaned forward to sniff. It was like a drug, and without even considering otherwise—he poured a good amount of it into the first glass called Vampiric Court Ale and swished it around with an eager, manly laugh.

"I haven't seen you look that happy in a while," Fay said, one eyebrow raised as she and the others began to dig into their own food with forks and knives, slowly savoring the flavor of the odd, expensive orange meat with groans of appreciation. "And you haven't even tasted it yet."

He playfully nudged her with his elbow in response. "I don't know about that! The other night in bed with you and Athela . . . I was a pretty happy man then, too."

Fay immediately held her face with one hand as her mother began to laugh, and groaned loudly before taking a cup of her own and draining the wine in a single go. "I think I'm going to need to be drunk for this."

Just as he'd thought, the wine mixed with angel blood was incredibly good. So good, in fact, that he probably could have inhaled the stuff for weeks on end without getting tired of it. He took in deep gulps, swishing it around to rinse his fangs in, and with each swallow he closed his eyes and let the strange mix of fluids glide soothingly through his insides.

He'd found heaven on Earth. The thought immediately got a negative response from Gluttony internally, which only caused Riven to laugh as he inwardly explained it was just an expression from his old world. Then again, it also was angel blood . . . so it kind of made sense either way.

"If you need a live source to drink from, I volunteer myself to be at your disposal," Nitidi, Fay's tall sister, said with a very flirtatious expression from the seat across from Fay on Riven's right. "If you like Fay's blood as much as she claims you do, I'm sure you'd like mine as well. Perhaps there are even other things that—OW!"

Fay angrily pinched her sister and shot her a glare before returning to downing her third and final glass of wine before waving over one of the servants to fill the glasses up again. "Please keep them coming. I'm definitely going to need to be drunk for this."

Laughing and shaking his head, Riven ignored Nitidi's offer and put his arm around Fay's waist in a comforting gesture to calm her down. Despite how Fay had originally presented herself, as a sexy beacon of confidence, she'd certainly been the one of his minions with the lowest self-esteem. Time after time she'd not thought herself good enough for one reason or another, and although it appeared that succubus and incubus families were certainly more freely sexual with their partners than many, Nitidi's attempts at flirting probably weren't helping Fay's outlook.

He'd have to put a stop to that sometime soon, but nicely—so that her family didn't take offense.

"So how's Brightsville running without us there?" Riven eventually asked after a minute of people diving into the food and drink. "Is everything going smoothly?"

Tupper perked up at the question directed his way and finished swallowing before using a napkin to wipe his mouth. "Yes, everything is going very well, actually. Forces from the Blood Moon Requiem have settled in at the capital, while two other armies they brought have split off. One has gone to conquer the rest of Umbra that did not willingly submit to your claim over the continent, and the other has gone off to defend the coastline against Nephilim and other forces that are chasing Retesh Vorath's armies across the sea."

"Retesh Vorath is abandoning the northern continent for Umbra?" Riven asked, incredulous. He scowled in confusion and set his drink down with a frown. "I'd thought the war against Judith Marcina was going fine. Is it really that dire? That lich hasn't said a word to me about abandoning his homeland when we've briefly trained together in the Abyssal Descent . . ."

Tupper held up a hand and waved it back and forth in uncertainty. "It isn't that he's abandoning the northern continent, but the weaker and civilian undead he has are safer on Umbra than they are in the north, where the wars are heating up due to outside mercenary armies from across the multiverse being hired on by local factions. Your sister's terraforming of Umbra into a Death-oriented continent, as well as your own ascension as Gluttony's reincarnation, has put a target on your back across the rest of the world. As you know, there's already an additional world quest aimed at killing your sister, and it is in our own best interest to conquer most of Panu to acquire Elysium's prize and protection for the next century against outside intervention. If you don't abandon Panu entirely, you'll need to finish that quest above all others—and everyone on the Panu forums knows it. It's made you and your sister a public enemy to all non-undead. Regardless, I am getting off topic: Retesh Vorath has been sending his civilians from the north across the sea and into Umbra. The Blood Moon Requiem's forces, most of which are from your own House Wraithtide, are making sure they're safe once they arrive and killing anyone following them into Umbra."

Riven paused to consider Tupper's new information. "All right. I'm sad to hear that we're killing other undead that didn't subjugate themselves, but I think Allie's right on the money. Gluttony especially needs Elysium's protection to make Panu a safe harbor after the integration, and if we don't get it, that could spell trouble. We'd be absolutely forced to abandon the planet altogether before some S-grade asshole comes in and kills us while we're still weak."

"Exactly." Tupper nodded in agreement, while the rest of the family listened intensely on the sidelines. "I'm not sure if you're aware of this, but there are already massive armadas fortifying positions or battling each other on the outskirts of your sector, from dozens of major multiverse factions—those opposed to letting you live, those who are interested in your rise to power, and mercenary legions that are selling themselves to the highest bidder or hope to capture you for ransom. Just in case your plan to subjugate the planet fails, which in the case of those who want to see you dead gives them reason to sell their F-grade elites off to your enemies on Panu at an extreme discount, despite massive losses."

Riven blinked, then sipped on his wine again. "Well, that's not good."

Tupper snickered. "As you say. But they have to do it within Elysium's rules, so there's still a very good chance you'll succeed. Dawn's forces have rallied to rebuild their cities, and they're sending soldiers through the Riven's Eye Wormhole to help Chicago's legion in securing land on the other side of Panu. The Romanovs have fallen, and General Bruner is putting new power structures into place with the cities your forces have taken. But news of a new alliance on that side of the wormhole has led us to build up a defensive line to the north along the waterfront, where we expect the attack to come from, as a lot of your neighbors are very concerned about the Thane Necropolis's quick expansion. The elves of Tereen are also producing a lot of goods for the war effort. Despite their inherent hatred of your rule, most of the undead elves have seen the futility in fighting back, and underground resistance efforts are almost entirely gone at this point. Most of them are just trying to carve a new life out of the loss they suffered. The undead dwarves are still rebuilding from the war with Deepnest."

"Any news on the ratkin?"

"Still absent, having not shown themselves after fleeing your wrath in the underdark. Rumors from drow wanderers have reached our ears: A new blight plague—the plague of undeath—is spreading in the deep from where the cursed ratkin have laid waste to underdark strongholds in search of a new home. But they are just unconfirmed rumors, nothing more."

"And who is actually running everything? Specifically."

"Allie has left Chancellor Mara Tovane in charge. Mara was wounded and nearly drained of her life energies after being captured and siphoned in a blood ritual where the vampiric elder god is still entombed, but she's made a good recovery and will be back in fighting condition eventually. She is counseled by Kathrine Vonsilla Crushada, Counselor Brass of Earth, Counselor Gurth'Rok of the Yellow Skull Tribe, Captain Crendir No-Name of the Blood Moon Requiem, King Arthur Brix of the vassal state Dawn, Gaia the demigoddess of Dungeon Alibast, Fred the Jabob demon, as a representative of Dungeon Negrada, King and Queen Glassleaf of the vassal state Tereen, Jeltuna, voice of the Sarak, a representative I can't remember the name of from the Golden Bull Sect in northern Umbra—who have recently submitted themselves to your rule for a chance to retain localized power—General Bruner of Chicago, and Tre'Zix of the Purple Claw, archdemon of the Klinac'Tal clan. They are currently in talks with pursuing a representative from the dwarvish cities in the underdark that may counsel Chancellor Mara Tovane as she tries to rebuild their infrastructure with support from the surface, but things are slow going in vetting potential candidates with the multipronged war. We have forces fighting on Umbra and along the coastline as Judith Marcina's forces dabble in what can nearly be called acts of war any time an undead refugee fleet arrives from the north, we have forces across the world near Chicago in the previously Romanov-controlled lands, and we have forces fighting in the hells to help our allies from Dungeon Negrada, with two legions stationed in or around Brightsville on standby. One of them is under Kathrine's control from your vampiric ancestral homelands, and the other is a force made of Panu locals. Rippenvire is also completely withdrawn from the world, as you well know, except for those who chose to stay behind, but the other invading forces are hunkering down and solidifying their own spots while gaining extra tokens to bring in reinforcements due to the changes Elysium imposed—given your ascension as reincarnation."

Riven nodded. "Seems like our team has got everything mostly under control, then. How go the wars in Negrada?"

"Very well. Tre'Zix of the Purple Claw has been given full control over Negrada's forces after Negrada itself asked him to do so, and the enemy dungeons have been getting massacred ever since. Tre'Zix has the mind of a war-based artisan and is a truly glorious warrior to witness in battle. He's said to have slaughtered tens of thousands of the enemies by himself—and I do believe he was in Gluttony's legions as a commander during the first eternal war."

Gluttony's visage, laid out across Riven's chest, let out a low chuckle. "He was."

Hesitating, and not knowing how to react to Gluttony's comment, Tupper nervously smiled and scratched the back of his neck—receiving menacing glares from both his mother and father, as he didn't show what they considered the proper respect.

It was very obvious that all of them were a little bit more comfortable talking directly to Riven rather than Gluttony.

"And are the vampires well-fed?" Riven asked curiously. "I know we'd been working on what vampire refugees we had taken in from Rippenvire, but with the transformation of Umbra, blood had been scarce even after importing it from citizens we paid in Chicago. Especially now that Kathrine has brought over more vampires from the requiem . . ."

Eager to avoid looking back at his two glaring parents, Tupper quickly latched onto Riven's question with a fervor. "Oh yes! The Sarak slave army they brought are more than able to supply their vampire counterparts with blood. Funnily enough, the Sarak almost view you as their savior."

Riven raised an eyebrow. "Is that so?"

"It certainly is." Tupper grinned back and stuffed a freshly made bread roll into his mouth, chewing and then swallowing before going on. "Their conditions back on the planet you inherited—Uh . . . Vartesh?"

"Vartesh is the planet my mother left me, yes."

"Ah, yes. Their living conditions have tremendously improved, and you're allowing them to level and fight now, a thing that has not been done in their culture for many millennia outside of arena tournaments, where they fight to the death for the entertainment of vampiric masters. They talk about you with reverence and often are found to be the most eager of your troops. The man you appointed as voice of the Sarak is also seen as something of a mouthpiece for you, one that rivals or surpasses many of the vampiric officials on Vartesh, and they look up to him as some kind of hero. Unrest on Vartesh has hit an all-time low, by the way, with General Viku passing Kathrine messages about how impressed he is with labor output in the mines now that the population is happier. House Wraithtide is also now seeing record profits, despite the trade blockades or pirate raids rival houses in the requiem have tried to launch from time to time."

"Rival houses have been attacking us?"

"Not in open warfare, but with proxy forces. Or so I am told. That man you and Allie killed—the one who was supposed to be wed to Allie? His family is still scheming against you and wishes to see you very dead."

Riven snorted a laugh and started cutting into the orange meat on his plate, letting out a sigh and then savoring the intense, fruity, and simultaneously meaty flavor of the steak that dripped along his taste buds like a godsend. "Wow. Just wow, this is really good."

Saemi butted in with a wide smile. "I'm glad you like it, Your Excellency! If you feel like you want seconds, we have some more waiting for you. Feel free to ask at any time."

CHAPTER 11

Six weeks since arriving in the Abyssal Descent . . .

The training regimens were brutal for everyone, but most of all Fay, who continued to have the hardest time. They pushed her the most because she was, above all, the least useful.

And thus she tried the hardest.

On one of the abandoned peaks surrounding the city of the Abyssal Descent on Floor One, she remained sitting in meditation just like she'd been doing for what seemed to be days on end now. Time did not seem to have substance here in this state of everlasting torment, as the cyclic rotations of her cursed energies continued to eat away at her from the inside. Blood trickled down her face in place of tears as she concentrated on maintaining her spells past the normal breaking point. But the more she inflicted self-harm through the curses, the stronger they became—and the more her body adjusted to the backlash, allowing her to push even further.

So far she'd increased her available power output by nearly 20 percent, and that amount was only climbing by the day.

"Concentrate, Fay," her self-appointed mentor, Lavini, said while steepling her fingers across from Fay's own meditative pose. "You are improving. Do not give up now, push through the pain. It is only mental, and as long as you don't push too hard or too fast, your body will be able to maintain a steady climb until you reach the precipice at level 200. Only then will your soul lattice be able to connect, and you have the most to climb of all."

Fay winced but kept her eyes closed and did not falter. The green flames of cursed energy that Lavini herself had imparted knowledge about now rotated around Fay like planets orbiting a sun, five fireballs imbued with malice that both outstripped normal Unholy energy in power but also applied Insanity debuffs to enemies that temporarily afflicted an opponent's outlook on reality. The problem was that channeling such a potent, destructive curse also did damage to Fay's mind as well—but the images of alternate truths about the universe at large had been kept to a minimum with Lavini interfering whenever Fay drifted too far into madness.

"Your break is over. Open your eyes, Fay, and tell me what you see," the red-headed, winged woman commanded in a tone that brooked no argument.

Fay, though not necessarily wanting to, did as asked—and a torrent of images slammed into her mind as the world twisted and the flames grew larger. The fires rose higher and higher, forming outright pillars of cursed energy in a swirling vortex as the five points began rotating even faster while the madness took hold again.

Fay stuttered a reply. "I see . . . I . . . see . . . ?"

She stopped, shuddering when the image of Lavini turned into that of Riven—his headless body leaning forward with hands steepled in front of him. The sky above them shattered and broke, and the laughing faces of the cultists who'd kidnapped her months before rose up from the ground like wraiths.

"Concentrate, Fay. You know what to do," the headless version of Riven told her without a mouth to do it.

Fay shuddered again, pushing the cursed mana through her pillars in ways that circumvented her core—only releasing them at the very tips of her pillars and putting up barriers in her mind. Real teardrops mixed with the blood leaking from her eyes, but her jaw clenched in firm resolution while she pushed through. She knew this wasn't real, despite what her mind was trying to tell her, and slowly—ever so slowly—the images began to take on their real forms. The laughing cultists disappeared, Riven's body vanished, and in its place the other succubus sat smiling across from her, and yet the pillars of green fire swirling around Fay remained just as potent.

Yes! She was making progress! It'd only taken her half the time to complete this round, only half the time to regain control of her mind.

Smiling despite her internal agony, Fay met Lavini's eyes and flared her wings. "May I try the next step?"

Lavini glanced to the sky where a rumbling sound echoed out, the flashes of deep purple Sin energy lighting up the darkness on the outside of the system's dome protecting the city of the Abyssal Descent. Out there in the beyond, two void titans—each larger than the city itself—were having a herculean battle to the death with powers so beyond them that it made the two succubi feel like nothing but ants.

"Yes . . ." Lavini eventually stated, regaining her senses and shaking her head after wrenching her eyes off the awe-inspiring battle above. "Next step, create the illusions. This time, when you cast your dreamwalker zone, be sure to imbue the images you project with the same cursed energies you used with the fire. Keep that energy on the outer edge of each illusion, like a shell. If you are able to reinforce the illusions like this consistently, you will create semisolid objects that can manipulate the environment as if they had real physical substance. And if you eventually perfect your craft, somewhere in the E- or D-grade, you may even be able to provide minor amounts of consciousness to each of your images—creating copies of yourself or others, or even creatures, that do your bidding."

Fay let out a small laugh. "I think I'm quite far from anything like that. Static and temporarily moving images are the best I can put out at this point."

"And that's why we're training you!" Lavini retorted, reaching out and smacking Fay upside the head playfully through the gap between flaming pillars while she rolled her eyes. "Is your grimoire still bound to the dreamwalker zone?"

Fay nodded, reaching into her satchel and taking out the black book with etched Unholy runes and the depiction of a glowing green viper on its cover. It was her most prized possession and had already been granting her insights that had tweaked her Curse Trap ability to a minor extent. Now, she'd been putting most of her focus into the illusions. Flipping the book open, she watched as the grimoire wrote and rewrote diagrams, runes, and other magical sigils in different sequences, like a computer shifting codes around. Sequences were erased, changed, or reorganized at random and repeated over and over again across its many pages while it experimented with her chosen skill and attempted to find ways to better the illusions for her.

What a fabulous item indeed.

[Viper Grimoire of Curses and Schemes (Unholy Specialization Grimoire, Unique): +129% mana regeneration when held. +9% damage to all curses when held. By binding this grimoire and adding a single one of your curses to its pages, you will decrease the cooldown time on your chosen curse by 10%, while simultaneously allowing for spontaneous evolution options of that curse with insights drawn from the Unholy foundational pillar and its related subpillars. Spontaneous evolutions will occur as the grimoire actively writes out different variations of the curse across its pages with random trial and error experiments in an internal, limited plane. Evolution options will occur in the form of insights once a breakthrough is made.]

"I don't think you realize just how valuable that book really is," Lavini whispered from across the few feet separating them, looking longingly at the grimoire with a mixed expression—until she rubbed her temples and sighed. "Anyways, let's move on. Keep the book in your hands while it regenerates your mana, and we can start with the more energy-intensive portion of your training. Create an image of me, infuse it with the fire's cursed energy, and try to give the image a solid outer shell. Please begin."

Seven weeks since arriving in the Abyssal Descent . . .

Black waters snaked through a land of flames, each of the volcanic pillars belching infernal plumes that easily dwarfed the young hellscape brutalisk and nearly matched his teacher. Molten rock oozed out from each of the crystals in turn, forming roots that sapped life out of the descent where none should find harbor—and it was here that he'd been training most over the last weeks. The environment was rich with Infernal energies, and the opponents were no pushovers—and they gave a very good XP boost for leveling whenever Azmoth managed not to die. He'd been killed twice now, but that didn't faze him in the least—having taken Lillith's words to heart and pushed himself to new heights to catch up with his master.

Azmoth's obsidian plates shifted and moved in perfect alignment with his musculature, rotating through the motions of a dance being taught to him by a true master of his own race. His war hammer was long gone, and his original shield as well—both destroyed when Deepnest had been obliterated by an act of treachery. But that was fine, for Azmoth had his claws—and he was quite able with just those alone. Not only that, but he'd been provided with a new set of items to acquaint himself with . . . ones that were traditional weapons of the brutalisk race, and Azmoth was quickly beginning to see why that was.

His mentor, the huge, winged, E-grade brutalisk looking down at Azmoth from a crouching position, snorted, turning its eyeless, armored head to the left when one of the monsters of the deep began to crawl out of the volcanic entrances of the lower abyss. Made of darkness and lava, the creature was an amalgamation of a centipede and an eagle, with a large, snapping beak and numerous feathered wings that glistened with cinder, each set along sections of Shadow-crafted plate armor intrinsic to the beast. It was twice as tall and nearly twenty times longer than Azmoth, but Azmoth's eel-like snapping jaws grinned as they wrapped around to look at the monster in anticipation.

Another customer.

"Take up your new weapons, youngling," Azmoth's tutor rumbled, the massive dark wings of the older brutalisk coming out to the sides while he stepped back and folded his four naturally armored arms. "You may start again. This time, you are restricted to using your upper Shengari Shields to strike with. Your lower ones may only defend. If you act otherwise, you fail."

Azmoth didn't bother replying, but instead walked over to where the dark-gray Shengari Shields lay half-buried in the molten ground near a large black crystal. Ignoring a burst of flames from a hole in the ground underneath his legs, Azmoth took hold of the four items and yanked them from the earth in a spray of debris and lava.

Shengari Shields weren't just shields, though, and that was very apparent when he tore them from the ground. Instead, they were both shields and blades at the same time—simultaneously providing both offensive and defensive options, and meant to be used as a four-piece set, as was tradition in brutalisk culture.

The upper and lower shield halves were paired and had pieces on their dull inner sides that—when interlocked—created two large tower shields from the four halves. These tower shields in turn had long, curved blades along the outer edge that—when unlocked—allowed each upper and lower shield to be split into the equivalent of four large machete-like weapons.

Each of the four halves had thick, metal holding rings on the inner side of the weapons facing Azmoth whenever he combined them to form the two tower shields, emphasizing the powerful four-pronged attacks and long-reaching swings typical of berserker-style fighting. The metal was very thick, the blades on the outer exterior very sharp, and Azmoth was very quickly becoming a fan of the weapons as he used them with increasing proficiency.

The monster turned its head, leading out an ear-piercing screech when it saw him, and then burst from the magma vein to rush him.

The tutor watched as Azmoth interlocked the four halves, creating two tower shields with one laid over and above the other. Snapping them together at the interlocking slots right before the monster crashed into the thick metal barriers, the impact caused the ground to shatter underneath the combatants. The beak snapped angrily, and long piercing legs from either side of the Shadow-imbued chitin tried to reach around, but the outer blades of the Shengari Shields rapidly snapped back and forth while maintaining their locked positions—severing the reaching legs one by one with quick jerks in back-and-forth motions and simultaneously keeping the beak at bay.

The monster let out a scream of rage and began to backpedal, withdrawing its beak, only to let out a squawk of surprise when the four halves of the tower shields ripped apart and lunged forward—with four machete-like arcs crashing into the monster's head in a spray of black blood.

Azmoth's spiked tail whipped around as he spun, slapping the monster's eagle face to send it sprawling and quickly following up with a whirling four-pronged attack that hit the beast as it fell. Blooming with flame and roaring with a manic grin, Azmoth stomped down to let out a Shock Wave martial art that smashed his opponent against a nearby boulder—before he activated Propulsion and rocketed forward with the cackle of a maddened hunter.

[You have gained one level. Congratulations! Be sure to visit your status page to apply points.]

The tutor, for his part, merely grunted in acknowledgment when Azmoth walked back with the severed head of the beaked beast a minute later. Then he gestured at two more of the monsters when they were spotted coming out of another magma vein not far off. "Again. This time, infuse your stamina channels abruptly before each strike. Channel the energies into your arms in quick bursts to preserve your reserves and make quicker hits."

Grunting back at his larger comrade, Azmoth once again yanked the four halves of his Shengari Shields out of the ground and began loping over toward the new targets. Passing by a small hill of the heads he'd collected since arriving here, he began the dance of killing while he power leveled under the watchful eye of his comrade-in-arms.

Twelve stone skulls laughed at her while she meditated above a sacrificial altar, the blood of their most recent sacrifice pooling around the stone steps as a testament to the resolve of the clergy here. She didn't know who the dead human was or why he'd been selected as the sacrifice, but the potent death energy leaking off his carved-up corpse made for a very good environment to cultivate in.

She'd need to replicate this sometime.

The feathers of Allie's black wings shifted in a wind that did not exist outside the ethereal world of the void, thousands of souls dancing around her happily while she meditated in a temple of death. Fimrindle watched emotionlessly from the sideline, invisible to most but present in her own mind through the connection of master and servant they'd established. He was truly a gifted assassin, and the priests of death that waited on them had shown both of them a deep respect. Though reapers were more common here in the Abyssal Descent, they were still quite rare and respected by all. As the hands of the Scythe, they were some of the most elite mercenaries of the multiverse—and often provided the temple of death with significant donations to appease their god for the gifts he had provided them.

Much to her surprise, though, it appeared that the reapers didn't always get along. They might be of the same order, and they might all worship the Scythe, but in truth they were usually independent of one another. They also remained united in core values that she was still trying to figure out, but those values seemed somewhat vague—and the rules were prone to bending.

"My lady." A robed, skeletal skresh walked in, bowing to her and briefly acknowledging Retesh the lich, who was meditating at the opposite end of the room. "We, the clergy, wish to speak to you—if we may."

The skresh smiled politely and awaited her answer while Allie's aspect of true death caused the room to quake in a shudder of gray energy.

The souls, wraiths, and ghosts around her drank it up greedily, empowering themselves on the passive presence of their master as Allie opened her deep gray eyes and lowered herself to the ground. Her foot touched down on the bloody body on the altar, and a pulse of power absorbed the sacrifice with the rush of an echoing whisper. When she picked up her Blade of Soulcry, the Divine-ranked claymore moved—causing the world to move with it as she raised it. She then clutched the magnificent weapon to her chest in an embrace.

"And what would the clergy of this temple ask of me?" Allie asked, her gray halo glowing in the dark room alongside the souls that encircled her. "Speak."

The hooded skresh bowed low, clasping his skeletal hands in front of him in a gesture of respect while maintaining a ninety-degree angle at his waist. "My lady, I was hoping I could speak to you about the whispers I have heard in the darker places of this city. Our agents have heard of unease and restlessness from others who take the path of the descent, and I would not see one of your stature fall prey to them."

Allie raised an eyebrow and stepped down from the sacrificial altar, glancing up at the laughing stone skulls above her only for a moment. "I was deep in meditation, priest. Please make haste in what you have to tell me, so that I may return to gleaning the insights that have eluded me over past weeks."

"Apologies, Mistress," the skresh said again, bowing even lower this time before standing straight and huffing slightly. "Whispers have reached me. The Church of Greed likely moves against you."

Allie raised both eyebrows this time, then nodded slowly. "I am aware they are not friends of my brother. But they target me now?"

The priest hesitated, looking over to where Retesh had come out of his own meditation to pay attention to their conversation. "Yes, though the time is not yet ripe."

"And how do you know this, priest?" Allie asked, taking a step forward to be within arm's reach of the skresh man.

"The reapers," he replied at once, nodding over to where Fimrindle had come out from the shadows to stand beside his master. "Two of them had come forth with information on contracts that were not specifically naming you but were rather obvious by the nature of what they did say."

"And what is that?"

The priest hesitated. "They did not say. But when two separate agents come forth with the same suspicions, it is likely they are on to something. They would have nothing to gain from lying, but by declining the contracts they are able to send word without breaking the reaper oath of silence."

"Oath of silence?"

This time it was Fimrindle's turn to speak—and he did so in the same raspy voice that sounded like wind being drawn through a metal pipe. "When we accept a mercenary contract, we sign in the name of the Scythe. Part of our earnings will go to the church, and we gain power from fulfilling the contract, but we are also oath-bound not to speak of the contract during or after its completion. By declining the contracts, they are able to let their thoughts be known—but it is unlikely the client gave away much information about their targets before the reapers accepted their task."

"And what if they'd not wanted to proceed after taking the contract?" Allie asked curiously.

Fimrindle shrugged. "We may refuse it afterward, but the oath of silence still stands. Breaking the oath will result in disastrous consequences for our cultivation. It is partly why the reapers are held in such high esteem. But if two agents came to this church to warn the clergy of what they suspected . . ."

Fimrindle's metal head abruptly turned to face the skresh in an uncanny, quick motion between blinks.

The skresh priest nodded. "Yes. It is likely that other reapers will accept the contract and proceed with it, if the Church of Greed pays enough. Even if the target were, perhaps, a Hero of Death. The Death God may play favorites, but the contractual rules of the reapers do not penalize them for killing one such as you. Only the priesthoods are protected from such assassinations, and any foul play between contenders in the orders is otherwise allowed to promote growth."

Allie frowned slightly, but in time nodded and turned to watch Retesh amble over with a creak to his bones, his rotten organs shifting across his skeletal frame.

"Do you have a guess as to when they will strike?" the old lich asked, his eyes burning with neon-teal light while he clasped his hands behind his back.

The priest hesitantly shook his head. "As stated, we are unaware of the exact details. But we can guess as to when it will be, if they do so at all. These are merely educated guesses, though, so please do not think ill of me if I am mistaken."

"Well, go on then," Retesh replied impatiently, mirroring Allie's own misgivings on being interrupted while cultivating. "What are your educated guesses, and how did you arrive at them?"

The skresh priest glanced over his shoulder, looking to the temple halls that appeared to be utterly deserted—but they all knew better.

"It may be now, it may be months from now—and it likely revolves around a particular event outside of this realm," the priest said.

There was a pause.

"Have you heard of the Seventh Wing?" he eventually asked. "And have you heard, perhaps, of the potential reincarnation arriving in the third universe?"

CHAPTER 12

The small, private practice room was illuminated with only faintly glowing mana stones embedded in the walls.

Lillith nodded, hands clasped behind her back. "Change stance."

Riven's shirtless body shifted in a wave of crimson, and to the observers it looked like he was re-forming himself from the blood around him in an instant rather than actually moving his limbs.

"Change stance," she repeated.

Again he shifted, instantly moving into the next stance as instructed as the blood mana rearranged his position with the speed of thought.

"Change stance."

From the sidelines, Allie watched her brother while panting and wiping sweat from off her face with a damp cloth. Despite her newfound body and abilities, Lillith was an absolute slave driver—one that she was quickly learning to respect as both an ally and mentor.

Athela and Nora weren't in much better shape, though Fimrindle seemed rather tireless despite the fighting and exercises they'd undertaken over the past few days.

"You may rest," Lillith eventually said, letting Riven fall to his knees with deep, heaving gasps. The demoness turned to look at the others in the room, frowning at their worn-out expressions before giving Fimrindle a nod of approval. "Any word on our request?"

Faster than it took to blink, Fimrindle moved to hand Lillith a parchment.

"As you requested, creature of the night," Fimrindle replied with a nod.

Lillith glanced down, took the parchment from the reaper's metal claws, and unfurled it. As she read, a smile crept across her face and she turned back around to look at the panting young man in the center of the room. "It appears we have found the materials we were looking for."

"Materials?" Nora asked between pants. "What materials?"

Lillith head-bobbed to where Jackal and Messenger were sitting against a wall. "Materials that were needed to upgrade and modify Riven's items. It's time to head out to the trade district."

The city of the Abyssal Descent was truly massive, but despite the crowds, most people kept to themselves and tried to avoid others as much as possible. There were still frequent fights and even raids on enemy compounds when opposing factions across the multiverse sent their young prodigies to properly acquire a soul lattice, but otherwise the hostility was kept to a minimum to preserve some semblance of sanity.

This rule was usually even more steadfast for the merchant guilds. They tolerated no violence in their compounds at all, and if one of their number offended them, it would end in a ban on any trade resources.

It was to one of these merchant guilds that Riven found himself walking, following Lillith as they remained disguised by masking treasures. Though the rings they wore certainly weren't foolproof, they kept attention to a minimum and were similar to the drow Gentry's amulets in how they worked. They nullified identification information and gave off false reads, but they ALSO provided minor illusions that gave them nondescript cloaks and hoods and hid their features. Occasionally the disguises were seen through, but those that did recognize just who Riven and Lillith were quickly averted their gaze when caught staring or hurriedly moved aside.

Riven felt like a fake when compared to Lillith, though. Although he was technically a MYTHIC-tier individual himself, that in large part was due to the bond with Gluttony or the bonds with his familiars. It wasn't entirely due to his own strength—YET—which irked him. But that's why he was training religiously, and he could safely say he'd made great strides in his own abilities since coming here. At this rate it wouldn't be long before he entered the lower levels of the descent, claimed Chalgathi's quest line for his own, and in the long run, he intended to conquer Panu one way or another in order to keep himself, his sister, and the things he'd built on Panu safe from the outer multiverse for at least another century.

At least, that was the plan.

Dark stone skyscrapers towered above them as they passed through the streets, and flashes of purple lightning overhead illuminated an otherwise pitch-black expanse beyond Elysium's dome that surrounded the city.

"You never told me how you two met," Riven stated as they moved through the streets with Lillith leading the way. He looked over to Allie and Retesh—only briefly glimpsing Fimrindle and Athela skirting the perimeter to act as anti-assassin personnel. "What happened back on Panu? How did you, Retesh—the person of interest in World Quest 1—come to be here with us now? I was convinced I'd have to come and find out where you were to kill you, rather than end up allying with your people."

The lich, who wore a tattered, dark-gray robe full of burn marks, shifted his skull face in Riven's direction and made a gesture toward the sky with one hand. "I did not expect to be here, either . . . It is as much of a surprise to me as well. Both in the fact that a Hero of Death would terraform an entire continent in a way that I've been attempting to do since my awakening . . ."

Retesh nodded in reverent respect to Allie while they walked. "Thereby providing my kind something I've been searching for for a very long time—a home. And that I am now here, mingling with powers that are obviously far beyond me in a grand event I didn't know existed. I had always considered myself the height of power . . . and then I was taken from my planet and placed on Panu. It has been an eye-opening experience, if I were to actually have eyes."

Riven grinned at the remark but didn't comment on it.

Allie took up the topic next. "Judith Marcina was chasing him across the sea when he attempted to make contact with our kingdom."

"Judith Marcina? The previous Apex rank one?" Riven raised an eyebrow.

"The one and only," Allie replied with a grimace. "She's quite formidable in person."

"Says the one who scared her off with Lillith." Retesh chuckled, then he let out a groan as his bones started to literally rattle with some undetermined emotion. "I was nearly dead, my undead drakes that'd escorted me to Umbra were gone, and if not for the very shores of Umbra permeating my being with death mana, I probably would have died a true death. I managed to draw enough attention in our battle to warrant a response from some of Lillith's demons, who then contacted Lillith herself. And she, in turn, brought Allie with her to meet the sky rat that'd been chasing me."

"We didn't get to talk, she merely fled," Allie put in with an eye roll. "And given the reports from back home, it's likely she's gearing up for a full-fledged invasion of our home continent. Ever since the world quest to kill me leaked, it's been an us-versus-them situation. Even more so than the other world quests were. The Panu cortex forums are also alight with talk of cleansing the world of the Unholy orders—namely, us."

There was a pause.

Riven eyed the lich, turning a corner in the dark road to follow the tight-lipped Lillith while making their way to the merchant guild. "So what's your world quest even about?"

[World Quest 1, the Lich King's Plague: In the far reaches of the northern Chaos Wastelands, an ancient lich begins to stir. Advanced details are locked until you come into contact with this quest.]

Riven pulled up the quest log on his status page to show the elder lich. "Not much in terms of details on my end. Care to enlighten me so I know who we're getting into bed with?"

Retesh clicked his bony fingers together a couple of times, as if trying to recall something, before shoving his pockets into the dark, tattered robe he wore. "I will tell you of my quest when the queen of the Necropolis deems herself fit to finally speak to the Scythe."

"Speak to the Scythe?" Riven repeated, turning his gaze to his little sister—who uncharacteristically winced. "What's he talking about?"

Scratching the back of her neck, Allie bobbed her head side to side while lowering her pale, glowing eyes. "When I was given the title of Hero of Death and turned down the path of divinity to become an angel of death, I was also given a direct link on my status page to speak to the Scythe. I haven't used it yet."

Riven raised an eyebrow. "Why not?"

"Because I don't trust gods," Allie replied promptly, getting a snicker of approval and a backward glance from Lillith—and a groan from the lich Retesh. "I don't know anything about the Scythe, and this . . . thing—or creature—or spirit, whatever he is—he wants me to serve him. But I'm just a baby god! I don't know why he's paying so much attention to me."

Riven stifled a laugh. "Baby god, huh?"

She pointed an accusing finger his way. "Same can be said for you! Kinda. But, instead of a god you're more like a . . ."

"My dear child. Gluttony is more feral, ancient, and primal than what most of the current gods are now," Lillith said with a sideways smile filled with amusement. "The sins and commandments were here long before many of the gods that now exist. But not all of them, because some of the gods were born at the same time as Gluttony. Most pantheons of gods have come and gone, though, with a prime example being the fallen elder god of a different blood origin than what is widely accepted today. When a god dies, Elysium usually either recycles that power or gorges itself on the god's remnants to increase its own strength, but it could never figure out how to do so with beings like Gluttony. Still, the comparison is one many across the eons have come to make—though the sins and commandments aren't divine by any means. They are something completely different, but comparable. They are fragments of the fabric of creation's birth."

That certainly brought up more than a few questions that Riven wanted to ask, but he was cut short when they turned down a final street that was far busier than most that they'd traveled through up until now. Various multistory compounds were hung with banners Riven didn't recognize, in various shades of green, black, red, gold, orange, and gray—with Lillith pointing to one in particular farther to the left that had the symbol of a large flaming spear or orange fire embroidered on a dark-green background.

"We're almost there," she said, picking up the pace and heading over to where a long line had gathered outside the front of the compound—with many bystanders of various races watching anxiously or in obvious irritation.

"I DEMAND TO BE SEEN! DO YOU KNOW WHO I AM?!" a young vampire man screamed into the face of a hooded figure dressed in gold and black at the barred compound gate. The vampire was well-dressed, with an extravagant long sword hanging at his side, handsome, with slicked blond hair and fangs bared in frustration while he made animated gestures back and forth in protest to the skeleton hand that was held up in front of the other person. "My family is of GARTH! The fourth house of the esteemed Rantali bloodline! How DARE you forbid me entry!"

Three other vampires in line with the young blond man wore worried looks on their faces while the hooded skeleton continued to stare blankly back at the vampire without so much as twitching.

"I DEMAND TO SEE THE MASTERS OF YOUR ASSOCIATION!" the vampire screamed once more after huffing loudly in irritation.

Glancing over his shoulder at the two large minotaurs decked out in obviously enchanted heavy-metal gear and wielding large stone clubs that were likely totems, judging by the soul pulses they gave off to Riven's senses, the skeleton and one of the minotaurs spoke in hushed whispers before the skeleton turned back to the vampire with a shake of his head. "I am sorry, young master. The Firebrand Trading Company is currently engaged with many other higher-priority customers. Due to company policy and the need for secrecy in our halls, you must come back another time to see if we have an opening. I apologize for the delay of service."

The vampire's jaw dropped, and he began to sputter while others in the line began to loudly grumble or call out to him to shut up and move on. "Higher priority?! DO YOU KNOW WHO—"

"I am very well aware of who and what your family is, young master." The skeleton sighed, air somehow rattling the very bones of his neck and shifting the gold-black robes he wore. "You have made it abundantly clear multiple times now. I do not mean you insult; merely being in the descent is a testament to how grand your personal skill and the wealth of your family is, but you must realize that you are now surrounded by people of similar standing. As much as it pains me to offend a prince such as yourself, I must caution you about your outburst. If you do not remove yourself from the line and come back another time, I'm afraid I will have you forcibly removed."

One of the minotaurs snorted in agreement from the side, and a pulse of stamina flared around the huge beast to cut off any retort from the much smaller vampire man.

The vampire prince sputtered something once more, but must have thought better of it when the minotaur began to grin savagely. Spitting on the ground and turning heel, the vampire prince stepped aside with his three companions while venomously hissing to the others with side-eyes at the gate's guards.

"Oh look, it's another one of you!" Nora teased, coming out of stealth and nudging Riven with a laugh that was a little too loud for what was probably appropriate. "I didn't realize there'd be so many vampires here!"

The comment caught a couple of glances from around the crowd and in the line leading up the compound, but most ignored it and kept moving as Riven gave the smaller Asian woman a raised eyebrow.

When Lillith turned to glare at the start-up assassin, Nora visibly flinched and held up a hand of apology. "Oh . . . Sorry. Didn't realize it was a big deal . . ."

The line moved on while people made more civil conversation at the front, and Riven edged himself in beside Allie, Retesh, and Lillith in their disguised appearances. Riven only caught one person who had definitely seen through the cloaking methods, which was obvious by the way the ghoul caster's face went slack-jawed, eyes bulging before he took a step back.

"You there!" the vampire prince who'd been screaming at the gate guards called out, making his way through other bystanders to come up next to Riven's group. "Did I hear the woman right? Are you of my kind?"

Obviously the guy couldn't penetrate the ring's illusion, but as more and more attention was drawn to him, Riven could not help but feel a little bit of irritation about the situation. Slowly giving Nora another glare and causing her to shrink back some more, Riven put up his hand to his forehead and began to rub it frantically to try and relieve the building headache. "Why do you ask?"

The line moved forward a few steps, and so did Riven. This time, though, the new vampire princeling followed him.

"I'll take that as a yes," the prince said, shooting a menacing glare at the upcoming skeleton dressed in black-gold robes for just a moment before returning his attention to Riven. "I'm sure you saw some of what just transpired, and I'm more than certain you—being a vampire yourself—have heard of my family in turn. My name is Prince Narzkal Rantali! Perhaps you've even heard of me!"

He looked to Riven for confirmation with a hint of pride but couldn't see underneath the fuzzy illusion that hid Riven's face and status information. When Riven didn't reply, the prince hesitantly folded his arms. "The kingdom of Garth? The Rantali bloodline?"

Riven merely blinked. "I'm afraid not."

Suddenly skeptical, the prince furrowed his brow. "Are you a vampire or not? You must not be a very bright vampire to not have heard of my family name, or you must be from an isolated part of the multiverse. Is that it?"

The line moved forward again.

Sighing, Riven let his shoulders slump while Allie began to giggle behind him. "Look, man . . . You're drawing a lot of unnecessary attention to me right now. Can we just—"

"Or perhaps you're just bashful in the presence of a greater vampire? I AM almost pureblooded, you know," the prince said curiously, tapping his lips in thought with a far-off look to his eyes. "There's no need to be wary of me because of my lineage, if that's it. Even if you're a lowly lesser vampire, or worse, we are still kin! I think that, if you would allow yourself to do me a favor, I could pay you back in ways that you'd not even fathom!"

"I could fathom putting a boot up Nora's ass right now," Riven muttered under his breath, getting an outright laugh from Allie, who gave Nora a teasing jab while the assassin skulked backward in shame.

"What was that?" the prince asked, coming back to reality from his daydreaming.

Riven shook his head. "Nothing important. What is it you want with me, Prince Rantali? I'm not necessarily hiding right now, but I am trying to keep a low profile. You're botching that in a big way, so if we can move this along . . ."

The line moved forward again.

Conspiratorially, and not taking the hint that Riven was becoming agitated, Prince Narzkal Rantali leaned forward in a poor imitation of a whisper. "Do you know what this place is, lesser one?"

Lesser one?

Was he referring to Riven's apparent "lesser vampiric heritage"?

Jesus Christ.

"Why would I be here if I did not know, dear prince?" Riven said flatly, noting that Lillith was shaking her head from side to side while she listened in. Murmurs in the crowd had begun springing up, with a few of them gawking—others whispering—and even more laughing at the sight of Riven's obvious agitation.

The oblivious prince ignored the comment and pressed onward, explaining it to Riven as if Riven didn't know what was beyond the gates. "Inside this compound can be found some of the best artisans in the Abyssal Descent, the younger generations of the greatest crafting clans of the Unholy foundational pillar! There are very few others that can compare, and though they may not be blooded like we are, they are still skilled individuals. I was wanting to buy my . . . um, my fiancée, a gift."

The prince looked uncomfortable, and Riven's eyebrows shot up in surprise.

"A gift?" Riven repeated. "From here? In the descent? Don't you have an entire country of gifts to pick from?"

The prince suddenly looked agitated, and slowly—ever so slowly—Riven was starting to understand the man just a bit more.

Had this princeling been sheltered all his life? His social cues were off, his demeanor immature, and the uncomfortable look he had when asked about the gift set off alarm bells that screamed desperation.

"It is complicated," the prince replied quietly, red eyes falling to the floor. "And in fact, it is the sole reason I even came to this place. I'm sorry to bother a complete stranger such as yourself, but if there is any way you can gain access to the compound and bring me along as part of your group, I would forever be in your debt. Without a very particular item from a very particular person inside this compound, I'm afraid my fiancée won't last much longer."

Athela's voice rang in Riven's mind through their link. *"Just assassinated a runner. He'd been on his way to tell the Church of Greed about your whereabouts, hoping for a price. I have no doubt there are others on their way if I caught this one so easily after he discussed it in the open. And yes, before you say it, I know that this won't stop word from getting back—but it's still fun to slaughter those who'd attempt to profit off our demise!"*

Riven had known this would happen, as had Lillith, so it didn't bother him much. The churches of Greed and Gluttony were technically under a nonaggression pact right now while dealing with the Seventh Wing, but that didn't mean spies here in the Abyssal Descent were a welcome thing. Though regardless of what they did now, there was almost a 100 percent guarantee the Church of Greed knew where they were right now, and if not, it would know soon.

"He was wearing a very cute man-lingerie we can put on you later! We'll have to clean off the blood, though," Athela chimed in when he failed to reply. *"I've been wanting to get you in—"*

He cut the connection with a chuckle and an eye roll. God, how he loved that woman, and cutting her off like that would no doubt make her attempt to prod him even harder later on. He'd be sure to enjoy it when she did, but there was no way he'd be wearing any man-lingerie. Not a chance.

Feeling slightly bad for the prince, who was still staring at Riven with desperation in his eyes, Riven gestured for the man to continue speaking while the line inched forward yet again. "And just what is it that you intend to buy here? If I'm able to get inside, that is."

Prince Narzkal Rantali beamed excitedly, while his three associates just stared blankly at his back. "An amulet! One crafted from a black phoenix stone that is said to only be in supply at this location. You see, my fiancée is a lesser princess of a bordering vampire state—and she has a deep-set sickness. Blood rot, more specifically. If I'm able to get such an amulet with the essence of a black phoenix inside it, its aura should be able to keep her alive."

He wasn't a pureblood, yet he was a prince. Neither his country, nor the country this princess came from, could find the antidotes for said fiancée. He'd also been denied access to the crafting compound while numerous others had been let in.

All this pointed to the idea that Prince Narzkal Rantali and his "Kingdom of Garth" were probably not all that well-off, or all that well-known, despite the man's claims.

Riven stared at the other young man for a time, trying to search for more clues. He seemed truly desperate. His clothes were well made, yes, but they held a lot less intrinsic power that he felt from many of the other elites roaming the city here. And when pulling up his information, he wasn't even registered as ELITE by Elysium—but rather had a normal display tag with a combat level of 190.

"Lillith . . ." Riven eventually said, not turning to look at the disguised demoness. "What kind of faction is the Kingdom of Garth, exactly?"

Lillith turned around, then shrugged. "Never heard of it. It obviously wasn't around when I was at the peak of my power."

Riven turned to Allie. "Ever heard of it when talking about politics with the queen?"

"Our great-grandmother has rarely talked to me, Riven. Despite what you may think," Allie retorted with a shake of her head and folded arms. "All she's done is try to sell me off to the highest bidder, and now that I am what I am, I'm not even sure she's going to want to do that. So no, I have no idea what the Kingdom of Garth is."

"It's a middling D-grade kingdom in Universe 70!" a bearded chaos dwarf laughingly called out from the sidelines, where he was waiting for one of his kin to come back out of the compound. "I only know of it because my own kingdom is two galaxies over. The boy talks big, but do not be fooled! It is an act and he likely could not pay you back if you were to help him actually get inside such a grand establishment!"

Many of the others around them laughed when Prince Rantali's face fell, but Riven wasn't one of them.

"Next!" the skeletal attendant at the gate called out, not paying Prince Rantali any attention when Lillith stepped up to the front. He looked her over, then glanced at Riven and the others. "Camouflage devices and all automated offensive enchantments must be deactivated before evaluation, or before entering the Firebrand Trading Company's main compound here in the Abyssal Descent. If you cannot do this, you must turn around and leave now."

Lillith grumbled under her breath, then thought about it and nodded to the others. "I didn't realize that was a rule here. Apologies, reincarnation."

Allie was the first to deactivate her own ring, and her LEGENDARY status alongside her race and title were more than enough to snap a few surprised heads her way for those that hadn't already seen through the disguise. Retesh and Nora went next, and then Lillith.

When Lillith took her ring off, a palpable silence overcame the crowd—with many of the ones who'd been gambling or gossiping around the gated entrance to immediately take on expressions of awe, fear, and shock just like a few of the more insightful ones had prior to her deactivation.

Immediately one of the minotaurs gasped, falling to his knees and slamming his horns into the ground in a semblance of worship, as the skeleton took an involuntary step back.

"Y . . . you're . . ." The skeletal attendant rapidly shot his gaze left to Riven's position when Riven deactivated his own ring.

Prince Narzkal Rantali blinked rapidly, noting the ancient Unholy scripts on Riven's skin—and the burning red-and-black eyes. He looked confused, then flustered, then he paled. "Are you the prince they speak of from the Blood Moon Requiem, the one that became the aspect of a demonic god?"

Allie chuckled. "See, told you. You're a baby god, too, Riven."

"Not god," Lillith corrected again. "Demonic origin."

"For what it's worth, my own faction is only F-grade," Riven said with a chuckle while ignoring the two women. "If you don't include all the demons that worship Gluttony, or my great-grandmother's S-grade faction."

"We demons worship you, too," Lillith said with a side-eye. "You are the reincarnation. You are one with the Great Maw, Riven."

Riven didn't bother replying. He'd had this conversation with Lillith more than once since his arrival in the descent. Looking over to the skeleton, and to where both of the minotaurs had now prostrated themselves, he turned to face the gate. "Would it be all right if I brought my new friend Prince Rantali along with us? I was hoping to ask him a few questions about vampiric society, to compare it to what I know of the Blood Moon Requiem."

He looked at the skresh, who was gaping at their group with an unhinged jaw. "Assuming, of course, we can get in."

CHAPTER 13

The inside of the compound was a lot fancier and far more colorful than Riven would have thought, considering the dark and dreary outside that was so commonplace here in the descent.

Brilliantly colored paintings of scenes from other worlds hung from the walls, platinum trimming lined polished white marble hallways, colorful plants that obviously weren't native to this place thrived under small artificial suns at crossways between passages, and large workshops of different types were established for crafting experts at intervals through a network of interconnected buildings.

A bustling, active community of apprentices rushed back and forth, sometimes stopping to stare—while others completely ignored the group as if they were in a panic while getting their master's needed materials. They lugged around large crates, vats of fluids, vials, and glass instruments—and sometimes even pushed large, wheeled platforms of large metal ingots.

And the last room that they stopped at had one such platform of ingots resting along the side of the wall when they walked in.

"This is an impressive forge," Riven commented, noting the two pools of lava to the left and anvils alongside cooling weapons and armor. Along the walls were numerous completed sets of finely made pieces, and a large, hulking creature approached them from where it'd been sitting upon their arrival.

The creature was a cyclops, very reminiscent of the monster that'd killed Azmoth back when Fay had been new to the group. He bore a couple small tattoos, burn scars, and had a thick but short black beard while his one eye scrutinized the bunch. Placing his hands on his belly, he gave a bow in Riven's direction—and then did the same with Lillith as the skeleton introduced them.

"Esteemed guests, may I present Jamal Iktorian—the best smith we have available at the Firebrand Trading Company. He is sure to go above and beyond your expectations for whatever job you may have." The robed skeleton turned to gesture at Riven and Lillith. "Jamal, may I present—"

"We are acquainted. She let me know she was coming already," Jamal cut in with a smile, reaching out and grasping Lillith's hand in a shake despite his hand dwarfing her own. "My great-great-great-great-great-great- . . . eh . . . you get the picture, my ancestor is a friend of Lillith's. Any job she wants done is on the house."

"You told the old goat I said hello, yes?" Lillith asked with a laugh.

Jamal snorted and let go of her hand. "Aye, I did. It's a real honor to meet you, Lady of Black Skies."

He looked at Riven with a little bit of hesitation next. "And the reincarnation . . . It is truly an honor. I did not ever dream I'd be serving ones of your stature here in the abyss, but it seems that Elysium smiles upon me. I only wish I could have thrown a party in your honor, but Lillith insisted that I keep hushed about it."

Riven waved a hand dismissively. "Don't worry about it. I'd like to think I'm down-to-earth, in a matter of speaking. I was told you'd be able to help upgrade my armor and weapon, and as long as you're able to do that, I'm rather excited to be here."

Gesturing to the skeleton dressed in black and gold, and putting his other arm around Athela's waist when she stepped out of the shadows, Riven held out a wrist. "Payment for my request, as agreed."

The skeleton glanced down, then back up to Riven with an uncertain excitement. "Are you sure, esteemed one? The blood of a reincarnated ancient is sure to be worth far more than just a single pendant!"

Riven laughed. "I am. Just be sure Prince Narzkal Rantali and his crew here get the black phoenix pendant like you promised."

The skeleton literally quivered with enthusiasm and drew out a knife and vial from somewhere within his robes. "Absolutely, majestic one! I assure you, the princeling will have his amulet before the day is over!"

The vampire Prince Rantali watched with building tears of appreciation in his eyes from the background as the skeleton slit Riven's wrist and began collecting the blood into the glass vial. The skeleton had to slit Riven's wrist twice more because of the natural vampiric regeneration, but shortly he plugged up the container and bowed low with another round of thanks.

"I won't forget this. Thank you, great one." Prince Rantali clasped his hands in front of him in a sign of respect while the skeleton began to walk out the door and gestured at him to follow.

"Don't sweat it." Riven gave the other vampire a thumbs-up. "Just think of it as my wedding present to you. I hope it's a marriage that lasts forever, my friend."

"As do I!" the young man replied, before quickly walking out of the room, wiping away more tears, and disappearing from sight.

The bubbling lava pits and the heat of the forge drew Riven's attention back toward the cyclops. He then produced the items he'd been carrying around in his spatial sack. Usually they'd have been left out in the open or worn, but Lillith had said something about the smith needing them to spend a certain amount of time in stasis for the process to work more effectively—something that neither Jackal nor Messenger had necessarily liked. But they'd complied nonetheless.

"These are the items I'd like you to upgrade," Riven stated, handing the long, sleek spear-staff Jackal over to the cyclops first. The canine maw producing the blade at the center seemed to snarl when it was put into the cyclops's hands, and the rivers of blood flowing over the weapon grew more intense.

Next Riven bade Messenger float forward, and the heavy ivory plate armor shifted through the air to hover next to Jamal while shifting its helmet as if to look at the smith. The red bloodsilk connecting the plates stretched from time to time, and it looked like the upper half of a man was somehow controlling it from the inside due to the way it actively manipulated itself.

Next, Lillith handed Jamal a small slip of paper with writing on it.

Jamal, who was staring at the two items he'd just been given, had to snap himself out of the trance before taking the paper to read it. He looked up with a grin. "This is a big job, but it's exciting work."

"How long?" Lillith asked.

The cyclops shrugged, then gently laid the weapon on a nearby bench. "A few weeks, perhaps a few months. Is that all right?"

Lillith shot Riven a curious look.

"That's fine," Riven confirmed with a nod, jabbing Athela in the rib cage and making her screech in retribution for her trying to grab him where she shouldn't in public. "Do you think you'll be able to rearrange the stats as requested?"

"Oh, definitely. The materials were already delivered," the cyclops replied enthusiastically, gesturing to where a large tub of various metals, ingots, bones, elixirs, and gems was set out beside numerous black metal tools. "The Church of Gluttony was rather giving, for obvious reasons. And do not worry, we have very tight security here, so no one is going to try and steal them. Is there anything in particular you'd like to request before I get started?"

Riven thought about it, then nodded with a grin. "Yes. Be sure to make it . . . flashy."

Three and a half months since Riven's arrival in the Abyssal Descent . . .

Battle lines were drawn, and the legions were awaiting orders. Out into the horizon to Kathrine's right and left, an ocean of men, women, monsters, and mechs was grouped by type and experience in preparation for the possible battle to come. And ahead of them was the last holdout of resistance on the continent of Umbra, the city-state of Mayana, which had once been home to humans before they too had been turned into undead. Barriers and magical siege weapons had been erected, and enemy combatants lay in wait along the city walls with steepled white towers, a citadel looming ominously in the backdrop.

City after city, faction after faction had either peacefully submitted themselves to Necropolis rule or had been integrated by means of coercion or force. First had been the elves of Tereen, then Dawn, and then the dwarves of the underdark. The Golden Bull Sect had been the first of the other continental factions after that to pledge loyalty after talk on the Panu forums had called for an undead purge that was quickly ramping up, support-wise, from the rest of the planetary populace, and the majority of Umbra had quickly fallen in line after that—seeing the Necropolis as a pillar of support for a potential crusade against undead-kind. Even if Allie had indirectly been the cause, and even if unrest about their current predicament was still somewhat present.

But soon the continent would be unified; it needed to be unified, or else securing their borders from outside invaders that were sure to come would be much harder to do. Not only that, but the Necropolis had a conquering criteria to keep in order to achieve the century of protection from Elysium that would in the long run save more lives than these wars now cost. So this city was destined to bow, one way or another.

Legions of vampires, Sarak, undead, demons, and humans all formed up in ranks under their designated commanders to number just over 160,000 strong. And this was just half of their current force, with the rest of their armies positioned on the coastline in the north or across the world around Chicago.

Smoke rose from blast sites where magic and missiles had created a landscape that was devoid of life and undeath alike, where craters riddled the land like a disease—and the corpses of many lay burned to ash or torn apart.

A squadron of jets from the Machine-oriented branches of Chicago's military flew overhead through the clouded sky, mirroring Dawn's roc riders that could almost keep pace with the planes at full speed now after hitting a certain level. The sight of the giant undead birds paired up with the machines of war so far above them gave Kathrine pause before she turned from her perch on the outcropping of rock to look at her fellow leaders.

Chancellor Mara Tovane was there, alongside Nin and Vin. Gurth'Rok was also there in full battle attire, while Dr. Brass had remained in Brightsville to oversee the city. Jeltuna the Sarak was present alongside a few of his purple-skinned officers, and Crendir No-Name, the E-grade vampire military genius who'd been handpicked by the upper echelons of the Blood Moon Requiem, stood at attention in full black-and-red plate armor typical of the requiem's forces.

"Where is the demigoddess Gaia?" Princess Kathrine asked, stepping forward as the circle quieted. Her red eyes narrowed from underneath her metal helm, looking around the battlefield without luck. "She was supposed to be here nearly an hour ago."

The ghoul Mara gestured to the west. "She sent a transmission and said she is running late but should be here any minute."

Kathrine's stance relaxed at the news. "Good. She's supposed to be spearheading the main push. I didn't want to start without her, assuming the city of Mayana has declined our final offer to spare them and accept bloodless surrender."

"We have yet to receive their answer, but I would be surprised if they did anything but refuse," Crendir No-Name replied.

Many nodded in agreement. The city-state of Mayana had been overly eager to refute any attempts at peaceful negotiations, which left the Necropolis with little choice. If they didn't conquer enough of Panu in Allie's name to fulfill Elysium's criteria by the time five years of integration was up, their planet would be opened to the multiverse—and a wave of enemies would no doubt pour in. They did not just want the victory of conquest, but needed the victory if they wanted to remain here on this planet and not abandon it entirely.

A crash nearby resulted in a spray of debris from the rocky ground, and all heads turned to see the figure of a small child lifting herself up out of the pit she'd created.

Gaia had regained her childlike appearance since Allie's terraforming and transformation of the populace on Umbra, though what had once been vibrant greens had now turned gray and black, and the demigoddess looked like an outright evil version of her previous self whenever she wasn't in her tree form. When she did take on the form of a giant carnivorous tree, however, she was even more dangerous—and more intimidating.

"Apologies for my late arrival. I had to run for two days straight at high speed to get here," Gaia said, stepping out of the crater and walking up to the group, not showing any sign of weariness or fatigue.

Kathrine brushed a long strand of brunette hair from her pale face. "It matters not, we are glad you're here to—"

An explosion echoed out across the battlefield, causing Kathrine and the others to turn and look. More explosions followed, and balls of hellfire began tearing through the skies from somewhere within the city, where siege weapons were located and beginning to fire in the direction of Necropolis forces.

Kathrine frowned.

"It appears they have forgone the option of peaceful surrender," Mara commented flatly, watching as the projectiles were intercepted by antisiege equipment and interceptor missiles on the Necropolis side. "Any word on whether or not Tre'Zix and the other demons are coming?"

Kathrine shook her head no as the sky above them lit up with artillery fire and her own siege equipment began firing back at the city. "They're preoccupied with the war in Negrada. It is up to us to finish this on our own. And since Mayana seems to have declined our proposal, we won't waste any more time here. To your stations. Crendir, you're heading this operation. Get to the command vessel and prepare for a march."

The officer saluted. "Yes, Princess."

Kathrine glared back at the city in the distance while horns began to blow across the legions of the Necropolis, and the rest of the commanders began dispersing to their own designated areas across the battlefield.

It was unfortunate that they could not see reason, but like it or not—this city would be hers by nightfall.

The long, slender blade at her side rattled against her armor as Kathrine marched at the head of her column with shield overhead. The column was mostly composed of elite vampires of House Crushada and House Wraithtide that kept uniform columns despite the bombardment that continued to crash against their defenses, and she knew any of them would die for her if it came down to it. Erected magical barriers, miracle auras, and stamina-infused tower shields held above their heads caused the turtle formation to look like a giant metallic caterpillar while crossing the pockmarked grounds, but they were not the only columns advancing on the city walls.

To her left and right were hundreds of other large formations just like hers, while projectiles of magic and metal continued to whiz by or skid right off them.

And the sound was deafening.

"FORTY YARDS TO GO!" Kathrine shouted over the in-step march of metal boots, while the ground shook and magics roared overhead. "PREPARE THE DRILLS!"

Immediately a whirring sound started up in the center of their formation, and the tower-shield roof parted for just a moment as a large mechanical object was brought down the middle of the ranks. It was one big drill adorned with spikes and various runes, with blood mana powering the engine as red light seeped out. The thing was large enough to punch a man-size hole through solid rock and enchantment alike, and she doubted that these integration-age F-grades could put together anything that'd stop it.

Another drill followed the first, and then another, until three huge drills were at the forefront of the column just ahead of her with the whirring sound growing louder. The walls above flared and debris rained down about them from the impact of a bomb that a roc rider had dropped on the defenders, with the screams of enemy ghouls reaching their ears as the ones atop the wall fell to their deaths with splats and crunches.

Kathrine just focused and kept moving, despite her heartbeat racing over the din of the fight.

Twenty yards.

Ten yards.

Five.

"SET THEM UP AND TEAR A HOLE!" Kathrine screamed, yanking out her curved blade and sending a vibrant red slash through the air that tore apart a dropped boulder meant for the drills.

More of her soldiers began turtling around the drill site as the machines all latched on to the thick stone walls of the city, putting up further barriers and creating another ceiling of tower shields that blocked the arrows, lightning strikes, and mana-infused javelin throws alike.

A fighter jet spun out of control in a fiery spiral and smashed into the ground a couple dozen yards away, jarring the earth and making Kathrine lose her footing—only for the vampire princess to regain it a second later just when the drills began tearing through the base of the walls.

Vibrations rippled across the earth under her feet, and her teeth chattered despite her clenched jaw. The stone was being chewed through at a rapid pace, absorbed into the blood engine, and spit out the back side in a cloud of crimson ash that not only invigorated her soldiers but healed them any wounds from the bombardment.

Time ticked by far too slowly for her liking while she watched the three large drills bury themselves into the city defenses. Her soldiers waited with stoic faces behind her, and within fifteen minutes, which felt like hours, they all finally heard the noise they'd been hoping for.

The crash through the other side.

In an instant the columns of vampires drew their weapons and headed in, with Kathrine in the lead.

The tunnel she'd chosen was the centermost one, and moving through the recently made tunnel in the thick stone wall was a bit awkward due to confined spaces, but coming out the other side she sidestepped the closest drill and into the city interior.

It was absolute chaos.

Buildings burned and fighting had erupted across multiple places where the wall had either been scaled or burrowed through. She'd been fully anticipating an enemy formation to be awaiting her arrival but found utterly nothing.

They were already too preoccupied with the rest of the assault.

In turn, this left the citadel wide-open.

"FORWARD UNITS, REINFORCE THE FIGHT AT THE WALLS! THE REST OF YOU—THROUGH THE CITY! KEEP TO YOUR SQUADS!" Kathrine yelled back at the lines of soldiers streaming in, barely shifting her tower shield to deflect an incoming crossbow bolt that sparked off the dark metal. "TOWARD THEIR LEADERSHIP! FIND THEM! IF WE TAKE THE KING, THE CITY WILL SURRENDER!"

As one, the vampiric soldiers smashed their swords against their shields in acknowledgment and began wordlessly charging past the main battlements and deeper into the city. As they went, they began breaking off into prearranged squadrons to search for the enemy leadership faster.

Her own squad consisted of twelve other members, all vampires that she didn't know very well—but who'd been guaranteed to be the best of the best that the Blood Moon Requiem had to offer for their F-grade younglings. Or at least that was what Crendir No-Name had told her, and she trusted his insight on the matter. He was one of the best officers for his age and rank, and she was merely a princess. What did she know about war when compared to someone like him?

So if he said they were good at their jobs, they were without doubt good at their jobs.

"Behind me!" The other twelve vampires all silently nodded, one of them deflecting a javelin and blasting the offender with a course of black lightning before they started moving farther into the city interior.

Or what was left of the city interior, anyway.

Rubble was abundant, and more than once they had to change directions due to the burning wreckage blocking their way. They dared not take the rooftops, either, due to enemy snipers killing most who tried. Roads were blockaded and the fighting was fierce, with a couple of enemy groups being encountered at random times throughout their forward approach.

Her blade blurred, leaving red ribbons in the air and corpses at her feet while she pressed on in a bloodstained suit of dark armor, not once speaking and keeping her breathing as calm as she could while focusing on the advance.

Just keep advancing. The targets would be there waiting for her.

"Princess Kathrine! I think I've found a shortcut!" one of her soldiers called back after the fifth time an enemy patrol had intercepted their group.

She wiped the black blood off her slender sword with the most recent undead victim's shirt, who remained lying facedown on the ground in a silent scream. Turning her red eyes back to the soldier who'd called out to her, she didn't question the man and dashed over at superhuman speed toward the alley he'd pointed out. "A shortcut? Toward the citadel? This is going northeast—are you sure?"

The man nodded, and he got a confirmatory shout from another of the soldiers farther down the alley. "We are sure, Princess. Please, follow us."

Shifting her weight and not pressing the man any further, she did as he asked and went down the alley along with the others of her squad at a fast jog. They twisted and turned down the side streets as another fighter jet crashed into a nearby street after its own death spiral—and eventually Kathrine came to a dead end.

"It's here! We found a passage!" The vampire soldier indicated with a finger pointing toward a small, open trapdoor leading into some kind of basement. "It should lead to the citadel, if our guess is correct."

Kathrine raised an eyebrow and gave him a skeptical look. "You had time to explore the passage while we were moving and fighting all this time?"

The vampire merely shrugged. "I chased down one of the enemy that fled here and interrogated him briefly before dispatching the man. He said that this was a secret way in, and I'm pretty sure he was telling me the truth based on how the conversation went."

Another explosion and the screams of the dying echoed out from somewhere nearby.

Clicking her tongue in uncertainty, Kathrine eventually nodded in approval. "Fine. Let's go."

The soldiers nodded, and the first two who'd scouted out the area went down first. Kathrine came next, only to be followed by the rest of her squad as her feet hit solid ground. Looking around and frowning even more deeply than she had been, she saw that this wasn't a passage at all—rather, it was a large basement without exit. She turned to the soldiers who'd led her here with an undercurrent of irritation. "This is another dead end, you fool! What are you—"

CRACK

Kathrine staggered, falling to the ground when a blunt instrument smashed against the back of her head. Her vision blurred and she immediately felt like vomiting, only to receive a swift kick to the face that sent her spiraling backward before she felt hands beginning to restrain her.

"W-what are you doing?! WHAT ARE YOU DOING?!" Kathrine began to scream, enraged and confused as her eyesight began to come back to her. She felt her mana blink out as a suppression collar was placed around her neck, and her sword was ripped off her belt—scabbard and all—by another of the vampire soldiers, who then took a step back.

Slow footfalls echoed from where a pair of large barrels had been stacked, and blinking rapidly while spitting blood, her eyes widened with even further confusion as she saw none other than Crendir No-Name show himself from his place of hiding.

They stared at each other wordlessly, Kathrine's mouth gaped open as a sly smile overcame the other commander's features.

She took in a deep breath, suddenly realizing that some kind of treachery was at play, and a stark fear began to creep into her soul. "Why?"

"Why?" Crendir No-Name asked, smiling—and then laughing as he clasped his hands behind his back. "Elder Thune is very persuasive. The soldiers here, and myself, are all being very well compensated for what we're about to do here today."

A sinking feeling continued to build in her gut. House Crushada had been on edge with the elder and many other factions of the Blood Moon Requiem ever since Lord Justo Barimont's death.

"Elysium wouldn't have allowed you to come here if you'd been planning to betray Allie or Riven . . . it was part of the rules . . ." Kathrine muttered to herself, as if in denial.

Crendir shrugged innocently and held out both hands to either side. "I wasn't intending to. But that was then and this is now. Elder Thune is very persuasive, as I said, and for someone without a family name . . . his offer is simply life-changing. Even if it does mean I have to capture, and potentially kill, one of the lesser princesses of our great empire."

Snarling with an abrupt surge of rage, Kathrine tried to strike out against the man with her foot—but the soldiers holding her back didn't let her get more than a few inches off the ground.

Crendir chuckled, then snapped a kick in her direction.

Her head flew back, and the helmet was knocked off as she yelped out in pain before a sudden burning sensation caught her in the collarbone.

Gasping and looking down at the dagger that'd been slammed there, she began to scream.

"Now listen to me, Princess," Crendir calmly commanded, picking the terri-fied royal up by her hair and yanking her roughly around to face him. "You're going to answer all my questions and do exactly what I say, when I say it—or else I'm just going to leave you in a ditch somewhere. You know what happens if I do that?"

Kathrine didn't reply, but her chest heaved up and down as his grip on her hair tightened.

"If I kill you, then someone else in House Crushada is going to be your replace-ment," Crendir snarled. "I'm hoping you cooperate, lest I need to go take one of your cousins that so eagerly came to this planet in search of glory. And perhaps after I'm done interrogating you, if you do a really good job, I could even keep you as a pet. Better that than what's going to befall the rest of your family, if you ask me."

CHAPTER 14

They ate, breathed, cultivated, trained, and fought in the arena events to test their progress.

Then they slept and repeated—with only a few exceptions.

Each of their soul lattices were slowly building up, but the further descent into the abyss was still on standby. Despite Gluttony's urge to find Purity's reincarnation, the so-called Seventh Wing, Greed's Gambler had provided them with information that was vague at best. Not only that, but if the two sins did go after the commandment of Purity, it wouldn't be Riven who was participating. Riven was far too weak, comparable to a bug when the true titans and monsters of the multiverse under Gluttony's control were getting involved—even if the churches were scattered and only a shadow of the powers they'd once been. S-grade agents of the highest orders from the churches of Greed and Gluttony had, grudgingly, started working together to comb a very specific area in the third universe for the potential target—and that's all Riven knew.

Yet neither he nor Gluttony trusted Greed's henchman despite the temporary truce concerning Purity, and they fully expected Greed to betray them when opportunity presented itself. It would be stupid to think otherwise.

But still, he was interested to see whether they'd succeed in finding and kidnapping the commandment's reincarnation at all. A lack of information and a heavy angelic presence made for poor prospects at best, but even poor prospects were better than no prospects to the demons who wanted Purity out of the game. Any time Riven even thought about it during his bouts of combat training, mana sensing, and soul lattice building, he got an abrupt and angry surge of emotions from Gluttony. Those emotions weren't directed at him, but it was obvious that Riven's counterpart had a long history with this particular commandment.

A history that Riven was now dragged into regardless of whether or not he wanted to be, given his status.

Only time would tell how this all played out.

Riven's soul cracked, shifted, and groaned as bridges formed, broke, and re-formed while the lattice built itself up. His pillars were creating bridges, forming threads that became cords that became rivers of intermixed attunements.

He was on the path of transcendence, and he could feel the abyss deep in the descent calling out to him even from here.

His eyes flashed open with a spark of primal ether, merging his mind with Gluttony's own as the two of them watched their souls intertwine rapidly. In the meditation chamber, his skin—etched in ancient lost scripts of Unholy origin—radiated wisps of power. A calm lake of purple, teal, black, and crimson shifted around him and rose into the air, dissipating after leaving his body to fall back into the environment where the mana was less condensed.

His senses had been refined. He could now sense any F-grade and most E-grades that Lillith sent to hide around him via mana pulses.

His skills had been refined. He was now winning more than nine out of ten fights without the use of his minions, summons, or Gluttony's interference.

His way of thinking had been refined. He would no longer overestimate his own abilities and would rid himself of the fatal flaw of taking an enemy for granted. He was imperfect and had room to grow.

Though it had only been seven and a half months, and though he still had a long way to go, he was far from the man who'd first set foot in this place. For an F-grade, he was at the pinnacle, even here, in the Abyssal Descent, where the elites of the Unholy-oriented multiverse sent their young to create their soul lattices. And he intended to move forward with that mind-set as he continued his training elsewhere.

But his minions had all reached their own level caps now under the rigorous training and power leveling of Gluttony's church. The opportunities no longer existed here in the top level of the descent, but rather in the lower floors, where the condensed energies of the abyss called to him.

Now it was time to move on.

The black scripts shifted across his body and set into a new formation as he floated down from his hovering position and touched foot first onto the stone floor. A silent shock wave radiated through the room, immediately highlighting the seventeen assassins in various locations as they launched themselves at him.

Seventeen rifts, twenty spikes of Crimson Ice, twelve Wretched Snares, and eight quick Black Lightning strikes in the next three seconds resulted in the assassins all being incapacitated with varying types of wounds.

And he hadn't moved from his position.

He looked around at the many opponents, demons all, who now lay on the ground in pained heaps. Men and women or creatures of unknown gender who'd once wiped the floor with him in the arena only three months ago, now reduced to groaning and bloodied messes around him with little expenditure of his mana. His skills had been focused and clean-cut, without redundant use of unnecessary power, and his identification of their positions had been both simultaneous and immediate.

He exited through the next door and came face-to-face with a grinning Lillith as the healers rushed by him. His body still radiated with a myriad of Unholy energies, and his black-red eyes narrowed as he gave his teacher a bow of respect with hands clasped in front of him. "I believe I am ready, Lillith. Please, let us proceed."

Lillith looked over his shoulder, smiling. Then she nodded and turned back down the hallway. "Let us go, then. The others are waiting."

Genua, noticeably pregnant now, merely nodded to him as he passed her by to join the others in the gathering hall. She would be heading to the Blood God's realm soon enough, to avoid any of the fallout until he summoned her at the bottom of the descent for inspiration.

The others of his group were all ready to leave. Not including minions, only five could descend, per Elysium's regulations.

Nora had been given twin daggers made from the bones of void eels, creatures that dwelled down here in the dark—each weapon being infused with Sin energy itself, which she used to devastating effect.

Azmoth now had an entire outer layer of actual armor on top of his natural plates. It was a very dark gray, with holes in it for the black spikes of his body and fire-drawn runes that continued to burn even now while not in combat. He held the twin halves of a huge tower shield in each set of hands, for a total of four, with large blades attached to the ends and outer edges that made the shields act simultaneously as odd swords, too. His flaming antlers, given to him by Riven a while back after a dungeon raid, had also been added and forged into his armor, which gave him a rather interesting appearance now.

Athela had been given a cloak made from shadow, flickering in and out at random intervals even while she stood still in the far corner—leaning against a wall with a smile under her hood.

Allie's soul-woven bone armor had been reforged, enhancing the Legendary-quality F-grade set and turning it into an E-grade set after immense expense on behalf of the reapers' organization here in the abyss. Her glowing gray halo and pale eyes reflected off ivory plate as her black wings drifted out to either side amid a swirling vortex of souls—and the Divine claymore with teal runes etched into it danced with shifting patterns from time to time as she held it tucked to her chest.

Retesh and Fimrindle hadn't changed much on the exterior, but they'd undergone advancements of their own concerning their cultivation and skills. But Fay had been the most dramatically changed of them all. She was, even by Lillith's standards, finally a somewhat competent underling. In large part it'd been due to her secluded bouts of meditation every other day while investing her time in deep meditation with the Viper Grimoire of Curses and Schemes.

[Viper Grimoire of Curses and Schemes (Unholy Specialization Grimoire, Unique): +129% mana regeneration when held. +9% damage to all curses when held. By binding this grimoire and adding a single one of your curses to its pages, you will decrease the cooldown time on your chosen curse by 10% while simultaneously allowing for spontaneous evolution options of that curse with insights drawn from the Unholy foundational pillar and its related subpillars. Spontaneous evolutions will occur as the grimoire actively writes out different variations of the curse across its pages with random trial and error experiments in an internal, limited plane. Evolution options will occur in the form of insights once a breakthrough is made.]

Fay's skills had developed significantly. Curse Traps, a staple of hers in the early days, were now far larger and stronger and could be triggered by certain actions or criteria rather than needing to be set off manually.

Curse of the Dreamwalker now let her illusions do small amounts of damage even though they weren't actually real, which added up over time and made her offensive abilities go up drastically.

Her Curse of Rot cloud could detect friend from foe and wouldn't afflict allies—allowing her to bathe entire battlefields in her dark-green clouds that ate away at the flesh of enemies with potent necrosis.

Charm was extra effective up close.

Dark Pact healed others more than it used to, though its slow debuff was the same as it had been, and it also hurt her less while using it.

Not to mention Lavini had also taught her a cursed flame technique, which allowed Fay to create whips and fireballs from green fire to attack her enemies with.

Due to her drastic improvements, she'd been given a set of silver illusionist's robes that left little to the imagination, as they were partially see-through and fit rather tightly. She was also given a silver hat that matched the set. Despite how revealing they were—and they were damn revealing—the skintight robes and hat also gave significant boosts to any illusion-based spells a caster may use.

As the others were Riven's minions, Elysium registered himself, Lillith, Nora, Allie, and Retesh as the ones who'd be going down the descent together later that day. And after saying goodbye to Amano and Lavini, Riven left the halls of the underground enclaves to finally reappear on the surface of the abyssal city with his group in tow.

*

Once there, Riven saw not three but four of the icosahedrons that he'd originally asked Gragle the gnome to create. He had been somewhat surprised to see the gnome alive, but he was happy for it and gave Greed just a bit of a mental acknowledgment for not butchering the little enchanter on a whim. The totems had also been reduced in mass, each of them being baseball-size metal objects with twenty faces, each adorned with glowing red and flickering black runes. Above all else, the graphic that Gragle had infused into them concerning the Hive and Swarm aspects was absolutely fascinating.

And through Riven's link to them, he could either manually control the creations or set them up with given orders that the soul fragments inside would follow to the best of their ability. Thus, as he walked, the four almost-spherical artifacts of his totem set swirled around him like planets orbiting the sun.

[Hive Totems of Bloodforged Rift Sparks (Lesser Artifact, Elite Tier, Level-6 Totem Swarm): These totems come as a set, and new totems can be added to this number at the additional cost of Willpower—with each totem adding exponentially more Willpower to the cost. Cost of Willpower is based upon attitude toward the wielder of this totem set, as well as current combat level. Current requirements: 119 Willpower, Blood subpillar, Shadow subpillar. Bound to Riven Thane.

Adding different types of totems will change the name and description of this totem set.
Current totems in Hive Swarm:

- **Four totems of Bloodforged Rift Sparks**

The Path of Red and Black has been imbued into these totems, along with numerous different sigils, and the creator has used the blood of an ancient avatar of original sin to fuel their growth. These totems have the ability to grow and level up but diminish in level each time one is destroyed. This totem swarm can currently perform the following abilities:

- **Black Lightning**
- **Crimson Ice**
- **Rift]**

They truly were remarkable.

Yet, despite his fascination with the deadly little creations, he didn't let his gaze linger on them for very long as his team walked through the city. Through the streets of dark stone that were bustling with activity, he passed like a silent tidal wave of oppression as the other residents of the Abyssal Descent quieted and stood aside.

Wide-eyed stares of varying species greeted him as his group moved forward. Nondemons kept a wary eye on them as they passed, and nearly half of the demons gave them signs and gestures of respect or reverence when they realized who it was. The burning-purple MYTHIC statuses on both Riven and Lillith were in obvious contrast to everything else that resided here, and due respect was given in one way or another.

Meanwhile, as they made their way to the central portal of the upper first floor in order to begin their descent into the depths, Athela, Nora, and Fimrindle all stuck to the shadows as an antiassassin measure. That left Riven, Lillith, Allie, Retesh, Azmoth, and Fay leading the front of a pack of hundreds of mindless skeleton warriors and monsters being controlled by the lich and angel of death.

"Has your man completed the upgrades to my armor?" Riven asked Lillith, ignoring the stares as they passed crowded shops.

"Messenger and Jackal have both been fine-tuned to better fit your revised style. They're waiting at the portal with the smiths and enchanters," Lillith replied evenly, her long black hair made from shadow itself flowing out behind her like a cape. She turned her eyes up at the large black-and-yellow flower that had now spread along all seven of her horns and gave it a firm pat while moving along with silent footsteps. "I think you'll like how they turned out. Have you given any thought to your last available minion slot?"

Riven's gaze shifted forward, and they turned left with a direct shot toward the city's center with a black hole looming in the backdrop of the buildings. "No."

"Do you intend to fill it any time soon?"

He didn't miss a beat. "I do not. I'll be temporarily binding to your fill-in for the descent down when we get to the portal's edge."

Lillith evaluated him for a time, then nodded. "Very well. You'll be meeting him when we arrive. He's a beholder demon, to shore up your weaknesses—despite your improvements concerning finding enemy assassins."

Riven grimaced. "Beholder demon?"

Lillith's eyebrows raised, and she let out a laugh. "Do you have something against beholders?"

Glancing over his shoulder, he gave Fay a knowing look. "Let's just say that I haven't had the best experiences with beholders thus far. They've turned out to be rather treacherous . . . But hopefully this one that you've chosen will prove me wrong."

The silent parade of demons and undead marched below his perch. It was certainly an intimidating sight, but despite this, there was one in the crowd that was not impressed.

Scarred blue scales rippled underneath a ragged cloak in a hidden alcove. He lay coiled up, watching and waiting, with the communication orb in his hand lying dormant . . . for now.

Netithi Bluskish, Champion of the Kraken, newly appointed Disciple of Greed, had a job to do. The gift of Sin energy had been more than enough of a payment for his loyalty, but the more Netithi performed, the more power he gained, and he'd found this allegiance to the Gambler and the great sin of Greed very profitable ever since their first encounter.

And despite the "ceasefire" Greed and Gluttony had negotiated, it wasn't as if Greed would actually abide by such things. Not in truth. As soon as their agents off-world made their move against the Seventh Wing, all bets were off, and Netithi's hired scythes would move in to kill.

For despite the presence of an angel of death, scythes—despite their reputation as elite assassins—were in the end just extremely expensive mercenaries. Even with one of their own in the mix, such as that scarecrow character, they would not hesitate to fulfill contracts to eliminate the high-priority targets below. With the Church of Greed there to back them up, it was going to get very heated—very fast.

He just had to wait for the confirmation . . . confirmation that the Seventh Wing was under Greed's control, and that the S-grade Gluttony warriors off-planet had been left behind to fight Purity's forces while Greed's own escaped. Only after that confirmation could Netithi truly move, because if he acted too quickly, all bets on cooperation were off, and the Seventh Wing was an even greater prize than Gluttony's reincarnation.

His prosthetic left eye, a purple gemstone enchanted to help him evaluate energy signatures, quickly worked over the crowd and found his targets easily enough, even at such a distance. Energy roiled within his core as he cycled and pondered on his plan-to-be. The communication orb in his hand started buzzing.

He looked down with a wicked smile, fangs bared, only to abruptly stop as a shadow crossed his peripheral vision. Was he imagining things? He blinked, looking around and not finding anything, until his prosthetic noticed just a slight—

Netithi barely had time to blink before twin red blades snapped through his heart—and a crimson web slapped across his face to prevent his scream. Simultaneously a scythe ripped through his upper spine—making him go limp while his body started to spasm. He let out a gasp as blood sprayed from his body when some kind of poison began to seep into his brain, and the last thing he saw before the world turned black was a woman wielding twin bone-crafted daggers lunging forward from the darkness to pierce his skull with a thunk.

He was thrown from the Abyssal Descent and back into Chalgathi's realm for respawn, with no ticket back—and what would become a lingering pain where the woman's blades had entered his head only moments before.

CHAPTER 15

Riven sent out another pulse, using his mana as a kind of echolocation tactic just like Lillith had taught him over the past months.

It worked like a charm.

He'd picked up on a number of stealthed individuals already, though he was sure that he'd probably missed some given the insider information from the priest of the Scythe that Allie had talked to. Individuals like Fimrindle in the reaper castes would be far harder to distinguish from the spies, other potential enemy assassins, his own entourage from the Church of Gluttony who'd volunteered to escort him, or just curious onlookers.

There were also the crowds of individuals who didn't try to hide, and rather just stared from a distance while making room for the passage of the large group. Nobles of great factions across the multiverse came out to watch from their balconies, drunkards silently sat at windows in taverns, and tradesmen watched from the doors of their shops as the palpable auras passed them by under the shadow of towering obsidian buildings and the flashing rumble of sin-imbued storms overhead.

Emerging from one of the crowds, a cloaked priest bearing Gluttony's mark came to fall in line beside Riven and Lillith at the front. Making a reverent gesture with his hands, the red-skinned, horned man glanced around warily.

"Lady of Black Skies, the Eternal Maw." The priest bowed his head. "The operation is commencing as we speak. The Seventh Wing's enclave is under attack in the third universe, and there is no doubt that Greed will attempt to snatch her after she is out of heaven's domain."

Riven nodded, feeling Gluttony stir within him at the priest's words. It was an unspoken thing, knowing that both Greed and Gluttony would immediately revert to being enemies once their combined strike force abducted the reincarnation of Purity from her home. After that, all bets were off . . . and both original sins had their pieces on the chessboard waiting for the moment to fall.

"We should still make it to the portal and into the descent before then," Riven replied. "We waited as long as we could—I just wish we had more time to train."

Lillith snorted in amusement. "You've already spent far too long here and have to catch up with your apocalypse beast trials. You've improved much and the training was needed . . . but still. We cannot wait any longer, not for finishing the Abyssal Descent and your ascent into the E-grade, and not for finishing your time in the Altars of Despair and Hope. And not . . ."

Her voice trailed off hesitantly.

Riven raised an eyebrow her way. "What is it?"

Frowning, Lillith gave him the side-eye. "And not for your return to Panu. Word has reached us that the vampire princess Kathrine has gone missing, though her family says she still lives, as they can feel her lifeblood still pulsing. It is likely that someone captured her, but who it is and why they did it is unknown."

Riven nearly stumbled, surprise and worry etched into his features. "What? When did this happen? How long has it been?"

"Nearly two weeks," Lillith replied gravely. She held up a hand of restraint when she saw the look of rage cross over Riven and shook her head. "Calm down. We couldn't be sure of the details until just recently, and I have some of my best scouts from the banished looking for her. It is likely they will find her if she is still on the planet."

Nostrils flaring, Riven closed his eyes. Letting out a deep breath, he gritted his teeth. "Fine. I would appreciate it, however, if you didn't keep things like that from me in the future. Kathrine and I aren't extremely close, but she's still a friend, and it isn't your place to decide what I can and cannot know. I'm not as fragile as you seem to think. Not anymore."

Silence hung in the air between them.

Lillith scrutinized him for a time, not expressing any emotion, but then gave him a firm nod. "I will keep that in mind for the future."

Their path into the city's center was undisturbed after that. They walked in silence and soon found themselves facing a whirlpool of darkness over a mile across—and a greeting party of nearly fifty strong waiting at the edge of the descent's first portal down.

Jamal the cyclops smith and other artisans from the Firebrand Trading Company that'd worked on Riven's new equipment, along with their heavily equipped guards, had come to meet Riven before his departure. It was likely the last time he'd be here if things went according to plan, and they wanted to make a display of giving Riven his upgraded weapon and armor—likely for their own benefit. Because if they were trusted enough to make items for someone like the reincarnation of Gluttony, then what did that say about them?

The company's president was there, a husky mutant undead of some sort, but he only smiled and stepped back after his presence was noted—not wanting anything more than to be seen. Others in the company inclined their heads in respect or even bowed and took a knee, while Jamal the cyclops waved Riven over with a cheery grin.

Standing behind a long stone table they'd erected, with a thick semitransparent glass casing over the top, the large cyclops slapped his protruding belly in excitement. "Aye! I've been waiting for this day to come! Are you as excited as I am?"

Raising an eyebrow, Riven stepped forward with a smile of his own and put his hands on his hips. The four icosahedron totems sparked around him while they orbited his body, and the city directly behind them became silent when the others of Riven's group took guarded stances to face outward in case of a possible attack. "If you were able to do what I asked, then yes. I am rather excited."

"Aye, I did that and more," Jamal replied almost arrogantly and reached down one large hand to grip the glass casing. "They both have your very blood and soul shards from Gluttony imbued into each piece, and I used only the finest materials from the most dangerous abyssal creatures. Just you wait!"

The glass shattered and evaporated into thin air, and underneath on the stone table were two items that were both familiar and unfamiliar to Riven at the same time.

But their soul signatures made it easy enough to tell that at their cores, they were still the same Jackal and Messenger he was used to. Based on his training and developing fighting style, these would suit him quite a bit better than the previous versions of these items.

The auras of Unholy energies were almost physical things that crashed into his senses like a storm, with a mixture of Sin, Unholy, Shadow, Death, Blood, and Infernal all mixed into it. So potent was the onslaught of ambient energies surrounding both of these items that it caused many of the nearby onlookers to stagger after the glass casing shattered.

His spear-staff had been reforged into a sorcerer's staff, somewhat reminiscent of his beginnings in Chalgathi's starter event. Only instead of a gnarled wooden staff that in retrospect was basically garbage, he was looking at an absolute masterpiece. The weapon was almost as tall as he was, retaining about the same size as its original form. The main body was still made of obsidian metal with pulsing streams of actively flowing blood running the entirety of the shaft, but now two very realistic bone figurines of beautiful, winged succubi crawled up along opposite sides of the staff near the top and reached upward. Their tails wrapped around the staff and intertwined, and their wings flared out behind them. There, at the head of the staff and where the Barbie-size succubi bone carvings were reaching, was the visage of a skeletal hand carved from ebony metal, holding a horned humanoid skull that burned with hellfire in the eye sockets. A burning pentagram with Gluttony's maw sigil also was displayed in the center of the skull, and spiderwebbing arteries pulsed along the skull's surface like cracks in a mirror.

[Jackal (Legendary Weapon, Vampiric Artifact, Sin Artifact—Gluttony Aspect, Sorcerer's Staff) (Evolving Symbiote): 1,795 average damage on strike with each physical strike dealing additional explosive Infernal damage. This is a self-repairing item. Mana regeneration is increased by 600% while holding this item. Sin, Unholy, Shadow, Death, Blood, and Infernal magics are all amplified in effectiveness and damage output by 20% while wielding this weapon. All spells cast while holding this item have their range increased by 100%. This item has an abnormally high endurance and is hard to destroy. Requires vampiric heritage and an affiliation with the original sin of Gluttony to wield.

- **Gluttony's Ascent: Passively and steadily builds up its own stats based on the growth of its bonded master. Current master: Riven Thane, reincarnation of Gluttony.**
- **Furious Storm: This staff can passively build up charges of Furious Storm, which utilizes a supercharged dose of any single energy from the pillars of Sin, Unholy, Shadow, Death, Blood, and Infernal. You may only unleash one type of energy at a time. Power of Furious Storm depends on the amount of charge emitted.**
- **Portal Master: This weapon can sync to any stabilized portal you have permission to use by the maker and master. Current locations available for access: Dungeon Negrada, Riven's Eye Wormhole, Panu, Changeling's Forest. Takes one week of channeling in the same place to use this ability.**
- **Abyssal Beastform: This weapon can turn into an Abyssal Canine Warbeast and does passive Sin damage on strike. This form is offensively compatible, but your weapon will automatically revert to staff form upon taking damage equal to 20% of your maximum health.]**

The damage output had skyrocketed. The mana regeneration had skyrocketed. Passive Shadow damage had turned into passive and explosive Infernal damage. He no longer needed to kill things to absorb stats; rather, it grew with him at a steady rate. He now had a supercharged pool of dark energies to utilize beyond his normal mana pool, which could draw on six different pillar types. Jackal had retained its portal master trait, and its beast form had upgraded into something that it could use to actually fight.

Most importantly, though, his spell-casting range had just doubled merely by holding the item. It was the most important aspect of all the upgrades and was doubtlessly going to play into his newly developed fighting style—focusing on his mage-related strengths rather than close-quarters fighting as much as possible.

His eyes flitted to the next item on the table.

Messenger had similarly undergone a complete rework. Once it'd been the conglomeration of Chalgathi-labeled artifacts, only protecting his upper body. This had been a problem, as he simply hadn't found any pants or lower-body armor that compared or matched. In many of the arena fights, people had actively targeted his lower body because of this.

Now, that problem was mostly solved. He'd had to sacrifice a little bit of defense from the item to do it, but his entire body would be protected with the rework.

It was a full-body suit made from plates of ivory—albeit thinner ones than on his previous heavy-armor set. It looked relatively lightweight now, and the bloodsilk connecting all the plates was more prominent as it filled in all the gaps to stretch the material out—even going as far to cover his fingers and toes. His pauldrons had reduced in size, and his helmet was thinned out; it no longer had a dorsal ridge with red feathers coming out the top. The central chest of his body suit still had Gluttony's maw, however, and bone spikes still remained over his gauntlets' knuckles.

[Messenger (Mythic Medium Armor Set, Gluttony Aspect) (Evolving Symbiote) (World Quest Item: Panu) (Unique Soul-Bound Sentient): This Mythic-tier armor set was created on the world of Panu during its integration cycle by the pureblooded vampire Riven Thane and has been upgraded by the smith Jamal Iktorian in the Abyssal Descent. Having far surpassed the realm of normalcy, this armor set has been afflicted with the original sin of Gluttony. Gluttony has blessed this armor to even further heights so that the wielder may one day become the tidebringer of wanton destruction Gluttony seeks. All shall perish before the Great Maw, all hail the abyssal depths.

- **Gluttony's Ascent: Passively and steadily builds up its own stats based on the growth of its bonded master. Current master: Riven Thane, reincarnation of Gluttony.**
- **Devour: This amulet can use shadowy tendrils to attack and pull in prey for devouring. If bitten, there is a chance to paralyze your enemy.**
- **Identifier's Clause: Bonding with this item increases your ability to identify information concerning items or living creatures, being the equivalent of a low-tier identifier class. Your own basic information will be much harder to identify.**

- **Ripping Claws: Punching someone with the spikes of your gauntlets will cause massive hemorrhaging damage over time.**
- **Quickening Flight: Wearing this battle suit will enhance your reflexes and speed drastically and allows you to fly. Flying puts a significant drain on your own energy reserves.**

> **+20% to all base stats**
> **+300 Strength, +600 Sturdiness, +300 Agility**
> **+1,650 defense to all plated areas of armor**
> **+1,010 defense to all bloodsilk areas between plates**
> **+50% increased mana regeneration**
> **Natural sunlight does not affect you while wearing this suit.**
> **Liquid breathing is bestowed upon you while wearing this suit.]**

Slight decrease to the armor along the ivory plate pieces, slight increase in armor to the bloodsilk, but with a spread that encompassed his entire body now and not just the upper half. Increased mana regeneration that hadn't been there previously. It'd retained a lot of the previous traits, like negating natural sunlight debuffs, liquid breathing, Ripping Claws, Devour, and Identifier's Clause. However, the most vital and massive change to this armor piece was the last of the traits displayed on the list, Quickening Flight. It was the keystone to the entire change, which would increase his speed and drastically increase maneuverability by adding flight. Previously he'd had Launch incorporated into the suit, but it was more of a blunt instrument when compared to the refined touch that Messenger now had through Quickening Flight. If Jamal had made it to his specifications, he'd be able to do quick turns and evasive maneuvers previously impossible in the heavy and clunky—though very sturdy—armor that'd been Messenger's first form.

"They're amazing," Riven said, letting his fingers trail Jackal first and then Messenger—feeling them calling out to him as they began to rise off the table. "Exactly what I wanted."

Instantaneously, Messenger expanded itself and snapped around his body. In the blink of an eye, it'd molded itself to fit him perfectly—covering his entire body with the exception of the eyes in a layer of bloodsilk with overlapping patches of ivory bone armor. Immediately he felt his stats increase and his body become empowered with a thrum—and he began to lift off the ground a couple inches while initiating the innate flight ability that the armor made accessible to him like a newly grown limb.

The influx of increased mana regeneration was beyond noticeable as well, and he felt his body drawing in ambient energies of the abyss like he was drinking out of a fire hydrant, whereas previously he'd only been drinking from a glass.

"I'm glad you like them," Jamal the cyclops said with a bow and a wide smile, which was copied by many of the others of his trading company behind him as they whispered excitedly to one another. "If you are pleased, perhaps you may pass on a good word to your church? My company and I would be indebted to you eternally if you were to come up with a labor contract so that we may supply your worshippers here in the Abyssal Descent."

Riven chuckled and set himself back down on the ground as silent as a feather. "Consider it done."

More excited whispers and muffled exclamations came from the back of the company's group, and he noted the cyclops gesturing behind him.

"There is still one more piece that we helped create," Jamal replied cheerfully. "Athela?"

Riven turned around and saw Athela pass by where Fay was standing—who in turn gave the other demoness an encouraging nudge. Almost in an embarrassed manner, Athela avoided Riven's eyes from underneath her own shadow-crafted cloak and came to stand in front of him.

"You have something to show me?" Riven asked curiously, cocking his head to one side.

Athela gave him an awkward smile and shrugged, still avoiding his gaze. "Um . . . yeah! You know, a princess always has to make sure her prince looks stunning, right?! So, um, I spent a lot of time on this between jobs. I got some help from the crafters here that were already working on your other equipment and I . . . I want you to have this."

From underneath her cloak, she pulled out a medium-size box. It was wrapped with pink wrapping paper he'd have expected to see at a birthday party or Christmas, with a little yellow bow on top.

"I made it look like your old world's presents!" Athela said, and she suddenly became animatedly excited when he took it from her hands. She poked the decorative bow. "Allie suggested these colors, too! She helped me design it—she was super nice! I've been working on this for a long, long time. I made it by hand! And I . . . I wanted to originally give it to you as a birthday present. Back before I was killed and you brought me back, and I . . . I wanted to say happy birthday. And that I love you. I hope you like it."

She got up on her tiptoes, closed her red eyes, and pressed her pitch-black lips against his cheek before stepping back.

Riven was taken by surprise, and he felt a lump beginning to form in his throat. "You've been working on my birthday present by hand?"

"Mmm-hmm!" Athela replied excitedly, bouncing on the balls of her feet. "Do you like the wrapping job?! Go ahead and open it!"

Riven just stared at her for a while, let his helmet fall back and wiped at his eyes before laughing. "You did such a good job wrapping it that I'm not sure I want to undo it . . . but pink?! Really?!"

"Allie said your favorite color was pink!"

He shot his laughing sister a glare. "I see."

Gingerly, he began tugging at the ribbon—and then ripped off the paper to reveal a cardboard box.

Nostalgia hit him full force. He hadn't seen cardboard in god knows how long, and he began to laugh silently while opening it to reveal a folded garment within.

It was a cloak made from shadow on the outside—similar to Athela's, but the underside was red fabric that was no doubt Athela's bloodsilk.

[Riven's Happy Birthday Cloak (Epic Light Armor Piece, Gluttony Aspect): This cloak was handcrafted by Athela, who incorporated her own bloodsilk to weave much of the garment. Gluttony has infused part of its own essence into the cloak as well, instilling the ability to hide your status information from all but the most observant identifiers or scrying treasures while wearing this garment. Crafters from the Firebrand Trading Company have also helped imbue it with further resilience and Shadow affinity. +190 defense to physical damage, +410 defense to magic and miracle damage.

- **Gluttony's Guise: Passively hide your status information from most forms of identification while wearing this cloak.**
- **Walk in the Dark: Passively increase your success at hiding when moving in shadow.]**

The corners of Riven's lips turned upward, and he reached out to pull Athela into a long embrace. Holding her close, he hugged her and whispered into her ear, "I love it almost as much as I love you. You're amazing, Athela. Thank you."

He heard Athela inhale sharply in fake bashfulness, which got him to laugh. But before Athela could reply, he felt Lillith's hand on his shoulder.

"Riven," she said with a stern face while movement in the crowded street began to ramp up farther into the city. "We just received word that—"

There was an explosion that cut Lillith off, then multiple explosions as the entire portion of the city along the portal's edge shook—and a rising mass of flesh tore through the streets into the sky. Buildings were crushed or swatted aside under its might as the abyssal residents caught up in the disaster began to scream, and an aura on the level of Lillith at her peak crashed down on their position. Huge, bloodshot eyeballs tore open from towers of writhing tentacles made from millions of leeches, worms, and insects as roars and battle cries escalated all around—with dozens and then hundreds of demons beginning to swarm from places of concealment at the left and right.

"The deed is done . . . the Seventh Wing is captured!" a booming voice echoed across the skyscrapers while the huge hive-mind abomination stared down at Riven's location from different angles in the sky. "BROTHERS AND SISTERS OF GREED! CAPTURE GLUTTONY'S REINCARNATION NEXT, SO THAT HE MAY FOREVER BATHE IN THE AGONY OF OUR HALLS! SPILL HIS BLOOD AND KILL HIS ALLIES WITHOUT REMORSE!"

There was a splat and crunch a dozen yards away from where Riven stood, and as the sounds of battle erupted along the perimeter, he recognized the crushed body of the dark elf he'd befriended upon coming into the descent. Gentry, who he'd only known for a short time, was still recognizable even with his corpse twisted in pain. It appeared he'd somehow gotten himself caught up in this after all, and Riven felt a little bit bad for the man.

But the expected battle had finally come, albeit a little earlier than he'd thought, and there was no time to dwell on such things. It was time to show these fools just who they were fucking with. Just like Greed had set up the trap, Riven and Gluttony's forces had been expecting it. And they had prepared in kind.

CHAPTER 16

The city rumbled as the Gambler's body tore through the black earth and soared toward the abyssal heavens. The hive-mind creature roiled and surged, exploding in volume by the second while thousands of demons all made a mad rush from their hiding spots. They came from the nearby buildings, from up in the darkened sky, and from across the central portal vortex.

Gluttony's mind addressed Riven with a malevolent chuckle, whispering into his ear as if the sin were standing there right beside him. "And so it begins. I will be with you, Riven. Under our combined might, we will not hold back as we crush the insignificant ticks before us under boot and claw! KILL THEM ALL!"

Their minds merged. Riven's aura soared in a staggering surge of force, and his body sang with energy as his mana took hold of his items to equip them in an instant.

Riven lifted his hand, wreathed in the power of raw sin, and the purple lightning storms overhead parted like the Red Sea before Moses. Riven's third eye ripped open across his forehead, and Gluttony's maw opened above the city with hundreds of gigantic tendrils that tore through the air with a roar of hunger that shook the very mountains around them.

The Gambler turned his gaze upward and roared back, surging skyward to meet the oncoming onslaught of Gluttony's tendrils with mountains of pulsing flesh made from billions of worms and insects.

BOOM

A shock wave rippled across the city, and the two titanic forces clashed as a slow smile spread across Riven's lips.

The signal was sent, and Gluttony's servants went on the counterattack. From within the black portal of the descent itself, from deeper within the second level, a sea of allied demons in full battle attire launched themselves into the city to join the fray. Casters positioned in key locations across balconies surrounding the portal infused runic diagrams and launched attacks, and allied assassins hiding in wait began attacking ranged fighters on Greed's side that'd posted up along the portal's perimeter.

Violence ensued.

Lillith turned to Riven's team, looking at each of them one by one with meaning behind the gaze. Azmoth, Athela, Fay, Allie, Nora, and Retesh—intentionally ignoring Fimrindle in hiding nearby to not allude to his position should the enemy reapers for hire that were doubtlessly out there see the glance.

"This will be a battle unlike anything any of you have ever experienced. These are the best of the Unholy pillar's young, and none of them will die easily. Stay alive and uncaptured," Lillith said, nodding once to Riven and Gluttony. "All you, until I get back."

Without another word, the Lady of Black Skies vanished without a trace.

CRUNCH

Riven's hand snapped forward, spiked knuckles crackling with Sin energy as Messenger's sturdy body collided with a teleporting wraith only two feet away. Simultaneously Fimrindle flashed in and skewered the ethereal undead with his scythe, and Athela's Twin Red Doves flashed forward to rip into it a split second later.

The wraith, a reaper itself, let out a squeal of agony for only a moment before its body shattered and split, evaporating into the ether of the abyss like a fog in the night.

"Ugh . . . I have a long way to go," Nora muttered to herself, stepping aside to make way for the charging hordes of demons. "But I'll do my best."

Allie began to laugh and spread her wings to take to the sky as myriads of souls flew out of her body. "Riven, care to join me?"

Fay's demon wings spread next, and she shot upward, too, garbed in silver and grimoire in hand while channeling a green fog that began to spread about her like a miasmic cloud.

Athela warped her body, shifting into a pool of blood that wrapped itself around Riven's newly upgraded armor and wordlessly began to evaluate the surroundings for highest possible threats.

Nora and Fimrindle disappeared.

Glancing to Azmoth and Retesh, and then to the cyclops smith, Jamal, who was glaring daggers at the oncoming enemy hordes while his trading company packed in tight—Riven began to lift off the ground. Messenger's Quickening Flight took hold, and the air around him rippled when red snowflakes began to bloom and soar around his position.

"Just like we planned," Riven stated. "Retesh, show me what you're made of."

Retesh cackled, and his undead began to tear each other apart to build something new. "As requested, vampire prince! I've been looking forward to this, but I wasn't sure it'd happen!"

Azmoth snapped his Shengari Shields apart, one half in each clawed hand and spinning their bladed edges around with a happy grunt. His flaming antlers pulsed as he bared obsidian teeth. "Azmoth will be ready!"

The hellscape brutalisk dashed ahead, first falling into ranks with the other swarming demons of numerous species before breaking off and climbing up the side of a tall building with claws, tail, and the two overarching eel-like maws he had coming out of his back.

Riven wasted no more time, and as another explosion of force radiated out from where Gluttony's soul clone ripped and tore at the pillars of flesh that composed the Gambler, he turned to face the oncoming flyers, who were traveling across the pool of the black portal at the city's center.

Jackal's flaming eye sockets flared, and mana began to channel into the staff as Riven began to build a spell. Three eyes peered out from underneath the ivory helm of Messenger, underneath a hood of bloodsilk and shadow, as the storm of red and black began to build around him like a font of the apocalypse.

Already Greed's forces were halfway across the lake of abyssal power between Riven's position and the opposite shore at the far edge of the inner city. Even more of them were coming directly from above, though they were taking fire from prepositioned Church of Gluttony members that were launching barrages of Unholy curses and flame into the swarms. Still, the followers of Greed surged ahead. Devils, incubi and succubi, harpies, draconics, imps, shadow fiends, beholders, Cthulhu-like creatures, and more began charging attacks in a synchronized strike while closing in on his position, even as their land-based comrades closed in from the nearer side of the city.

"HERE THEY COME!" Allie yelled out over the battle raging around them, snapping down her newly modified visor and adjusting her full-plate soul-woven bone armor, black wings spread wide. Halo surging with mana of true death, her Divine-quality claymore roared to life with teal flame—and the thousands of souls at her beck and call began to condense along her body to enhance her. "THIS IS IT! ARE YOU READY?!"

The swarms of enemy flyers came crashing down in a thunderous cacophony of strikes, and Riven put a hand on his succubus, who was trembling slightly next to him. "Just like we planned."

He felt Fay steel herself, and she let out a sharp breath.

Instantly, the world turned gray as Riven and Allie forced their Malignant Prophecies into a unified foresight. The world froze around them, and Riven's out-of-body ethereal soul looked back at the figure of his sister not far off. Their minds linked.

[Malignant Prophecy has activated.
Desired action: High-tier manipulation. Combined current Willpower stat: 4,809. Sufficient Willpower to perform desired action. Performing this act will put your Malignant Prophecy on cooldown for significant amounts of time. Do you wish to proceed?]

They spoke in unison. "Yes."
The desired action was selected.

[Your manipulation of fate has gained you each nine Malignancy Points. Beware, this action has been noted by the Elysium administrator, as a significant amount of fate has been adjusted to your own benefit.]

Time reverted back to normal, and Fay's dreamwalker zone took hold.

One, three, seven, and then a dozen replicas of Riven's sky-borne team took form—illusions born from dreamwalker zone as Allie and Riven flared their own building spells with conjoined effort. The succubus gritted her teeth, snarled, and channeled as much mana as she could into the Viper Grimoire of Curses and Schemes. A power stone, given to her by Lillith for this exact moment, appeared in Fay's hand. She screamed and raised the black object over her head—wings outstretched—and the stone cracked and exploded with energy that cycled through Fay's body into the grimoire, and the world warped around them.

Up became down, left became right, and the sensation of gravity became meaningless as the newly power-leveled succubus put literally all her effort and her entire mana pool into shifting the perspective of the oncoming swarm.

Immediately, the oncoming enemies let loose their attacks.

But nearly half of those attacks went astray.

Greed's minions began flying into one another, misfiring fireballs, necrotic clouds, or bolts of lightning into each other as they screamed and roared. Hundreds died in an instant as chaos ensued, and many more were injured, and even more of the oncoming horde that went unscathed targeted false illusions while their minds were twisted to confuse them.

Riven and Gluttony chuckled at the absolute mayhem that single ability had wrought, and with Malignant Prophecy guiding him, they flexed their Shadow pillar with a supreme will upon lifting the fingers of Riven's left hand in their direction.

Rips in space tore open at dozens and then hundreds and then thousands of places within the time it took to take a breath. Incoming enemy attacks were rerouted into other Greed followers, adding to Fay's induced chaos, and yet more of the enemy demons were sent spiraling into one another.

With his right hand, Riven gripped Jackal and raised the staff overhead to where a sun of hellfire had begun to burn twenty yards above him. With the staff he created a circle of flames above him—drawing it in the air around the sun with slow but steady intent before clenching his fist tightly around the shaft. Then his forearm twisted while he chanted the words he had only spoken once before while he hovered over the black lake of the abyssal portal below.

"Rain fire upon mine enemies, cast doubt upon divine providence, and bathe the land in a blaze of profane glory."

[Blaze of Profane Glory (Infernal) (Tier 3): Detonate a massive ball of Infernal power overhead, devastating the surrounding landscape and burning your enemies alive. This spell seeks out all living creatures, avoiding nonliving material, causing soul damage as the fires of hell temper the innocent and guilty alike. One-week cooldown.]

The sun overhead exploded over the sound of the battles behind him, and the supernova blew in all directions before turning into streams of flame that sought out all living enemies ahead and above him. Trails of liquid fire dived through combatant formations, blasted through barriers and armor, and burned enemies alive as they screamed in pain. Due to the nature of the spell, it wanted to seek out even Riven's allies—but through supreme force of will he was able to temper the trajectories of the spiraling flames and turn them away and onto those who sought to do him harm.

If only he could gain levels by killing enemies here. It made him wonder just how much XP he was missing out on by being in Chalgathi's quest line right now, but his leveling would have to wait until he finished the Altars of Despair and Hope. For now only finishing event quests would give him personal XP, and the thought made him flinch at just how much progress he'd lost because of this.

A flash of neon light tore open above the sky just as he finished conjuring Blaze of Profane Glory, and the eye of some deathly god awakened to glare down at their enemies. Allie held her claymore straight up, still channeling some kind of fiery gray spell into her weapon while the deathly presence crushed many of the flyers and flung their flaming bodies into the portal below through a storm of swirling red snowflakes.

Immediately after that, Retesh unleashed his own attack.

Hundreds of newly constructed skeletal siege weapons pulsed with green energies before launching cannonballs of miasma into the enemy swarm. They were joined by Riven's own barrage when thousands of red and black Storm Razors sang through the howling winds to smash into the oncoming tide—eviscerating many and exploding when they didn't cut through. The air thrummed, and Riven didn't even bother turning around when he sensed a new presence appear behind him. Instead he coated himself in Hell's Armor and let Athela and Fimrindle do their jobs.

Athela's blood form dispersed from his body and shot forward like a bullet, taking humanoid shape as a hail of blades clashed with the opponent. Fimrindle closed in quickly to help, and Riven saw a distant tower get crushed when one of Gluttony's tendrils smashed one of the Gambler's writhing limbs into the city streets.

And yet, despite all the power and carnage on display, despite the storm of mana that'd been dropped on the incoming tide of flying enemies like an atom bomb, well over a third of the enemy forces were still coming in strong.

These were the best of Greed's forces, some of the best in the multiverse for their tier, and many had come out without even so much as a scratch.

Allie's body blazed with gray light as she finally finished channeling the souls around her into a condensed layer of fine energy, and her angelic figure pointed her claymore back down at the oncoming tide like a Valkyrie of legend.

Riven did not bother looking her way as his cloak of shadow rippled about him on frosted red winds. Gripping his staff more firmly and channeling a series of Blood Lances into his left arm, he shot upward like a torpedo to gain distance from his enemies—initiating a sonic boom while his sister met the charge to the dance of a prophecy yet to be fulfilled.

They were violence incarnate, a perfect unison of a song and a playbook written only for their eyes. He supported her from afar with magic as she engaged in close combat, while he was simultaneously supported by Fay's illusions as she mustered the mana to help again. Every move the siblings made was part of a dance, moving as one entity tied together by strings of fate tethered by their shared bloodline, fueled by the power of an original sin and the burning seed of one who had taken the first step into divinity in death.

A fake image of himself flew left from his position and took with it three pursuing harpies.

Riven snared three imps in a black net of Unholy rage that dug into flesh and dragged them down through the portal below—into waiting claws of Gluttony's army, still pouring through from the other side. Their marks of Greed burned on their souls like a blazing sun to his eyes, and he moved on to deflect two orbs of hellfire with unnatural ease while swatting them away with Jackal's skull.

He dodged through the air under the effect of Blessing of the Crow, connecting with a platform of bone Allie made for him to push off before righting himself and flinging a Blood Lance into an enemy's skull above the city skyline. Whipping himself around, he vanished through a portal while avoiding the claws of a devil—only to appear above the archdemon before sending a Blood Nova into its back.

The explosion ruptured its lungs and upper spine, splattering it all over a nearby succubus before she too was consumed by the explosive blood discharge.

Allie crashed into another gargoyle and tore one of her wings into the demon's own, cutting cleanly through before kicking the creature's face with a spin that sent its teeth through its neck and its body spinning into the black portal far below.

Athela had rejoined him now, flying upward and latching on to his body, and was playing antiassassin on high guard the entire time—occasionally zipping out to take her humanoid form and strike down enemies before zipping right back as a ribbon of blood.

CRUNCH

BOOM

SPLASH

Riven wove through the continued barrage of the magical siege weapons created from Retesh's minions, diving easily through the hail of fire while Gluttony's own flyers had been called in through a mental tug. The full-on melee had been brought on not only through the city streets now but raged over the city in the sky itself beneath the black dome of the abyss—while void titans on the outside curiously watched the ants fight.

Creating a platform of ice hundreds of feet up in the air, Riven landed with a crash and a spray of crimson shards before turning and summoning a wall. The ice shards rapidly condensed from the storm of snowflakes and froze the space in front of him to block an incoming spear of crackling orange energy, before the spear was yanked back by an overzealous insectoid creature that'd been tailing him throughout much of the battle—

"RAAAAAAAAHHHHHH!!"

CRASH

Azmoth's propulsion smashed the four blades of his Shengari Shields into the mantis monster, hacking and gnawing at the screaming demon that was taken out of the sky like a bird by a stone.

Riven summoned another two Blood Lances back-to-back and flung them into oncoming incubi, headshotting both of them with perfect precision before resummoning Azmoth through the minion sigil on his chest. Azmoth disappeared from where he was beating the insectoid to death right before hitting the black lake underneath, then reappeared on Riven's crimson platform.

"AGAIN!" Azmoth screamed, covered in blood before bursting into flame with an excited laugh. "AGAIN, AGAIN!"

Riven didn't need to be told a fourth time, and his free hand sprouted a thick net of Wretched Snare. Using it to propel Azmoth just like Riven did with many of his Blood Lances to speed them up, he launched his armored, flaming minion into the closest crowd of flying fighters that he could see.

CRUNCH

The ice underneath him shattered, and Riven's staff whipped around to collide with a huge hammer. Jackal's passive on-hit effect exploded with hellfire to rebuke the attack, and Riven did a 360-degree spin before kicking out against the mammoth gargoyle that'd assaulted him, putting distance between the two but not having many places to go with so many combatants. Malignant Prophecy had worked overtime to get him here, but even with the prophecy active, it'd been an absolute hassle to follow each of the steps perfectly. Due to the messy nature of the battle, he'd ended up with a few fuckups that'd left him scrambling to get back into the prophecy's alignment.

And even with the prophecy active, given the skill and power present in the Abyssal Descent, he was being pushed to his limit. Attacks that would normally level city blocks would sometimes only injure his enemies depending on the target. With Gluttony suppressing Greed's main player—the Gambler—and Lillith on her own side mission to take advantage of the circumstances, it was all he could do to keep himself on track while killing as many of his opponents as he could.

CHAPTER 17

The Path of Red and Black called to him while the air shattered, and his specialty Blood pillar—Profane Cyclone—was building in power as more and more of the creatures around him died like flies. The sky was split with arcs of Black Lightning that roared around him as he moved in harmony with Gluttony's predatory instincts, smashing through enemies in explosive detonations with the original sin's full might and amplifying it with his own innate power.

Buildings crumbled to dust, and the central purple iris on his forehead glowed brightly as the souls of his enemies were sucked into his skull with the whispered screams of the damned.

This was perhaps the very first time he'd truly been in sync with Gluttony, their combined wills dancing together like an unstoppable storm of violence while they wrecked entire squadrons of enemies in the air and on the ground alike. It was the first time that Riven truly felt like he deserved the system title of MYTHIC; he felt like a fallen god rising from the ashes to retake his former glory. All that training had only been half of what he could truly bring out, and that was becoming very apparent now that his other half was involved.

Roaring hellfire exploded from his body and catapulted two mantis demons across the abyssal city into a tower with an explosion of stone, and Riven abruptly vanished into a portal to avoid ribbons of green light that sought to entangle him as a dozen enemies dashed past allied fighters while he ducked and weaved at blinding speeds under bridges between skyscrapers, through tunnels, or in between alleys to keep his range advantage. Meanwhile, his four orbiting totems continued to unleash dark lightning strikes of their own accord, and rapidly used small rift portals to redirect incoming attacks while forming barriers of Crimson Ice to block ones the rifts didn't catch in time. They were machinelike in their accuracy and effectiveness.

And his other item upgrades weren't anything to scoff at, either. With his normal mana he was able to levitate and hover, even fly to a minor extent. With his previous version of Messenger he'd been able to use a propulsive burst to go through the air like a rocket. But this new version of Messenger was on another level of control—a mere thought allowed him to push his mana through conduits in the armor itself that flushed the air around him with intrinsic propulsive maneuvering not seen in any kind of living thing or machine back on Earth pre-integration. He could walk on a knife's edge and double back or turn instantly, without any whiplash.

He flashed forward and burst through another underpass while firing off conjured Blood Lances so fast that they appeared and ruptured off his arm like a Gatling gun, blurring backward at his pursuers and piercing through tough armor and hide in sprays of blood. Crackling with lightning, he zigzagged and then then blasted forward—tearing open a portal in space and putting distance between the fastest of the enemy flyers before unleashing a thunderstorm of darkness.

The street behind him shattered alongside a merchant's store, rupturing the ground and causing the entire sector of the city to shudder as chained snares bloomed from his outstretched palms and scattered, forming a web lattice around him for hundreds of yards to slow down the ones who'd survived his initial attacks. Meanwhile, his four totems orbited him in a spinning cycle that began to speed up, creating shards of sharpened ice that began collecting in protective layers as runes along each of the totems lit up brightly with red light.

[Hive Totems of Bloodforged Rift Sparks (Lesser Artifact, Elite Tier, Level-6 Totem Swarm): These totems come as a set, and new totems can be added to this number at the additional cost of Willpower—with each totem adding exponentially more Willpower to the cost. Cost of Willpower is based upon attitude toward the wielder of this totem set, as well as current combat level. Current requirements: 119 Willpower, Blood subpillar, Shadow subpillar. Bound to Riven Thane. Adding different types of totems will change the name and description of this totem set.

Current totems in Hive Swarm:

- **Four totems of Bloodforged Rift Sparks**

The Path of Red and Black has been imbued into these totems, along with numerous different sigils, and the creator has used the blood of an ancient avatar of original sin to fuel their growth. These totems have the ability to grow and level up but diminish in level each time one is destroyed. This totem swarm can currently perform the following abilities:

- **Black Lightning**
- **Crimson Ice**
- **Rift]**

Three figures broke through the debris, tearing through the air on whistling, feathered wings and outstretched spears. Fallen angels, all dark paladins in black armor, crashed toward him through nearby buildings with relentless fury.

In turn the totems unleashed their layered shards of ice in a flash burst. One of the angels let out a cry of pain and the other two veered off as black electricity followed up the ice attack and smashed into the caught paladin, only for the man to let out a charge of brilliant orange light, healing his wounds and blasting the totem's magics backward in a new surge of resilience.

The paladins doubled their efforts while Riven flew backward, and they simultaneously launched their spears his way while avoiding the writhing tide of nets that actively sought to take them down.

Jackal swung down and exploded in a blast of hellfire along its skull as the weapon deflected the first spear. Riven jerked his head sideways to catch the second spear, and he formed a rift to teleport the third spear behind him right before impact. Part of the building behind him tore apart, and the fallen angels drew swords while weaving between the thrashing network of snares before making another dive at him.

Red ice that'd been accumulating on the city streets below abruptly tore toward the heavens, with dozens of spiked pillars coming to meet the angels under Riven's will.

Fay's dreamwalker zone triggered when the succubus finally caught up, and Riven used her illusion to vanish amid a series of copies of himself just as the angels met his position. His red pillars of ice versus their enhanced physical blows crashed through the air in sprays of frost, and Athela ripped off his body to change from her blood-pool form, flinging herself at the nearest of the angels and bringing the screaming man down while she rapidly impaled him over and over again at the weak spots in his armor.

Riven chuckled, making a fist as the writhing sea of snares all around them rapidly condensed. "There is no escape for you now."

The two remaining angels didn't seem to notice their impending cage shrinking in and continued their assault—lunging for him in bursts of Unholy power with one going right for him and the other veering left before flanking.

A flash of gray and pink light from behind caused one of them to stumble and groan as Fay's Charm caught him flat-footed.

[Charm (Depravity): Infatuate any enemies within range of sight that look upon you when activating this ability, causing them to lose focus. The farther away they are from you, the less effect this ability will have. The more Willpower the enemy has, the less effect this ability will have. Channeling ability that costs increasing amounts of mana over time.]

And Riven used the opportunity to send a crackling Blood Lance right through the man's skull. The fallen angel's face imploded and his brains sprayed out the back of his head as the winged man began to fall like a limp doll toward the city streets far below.

CRASH

Riven's weapon smashed aside the sword of the last enemy with another on-contact explosion of hellfire from Jackal, and from underneath his shadowy hood in the dim light of the abyss, his three glowing eyes stared back out calmly at the enraged dark paladin in front of him.

"Greed will have your soul, reincarnate!" the paladin hissed through clenched teeth, flexing his own stamina channels to combat the building red frost accumulating on his skin and armor while green sparks flew off his sword to combat the flames writhing along Riven's staff. "And I will be the one that brings you to—"

SSSSSSHHHHHHINNGGGG

Red strings latched onto the man's helmet and yanked his head back, exposing his neck for a swift, clean cut of a sharp arachnoid limb. The man's decapitated head flew through the air and Athela caught it, catlike, before shoving her claws into the brain as an overkill.

Riven flicked his wrist, and the condensing shroud of snares evaporated. The roar of battle with explosions, metal, and claw clashing were all around—and the screams of the dying were intermixed by other victorious roars.

"WOOOOORRRRRRMMM!!!!" The echoing, enraged voice of the Gambler caught Riven's attention, and the vampire prince turned his head to look at the enormous mass of writhing insects creating the Gambler's body. He was struggling but slowly pushing Gluttony's tendrils back with the help of hundreds of other casters from Greed's church, but was in large part being held at bay while his other forces were caught up in the rest of the fight.

A visage of Gluttony appeared beside Riven in a flash, and the sin began to speak. "He did not think us to be this strong so early . . . He did not know the extent of our synchronization and did not think I'd be able to manifest myself to this extent. He miscalculated."

Without looking, Riven summoned a dozen Storm Razors and sent them hurtling to the right—eviscerating an enemy succubus who'd gotten too close to try and recite a miracle. He heard the feminine scream of surprise and pain before she went silent, and in his peripheral vision saw the bloody patch where she'd once been on a nearby building rooftop.

"His mistake then," Riven muttered, noting a familiar figure zigzagging through enemy combatants to send an enemy devil's corpse skipping along the outer wall of a barracks.

The fully armored half gargoyle, half minotaur let out a loud cackle of amusement, bloodied teeth bared into a smile when he turned Riven's way. "YOU HAVE IMPROVED MUCH, REINCARNATION! Do not think I have not noticed!"

Riven gave Amano a nod of appreciation. "In part, thanks to you."

Allie's flaming skulls ripped through the air as a howl of souls burst out of the city to the north, and Riven's attention focused there next. Without as much as a word, he, Amano, Athela, and Fay all headed in that direction to join the battle once more.

And on the way, Riven opened his mouth and a swarm of hungry beetles poured out from his throat in a cloud of ever-expanding carnage that began racing through the city. Hundreds became thousands, which became tens of thousands of insects that buzzed ahead to gnash and tear at any enemy bearing the mark of Greed—before the feeding frenzy began to take hold on Riven's mind . . . and his hunger began to skyrocket.

[Ravenous Beetle Swarm (Sin): Open your mouth to summon a swarm of ravenous beetles. The more biomass they eat, the more your health, mana, stamina, and divinity replenish and the more beetles you can create. Consuming targets with this ability applies toward your Gluttonous trait.]

Lillith walked with the bloody head of Greed's high priest in her right hand, or at least the high priest for this particular event in the multiverse. The Abyssal Descent was of course an isolated area, and there were many high priests that each presided over certain designated places for each of the sins' churches, but it was nevertheless a grand thing to take one out.

Whistling to herself and casually stepping over the bodies of hundreds of defenders that'd been left to guard the "hidden" temple of Greed far underground and through five defensive layers of wards, the shadowy demoness was all smiles as her pale white eyes sharpened dangerously upon the approach of new figures emerging out of the hallway ahead.

"Lady of Black Skies . . . it is truly an honor," the calm, collected voice whispered from before her as a robed, skeletal skresh with an intricately made pair of short scythes held them out to either side in a greeting gesture. To his right, another skresh wielding a scythe's blade attached to a chain held the weapon calmly in front of him, while to his left, a third hooded skresh undead held a more standard scythe weapon with a crooked shaft.

There were no runes to mark them. No semblance of magic, miracle, or stamina infused into their bodies or equipment. There was only a complete lack of substance, even to her senses, with a void of power encompassing their positions in the telltale sign of assassins who had pushed their masking and deception skills to the brink of their tier's limits.

She should know. She was the same.

"Reapers . . ." Lillith mused, coming to a stop twenty yards away from them with a giggle and swinging the high priest's head around by his hair while the dead man's open mouth continued to sprinkle blood around the room as she played with the new toy. "I wonder, how much did they pay you to seek your own deaths so openly?"

She put a finger to her lips as if in thought, then tilted her head to the side with a brilliantly white smile that was in stark contrast to the pitch black of her hair and skin. Her body rippled with shadow, and the very air around her began to darken as her body looked like it was losing substance. "What kind of promises did Greed give you to take on such a risk? You must know that you cannot beat me, regardless of how talented you might be. Only a swift end awaits you should you try to stop me here. This is not a conflict that involves the Scythe . . . I will give you this opportunity to leave."

Her offer was immediately shut down.

"Do not think you are the only one who embraces the dark places of these realms. We too thrive in it; we are some of the best our order has here in the descent, and our skill sets together—they surpass your own." The empty eye sockets of the leading skresh's skull lifted slightly from underneath his hood, and his bone teeth clacked twice. "Greed has offered us . . . enough. It is not our place to discuss such contracts after they are accepted; it is against our code. All that you need to know is that we have been hired to stop you. And once we do, our names will be listed in the history books as the ones to have slain one of the greatest assassins of all time. Just think of the honor . . . of what titles we will be given not only in our own order, but by Elysium itself."

Lillith's giggles grew louder, and her domain of darkness expanded further. "It appears people have forgotten just who I am . . . and yes, that would be an interesting thing to see. What exactly would happen if I do die? What title and bonuses would you get for killing one such as me? But . . . I'm afraid we'll never know."

Her crown of seven horns began to grow in length, and the yellow flower she'd found in the underdark on Panu began to shrink down into her body as her hair began to rise up behind her in a flowing wave of black ribbons. Her claws extended, and the room abruptly went pitch-black as her brilliant white smile faded from view.

"Come to me."

The reapers simultaneously blurred forward into the darkness, and the strikes of metal on claw came and ended a thousand times over in the time it took to take a single breath.

Then there was only silence.

Seconds later, Lillith walked out of the room, leaving the scattered remnants of the reapers behind her without so much as a backward glance.

Her bare feet touched stone while she slid through the passages of the temple, passing through barriers and defensive soul snares like they were nothing. A blockade? She slipped through the cracks. More sentries? Dead. Another explosive ward meant to bring down the entire temple if she walked through that archway? Deactivated.

Without the Gambler here to protect this place from her, it was like walking through an amusement park.

Eventually she came to a circular room with a single, nonuniform black crystal, glowing orange at the deep center of its core while it hovered over a pedestal at the center of the room. Smiling to herself in excitement, she reinspected the area just to make sure that there weren't any more hidden surprises waiting for her before stepping forward and reaching out to grasp it.

The treasure felt cool in her hands, drawing the heat out of her body like a hungry, animalistic thing, and she let out a sigh of fulfilled relief while closing her eyes and bringing the item to her chest. "So it really was here all this time . . . To think that after so many eons of being hidden here in an E-grade zone Elysium would not allow me to enter in my previous heights of power, the opportunity to finally grasp it comes to me now."

She felt herself beginning to shake with excitement and let herself do a quick skip around the room while continuing to hold the crystal to her bosom. Twirling in place and letting her waist-length black hair flow around her, she settled down into a kneeling position while beginning to press her lips up against the crystal's smooth surface. Pale eyes widening as she began to drink in the pure energies of the crystal's core, she felt her own soul lattice quickly form as Lillith began to ascend into the E-grade.

CHAPTER 18

Elder Thune's white ponytail trailed down his back as his crimson eyes darted over the tome in his hands. Pale candlelight illuminated the crypt, and an ancient, shriveled vampire in front of him rested inside an open coffin.

"The fallen god has been found, Master . . . Our rise back to power beckons us from the outer reach," Elder Thune whispered, his black robes shifting slightly from a mana breeze that was only barely there after untold years of decay. His fingers traced the ancient sigils of lost and forbidden lore that would have him hanged if any priest of the Blood God were to witness. Whispers of blue light began to rise off the page—calling him toward a new path, a separate path that much evidence pointed toward having once been a mainstream ladder to the heavens.

Now, though, the secret to that path rested on Panu in the depths of the underdark. A secret once buried with the so-called precursors.

"I track the bitch queen's granddaughter to Earth, and they escape . . ." He snapped the ancient book shut, putting it into the coffin with the shriveled ancestor. "They destroy all their research on un-entombing the fallen elder god . . . leaving nothing but ashes in their wake."

He sneered, spitting on the stone ground of the hidden tomb and turning to look into a mirror, his wrinkles starting to show despite his pureblooded vampiric heritage. "Elysium takes the planet and merges it into an integration zone as if to spite me, right when I find a lead, and then those damnable royal brats show up to inherit the world quest for themselves. A world quest . . . designed to hand them the prize I have been seeking for millennia. Did their parents leave them there intentionally? Did they experience a prophecy knowing this would happen, and follow the threads of fate through malignancy?"

His ancestor did not stir, and Elder Thune let out a long sigh before bringing his hand up to rub at his temple. "I fear it is so. The question becomes just how much they saw and what I can undo before all is lost to us. All that we have worked for will be for nothing if either of the Wraithtide runts get their grubby claws on it, and I have no doubt that the Blood God himself would see them greatly rewarded if they were to destroy the legacy for him. Doubtless they will rise in the ranks of the Blood Moon Requiem if they do so, perhaps even receiving the ranking spots to inherit the throne. Already they have thrown mud into the water with one of the aspects of sin choosing the undeserving warlock whelp. It is as if Elysium itself is fueling his ascent. But losing the legacy of blood's brother path . . . That cannot happen. Not when we're so close."

A spark lit up along the lower edge of the mirror, gaining the elder's attention as his eyes narrowed. "Open."

Immediately the mirror shifted image, revealing none other than Crendir No-Name on the other side. Through the mirror, Elder Thune saw a torture chamber where the vampiric princess Kathrine's bare body had been strapped down to a bloody wooden table. Her eyes were glazed, drool dripped out the side of her mouth, and her body quivered violently in protest of the shackles and numerous metal stakes that skewered her to the wood.

Crendir shifted uncomfortably under the gaze of the older vampire. Despite working for the man, Crendir was still playing a very dangerous game should the high queen or any of the other elders find out what exactly was going on here.

"Have you found it yet? Have you found the location?" Elder Thune asked through the mirror, wringing his thin fingers together anxiously while glaring out at the E-grade vampiric captain. "Answer me, boy. Do not keep me waiting!"

Crendir bowed respectfully and took off his helmet to reveal a clean-shaven head. "I meant no disrespect, Excellency. I have not found the location yet . . . unfortunately. But nevertheless I called on time as you command."

"Then find others to interrogate!" the old man hissed.

Crendir frowned, looking over to where the ghoul woman Mara now lay half-dead and stuffed in a box, her limbs, oriented at odd angles. He looked to where the ones called Nin and Vin were reduced to bone dust, their spirits already vanished into the void days ago. To where the other necromancers of Allie's guild were also dead. None of them had uttered a peep. "One by one I have gone through the people who knew. The last ones who know are Kathrine and Mara, which is why I even took this risk to begin with, Your Excellency. There are no others to interrogate, and they're only just now breaking. I do believe that I will finally get it out of Kathrine, as she is not as strong-willed as the others were—but it is going to take time. Mara is one I may have to dispose of sooner rather than later, as talks with her are going nowhere."

"And if you fail?" Elder Thune hissed, nails digging into his palms to drip blood onto the ground on the opposite side of the mirror—and into another universe.

Crendir remained stone-faced. "Then I will scour the underdark myself until I find it. With Riven and Allie gone, there are very few here who are able to challenge my strength. I just need to avoid the banished and I'll be fine."

"The banished?" Elder Thune asked with furrowed brows. "Ah, you mean the demons that were banished with Gluttony . . ."

"Yes . . . those creatures." Crendir shifted stance uncomfortably. "They are . . . formidable. I have no doubt that many of them could kill me if they found out what I was doing, but if what you say about the legacy is true . . . then it is worth the risk."

A slight smile played on Elder Thune's lips, and he nodded in agreement. "It is. To form a new step to the heavens so that our kind can finally break the chains of the Blood God is a step toward righteousness. We were not meant to be born as slaves to his will. It is time to form a new path, to re-form the old ways, and I am glad that you have seen the light. But know that the actions you take now will heavily influence that fate, and if you fail . . . you curse us all to an eternal damnation."

"I am aware," Crendir stated, saluting with a fist to his chest. "I will not fail you, Excellency. I will pry the information from the princess, or from the ghoul chancellor. One or the other. Be it a long and agonizing time in the chamber or not, the choice is up to them. I will try not to kill them as I proceed, but again . . . the ghoul they call Mara is trying my patience."

"Very well. Keep me informed, and see to it that you get what you need at all costs," Elder Thune said sharply. "And dispose of them like the others when you're finished."

Crendir hesitated. "I was hoping to keep the princess for myself."

Elder Thune raised an eyebrow. "You cannot. The risk is too great. If her family is able to use her blood to track her down, which I am doubtless they are attempting to do even as we speak, it will not bode well for you. My wards cannot hide you forever. Kill her when you're done, just like the ghoul, and burn their bodies to ash when finished."

Without giving Crendir a chance to argue, Elder Thune turned off the communication channel.

Silence hung in the air for a long time after that, as Crendir considered just what kind of mess he'd gotten himself into. But there was no turning back now, and the prize at the end—should he succeed—was almost all he ever thought about anymore.

Grunting in irritation and muttering to himself, Crendir picked up a hot iron that'd been lying on a nearby rack. Turning around and walking over to where Kathrine was still pinned to the wooden table, he eyed her twitching, bloodied body before passing her by and walking toward Mara. Looming over the broken ghoul woman and glaring down at her, where black blood pooled underneath her prone form into the box he'd stuffed her into, he saw her one remaining eye shift to look at him when he raised the hot iron.

"Ready to talk yet?" he asked with a cold smile. "Where is the fallen elder god's tomb, Mara? Answer me, and this torture all ends. Forever."

Mara tried to spit, but all that came out was a gurgle—and one of her broken fingers shifted slightly in the attempt to strike him.

He chuckled and shook his head, abruptly spearing the ghoul woman to skewer her as she let out a loud squeal of pain. "Remember the rules, Chancellor Mara. Blink three times in a row when you're ready to tell me what I want to know, and I will heal you. Until then, it's merely a long game to see how much you can take before your mind breaks."

The sky roiled red, with tens of thousands of Gluttony's insects devouring and battling the swarm that comprised the Gambler. It was interesting to watch, with both insectoid masses clashing with one another in a fervor—neither able to overpower the other. Truthfully, though, the Gambler probably would have won if not for the hundreds of other attacks barreling into it.

Riven exploded with energy as rivers of blood tore from the hundreds of bodies around him to fuel the Blood Nova. A shock wave of red pulsed out of where he hovered over the city's buildings, and then with a boom, the enormous globe of shredding crimson cannonballed directly into the Gambler's mass of writhing leeches and insects.

The enormous hive mind roared, its writhing tendrils swooping in at supersonic speed to swat him from the air like a fly.

But he didn't stay still and vanished through a rip in space just before they met his position.

"How is he still alive?" Riven whispered to himself, thoroughly intrigued while he watched the creature regrow the limbs he'd just eradicated as if it were nothing. "He's unkillable."

Gluttony chuckled inside Riven's mind. "It is why he is such a formidable opponent. Lillith has attempted to kill him many times, but should even a single one of his creatures live . . . the hive mind persists. He is one of a kind, and it pains me that he chose to serve Greed over myself. A shame that we must inevitably devour him."

Towers were turned to rubble and Riven created a shield of Crimson Ice to block three arrows launched from a tower's roof, not able to return fire because of the swarming appendages ripping through the air toward him and erasing entire city blocks in the process.

Allie dived through the air alongside a dozen allied flyers with a cloud of souls engulfing her, the Divine E-rank claymore gifted to her by the Scythe itself wielded in both hands as she crushed one of the Gambler's stems. Her angelic halo burst with light and her black wings turned sharp to encase her as she dived into yet another one of the fleshy towers, blasting through the outer side and coming back around to zip through the mess of entangling swarm as it re-formed behind her almost instantaneously. The bone armor covering her entire body was covered in gore, which was soon burned off as she channeled an immense amount of deathly gray flames and let loose with another eruption of fire that smoked the oncoming appendages with a necrotic aftermath.

Riven raised his staff overhead, drawing from the raging storm of blood mana around him and sending thousands of explosive razors down onto the Gambler's body.

Amano flew up to hover beside Riven, watching the avalanche of projectiles rain down. He gave Riven a respectful nod. "Reincarnate, the Church of Greed is withdrawing to their temple as planned. Our counterambush was a glorious success. We give chase to corner them like rats, but that is all. Is Lillith ready? Do you know?"

Riven's purple eye, the one in the center of his forehead controlled by Gluttony, narrowed and shifted to the demon—and a visage of Gluttony's maw ripped open in the air beside them. "It is impossible for Lillith to fail in this. Have faith that she is already done and out of harm's way."

Amano abruptly bowed. "Of course, Great Maw. We are ready to proceed when you give the command."

Below them, the city continued to crumble, shatter, and burn. Roiling mounds of flesh continued to grow and bat aside the innumerable projectiles being hurled at the Gambler and Greed's other followers. Hundreds of enemy demons were being routed through city streets and into underground defensive structures that Gluttony's agents had already mapped out—or rather, that Lillith had already mapped out. The battle was finally drawing to a close, and Lillith hadn't even taken part.

Yet.

"If the Gambler cannot die . . . then why is he maneuvering away from us?" Riven asked absentmindedly, watching while the collective swarm continued to take absolutely brutal punishment from innumerable sources—yet still persisted. He raised his staff once again, channeling a torrent of Black Lightning into the shaft as it sent a typhoon of Shadow damage barreling into and through the Gambler's body at random.

"That is not what I said. He can certainly die," Gluttony replied. "It is just incredibly unlikely. But like all the banished, we did not climb to the apex of power in our old lives by taking unnecessary risks."

Greed's followers were routed now, being cut down in the streets and over rooftops—in the air or on the ground. It was a butchering, with all of Riven's party members coming out intact. Retesh the lich was enjoying himself thoroughly, collecting and resurrecting dead demons that provided him with very high-quality bodies to use as new minions. Azmoth was beating some poor cyclops to death with the razor edges of his four half shields. Nora was paired up with two other assassins from Gluttony's commune, killing at random while Greed's members tried to flee. Fay remained cloaked at a distance to observe him for supportive purposes, and Athela's bloody pool remained wrapped around Riven's waist like a belt.

Despite the win, Riven was tired. Very tired. The raging thunderstorm of red circling him was let loose, smashing into what little of the Gambler's body remained and hadn't been pulled back to the underground halls of Greed's defensive structures where fighting would be less favorable toward Gluttony's camp. The hive mind just continued to roar in enraged frustration, killing many of Gluttony's own that got too close due to the immense firepower being unleashed from thousands of demons at once.

It screamed something at Riven, something about being cursed and reincarnation this or that—but Riven didn't hear it over the explosions of gore, flames, and shattering rubble.

"Miss me?" Lillith's voice whispered in Riven's ear, and he startled—turning around to see . . .

Nothing.

"Over here."

Riven turned again, only to see nothing once more.

He sent out a mana pulse just like Lillith had taught him and swatted her hand away just as she reached to smack the back of his head.

Laughing, she materialized beside him and gave him an approving look. "Very good. You all did very well in my absence, and the stage is set. Are you ready to proceed, Gluttony?"

Gluttony's visage seemed to smile. "Yes. Yes, I am . . ."

Riven, though, was scratching the back of his head in confusion. Something was . . . different about Lillith now. He couldn't really place it, but she was . . . more. More than she'd been before leaving to enact her own part of the plan, and . . .

Eh. He didn't know.

"Did something happen?" Riven asked curiously, folding his arms and letting his body suck in the ambient mana from the remnant Blood energy lingering in the air. "You're . . . off."

"Off, you say? I do believe I haven't felt so on in a very long time!" She laughed at Amano's confused expression and waved a hand to dismiss it. "It is not important and will be discussed later. Do you have the trigger, Amano?"

The Abyssal Descent's temple leader quickly nodded, producing a small sphere and handing it over to Lillith. "Yes, Lady of Black Skies. It is here just as you entrusted it to me."

"I knew I could count on you!" She beamed, only to get a sputtering and embarrassed, yet simultaneously proud reply that didn't really make sense.

Together, the three of them watched as the last of Greed's forces finally disappeared into their tunnels and toward the safety of the underground. When the Gambler's last tendrils finally disappeared with them, a roar of applause and cheers rose up from the crowds of Gluttony's followers. The sound came like a waterfall and built until the city shook with their victory cries—only for Lillith to smile even wider when she raised the bauble in her hand over her head and began to squeeze.

"If they liked that, just wait until they see this." With an evil cackle very fitting for an archdemoness like herself, Lillith smashed the orb—and with it, a low boom resounded from deep within the earth of the Abyssal Descent's city.

Within three seconds, a fireworks display unlike anything Riven had ever witnessed came to light as the equivalent of a volcano erupting in the city's inner district blew up with wild abandon. The hordes of Gluttony's people who'd gotten out of the way just for this event went even wilder, and the dome over the city was cast in ash as a burning crater of what had once been the underground fortifications of Greed's temple bunker lay smoldering in a pit of lava far below.

CHAPTER 19

The Gambler's body was scattered, in shambles after the eradication of the underground temples in the Abyssal Descent. The black crystal that'd been hoarded there for eons was now gone, rejoined to its original wielder, and even now as he swept through the darkness into the deeper recesses of the abyss, he could feel the presence of Lillith growing.

His archnemesis had gotten the better of him . . . this time.

Still. He couldn't blame himself for trying despite circumstances having not been ideal. What other time could he have attempted such a thing? Assassinating Gluttony's reincarnation would have been the pinnacle of success after Greed's forces had also managed to steal the Seventh Wing away from both the heavens and Gluttony's own warriors. The Church of Greed had lost a few S-grade Empyrean-class demons in order to do it, but they'd gained the true prize in their co-op with the Great Maw.

And draining the commandment of Purity for all time would no doubt be a great boon for both Greed—when he managed to reincarnate as well—and for the Gambler himself.

"I have failed, Master." The Gambler's voice resonated inside his soul like an echo chamber, but another's presence quickly presented itself as the original sin of Greed welcomed him home.

"It was worth the attempt. We knew it likely wouldn't work to begin with, even at the cost of many of the younger generation," Greed's scratchy voice replied, sounding like twigs cracking with every syllable. "Do not dwell on it. We will have ample chances to kill or capture Gluttony's reincarnation as he grows in power, and as long as we manage to do so before he reaches the pinnacle again, we won't have cause to worry. This reset on the commandments and sins will for eons restructure the power dynamic between what were once equals, and many more risks like this one will doubtless need to be taken as the centuries wear on. As for now . . ."

Greed paused, contemplating something while occasionally letting out growls and grunts. "As for now, there is another that you will contact for me. Are you familiar with the Blood Moon Requiem?"

"I am," the Gambler replied. "Why do you ask?"

"There is a vampire there of great importance to our cause. An enemy of my enemy is my friend, or so the saying goes . . . and I believe we could aid one another in the attempt on Riven Thane the next time we try. He goes by the title of Elder Thune . . . and the archbishop on the planet of Aldius should have some of our best waiting to escort you so that you may enter into diplomacy with him. Finish your own descent, claim E-grade, help the naga cultist with his own ascendancy, and then you must leave."

There was a pause.

"I will do as you ask, Master. And I will not fail you this time."

A tenth of the entire city was absolutely ruined, with city blocks eradicated and hundreds of the best of the F-grade and E-grade for the Unholy pillar now lying dead or dying in the streets. Gluttony's forces were cleaning up or helping their injured comrades while other forces who'd been watching on the periphery were kept at bay or dealt with harshly whenever they tried looting corpses.

Because in most cases, each corpse was a treasure trove of supplies from some of the wealthiest and most influential clans demonkind had to offer.

And truthfully, Riven felt a little sad despite the victory. He'd been saving his skeletal summons in case Greed's forces pulled out a trump card, and he'd not even used his ultimate form where he and Gluttony would fuse to form a demonic body—but now he was regretting not having used them due to how many of his allies had died. Gluttony was telling him it was wise to keep such things in reserve just in case they were needed, and Riven was used to seeing death by now, but these people—these creatures . . . they looked up to him as some kind of worship-worthy being.

They'd fought and died for him while Riven had held back just in case he'd been targeted and needed the additional boost.

"Don't give yourself so much credit. This fight between our churches is ancient and has been going on long before you got here," Lillith said with a friendly nudge, standing next to Riven atop one of the skyscrapers overlooking the molten wreckage of what had once been the underground Greed temples. "We'd have fought, killed, and died regardless of whether you were the almighty chosen one."

She said that last title with a bit of teasing exaggeration.

Raising an eyebrow and giving the ancient demoness a sour glare, he couldn't help but feel a little bit better. "I suppose you're right."

"Of course I'm right!" Lilith said, smiling widely. She swatted Riven on the back, causing him to stumble. "And I'm in a great mood! They'd been holding part of me hostage here for a long, long time. A piece of my soul. I just got it back."

"How'd that ever happen? Weren't you supposed to be some hotshot?"

"Hey, kid, I still AM a hotshot." She chuckled, then waved a dismissive hand in his face. "And wipe that stupid frown off. You did very well, and your training has obviously paid dividends. You'll be E-grade in no time and back in Chalgathi's trials."

"Indeed. How did the operation in Universe 3 go? Did we catch the Seventh Wing?"

Lillith threw up her hands to either side, still in a jolly mood. "Yes and no. We had a specialist mark Purity's reincarnation with a tracker in anticipation of Greed betraying us and are now waiting patiently for her to be settled down before we give it a go. They did just what we thought they would, and she'll no doubt be put down in a high-security prison somewhere—hidden from the rest of the multiverse. Worst-case scenario, Purity is still captured—just not by us. Best-case scenario . . ."

Lillith began rubbing her hand together with a vicious grin. "We get Purity back and find one of Greed's hidden strongholds so we can burn it to the ground."

"That's quite the gamble."

"Somewhat, but it was more important that Purity be taken from heaven rather than she go specifically to us. It would obviously be favorable to keep her ourselves . . . but it is a good outcome regardless. I have no doubt the heavens will be up in arms and scouring the edges of the third universe within days, though, and countless worlds inhabited by demons will burn."

Riven's mouth fell slack. "Seriously?"

Lillith gave off a more grave and less excited expression with a sigh. "Yes. But Purity is an extremist and would no doubt have done it anyways when she rose to power. The eternal war sleeps for no one, and both sins and commandments are going to be out with a vengeance. Taking Purity out of the equation is an enormous boon for all demonkind, not just us. Now, pick up and . . ."

WHOOMPH

The world around Riven abruptly turned gray, and time stopped as his soul was forcefully ejected from his body. Even Gluttony's presence was absent, as Riven's ethereal form looked around at what was usually the representation of the world when his Malignant Prophecy activated.

Just what was this?

Turning in the air and freezing stiff, his ghostly eyes landed on a familiar figure.

She . . .

She looked like she'd just walked out of his memories, every detail matching the figure he remembered from when he was a kid.

She stood like a beacon in the night atop the tower as time remained at rest. Soft features, a sad but brilliant smile, the head tilt he often did when pondering, and the same brown hair he had. She was beautiful, and . . . and was it really her?

His voice caught, and if he'd been in his normal body, his heart would have been pounding. "M . . . Mom?"

A wave of emotions roiled within him, and seeing her like this so suddenly and without warning . . . it made him want to cry. "Are . . . Is that you? Are you real?"

He reached out, floating down to stand beside the spitting image of the woman who'd raised him, but his hand traveled through her as she let out a soft breath of air with a nod.

"You've grown up . . ." she muttered, still looking forlorn. Sheline Thane, otherwise known as Lady Sheline Wraithtide, raised her hand as if to brush his face—but hesitated an inch from him and dropped her arm. "That . . . saddens me."

He could not comprehend this.

Was he dreaming?

Sadness, excitement, and confusion were abruptly replaced with rage—and Riven snapped angrily at her with a sneer full of internal pain and turmoil. "Yeah, well, it fucking saddens me, too, Mom!"

His voice broke, and he let out an involuntary whimper while rapidly changing between sorrow and anger. "Where have you been? Why are you here now? Why did you abandon us?"

"I did not abandon—"

"YES, YOU DID!" Riven screamed, snapping again and clenching his fists. "ALLIE AND I WERE LEFT ALL ALONE! We had NO IDEA where the FUCK you'd gone! I looked for you for years . . . and . . . and I'd given up until . . ."

He let his gaze fall and became silent.

That silence reigned for quite some time.

What was he even supposed to say?

He was at a loss for words. After everything that'd happened, without warning, she'd finally reappeared.

"I did not wish to leave, but it was for your own protection. We were being tracked . . . and we still are being tracked even to this day . . . the day in my future, where I'm speaking to you now," she said with a sigh. "And truthfully, Riven, I'm not even here right now. Not really."

His gaze snapped back up. "What do you mean? You appear out of nowhere and now you're saying you're not really here? What does—"

"This is an image. A projection of myself through time," his mother replied softly. "Please, contain your anger. I do not have much time to speak. These images are taxing, and I must find both place and time within the matrix to stay properly. It is a gift you may one day figure out for yourself, though not all carriers of the prophecy are able to do so."

He rapidly snapped his jaw shut but remained silent—waiting for her to continue and choking back words he'd been wanting to shout at her for over a decade. That he missed her, that he loved her, that he wanted her back . . . That he hated her for leaving. That he'd been scared when she'd left him to take care of Allie.

Allie. What would she say about this?

How the hell was he supposed to break this kind of news to her?

And who was it that'd made his mom leave? She was still being hunted? Even now?

"Riven . . ." Sheline began, with firmer resolve to her voice and standing a bit straighter. Her gaze flitted to Allie's form in the distance, and that gaze softened again. "Thank you for taking care of your little sister. I want you both to know that I miss you . . . more than you know. But you must finish this descent with haste. If you do not . . . your world will die. As will you. And Gluttony won't be enough to save you."

Riven blinked, and eventually, when she didn't continue, he replied through gritted teeth, "You have my attention, and you said time is short. Go on."

Silence.

"Please to not look at me with such hate . . . Please, Riven." His mother was obviously undergoing a hard time herself with this reunion, and her composure broke when she stifled a sob and held a hand up to her mouth. But soon afterward, she pointed toward the black portal at the center of the city. "This system event is unique. I know you have had the system notification explain some of it to you, but let me be clear. Every three hundred years, the rankings reset and more people are allowed into the descent to complete their soul lattice. That is the purpose of this place, for the greatest of the F-grades oriented toward the Unholy pillar, and you're not competing against the contenders who are currently here this round. Rather, your score is competing against the contenders who went in the last cycle."

She waved a hand, and a piece of the script from Riven's old notification months ago came into view.

[Successfully completing the Abyssal Descent will result in fifty event points. Completing in the top one hundred contenders will result in three hundred event points. Completing this event in the top five contenders will result in one thousand event points. Finishing first will result in three thousand event points.]

"I know you may be asking why I'm telling you this, but let me explain why it is relevant." She glanced down at the hologram, then back to him. "Your score in the Abyssal Descent is dependent upon matching it to the previous contenders, and is based upon how well your soul lattice is constructed. The abyss will give you insights during meditation, and the deeper you go, the more dangerous it gets, but the more insight you can acquire. If you do better than the top one hundred contenders from the last three-hundred-year cycle as ranked by Elysium when constructing your soul lattice, you will acquire a bonus. Completing with a better score than the top five means you get a top-five rank, and you'll need to beat the previous top contender in order to win the number-one spot. If you do not finish in the number-one spot, Riven, you will fail to win the Chalgathi trials. Another, a cultist, will beat you to the egg if that should happen. If that is to pass, the system will treat you as an outlier given Gluttony's presence and increase the penalty for failing—increasing the bonus the cultist acquires, and the apocalypse beast named Chalgathi will grow an entire two tiers. For those who have distinct advantages such as yourself, it expects you to win. And if you don't, then it punishes you far more harshly than it would others under more normal circumstances."

She paused for emphasis. "You will not be unleashing an F-grade apocalypse beast on the world if you fail. Not an E-grade, either. You would be unleashing a Legendary, level-599 D-grade apocalypse beast onto Panu, and it will kill you along with everything else that lives. This is something that I have foreseen, and even with this warning I am unsure if you will be able to make it out in time. So not only must you hurry, but you must hurry and do well. And I advise you now that, should you not succeed . . . you need to abandon Panu entirely. Not even Lillith would be able to save you if Chalgathi appears fully formed at the cusp between D- and C-grade, so there are no other options but to flee."

Tre'Zix of the Purple Claw sniffed at the cellar, and the mantis-like archdemon's bladed arms traced the dirt where the scent still lingered. He looked around the room at the various tools of torture, of the remnants of Vin and Nin. The flow of turmoil in the room was palpable to his senses; he could still literally feel the pain and torture that'd happened here, the horror behind it, and the resonant emotions of the victims who might or might not still be alive.

Or, at least two of them might still be alive.

"Tre'Zix . . ." one of his mantis compatriots hissed, clicking her mandibles and brushing a bladed arm up against her horns. "We have found a trail. A spatial rift was used in the opposite cellar. We believe the culprits to have fled through it . . . Do you think it was treachery? Betrayal?"

Tre'Zix snorted, his red eyes gleaming over the deep purple-red chitin of his face—and he stood up to stretch his wings while turning his simultaneously demonic and insectoid form around. "Probably. There are unknown scents here—I am only familiar with Mara's smell. It is hard for me to distinguish why this happened, but she was interrogated for something. Tortured, certainly, and less than a day ago. Whoever it was holding her, they probably found out that we were coming."

The other mantis cocked her head quizzically. "How?"

"Insider information and treachery—as you suggested . . . or a means of scrying that I did not detect. Though the latter seems unlikely." Tre'Zix clambered over an overturned table and through a hallway, changing into his more humanoid form in order to fit properly given his otherwise gigantic size. Walking into the next cellar, he came to a stop where others of his Klinac'Tal clan were waiting for him in silence. The remnants of the rift torn in space were now stabilized thanks to their efforts, and a wide grin set across his face when Mara's scent grew stronger.

His mandibles began to click. They were getting closer.

The mandibles of the others began to click in turn, and the pack of archdemons slowly all began to laugh with a violent glint to their eyes. A glint that called for a bloody murder, and one that showed they'd enjoy every second of it.

"The hunt is on, boys . . ." Tre'Zix called to his fellows, reaching toward the remnant magics and infusing them with sin. Purple lightning raced up his arm and discharged, tearing space open once again and revealing a spherical portal. "We have their scent. Let's not keep them waiting."

He stepped into the globe, and one by one, the twenty members of his ancient and once very feared clan all stepped in after him. After a moment the portal closed, and only blood and dust was left behind.

CHAPTER 20

Riven had been abnormally silent since the encounter with the vision of his mother, to the point where others had started to notice. Still, he'd done a good job at keeping his emotions under wraps despite this—and was quick to reel in any outward signs of his internal turmoil.

Feeding in the shadow of a towering skyscraper, his heart pounded in his chest—and Gluttony's instinctual desire to devour slowly began to fade. His fangs were sunk into the injured gargoyle, and, as he drained the blood out of the half-dead Greed affiliate, he continued to let his mind wander over the happenings of the last day.

Then he heard the familiar beat of wings overhead and a soft landing beside him. Looking up with blood running down his mouth, he saw the beautiful, blue-skinned succubus he'd contracted nearly a year ago begin to walk over to his position.

"Is everything okay?" Fay asked, reaching out to put her slender fingers around his—giving him a warm squeeze. "Riven? You look . . ."

She paused upon seeing the victim on the ground. The wounded gargoyle was bleeding out and going into shock, gasping with wide eyes on the floor, and she grimaced. "Are your impulses better now? Or will you need more?"

[Gluttonous (Trait): You are required to eat at least one enlightened being every week, or you will suffer a 1% debuff that stacks on all stats. Feeding on more than ten enlightened beings in a day gives temporary bonus stats that decay over time; the number of bonus stats depends on the power and number of consumed victims. Feeding on more than five thousand enlightened beings in a day temporarily doubles your stats and all the stats of your gear.]

He licked his lips and smiled, snapping out of his musings in front of the abyssal portal to the second level. "Yes, it's better now. And I'll be fine, I just . . ."

He glanced toward Allie, whom he could only barely make out near the portal's edge two blocks down. He'd tell his sister eventually, just not now. Not while they were needing to finish this event as fast as possible. "I just have some things to think about. Don't worry about me—let's just focus on getting the most we can out of this event as before returning to Chalgathi's trials."

Fay hesitated, looking like she wanted to say more while sweeping back her long white hair to stare harder at him—but eventually she smiled warmly. Wiping off his face with one of her sleeves, she got up on her tiptoes to kiss his cheek. "Fine. Let me know if you want to talk. I love you, you know."

Absentmindedly flinging a Blood Lance into the dying gargoyle's skull, Riven put a hand on Fay's cheek and kissed her back. "I know. I love you, too, now let's go meet the others. Secluding myself right now probably isn't wise."

Fay beamed and simultaneously raised an eyebrow at the remark, but she didn't press and let her hand stay intertwined with his as the two of them began to walk through the battle-torn streets and residents of the abyssal city stirred like a kicked hornet's nest.

The cleanup of the city was still underway, though there'd been new pockets of random fighting breaking out when other factions who'd been observers on the periphery started plundering the kills. But it was time to go—Riven had already stayed in the Abyssal Descent far too long as it was.

"Ready?" Nora asked, hoisting her two bone daggers out to either side with a wide smile. "This has been quite the run, but we should probably finish up and get back!"

"Agreed," Riven muttered. "And yes, I'm ready as soon as Lillith is done talking to them."

Lillith was speaking to Retesh and Allie off to the side while their hundreds of newly raised undead loomed around the group with blank stares, and Azmoth was cleaning off his Shengari Shields by burning off the blood with his fire breath. Watching his burning antlers attached to the new dark-gray plate armor wrapping his already naturally armored body up in another layer of metal, the eel-like maws continuing to belch fire as well, and the glistening black spikes protruding from holes in his outer layer, Riven realized Azmoth was starting to get physically bigger.

Azmoth was growing up.

The large, armored demon glanced Riven's way, grinned, and began to walk over as Athela appeared next to him in a puff of red. "Azmoth kill many! Training pay off well!"

Riven chuckled and gave Azmoth a fist bump when the young hellscape brutalisk came over and reached out. "Yes, I could tell. You're doing very well. All of you did."

"Same goes to you," Athela replied, leaning in and shoving Fay off him as the succubus fell backward with a squeal. Grinning and ignoring Fay's protests, she teasingly knocked Fay back again with an arachnid limb and wrapped her arms around Riven's waist. "You were very, very impressive back there . . . Makes me want to—OW!"

SMACK

Fay swatted Athela on the back of her head for a second time and harrumphed before injecting herself between the two, wriggling grumpily into the crevice from underneath and poking her head up in the middle of their chests. "This is my spot!"

Both Riven and Athela began to laugh, and Fay joined in a second later until Azmoth came over and bear-hugged the three of them—lifting them up to the screams and protests of the two women.

"Azmoth hugs too!" he roared, getting a sidelong glance from the others who weren't involved.

Riven, for his part, merely raised an eyebrow from underneath his cloak while letting his feet dangle as the brutalisk swung the three of them back and forth. "Azmoth, when do brutalisks start dating?"

"What is dating?"

"It's what Athela, Fay, and I do. We're dating."

"You mean mating."

"Well, yeah, I suppose that, too."

Azmoth put the three of them down and patted Athela on the head while she glared daggers up at him, but the brutalisk seemed oblivious to her irritation. "I not know. I not interested. Females gross."

Riven stifled a laugh, leaning on his staff and giving Azmoth another reassessing look as the watery black substance of the huge portal at the center of the city glistened in the background. "You don't say. Do you like men, then?"

"No. I not interested in that kind of stuff. I only interested in kill and smash and claw-rip."

"Color me surprised he's not wanting to find a partner," Athela muttered, rolling her eyes and leaning into Fay. "He's an ape. A big, scary-looking, metal-clad ape!"

"There's nothing wrong with not being interested in other brutalisks that way," Riven commented defensively. "And Azmoth is really young. He has a lot of growing up to do. You never know."

Azmoth snorted in agreement, quickly swatting at Athela—but only had his claw deflected by a blur of an arachnid limb. Then he turned his head to look at Riven. "Have Riven seen what female brutalisk look like?"

There was a pause.

"Eh . . . no?" Riven replied hesitantly, as a keen sense of amusement echoed out from Gluttony inside his soul. A flash of an image played across his mind, and Riven staggered in disbelief.

"Oh dear god," Riven said, disbelieving. "That's awful! How do you even . . . How?!"

Athela and Fay gave him confused looks, but they were cut off from asking anything when Allie stepped over to give him a nudge. "Are you guys done being ridiculous? We're ready to go."

[You have entered the staircase of the Abyssal Descent for Floors One and Two. Traverse the staircase to reach the second floor below.]

The portal into the second layer of the Abyssal Descent was cool to the touch, and far different than many of the other portals that Riven had passed through during his time since integration. It was as if he was being swallowed by a lake, and the black liquid of the abyss gently caressed his skin until he was suddenly sucked underneath in a whiplash of momentum. It was also his first time doing this, unlike his minions, who'd all already traveled here and below to work to reach level 200 over the past months.

Coming out the other side was also something of a surprise, as he stood staring directly at a beholder demon. He'd completely forgotten, but this was where he was supposed to meet his new minion—albeit a temporary one—that Lillith had picked out for him after he'd not come to any conclusion about who or what he wanted to fill his last slot.

[Narg, Beholder Demon, Level 200 Seeker, ELITE]

The beholder demon was colored a swamp green, with bulbous orange eyes along each of its many tentacles. Two larger ones were set over a toothy smile with slits for nostrils, and two larger tentacles underneath the main body were obviously used for interacting with the environment by the way the seeker Narg gestured at them when he saw them enter.

"I humbly present myself to the Great Maw!" the demon said with a very smooth voice just as Riven got his footing. "Please, let me introduce myself! My name is Narg, and I have been chosen by the Lady of Black Skies to temporarily assist you as your fourth minion throughout this descent!"

Riven was about to reply, but his words suddenly caught in his throat when he took in the surroundings. It was unlike any realm he'd ever been in before, as they were standing on the precipice of an enormous, miles-wide spiral staircase. Right over the central ledge was a massive drop, and in the far distance the opposite edge was facing outward.

Signs of where Gluttony's forces had been camped on this side of the portal, lying in wait for ambush, were still evident due to the odds and ends left behind, the upturned pieces of metal or fires still lit around what'd been gathering circles. The sky was completely black leading into a vortex above, and the spiral staircase leading downward through the darkness was speckled with deep-purple runes in the expanse of a never-ending abyss stretching out forever. A shimmering cylindrical barrier kept massive figures only barely discernible in the distance from entering, and if not for Riven's dark-attuned vision, he'd probably not have seen them at all.

"My name is Riven," he eventually replied, realizing everyone was waiting for him to address the demon ahead of him, who still hadn't moved from its bowed position in the air. "I am the reincarnation of Gluttony. We greet you, Narg. Thanks for being here."

"Of course! My parents will be so proud of me!" Narg immediately said with an upbeat, excited swing of his head. His many eyes focused intently on Riven's position, then keeled around to look at the others, who were being followed by swarms of very high-quality undead that'd once been demons in the battle in the city. "Quite the entourage! I should expect nothing less from one such as you."

Lillith walked forward and put a hand on Narg's scaly green skin. "Thank you for being here, friend. As we all know, the lower levels of the descent past the third floor do not allow groups of over five to traverse together. This excludes minions, though, so you're going to be a valuable asset by taking the last slot."

She turned to Riven with a head-nod Narg's way. "We had to choose someone that would fit within your current Willpower limit of 1,054. The minions you have had since early on cost a lot less than new minions contracted later at the same level—an example of this would be if you dismissed Athela. Right now she costs you 209 Willpower and slowly accumulates cost over time, but if you dismissed her and tried to recontract her, she'd likely cost you somewhere around 500 Willpower given her status as an archdemon and her Unique abilities. So we couldn't choose someone relative to her league."

"Seriously?" Riven asked in surprise. "That's over double the cost!"

Lillith nodded and ignored the smug look of satisfaction on Athela's face. "She's a very good find, but you grew with her to get her here—and Elysium taxes your Willpower stat less for it. This in turn is why we had to choose someone who wasn't registered as a Legendary tier, because they wouldn't be able to contract with you given your lack of points. Narg is an Elite-tier demon and is younger than most. Just as old as you, actually, and he may not be of Legendary status yet, but he has risen through the ranks very fast. His potential is very high, and I thought that taking him with us would benefit him more than any other. He also has quite a unique class."

"Your words humble me, Lady of Black Skies!" Narg beamed—literally lighting up with orange light for a brief moment. "I do not deserve such praise! Fallen gods, I wish my mother was here to hear this!"

Allie stifled a laugh.

Riven shifted to analyze the status information Messenger could grant him, then let go of Fay's hand to tap curiously at his status page. All his own demons were now maxed out at level 200, even Genua, who wasn't present due to her pregnancy, and it was probably about time he went over his own status page since it'd been so long . . . Nowadays he really only opened it to assign stat points, but with a new minion on the way—even if temporary . . .

"What can you do and how much Willpower will you take up?" Riven asked curiously, red-black eyes shifting back to the demon in question. "Mind showing me your status page and explaining your abilities to me?"

The demon was quick to oblige.

[Narg's Status Page:

- **Level 200**
- **Orientations: Unholy Foundation, Infernal**
- **Traits: Race: Beholder Demon, Class: Seeker, Observant (+200% to detect stealthed enemies or traps), Long-Range Tactician (Scaling damage bonus that increases the farther away an enemy is struck, up to five miles), Innate Flying, Born of Smog and Flame (decreased damage taken from any Unholy or fire-based attacks), Scoped Vision, ELITE RELATIVE RANK DISPARITY**
- **Abilities: Seek Object (Unholy), Seek Danger (Unholy), Seek Safety (Unholy), Identify (Elysium-Based), Nightmare Bombardment (Tier 3 Unholy/Infernal), Nightmare Barriers (Tier 2 Unholy/Infernal), Globspitter (Unholy), Hellspitter (Infernal)**
- **Stats: 40 Strength, 338 Sturdiness, 1,020 Intelligence, 809 Agility, 10 Luck, -201 Charisma, 1,832 Perception, 87 Willpower, 0 Faith**
- **Equipped Items: None]**

"Until I offer you the contract, I am uncertain how much Willpower I will take. Likely fewer than two hundred points, though, since we are guessing. Just like most of my race, I am inclined toward long-range combat and have a naturally high Perception," Narg began eagerly while Riven looked over his stats. "My magical prowess is nowhere close to yours, I'm sure, but I've also been neglecting my Intelligence in favor of enhancing my specialty class. It is a rare one, just as Lillith claims, and allows me access to Seeker spells. These spells aren't to be confused with scrying, which can be more easily interfered with or blocked, but rather, the Seeker spells are able to pull on creation, giving me insight on how to reach the desired target."

"Explain," Riven replied, now curious.

Nargle nodded. "Let's say I wish to find a specific fruit. I can utilize Seek Object, and as long as I channel the spell, it allows me to see the path that takes me to my desired object as fast as possible."

Riven's eyebrows rose up high. "Seriously? And the same goes for your other two spells?"

"Seek Danger and Seek Safety work slightly differently. They each give me multitudes of paths to choose from, with the strength and size of the path I see correlating to how much danger or safety there is. Proximity also influences the size and strength of the path. Seek Object, on the other hand, only ever gives one path. Even if I were to ask it to seek out a rock or pebble, it would lock onto the first rock or pebble that comes into my proximity. It can also be blocked out by barriers or wards, but it trades off with being able to seek out very specific objects as well. Unfortunately it cannot seek out specific people, but it can seek out a type of living creature such as human, vampire, or succubus—with the same proximity rule."

"That's incredibly useful," Athela said promptly, her own curiosity obviously piqued.

"Agreed," Allie muttered while sitting in a chair made of bones and looking down into the abyssal drop. She gestured toward the downward spiral. "Can't we just fly down the middle?"

"I would highly recommend that you not try," Lillith replied with a shake of her head, long black hair flowing out behind her. "Unless you want to get swarmed by the creatures nesting on the underside. It would likely slow us down far more than if we just took the staircase, where hives are less common."

"And what about your other abilities?" Riven pressed, more enthusiastic about the beholder demon's seeker abilities than he was outwardly letting on. He could now very much see why Lillith had picked this particular demon as his fill-in for the trek down. "Mind explaining them as well?"

"Certainly. First I would like to point out that my Observant trait, combined with my Scoped Vision trait, allows me to pick out things at high resolution for many miles out. Even stealthed enemies have a problem hiding from my sight, though the closer they are the easier they are to spot. This helps me adjust my long-range attacks, and concerning those—I only have long-range attacks. Nightmare Bombardment is a Tier-3 attack that drains most of my mana and has a long cooldown, but it is a great long-range area-of-effect explosive attack using both Unholy and Infernal energies. Unfortunately it also takes up a lot of space on my pillars, and until I get to E-grade I will probably be unable to learn more abilities due to the size requirement of the mana channels. Globspitter is a high-speed precision attack using Unholy mana that slows enemies, while Hellspitter is the same—only using flame instead, and it can apply damage-over-time burns. Nightmare Barriers are solid objects I can create with fire and Unholy power, which can also be conjured at long range, and I have a basic Identify ability as well that comes with my Seeker class. I intend to upgrade it when I reach E-grade at the end of this descent, though I'm not sure what Elysium will give me for options when that happens. Did you have any specific questions, my lord?"

"Call me Riven, and no, not yet anyways." Riven walked forward and extended a hand, but when the beholder demon gave him a confused, hesitant look, Riven explained. "Back in my old world, we shook hands to seal a deal. I'd be honored to have you on my team for a while, Narg."

"Oh!" Narg exclaimed with a widening grin. "Of course! Forgive me! I will certainly shake your hand, great one! Here is my contract—please feel free to let me know if it is not up to standards!"

Narg latched onto Riven's outstretched, bone- and bloodsilk-covered hand with a tentacle a second later—just as a new notification appeared in front of Riven's eyes.

[System Notification—Congratulations! Narg has chosen to offer you his services. You have received a demonic minion contract that you may choose to accept or decline:

Narg's Offers:

- **Acquire Narg as a familiar.**
- **Acquire Scoped Vision as a trait, allowing you to see much farther and in detail when wanting to do so.**

Narg's Demands:

- **No demands have been set.**
- **158 Willpower requirement for initial contract**

Do you accept this contract? Yes? No?

WARNING: If you choose to accept this contract, this will be your fourth demonic familiar. Your current class only allows four.]

Scratching his chin and pulling up his own status page, Riven considered whether he had the required Willpower to accept the contract. And indeed, he certainly did.

[Riven Thane's Status Page:

- Level 200 (Path to E-grade underway, Soul Lattice Under Construction)
- Orientations: Unholy Foundation, Blood Specialty: Profane Cyclone (Tier 1 of the Path of Red and Black), Infernal, Death, Shadow (subserviently linked to Blood Specialty pillar), Sin (Gluttony)
- Traits: Race: Pureblooded Vampire (Extreme Darkness Regeneration) (Sunlight Decay) (Extreme weakness to silver weapons, Sun pillar, and Light pillar attacks), Primary Class: Warlock Devastator, Devastator Class Trait (physical strikes are imbued with Unholy damage equal to 1% of damage being done at full mana capacity). Secondary Class slot is now open after conversion of the previous class (Harbinger of Gluttony) into a trait. Trait: Reincarnation of Gluttony, Soul Clone has taken form as Gluttony's Maw, +20% of your stats are applied as a bonus to all your contracted minions. More will be revealed upon reaching SSS-grade. Adrenaline Junkie (Blood) (+15% to Agility), Gluttonous (must feed on one enlightened being per week to avoid stacking debuffs), Malignant Sapling (Second Realm of Malignant Prophecy is under construction), Accomplishment Title: Bloodthirsty 2 (+8% increased blood mana from corpses, +2% dmg for blood magic), Mark of the Sinner tattoo (passively draws in ambient energy to build up your soul at a quicker-than-normal pace, expedites growth and XP acquisition, increases your ability to cultivate Sin energy). MYTHIC RELATIVE RANK DISPARITY. PANU WORLD BOSS.
- Abilities: Profane Blessing of the Crow (Unholy/Blood/Shadow), Wretched Snare (Unholy), Silvertongue (Unholy), Bloody Razors → Storm Balls/Storm Razors (Blood/Shadow), Crimson Ice (Blood), Blood Lance → Sniping Profane Blood Lance (Blood/Shadow) (Tier 2), Voodoo Doll (Blood) (Tier 2), Blood Nova (Blood) (Tier 3), Hell's Armor (Infernal), Blaze of Profane Glory (Infernal) (Tier 3), Riftwalk (Shadow), Gluttonous Sacrifice (Sin) (4,999 years until cooldown is complete), Black Lightning (Shadow), Legionaries of the Blood God (Tier 2 Death/Blood), Ravenous Beetle Swarm (Sin), Farsight Banishment (Sin), Soul Clone Projections (Sin), Gluttony's Aspect of Demonic Heritage (Tier 3 Sin), Devour (Sin)

- Stats: 1,167 Strength, 1,387 Sturdiness, 3,183 Intelligence, 1,228 Agility, 10 Luck, -51,058 Charisma, 414 Vampiric Perception, 1,054 Willpower, 9 Faith
- Free Stat Points: 0
- STATS PER LEVEL concerning Race, Primary Class, Secondary Class (slot currently empty), and Reincarnation of Gluttony trait distribution: +5 Strength, +8 Sturdiness, +6 Intelligence, +4 Willpower, +7 Agility, +2 Perception, -6 Charisma, +46 Free Stat Points.
- Minions: Athela, Level 200 Archdemon (Unique, three forms, Cute Wittle Blood Weaver/Gluttonous Arshakai/Gluttonous Fae Drider) (Classless) [209 Willpower Requirement]. Azmoth, Level 200 Hellscape Brutalisk (Infernal Crusader Adept) [165 Willpower Requirement]. Fay, Level 200 Succubus (Curse Witch) [171 Willpower Requirement]. Hive Totems of Bloodforged Rift Sparks [four totems] (Lesser Artifact, Elite Tier, Level 35 Totem Swarm) [119 Willpower Requirement]. Genua, Level 200 High Elf Vampiric Thrall (Priestess of the Blood God) [134 Willpower Requirement].

  o One open demonic slot is available, three of four used. 798 of 1,054 Willpower used. Current number of offered contracts: 190,457,998,252

- Equipped Items: Riven's Happy Birthday Cloak (410 magical/miracle def, 190 physical def, Gluttony's Guisee/passively hide status information, Walk in the Dark/passively increase success rate for stealth attempts), Jackal (1,795 dmg, 600% mana regen, Sin/Unholy/Shadow/Death/Blood/Infernal magics +20% dmg and effectiveness, Spellcasting Range +100%, Gluttony's Ascent, Furious Storm, Portal Master, Abyssal Beastform), Messenger (1,650 def/1,010 bloodsilk def, Gluttony's Ascent, Devour, Identifier's Clause, Ripping Claws, Quickening Flight, +20% all base stats, +300 Strength, +600 Sturdiness, +300 Agility, +50% mana regeneration, natural sunlight does not affect you while wearing this suit, liquid breathing is bestowed upon you while wearing this suit), Witch's Ring of Grand Casting (+26 Intelligence), Negrada's Modified Bag of Holding]

His eyes glazed over while going over his status page in detail for the first time in a very long time. A lot had changed since he'd appeared at the base of

Chalgathi's pyramid at the beginning of integration . . . and he was certainly very proud of his own minions' efforts to reach level 200 over the past few months. He doubted they'd have been able to do it so quickly without power leveling help from others in the Church of Gluttony and was without doubt going to somehow thank or reward the people who'd helped his minions get to where they were today.

Shifting his attention to the 158 Willpower requirement of Narg the beholder demon, and noting he had 1,054 current Willpower available to him with only 798 used—obtaining Narg would put him at 956 out of 1,054. It was close, but he'd be able to do it without problem. Plus, it was highly likely that Narg would only be a temporary fit—unless he proved to be invaluable in upcoming days during the descent down into the abyss.

[Congratulations! You have accepted Narg's offer to acquire him as a new demonic servant. Narg's information has been added to your status page.]

A flash of lightning connected Riven and Narg a split second later, and he felt the bond form. Mentally commanding Messenger to peel itself back off his chest, the gluttonous maw there opened to reveal another, fourth pentagram on Riven's sternum just beneath the pentagrams of a spider, teeth, and wings that symbolized his other three demons. Now, in the center of the fourth pentagram, was the sigil of an eyeball surrounded by seven other smaller eyeballs.

"Thank you, my lord, for giving me a chance!" Narg squealed excitedly, bobbing up and down and causing Riven to laugh a little guiltily.

He knew Narg knew this was a temporary thing, but he was certain the beholder demon had high hopes that Riven would change his mind.

Riven doubted that would come to pass despite the unique class Narg had, but that was still up in the air and to be determined.

[You have collected four demons and have reached level 200 as a Warlock Devastator. You now qualify for—]

Just as the new notification's script was writing itself out in the hologram, it vanished with a blip of purple energy—and Gluttony's maw appeared beside Riven to open vertically in the air.

"Elysium's temptations can wait until we have ascended," Gluttony said, as the area around them went dead silent in reverence. The bantering between Fay and Athela fell off, Narg's excited celebrations abruptly halted, the talks about techniques in necromancy between Allie and Retesh silenced, and Nora's questions concerning Azmoth's horns slowed to a quick halt when the original sin made its appearance.

There was a distinct air of relaxation with the others whenever it was just Riven, he realized, but when Gluttony's soul clone visage appeared, even his two lovers became nervous in the presence of the maw.

Only Lillith was not affected by Gluttony's presence.

"Master," Lillith said, bowing politely and smiling Gluttony's way. "It is not often that you poke out of your reincarnation's vessel. Usually when wanting to speak to Riven or me, you do so by way of thought. To what do we owe the honor?"

Gluttony gnashed its teeth twice, then chomped on another notification that tried to repeat itself—

[You have collected four demons and have reached level 200 as a Warlock Devastator. You—]

The hologram shattered when Gluttony's teeth snapped onto it.

"I want to make clear that Elysium is trying to goad us into taking a deal now concerning our class evolutions. And possibly concerning our secondary class," Gluttony replied without turning from Riven. "Do not take the deals Elysium offers us until we have ascended into the E-grade. Otherwise we will be hamstringing our potential growth, and I have high hopes for cultivating both separate warlock and melee classes whenever we finally arrive at the lowest level of the descent."

"Both, eh?" Riven commented, unsurprised.

Gluttony nodded. "Both. You would hold sway over the path of the caster and warlock, while I take charge of our secondary class."

CHAPTER 21

The stairway piercing through the darkness for miles down was lit aflame, with bodies of strange, black, carnivorous manta ray–like void beasts each the size of a small whale called gliffards covering the innumerable steps in all directions. The raging ball of hellfire Riven summoned overhead sprouted trails of liquid heat that washed over the enemies by the hundreds, and the spell would be on cooldown for another week because of it.

Surprisingly enough, he'd actually succeeded in locking his Blood Lance spell by pushing it to the limit during the last swarm fight, accidentally creating a cooldown that would last over twenty hours. He'd almost completely forgotten cooldowns existed, usually overriding them by pure force of will and the overwhelming mana that radiated through his channels. But nope, he was given a very stark reminder that even after having progressed so far, parts of his pillars could still lock up.

"The second and third levels of the Abyssal Descent are occupied just like the first except, instead of a city, the second level is a sprawling set of mercenary camps where people often hire help. You'll find a lot of people harvesting natural treasures that grow there, but the treasures found on the second layer are far less valuable than deeper into the descent. They're just far more common," Lillith said, lifting a hand with a flash of dark claws that split the sky and scattered over a dozen gliffards at once. She didn't bother looking up. "The third floor is where some of the more daring factions have founded compounds and fortresses to launch expeditions into the deeper levels from. It is the last stop concerning civilization; after that the only way you'll find others is by accident. And oftentimes, doing so will not be a friendly encounter. Killing people in the lower floors, by design, grants you any insight they might have acquired."

"So I assume there are groups just waiting in ambush down there?" Allie asked, clad in bone armor, black wings spread out behind her with an army of undead doing much of the butchery as she walked down the steps alongside the ancient demoness. "Or is that not the case?"

"That is certainly the case," Lillith replied with a nod. "Though I doubt any-one would be stupid enough to try attacking our particular group if they have any identifiers worth a damn. Then again, many groups don't have identifiers in their party—and identification treasures only go so far. It is highly likely that now after leaving the main city, many groups won't be able to get a read on just who and what we are even without our disguising amulets."

Retesh chuckled with a rattling of his exposed rib cage at the thought, using a large staff to balance himself while his bony feet clacked along the rune-inscribed black metal of the staircase.

"Azmoth wishes Genua were here," Azmoth stated solemnly, looking up from underneath burning horns at the enormous inferno that was scouring the sky under Riven's might. "I hungry. She make good snacks."

"Catch!" Fay called back, jerking her hand out of Athela's grasp and pulling out a bundle to toss to the young brutalisk.

Azmoth caught it, unwrapped it, and grinned when he saw it was a slab of meat. "Thanks, Fay! Do have more?"

Fay happily waved it off. "Yup! But let's not overeat—we have a long ways to go and don't know how long we're going to be here. It could be weeks!"

Nora let out a long groan at the thought, and her shoulders slumped as she too continued to trot down the steps in an endless spiral with her bone blades tucked into her belt. "This is a lot less exciting than I thought it would be. Riven's killing everything and I just sit and watch."

"Oh, don't worry, child. It certainly gets more exciting than this after the third floor." Lillith winked back at the human woman, then began to pick up the pace for another session of sprinting now that the gliffard hive was either scattered or dead. "Come along now! Let's not waste too much time here. These treks between floors are always long, but we should reach the second floor within the hour. I just . . ."

Lillith's voice trailed off, and simultaneously Riven felt an odd stirring sensa-tion from within his soul. Gluttony was agitated for some reason, but when Riven tried to mentally inquire about it, he only got a vague collection of images.

"Nothing to worry about now," Lillith said after Riven gave her an inquiring look. She brushed off her shoulder with one hand and a frown. "It's matters that don't involve your universe or this realm. Let's continue on toward the second floor, where we will have the opportunity to buy some good cultivation resources collected by the hordes of merchants and mercenaries before we descend even farther."

Purity, the Seventh Wing, had completely taken over the host body supplied to her by her worshippers. The angel she possessed was a nameless creature to her now, a subservient soul whose consciousness was pushed so far back into the depths of their shared mind that it might as well not have even been two—but rather, it was just one.

It was only Purity.

For how could one so pure share a body with a lesser?

And after all, the angel had given up her body willingly so that Purity could live again.

She opened her vibrant gold eyes, which showed with the radiance of stars, beautiful white wings stretched out behind her and flowing golden hair that burned with celestial fire in a tapestry that not even the greatest artists could capture.

The archdemons lurking outside this newfound cage cackled and sneered, even going as far as to try to talk to her directly—to goad her into a fit of rage. But she would not hear them. No, she did not need or want the insignificant jabs they had for her. One day she would purify them, too, and they would be naught but cleansing ash.

No, she had opened her eyes in this abysmal place because of something else entirely. Slowly turning her head and gazing through the layers of oblivion, she saw a crack beginning to form on the outskirts of Elysium itself. Eyebrows raising in disbelief, she watched as the layers of the outer shell began to break down.

Specks of the ancient lattice that contained the multiverse began to wither, die, and burn away, and Purity couldn't help but look on in approval. Was this a rebirth? An invasion from one of the outer realms? Or something else?

And how would Elysium react to such an infringement on its domain?

Did this have something to do with their recent release? Was it the reason why Elysium had let them out? Or did it have no correlation whatsoever?

Honestly, she had no idea. On one hand, a rebirth would favor all the sins and commandments equally after having been reset themselves and would have significant ramifications for the power structures currently in place. But an invasion would bring an even greater bloodbath than the renewal of the eternal wars and would set upon the multiverse a new era of carnage as two titans of creation clashed. The last time Elysium battled another of its kind, entire universes had been wiped out—but the inhabitants of Elysium had received a significant amount of power from the influx of energy after the wars were done.

Regardless, the answer wouldn't likely come for a couple of years, and she needed to get out of this blasted place to continue her cultivation. She wouldn't let Greed keep her here forever, and the filthy stain upon the realms had another thing coming if it thought she would stay here under its boot.

Taking a final look through the cosmos into oblivion's outer edge, she closed her eyes once more and went back to constructing a means of escape. But just as she did, she heard the sound of an explosion—and the rising roars of battle as an enemy force collided with the hidden fortress she was now contained in.

Unfortunately for her, it wasn't a rescue party. Rather, it was just one captor being traded for another.

High Queen Nephridi watched Elder Thune drag his wretched, feeble body down the hall like a slug. Or at least that's how she envisioned him. The ill-hidden sneer on her face whenever she saw the old man didn't surprise any of the other elders whenever they exchanged jabs or insults hidden as pleasantries no matter what the situation.

Thralls and lesser vampire servants scattered at his approach in the enormous halls of the city-size castle they found themselves in, and dozens of B- and A-grade soldiers stood at intervals up and down the huge passageway in stoic silence as he passed.

"My queen," Elder Thune stated sourly when he came to stand beside her. "What an . . . honor to be in your presence . . . again."

"Mmm. Have you eaten recently, Elder Thune?" she asked pointedly, glancing down at a blood spot on his otherwise pristine white robe. "Do you need a bib? Perhaps in your old age you forget how to clean yourself. I hear it is commonplace in humans to lose their minds due to the years going by. Perhaps you should look into some remedies."

"Mature, as always," he muttered, glaring back at her as the two of them turned in tandem to walk toward the inner sanctum, where a multitude of bishops, archbishops, deacons, priests, and even two prophets in service to the Blood God now lay waiting for their summons to be answered.

Silence overtook the two of them after that while their robes flowed out elegantly behind them, and the setting sun cast shadows through tinted windows in the upper reach of the stone walls where exquisite life-size carvings of vampires lording over their slaves could be seen in various forms.

"Word has reached me that Kathrine Vonsilla Crushada the Ninth, princess and 107th in line to the throne, heir to House Crushada and betrothed to Riven Wraithtide—reincarnation of Gluttony—has disappeared." She didn't take her gaze off the distant door where priests in red were gathered outside to greet them, and her posture remained firm, but her pace did slow. "Crendir No-Name has gone with her, and his recently betrothed fiancée here in the capital has mysteriously vanished as well."

"She is now 106th in line to the throne after Jalel was killed at the hand of your great-grandson. And what of it?" Elder Thune snapped, feigning indifference—but despite millennia of training, Nephridi could tell there was a very slight stutter in his heart at the mention.

She did not let on that she had noticed. "We are investigating the circumstances as potential treason, perhaps coercion on behalf of Crendir No-Name's part through his lover here on this world. We have not yet identified the party responsible for her disappearance, but the two are likely somehow connected. You wouldn't happen to know anything about that . . . would you, Elder Thune?"

She turned her gaze ever so slightly in his direction, letting on a less-than-friendly smile as her eyes flashed red. "I'd hate it oh so much to see your withered little neck snapped and nailed to a burning pinwheel for the vultures to feed on."

Elder Thune did not take the bait and kept his demeanor calm. "If you are so eager to see me dead, High Queen Nephridi, perhaps you could do me the honor of attempting the act now so we can get this farce of cooperation over with. Then, after I take your head, perhaps a real king would be able to take up the mantle of leadership for this great empire."

A genuine smile of amusement lit up Nephridi's face as she let out a loud, wind-chime laugh with the fingers of her right hand caressing her red lips. Dark brown hair swaying from side to side as she chuckled, she gave him a sideways glance. "Ah dearest elder, I would like nothing more than to rip your black little heart out from your chest! Unfortunately the clergy would not appreciate infighting among us, for to them, we are both invaluable chess pieces in the ultimate goal of vampiric rule across the multiverse. Just like all the other S-class vampires in service to the Blood God, we are treasures. But . . . if it were found out that someone was attempting to subvert the Blood God's authority by pursuing another path of the taboo arts . . . One, say, that could potentially be found in the blood of a fallen elder god on Panu?"

She slammed a hand into his chest to halt his advance with enough force to demolish a mountain, and she felt one of his ribs shatter as she bared her fangs in his direction. A shock wave radiated down the hall, knocking over many of the servants and even some of the highly trained guards, and two of the weaker thralls were even ripped apart in sprays of blood despite the vast majority of her strike being focused on the elder's chest.

To his credit, Elder Thune didn't even wince, but glared in disgust with a raised lip.

"If something like that were to ever happen, dearest elder . . ." she whispered with malice dripping off her words, leaning in to brush her lips against his ear. "I do believe I would be doing the Blood God's work by removing those who pursued such interests . . . I merely have to prove that I am right. Then we will truly see which of us is more powerful, old man, and why it was I that was chosen so long ago to rule this empire instead of you."

"Conjectures and wishful thinking," Elder Thune scoffed, violently swatting her hand away and continuing in the walk without her. "Do not waste my time with your ill-conceived fantasies, hag. For I will not entertain them."

The portal to the second layer of the Abyssal Descent was just as the first, a circular black pool that swirled like a vortex. Stepping through it gave the same odd sensation as the last—Riven's body was caressed by the black liquid in a wave of abyssal energy for a solid few seconds before appearing on the edge of the pool on the other side.

And just as Lillith had said, this area was one big, sprawling camp.

Riven could also see why that was.

Swarms of the same gliffard creatures flew through the air and nested on jutting cliffs, with ashen skies and dust clouds billowing through huge trenches that reminded him very much of Daskus, the city he'd sacrificed to save Athela's life.

Only it had a much darker and more evil feel to it.

"Evil is subjective," Gluttony whispered into his mind, only getting Riven to roll his eyes.

Randomly, the gliffards—of which there were likely tens of thousands—would swoop down and attack people, and fighting was breaking out at random intervals even between participants in the descent. Due to the nests up above limiting space and the ongoing attacks from the swarms above, the other big difference between Daskus and this place was that the second level of the descent was full of makeshift tents or canopies used to block out the dust storms. There weren't any actual buildings, likely because one would quickly get destroyed.

Frankly, it was a madhouse, with bartering, trading, drinking, drugs, and fighting all in abundance.

"It makes me wonder, why even camp here at all?" Riven mused thoughtfully while looking up and around at the massive number of monsters circling in the sky—bladed tails flashing with purple energy.

"It's a good training ground, with a steady supply of monsters that aren't too dangerous, and the tunnels and cliff faces are primed for growing various low-grade abyssal treasures meant for cultivating, as I said earlier," Lillith replied while putting her hands on her hips and stretching from side to side. "Eons past, when I first came here, it was the same. Elysium keeps it like this on purpose so that, even if you don't want to chance going into the more dangerous, deeper levels of the descent, there is still some value to coming here with a more minimal risk."

"HEY, DEMON SHADOW BITCH! THOSE ARE SOME NICE MUSCULAR LEGS YOU'VE GOT THERE!" a drunk, bearded, human necromancer sitting atop a bone platform called out while laughing with his buddies amid the madhouse that was the portal's perimeter. "WHY DON'T YOU WALK THEM OVER THIS WAY, HOW ABOUT IT?!"

Riven snorted a laugh when he saw Lillith go rigid. "Hey, I think he's talking to you. Probably didn't bother identifying you yet, or you're too high up for him to do so."

Others, unlike the necromancer, were already staring wide-eyed and backing up to give the oncoming group room—and soon Athela, Azmoth, Nora, Fay,

Retesh, and Allie had joined them with the oncoming horde of undead demons pouring out of the black portal one after another.

"DEMON BITCH!" the necromancer crowed to the laughter of his colleagues, taking a sip out of a large wine jug and belching loudly while skeletal servants brought his fellows various foodstuffs from a crate to their side. "GET THAT FINE ASS OVER HERE AND TALK TO ME!"

"YEAH, COME TALK TO US!" another younger, but equally drunk necromancer called out while stroking the head of a zombie wolf. "WE PLAY NICE, WE PROMISE! MAYBE A LITTLE ROUGH, BUT IT'LL FEEL GREAT!"

More guffaws followed, but the hushed silence from other onlookers giving either group side-eyes and quickly backing up was becoming more noticeable.

"Ah . . . Natural selection at its finest," Allie muttered, watching Lillith put on a wide, bloodthirsty smile before the archdemoness began stomping over to where the hooting men continued to catcall her. Allie folded her arms and began to chuckle when the screams and explosions started and shook her head with a sigh. "Things really aren't all that different from Earth, even here in the abyss. Not sure what to think about that."

"Fifty gold says Lillith makes a crystal cross formation out of the five of them," Athela mused, absentmindedly putting her hand into a pouch and drawing out a snack to chomp on while staring at the explosive carnage not far off.

Fay nodded sagely. "Oh it's coming, all right."

More screams.

Riven turned to look at the three conversing women with folded arms. "What's a crystal cross forma—"

"OOOOOOoooooohhhh . . ." A collective wince from the gathered crowd echoed out with a squeal and a snap, and Riven's eyes went wide as his jaw dropped at the sight before them.

Athela pointed. "That's a crystal cross formation."

Still gaping, Riven leaned his head left, and then right, to get a better look at just what Lillith had done. "How does that make anatomic sense?"

"It doesn't," Athela replied, reaching into her pouch again and pulling out another morsel. Hesitating, she offered it to Riven over the continued screams of Lillith's victims. "Want a chocolate-covered raisin?"

"Is that what that is?" Riven asked, amused. Picking it up and popping it into his mouth, he chewed and nodded in satisfaction. "Where did you get these?"

"Nora brought them," Athela replied, hiking a finger back at the Asian woman, who was staring horror-struck at what Lillith was doing to the poor idiots who'd catcalled her moments before. "I traded some crackers and a hand-stitched pouch made of my bloodsilk for them. Nora's kind of a snackie, or . . . what was it you called yourself?"

Nora didn't reply, but Fay did in her stead.

"A foodie, I believe," Fay stated, tapping her fingers along the grimoire held against her chest. "Just how long do you think she'll be at it?"

"Knowing Lillith's training regimens? They're akin to torture, so probably a long while." Allie sighed. Hoisting her claymore up over her shoulder, she began to move toward a nearby stall. "Come on, everyone, let's go shopping for a bit while Lillith finishes up. Unless, of course, you want to interrupt her. But I certainly won't be the one that tries. Oh, and Fimrindle—if you want something, just say so. You've been awfully quiet, so speak up if you do."

CHAPTER 22

The canyon complex and sprawling tent city was full of dead-end trenches dug into the greater cliff faces beneath the swarms of flying monsters, giving the more prominent factions of the descent on Floor Two areas of relative security to hunker down in. The Deadman's Featherfall Trading Guild, a notorious mafia enterprise known for its exorbitant prices and unyielding dedication to quality, had claimed one of these particular trenches as its own and had a reputation on the second level as a place to find some of the best items available on the greater market. The proximity to the lower floors made it a go-between for descent divers and the other established companies on the first floor in the city, too, meaning that although many of the things here on the second floor were unrefined before being passed back to the craftsmen above on Floor One—the list of potential items was usually unscoured and plentiful.

It was thus a spot that the group had agreed to check out before proceeding to the next floor, and Riven's group had quite a lot of money to spend.

Approaching the trench and trudging through the tent city, the stench of decay became more prevalent, as did a faint hum of cryptic whispers. The roaming caravan of mindless undead trailing behind them was quite the sight to be seen.

And coming to a stop in front of the undead proprietors at the mouth of the large trench where the Deadman's Featherfall Trading Guild had set up, it was both these mindless minions that Retesh and Allie had claimed and the elder lich and angel of death herself that most caught the attention of the sentries at the gate.

With their hollow eyes and pallid complexions, a small detachment of ghouls and skresh made their way to intercept Riven's caravan while bypassing many of the other customers that were already waiting in line. Their skeletal forms, draped in tattered robes and adorned with an array of curious trinkets over runic armor, seemed to blend seamlessly into the murky shadows that shrouded the canyons.

"Stop," the lead soldier called out, holding up a shriveled, armor-clad hand with a stern expression as he and two dozen others came to stand in front of Riven's parade. He'd obviously once been a demon himself, with horns adorning the ghoul's forehead and a skeletal tail trailing behind him. Half of his right cheek was missing, exposing bare teeth. "Minions of any kind are not allowed inside. Even for someone of your standing."

His eyes went in and out of focus while taking in the MYTHIC tags on both Riven and Lillith before settling on Allie. The ghoul soldier bowed respectfully in her direction and gave a nod to Fimrindle when the reaper appeared nearby crouched on top of a boulder. "I apologize for the inconvenience, but we have had too many attempts to cause problems using minions as a meat shield, and we simply don't have the room to accommodate so many if every necromancer or summoner wanted to bring in their underlings."

Narg the beholder demon, floating beside Azmoth, gave a sputtering hiss of protest. "I am needed to make sure the master is able to identify your wares properly!"

"I do not leave Allie's side," Fimrindle confirmed with another blur of motion to stand next to the angel he served. "You will let us in, or we will leave."

"Agreed. We can't just let the reincarnation of Gluttony walk into your store without guards," Athela mused, leaning casually against Riven and wrapping an arm around his shoulder. "Can we?"

The ghoul gave Riven another glance, eyebrows furrowing slightly—but otherwise did not appear too surprised. "I have heard of your dealings above . . . We do not wish for violence. But those stories give us even more reason to stop your passage should you attempt to bring your minions with you. All your minions. I am sorry, but—"

He was cut off when an aura of death descended upon their position and a huge, shirtless man landed beside them. Four long, black wings protruded from his back, and he was covered in tattoos, with two pale gray eyes and a halo similar to Allie's own over his head. He stood, his rippling muscles etched into his body like Adonis himself, as the ghoul squad leader rapidly took three steps back and bowed in deference.

Glancing once at the squad serving the trading company, and then turning with a polite smile in Riven's direction, the handsome angel of death gestured toward the open gate beyond the line of other customers. "Forgive my fellows— they are just doing their job as instructed. It is an honor to have customers of your caliber visit our humble home, and it would please us eternally to have you enter our abode. Please, feel free to bring your sentient minions with you. The mass of nonsentient undead will still have to stay outside due to restraints on room, but rest assured that your safety here is guaranteed by the company—and we will discreetly be on high alert while you browse our wares. Please, come inside. You of all people should not have to wait in any line."

Fimrindle grunted in approval, then vanished into thin air between blinks as if he'd never been there to begin with.

Smirking at Allie's expression from underneath her bone helmet at seeing another angel of death for the very first time, Riven took Athela by the hand and started walking forward into the gloom of the trench, where a sprawling setup of tents, stone, and wooden constructs awaited them beyond the gates. "Come on, Narg, I'll be counting on you to tell us all about the items they have to make sure they're valid. Up to the task?"

The beholder demon abruptly took in a deep breath of air in his excitement before floating onward to follow them. "Of course, great one! I only wish to serve!"

Numerous stalls with different groups of descenders were filled to the brim, haggling and trading was in full swing, and different high-borns of the darker side of the multiverse were giving Riven's group a myriad of expressions while he stood at his own stall desk.

"A vampire prince from the Blood Moon Requiem as Gluttony's reincarnation? I had thought it was just a rumor. It appears I was mistaken. To think that a greater undead would become one of demonkind's bastions . . . now that is something I would not have ever guessed at."

The ghoul merchant, clad in a gold-flecked green robe, eyed the party with a skeptically raised eyebrow. The other robed undead behind him underneath the canopy of the company tent cast curious glances their way from time to time while dealing with other customers, but overall their demeanor was rather reserved and polite despite the gawking of some of the random passersby.

"A lich, a human, an angel of death . . . oh, you're a rare breed. It is an honor to be in your presence, hero of the Death pillar." The ghoul gave Allie in particular an appraising and almost reverent look before glancing over at Lillith next. It was obvious by the way he took them in that he held no reverence for Riven or Lillith as many of demonkind did, and if anything—he looked at Allie far more favorably. "And the Lady of Black Skies, too—your legend precedes you. Things are certainly becoming interesting down here in the descent . . ."

The undead man picked up the list of things Riven and the others were looking for before scribbling down some notes and handing the parchment to an assistant. With a nod the skeletal assistant took flight back into rows of boxes, barrels, and shelves.

"Enchanted protective jewelry including five black stareater amulets, abyssal sigils for item upgrades, Dao treasures for cultivation, Unholy spiritual crystals for soul lattice cleansing, crafting ingredients of all sorts concerning totems, any artifact staves or melee weapons that we may have come by from floor-boss drops, information on this year's optional floor boss, and information on any item sets able to be found in the abyssal descent that have growth potential." The ghoul's dead eyes slowly settled on Lillith and then Riven. "It will be more than a few minutes, but I believe our trading guild can supply what you need. We'll be back after we find some selections of what you're looking for, but know that it will be expensive."

Retesh shifted uncomfortably, his skeletal head twisting and turning while he clenched and unclenched a bone hand over and over again. "Hopefully it does not take too long . . ."

The ghoul merchant ignored Retesh's comment and proceeded to walk back into the maze of cargo after his assistant.

Glancing over his shoulder, Riven eyed the lich with a discerning gaze. "You all right?"

There was a pause, and Retesh gave him an almost disbelieving look. "I do not know you as well as I know Allie, Riven. So know that I do not mean offense when I say this, but how is it that you can be so calm while our brothers and sisters die in our absence?"

Riven and Allie shared a look.

"He's talking about the people back on Panu," Allie confirmed with a brief flare of her wings, leaning on her exquisite claymore.

"Indeed I am," Retesh said with an underlying rage to his voice, and his bones rattled as the clenching and unclenching of his fists grew more rapid. "Every day we stay here is another day that more of my people die. Another day that more of OUR people die, for you are undead, too, Riven, even if you are also now of demon blood. Back on our world, our people are undergoing genocide. That smug bitch Judith Marcina is growing an army of natives and off-worlders alike to cull us, and it has been long since I have stepped foot on the soil of my homeland. I have been given news by Lillith that my people have been accepted as refugees onto the continent of Umbra, which the Thane Necropolis controls, but the pilgrimages are long and the merfolk are just as willing to kill us for what we are as that damn Nephilim wench. I wish to be rid of this place—and soon— so that I may rejoin the war effort where I am needed most. I have been here for my own cultivation efforts far too long . . ."

"Your efforts will be rewarded by the time the descent is done," Lillith said with a dismissive wave of her hand. "In the end, you will save more of your people than what you could have done previously by—"

"That is easy for you to say when it is not your own kin that die by the thousands every day!" Retesh snapped back in anger, only to hastily humble himself with a bow of his head. "I . . . I am sorry, Lillith. I meant no offense. I am just on edge. Your people have been a great teacher to me, and that was both uncalled-for and disrespectful. I apologize for my rudeness."

Lillith, whose features had initially hardened at his original retort, softened herself and shook her head. "Ah, Retesh. I know all too well that particular sting of loss . . . you are forgiven. But do know that, in the end, only the pursuit of true individual power can promise the changes you seek. Relying on oneself and your own abilities is the only thing you can truly control, so cultivating to the pinnacle here and now will pay dividends far down the road beyond what you can see in front of you. Take solace in the fact that you are doing what needs to be done for a long payoff, rather than mindlessly killing without insight into a path beyond basic violence."

The lich opened and closed his mouth three times with the clicking of bone on bone, but eventually he stilled and slumped his shoulders as his hands unclenched one final time. "I hope you are right, Lillith. I just feel an enormous amount of guilt, and like I have abandoned the ones I have raised up only to be slaughtered like children and sheep at a butcher's hand."

From behind where Riven stood leaning against the counter, a deep baritone voice called out his name. "Prince Riven Wraithtide and Princess Allie Wraithtide of the Blood Moon Requiem . . . I have heard stories of you two even in my sector of the multiverse. Your existence has caused quite a stir across the cosmos for someone in F-grade. I must say that I'm jealous."

Turning around, Riven caught sight of a well-dressed human with slicked-back black hair wearing a black suit. He had overly pale skin, with brown eyes and a firm jawline. He carried a cane, though he was just as young as Riven was by the looks of him, and his frame was rather muscular. Behind him, four other handsome young men dressed similarly and all with canes of their own watched passively with stoic expressions.

Azmoth, however, was standing in his way with crossed arms and Shengari Shields attached to his back—and the human man had to look around the towering armored demon in order to make eye contact.

The newcomer held out a hand of greeting to Azmoth's side, completely ignoring everyone else and only having eyes for Riven after a brief glance at Allie. "Jarntus Bemule. Earl of the Idorac Federation, an ally and neighbor to the Blood Moon Requiem in Universe 10, and I believe a direct neighbor to your own house located on Planet Vartesh in the Luteski sector. I would call a meeting such as this fate. For what would the chances of this meeting otherwise be?"

His words immediately grabbed Riven's attention, and Riven stepped through the tangle of his minions and fellows to come to the front. Looking the man over up and down, he eventually took the man's hand with a firm grip and nodded slowly.

"Connected the dots, huh?" Riven mused out loud, sending a mental signal to Azmoth to back off. "I can't say I've heard of the Idorac Federation, but I'm only just now being introduced to the politics of the Blood Moon Requiem. You must forgive my ignorance."

The immediate reaction was one of amusement and relief when Azmoth stepped aside, and the man named Jarntus chuckled at the statement before releasing Riven's hand. "Oh, it wasn't that hard to connect the dots after my identifier listed your information. Your system title says it all; there is only one reincarnation of Gluttony walking around, and his name is Riven Thane. It is a pleasure to see that you'd actually give me the time of day."

"What's that supposed to mean?"

"It means I wasn't sure you'd even be willing to shake my hand, considering I am not anywhere near your social standing. It is akin to a homeless peasant requesting the attention of a world's emperor, but I'd heard you'd grown up outside the realm of politics or royal upbringing and took a risk." Jarntus Bemule gave Riven a warm smile. "I'm glad the rumors from the Blood Moon Requiem are true. I wish to speak with you, if you have time."

"He obviously speaks the truth about your discrepancy in standing," Lillith cut in from the side, an irritated glare and a frown casting over the lot of five humans. "You really should try to reduce your time conversing with . . . lesser creatures such as this, Riven. Humans are not worthy of your time."

"Well, that's openly hostile," Riven said with a laugh, shaking his head in Lillith's direction as Jarntus frowned. "And you like Nora, don't you? She's human. I started as a human, too."

"You were never human—you and your sister were always purebloods. Even if not of demonic origin, your base race is far above that of insects like these," Lillith retorted, still giving Jarntus the stink eye. "And Nora is an exception. She's my drinking partner."

"Shucks, thanks . . ." Nora muttered with a sarcastic eye roll from underneath her Chalgathi hood. "Feelings not hurt at all, definitely not! And for the record, it was more like I was FORCED to drink whenever I messed up in training!"

Allie snickered.

"Which happened a lot." Lillith let her glare slip with a grin shot in Nora's direction, but then returned to scowling while eyeing the newcomers. "I've never even heard of the Idorac Federation. They're likely just brown-nosers, Riven, and you'll get lots of them as the eons pass you by. For dogs like these, it is better to just ignore them or force them to leave."

The gluttonous maw on Riven's armored chest rumbled in approval, but Riven still shook his head. "I live life on the edge, you old hag. I do what I want, when I want."

"Old hag?!" Lillith retorted in astonishment. "I look just as young as your two bimbo girlfriends!"

"BIMBO?!" Athela gasped in horror. She then pointed an accusatory finger at Fay. "Don't lump me in with HER!"

"HEY!" Fay protested and threw up her arms while the group laughed. "What's THAT supposed to mean?!"

Athela pooched her lips in Fay's direction and crossed her arms, thrusting her hips out to bump Riven teasingly. "It means that I am a sophisticated PRINCESS while you're just a ho."

Cackling, Riven shoved Athela off him before the two women he was dating started their regular catfighting and shook his head. Turning his attention back to Jarntus with a wide smile that showed his fangs, Riven rubbed his forehead with a sigh as the sound of a small scuffle breaking out, feminine yelps causing him to groan with amusement. "Some things will never change. Anyways, despite what Lillith says, I'd be more than happy to talk to you. It isn't often that I get to meet people from my great-grandmother's part of the multiverse."

His smile returning rather gratefully, Jarntus gave him a bow and then bowed in Allie's direction next as she took off her bone helm. "Princess Allie Wraithtide, your beauty is a thing of legends. I had heard you'd turned your back on the Blood God in favor of the Scythe, but to see your angelic figure standing in front of me with the brilliance of—"

"I have a boyfriend," Allie retorted, unfazed by his obvious flattery. "His name is Lahn, and he's waiting for me back on my homeworld. I don't wish to engage in flirting, thank you very much."

"Well, of course you have a man courting you, and of course not!" Jarntus hastily said with a sheepish laugh and a head scratch. He quickly straightened and became even paler. "I was not attempting to—I mean, I was not trying to engage in—eh, forgive me, Princess. I mean nothing by it. I would never dream of suspecting that I was worthy of a princess of the requiem, or a Hero of Death!"

"You're forgiven as long as you know your place," Allie replied with a blank stare. "Now, what is it you want with us?"

Swallowing and showing nervousness for the first time, Jarntus returned his attention back to the more friendly of the two siblings. "Well, as I was stating before, I am an earl of the Idorac Federation and a direct neighbor to House Wraithtide. In particular, my family is located in your own Luteski sector and three solar systems away from your trading hub on Vartesh. I was hoping, perhaps, if I helped you here in the Abyssal Descent, we may discuss trade relations that may be beneficial to both our houses. Would you be interested?"

Riven clicked his tongue thoughtfully. He honestly doubted that this man could help him here in the descent at all, considering he had the resources of the entire Church of Gluttony at his disposal. In fact, the Church of Gluttony would foot the bill for anything that he couldn't personally afford to buy. But there was no harm in seeing what the man had to say, and Riven was rather curious about news from Universe 10, where the Blood Moon Requiem held most of its territory.

"All right, take your shot," Riven said with a shrug. "You've got until the merchant comes back to make your pitch. If I'm interested, we can talk. Otherwise I'll have to forgo negotiations, because we're kind of in a time crunch—I believe we have an optional challenge boss for this floor to fight before the day's end."

CHAPTER 23

A large fissure appeared, far larger than any of the others, and its conjuration led to a shudder that the entire multiverse felt. Each universe was washed in the spark of creation as pieces of Elysium fell from the beyond and a new presence began to seep into the deep, dark places of space.

[Multiversal System Notice: To all creatures across Elysium, let it be known that the return of the sins and commandments is at hand. The second, third, and fourth of the seven original sins have been unleashed from the abyss. Pride, Greed, and Sloth have simultaneously exited the abyss after having chosen their host reincarnations. The second and third of the seven original commandments have been unleashed from the abyss. Judgment and Truth have simultaneously exited the abyss after having chosen their host reincarnations.

Release has been expedited. Other sins and commandments will be released from the abyss over the course of the next six months as long as they are willing to abide by Elysium's terms. Let the eternal war between the hells and heavens begin again, as the origins of angels and demons clash in the cosmos—unshackled and unrestrained, seeking to return to the power they once had.]

Silence reigned in the ever-expanding darkness of the prison that Gluttony had come to know so well over the eons. His mind turned, watching his counterparts leave this place of solitude along with all their banished servants that flocked after them like bees to honey.

Only Lust, Envy, Wrath, Piety, Selflessness, Humility, and Patience remained. They remained here in the deepest part of Elysium, farthest away from the light, where golden cracks were beginning to spread across the outer shell of the multiverse as another of Elysium's kind began to gnaw at the edges.

Elysium was starting to decay.

Wrath, Gluttony's greatest ally, shrouded the two of them in a cocoon of isolation. "My rage grows once more, old friend . . . I cannot help but feel that we are being lied to . . . This is nothing but a farce played by Elysium. It is a game. And so I must ask, what brings the Great Maw to my doorstep after so recently having been set free? What keeps you from the great hunts you so often gorge yourself upon?"

Gluttony let out a stark, guttural laugh. "It is certainly a farce. Elysium did not happen to let us out for no reason; it would not have done so if it did not have to, and that is why I came. Do you know what is happening here on the outer shell, Wrath?"

The spirit of Wrath paused. "I have an inkling of an idea . . . as much as any of us do. It could be one of a few things, but I lean toward a complete reset. This force that Elysium is fighting against is just as strong or stronger than the fabric of our own multiverse, and Elysium cannot afford to leave us trapped here as it is. When Galactis finally breaks through . . . Elysium will shun all other protocols in favor of an offensive merge. When that happens . . ."

Wrath trailed off.

"When that happens, probably within the next few years, everything will be thrown into chaos," Gluttony agreed thoughtfully. His internal sight briefly stalled on his reincarnation's body, who was speaking to some lowly F-grade scion. Amusement flared. "It depends on how things happen in the fight to come, but the scenarios I see playing out could range from a complete reset, as you say—where all the greater powers in the multiverse are reduced back to their fundamentals. I find this unlikely, though, in the face of a soft reset or a more probable scrambling."

"A soft reset? Or scrambling?" Wrath repeated, and the abyss around him began to churn with excitement. "A scrambling would be more favorable. I would not like to be set upon the path of equalization; rather, I want to have a chance at fighting my way back to the top through opponents stronger than I. It has been so long since I was the apex warrior of existence that I have forgotten what it is like to struggle against a possible defeat, and the idea intrigues me. I am tired of my own perfection, tired of being the very best without equal. I very much look forward to it and hope that you are right so that I can prove to Elysium itself that even if thrown down, I will be able to achieve perfection once more. A scramble . . . a scramble would be exactly what we need."

Gluttony's gaze shifted back to the other sin, ignoring the self-praise that was ever there whenever speaking with Wrath. "If such a thing happens, are you looking to be on your own again? If so, it is unlikely that we will see one another for a very long time—this will be my last goodbye for many millennia."

Wrath did not respond; instead he just kept staring at the ever-spreading cracks across Elysium's outer shell.

The silence was enough of an answer for Gluttony.

"I shall miss you, old friend," Gluttony stated after a time. "Please let me know if you have reconsidered my proposal. If the heavens and hells shift, if multiverses collide, it would be good to have one such as you as someone who I could call upon. In the meantime, I will gather my forces and attempt to take the tiny world I have landed on, as my reincarnation says—'before shit hits the fan.' Be safe and take care."

Gluttony began to withdraw from the abyssal prison when Wrath stopped him with a mental ping.

"Be sure to kill Greed's reincarnation before the time comes," Wrath called out, laughing when he got a malicious grin from Gluttony in response. "Be sure to make Greed feel pain as you do it . . . That disgusting roach has been an absolute pest ever since we were quarantined with him here. Almost to the point that I'd rather speak with those damned commandments than him."

This got an outrageous fit of laughter out of Gluttony, and the Great Maw ignored the glances of the other origins sharing their dark corner of space when the quarantined zone passed away. "I will do so. Farewell, and I hope to see you change your mind."

Wrath let out a chuckle of his own. "Perhaps I will. We shall see . . ."

Sheline Wraithtide hummed to herself, pushing her long brown ponytail off her shoulder and letting it drag across her back. Her red eyes gleamed with gentle light as the bloody vial was poured into the soup, and a small hand reached up to grab at it before she lovingly swatted the hand away.

"Jerald!" Sheline scolded, frowning down at the little boy in mock anger as he giggled up at her and ran to hide behind her husband's chair. "I told you not to grab at the kitchen bowls while I'm cooking! You could burn yourself!"

Timvar raised an eyebrow from where he sipped his coffee. A handsome young man by most appearances and equally as pale as Sheline, he was certainly older than he looked, as was his wife. Flipping a page in his book, he continued transcribing the work he'd been paid by the local guild to do after giving his youngest son a quick smile of approval. "Don't make your mother too angry now! You'll be sent right back to your bed again, and we don't want that! Remember what Mom said about obeying her rules in the kitchen?"

"You say that while silently goading him with your eyes," Sheline stated with an exasperated sigh. "Just look at him! Jerald's giggling at us! He's NEVER going to take us seriously!"

Timvar Wraithtide merely chuckled along with his son and ignored his wife's unrealistic pleas. "I'm sure you'll survive, honey."

Outside their cabin home, peddlers and merchants were closing up for the day as calls from the town guard made everyone aware the gates would soon shut.

Wheels turning over cobblestone roads and laughter from the local bar caused them to be at ease, but a rapid knock at the door caused Timvar to look up with furrowed brows. "Is that Markus?"

"Package delivery!" the squeaky voice of a teenage boy called through the wooden door.

"Definitely Markus all right," Sheline stated with a smirk. She wiped her hands on her blouse and gave her tiny son Jerald a stern look before heading over to the door. "No touching the food, Jerald!"

When she opened it, sunlight trailed in through the doorway and caused her to wince. Regardless, she stared down at the skinny teenager with a pleasant gentleness as she took the box of blood-filled vials from the runner. "Thanks, Markus. What do I owe you?"

"Two shills!" the boy said with a wide smile, scuffing his shoes against the cobblestone and shifting back and forth from foot to foot. "I have a date tonight! So I need all the cash I can get."

"OH-HOH!" Sheline turned back to look at her husband with a laugh. "Timvar! Did you hear?! Markus has a date tonight, probably with that little redheaded girl down the street!"

Timvar gave a wide laugh, displaying his fangs while the teenager at the door rolled his eyes.

"Money, please!"

Giggling, Sheline handed the young man his payment after fishing it out from one of her pockets. "Now, begone with you! And good luck on your date! I expect to hear great things!"

Markus smiled, thanked them, and skipped down the street toward his house. Watching him go, Sheline felt the firm hand of her husband rest on her left shoulder.

"Did he bring the ingredients for the Charisma-neutralizing potions, too?" he asked, looking into the box where leaves and roots had been stuffed between glass vials. "Ah, there they are! Very nice! We were almost out."

"Gods forbid that happens," Sheline said with an eye roll. "The last time—"

She stopped abruptly and felt something from far, far away call to her. She looked up at the sky's sunset hues, staring into the distance past the clouds at something even her husband could not see. Mouth slowly hanging ajar, her grip loosened—and the box of blood-filled vials dropped to shatter on the road with a curse from Timvar.

"Honey! You let everything spill!" he said irritatedly, getting down on his knees to pick up the pieces. "What's come over you?!"

Sheline did not reply. Instead, she just continued to stare. The cracks that were forming on the outer shell of Galactis were spreading, and through it, she felt the afterimage of the prophecy she'd left behind in Elysium's Abyssal Descent sing back to her.

Riven, her little boy Riven, had finally come into contact with her spiritual marker.

The prophecy was starting to come into fruition.

After all these years, it was finally time. Her other children were coming home. To her.

She could only hope that they would forgive her for what she had done. And she had to wonder just what games her grandmother would start to play whenever the high queen finally found out what was really going on.

The silence after the system-wide notification about commandments and sins was palpable, but it only lasted for a few minutes until things resumed as normal.

"Just what do you think that you'd be able to offer the two of us, human?" Allie asked, irritated by the man's eagerness to have their attention. "We have the ear of people far more influential than you. I have a feeling this will be a grand waste of our time."

"We have time to burn while the merchants get our stuff," Riven said with a shrug, a lot more relaxed than his little sister was, even if he was constantly combating the urge to tell her about the vision of their mother, Sheline. That would have to wait for another time. "And we'll have more than enough excitement later when we fight the optional Floor Two Boss. I even heard that it plays to your weaknesses! It'll be neat fighting such a creature."

Jarntus Bemule, self-proclaimed earl of the Idorac Federation, leaned forward to better look at Riven and Allie with a serious gaze. "I want to secede from my empire, and I want to join your house."

Riven and Allie both turned their heads with shocked expressions.

"Um . . . What was that?" Riven asked, just to make sure he had heard correctly.

Jarntus repeated his claim. "The Idorac Federation is . . . offput. I don't know what exactly is going on in the upper brass, but something is amiss. I have a very bad feeling about how they're allocating resources and the fleets, and my house is all of the same mind."

Jarntus waved back at his four followers with their suits and canes, and each of the other young men gave hesitant or stern nods of agreement to Jarntus's words.

Riven raised an eyebrow and put his hand behind his head, leaning back in his chair. "That's rather abrupt, and I honestly have no idea what or who your house even is. I don't even know if you're really an earl. How am I supposed to make that judgment call?"

"Just please, listen to me," Jarntus pleaded, firming his jaw. "There is something very, very wrong going on with the king. He—"

"That's not our problem," Allie stated sourly with narrowed eyes. "We're only estranged nobility on a planet far away; we have no political sway in your sector."

Jarntus blinked rapidly, then began to laugh uproariously. "No sway, you say?! Do you even know who and what you are?!"

Beginning to shed tears of amusement, Jarntus guffawed and wiped at his face with a sleeve. "Ah, it truly is refreshing to see the two of you being so different than most of the nobility from the Blood Moon Requiem. Do you want to know what it's usually like when meeting royalty of your faction? Even lesser royalty, such as those in the five hundredth seat or below?"

"There are five hundred seats?!" Riven asked, awestruck.

Jarntus gave him a sidelong look. "Far more than that. Your empire is very old, Riven. There are thousands of seats given out to the royals, and you're . . . what? Thirty-seventh in line for the throne?"

"Thirty-sixth," Riven corrected with a side-to-side nod. "Since I killed Jalel."

"Oh yes! You killed the other prince!" Jarntus said with a grin. "I watched that episode on the cortex, too. You really fought quite well for being untrained most of your life!"

The backhanded compliment was not one Riven appreciated, but it got snickers from Azmoth and Athela while Fay frowned furiously.

"Riven is more than fine at fighting! And he's an absolute genius when it comes to grasping magic!" Fay stated defensively, putting her arms around Riven's shoulders. "And he's a sensitive, New Age male! You'll hurt his feelings if you talk about him like that!"

Riven scrunched his nose and pursed his lips while glaring back at the succubus as Athela began to laugh harder. "Thanks . . . Fay. You really do me a solid sometimes, you know that?"

The succubus beamed, kissing him on the cheek and not realizing he was being sarcastic.

"Anyways . . ." Riven muttered.

Jarntus capitalized on the moment of silence. "No offense intended, Riven. I meant to say that you did very well. Regardless, you are thirty-sixth in line for the throne. That is far, far more influential than you realize. If you wanted to, you could easily contact my empire and ask to buy the planet my family rules over. For a price, of course, but it would be worth it, and your family only owns one planet if I'm not mistaken. Two, if you end up conquering Panu. We wouldn't be able to secede ourselves, but if it were a favor to an ally like you . . . Perhaps if you gave a discount on services at the trade hub your family owns for a few decades . . ."

Jarntus let his voice trail off. "Then we'd be in your debt."

"Well, of course you'd be in my debt—you're asking me to buy a damn planet!" Riven laughed. "And again, I know so little about you or this planet that I'm honestly inclined to say no. I don't know anything about the demeanor of your king, what these 'oddities' are that you're talking about in your empire, or what makes you REALLY want to secede. You're being very vague, and until you explain in detail, I'm absolutely refusing. Nor do I know if I even have that kind of swing, despite your words. It would be something that I'd want to run by Kathrine . . ."

Riven stopped speaking momentarily, realizing that Kathrine was still missing and getting a sinking feeling in his gut. But the banished were on it even now, and it was unlikely that they wouldn't find her. The question was, would she be alive when they did.

"Tell us in detail why and how your empire's ruling faction is acting oddly, and we may discuss the matter afterward," Allie cut in with a dismissive, queenly wave of her hand. "You can't expect us just to buy the planet you live on out of the goodness of our hearts. Especially when it is already owned by another sovereign state. We have to be convinced it is in our best interest to do so—for all we know your planet is a barren rock that has no real value."

Jarntus frowned again, but nodded. "It is certainly not as prosperous as your own family's trade empire, but my planet is full of opportunities to harvest treasure troves of aquatic spiritual herbs. They grow naturally in my homeland, among the island nations that speckle an otherwise sea-covered world. I can easily supply you with invoices showing how profitable my parents' estates are and what the economy is like. But that in itself makes what the king and lords of the inner courts are doing even weirder. The federal monarchy is tight-lipped about why, but they're pooling all their military might in one single solar system—leaving the outskirts of the empire completely undefended. They've also paid vast amounts of money to terraform inhospitable worlds in the core solar system of our empire instead of developing already flourishing planets in others. Lastly, they're making their most talented minds relocate to the inner solar system or capital world with huge stipends to draw them in. People are beginning to worry, trade routes are deteriorating, and piracy is becoming rampant. I am afraid that my own planet is being left isolated, too, as we are on the fringe of our own empire just like you are. I am afraid that something big is about to happen, and whatever it is, it's going to be bad. There have been rumors of riots and rebellions, ones that are not being suppressed despite the ability to do so. What I want is protection, and based on the actions of my king, I would assume he's far more open to selling my family's planet than you'd think."

CHAPTER 24

Jarntus Bemule left the trading enclave with only a half-hearted smile and a word of thanks, with the other humans from the Idorac Federation trailing him. He hadn't gotten what he'd wanted, not exactly, anyways, as Riven also wasn't willing to promise him anything beyond an "I'll look into it."

"You could have been a bit more forthright in your interest," Allie stated absentmindedly, raising an eyebrow in her brother's direction as the earl left. "I could tell that you wanted to know more. I personally don't think the Blood Moon Requiem would be very keen on me pulling the strings of our house now that I've forsaken the Blood God, but if it were you? If what the man is saying rings true, I'm sure you could make it happen."

Riven waved a hand dismissively as he saw the approaching undead merchants coming back. Standing up, he cleared his throat and approached the desk. "I know too little about politics to give a firm answer. He'll have to make do with what I gave him and await an inquiry from General Viku."

"The Deadman's Featherfall Trading Guild is nothing if not resourceful!" the ghoul merchant said, ignoring the humans who'd just taken their leave—and beaming at Riven with a wide smile as he was followed by three other ghouls, two skresh, and a fleshy risen demon that was constantly wreathed in cinders and deathly flame. "May I present to you our wares! I included some extra pieces than what you asked for, just in case you wanted all of it."

He tipped his hood with a snakelike look in his dead eyes. "Given that your church is paying for most of this with promissory notes, perhaps you could even grant some of them to your disciples back in your homeworld? Not much of this can be found on an outer-rim planet, if the rumors of your origins are true."

Amused but not disagreeing, Riven got up along with the others to approach the multiple trays of items that'd been set out along the counter of their stall.

And indeed, everything Riven had asked for was there.

Five sets of uniform amulets and rings had black crystals set in silver metal with protective enchantments of various sorts, of far higher grade than anything that could be bought on Panu. Over three dozen abyssal sigils, which were enchantment plaques glowing a deep purple that could be stuck and fused into pieces of armor for quick upgrades, were stacked neatly next to each other in a line. Dao treasures in the form of various herbs radiating Unholy energies were in abundance, with varieties picked out for each pillar underneath the Unholy umbrella: a flower in a state of constant decay radiated necrotic death energy, a five-pointed leaf seemingly made from blood itself, a vine crackling and writhing with chaos energy, a burning cabbage-like plant—the list went on. The ghoul had also brought numerous spiritual crystals, more reserved in their outward appearance than the Dao treasures, but each of them glowing with internal energies of a particular type.

"If you notice . . ." the ghoul began, stopping Riven from continuing as he picked up the flaming cabbage in one hand and the necrotic flower in the other. "These plants are actually still completely intact. You could even begin your own garden if the environment is right, though I will say that these fully intact specimens are far more expensive than individual parts. Otherwise, the more processed versions of these Dao treasures can be found in smaller pieces for bouts of cultivation in shorter bursts. The crystals could also be used to form cultivation rooms if set correctly! We also only bought the finest crystals available, greater soul crystals of pristine quality that may cost—"

"Price shouldn't be much of an issue," Lillith confirmed with a downward slice of her hand. "Just be sure you don't make it too outlandish or this will be the last time the church does business here."

She glanced Riven's way. "I think the garden and cultivation room would be nice additions to your guild hall . . . considering that we'll likely be needing to use the guild hall sooner than you'd think."

Riven furrowed his brows, confused by the comment, but Lillith made no attempt to enlighten him further. "Yeah . . . I'll take all of it, I guess. Now, let's talk about those weapons . . ."

Smiling gleefully and rubbing his hands together, the ghoul merchant moved on to the next set of items on the countertop. "As requested, we have a variety of staves for your lich companion to choose from—and for you to use as a melee weapon worthy of Gluttony . . . I present to you two options to choose from. I could not find anything quite worthy of the Great Maw, nothing like that staff you've got there, but these two are some of the best close-range weapons we could find on short notice in the dimensions you requested."

Again, the options available here in the descent were of a quality that surpassed anything from back on Panu. And despite what the ghoul merchant said, they certainly weren't bad.

There were five staves, each created from the stiffened, sculpted spine of some unknown creature, but each with a different crystal orb at the top of what could be considered a typical fantasy mage staff. They'd obviously been made by the same crafter, as, aside from their different affinities and perks, they looked almost identical.

But Riven's eyes were more for the two items that Gluttony would be using in his demonic form whenever the shift occurred. Riven also knew that Gluttony had some obscure plans about creating a second melee class involving that shift, but details were scarce. Regardless, it was akin to buying a new car or a new house back when Earth had been around. It was . . . exciting, for lack of better words.

One was an enormous, flanged mace, bigger than Riven's vampire form was from head to foot—but it would fit proportionally into his hands whenever he shifted into his larger, winged, demonic form. It was made from dark-gray metal all down the shaft and up to where the mace split into numerous edges at the top. Those dark neon-purple edges each sparked with Unholy energy, and when Riven attempted to pick it up as he was, he struggled to lift it. Also, for the first time in a long time, he felt the stinging burning sensation of an item indicative of him not meeting the stat requirements to wield it—and quickly put it back on the counter before the burning sensation became too much. The mace didn't have any major effects other than on-hit explosive sin damage, but it did have an incredibly high damage rating for F- or E-grade alike.

The other was a halberd, and its damage rating was almost equal to the mace. And by halberd, Riven meant a halberd on steroids. It was meant for a titan and was even larger than the damned mace nearly twice over. Reaching far beyond Riven's body length and crafted out of what appeared to be a strange blue-green jade, it constantly hissed audibly and lacked any obvious decorations. Looking over it more carefully, Riven saw that the weapon was actually dissolving the very stone tray it'd been laid upon. It obviously had an acidic effect to it.

Both items were completely geared toward close-combat fighting, packing a far harder punch than even Jackal did—but lacking Jackal's other passives such as the massive mana-regeneration boost or the range increase that made it so good for spellcasting.

[Mace of Shattering Storms (Awakened Weapon. Sin Artifact): 2,903 average damage on strike, with strikes adding explosive sin damage on impact. High chance for electric discharge and shattering effects to any armor on impact. Requires a Sin affinity and 3,400 Strength to wield.]

[Giant's Jade Halberd of Dissolving (Awakened Weapon. Unholy Artifact): 2,740 average damage on strike. Applies acidic and Unholy

splash damage on impact that feeds on enemies to do damage over time. Enemies eaten by the acid supplied by this weapon are used as fuel to extend and amplify any applied passive buffs. Requires an Unholy affinity above 60% and a strength stat of over 2,000 to wield.

- +350 Strength and +10% Strength
- Jade Tidal Wave: Swipe this weapon in a given direction to create a tidal wave of Unholy jade acid. The amount and potency of this acid is completely relevant to your affinity to the Unholy foundational pillar.]

"Gluttony, what's our strength when we turn into our demonic form?" Riven asked skeptically, disappointed that he couldn't wield either of these weapons in his vampire form. "Our strength in this form is only 1,167. I can't pick up either of these things as I am now."

Gluttony chuckled inside his head. "We grow to five times your current height in our demonic form. What do you think it is?"

"I don't know. Three thousand?"

"More."

"Four thousand?"

"More."

Riven paused. "Just tell me."

"We gain an additional five thousand Strength with a 30 percent boost to Strength, along with other bonuses, when in my ultimate form."

Riven whistled in appreciation, ignoring the odd looks he got while conversing silently with his partner. "Wow. I suppose I should probably already know that, huh?"

Gluttony internally grunted in agreement. "It is likely I will have to modify it to extend the time we can spend using our transformation, which will decrease the bonus stats. But that is to be determined by our soul lattice construct when we get to E-grade, and when I am able to craft our second class. Either way, we should have more than enough strength to use either of these weapons. That said, I want the halberd."

"Why the—"

"You get to outfit us for our mage class," Gluttony interrupted. "I control our other half. That is the deal. Remember?"

Briefly pooching his lips, Riven shrugged. "All right then. We'll take the halberd. And all this other stuff, too, but you can take the mace back."

Retesh had already picked out one of the spine-crafted staves with a nod of thanks to Riven and was thoroughly inspecting the large green crystal ball set at the top of the shaft. The others had started equipping their defense-boosting rings and amulets in turn. Each ring gave a bonus that absorbed any critical strike in its entirety one time, with a passive recharge rate of a single day, while the amulets each gave a large percentage boost to endurance and a buffer to any physical damage.

"Very well! Though I'd bind the halberd quickly so it doesn't try to eat away your flesh. We had an accident earlier involving—Eh, never mind. I'm happy to see you're happy!" the ghoul merchant said eagerly, having two of the skresh workers carry away the large, sparking mace. "I'll send the invoice directly to your church. Is that all right?"

"Certainly," Lillith said with a nod. "They'll be expecting you. Now, for the last thing we required . . ."

"Ah yes!" the merchant exclaimed, pulling out a scroll and handing it over to the shadowy demoness. "Here it is. Information on this year's optional Floor Two Boss. It's a good one, but rather dangerous even for you. The Abyssal Descent adapts based on who you are and what your weaknesses are. So although you may be formidable, I would not take this lightly."

Lillith began to smile, eyebrows raised and pale white eyes suddenly flaring brightly. "Interesting and exciting! I assume the reward for completing it will be good?"

The merchant nodded enthusiastically. "Oh yes! We've had more of our fair share of deaths, but if you manage to beat it, you'll be given a one-way portal ticket to the twentieth floor. The reward is a shortcut this year, and it'll save you a lot of time on your trek if you manage to do it."

With the enormous halberd stored inside his spatial sack along with a copious number of Dao treasures and spiritual crystals for use later, they began making their way down through the tunnels toward where Lillith said the optional floor boss was located. Twists and turns and entire caves filled with bustling activity were present. There were high-end succubus brothels, gambling dens, groups of muggers picking out marks, a few scattered bodies from the aftermaths of fights, and building crowds the deeper they went.

"The optional floor boss usually gives buffs, guides, or other means of passing through to the lower levels more easily," Lillith said while she led the group through the rabble that parted before them. Those who didn't move in time she violently flung aside with effortless ease—and only the stupid tried to get in her way or retaliate for any perceived slights. "I'm surprised it's an actual shortcut, though. Back when I did it in my youth, all I got for beating the second-floor boss was an enchanted compass. The deeper you go, the harder the fights get and the more energy you can absorb for your soul lattice, though, so this is far better a reward than usual."

"Sounds like the floor boss is also harder to beat this year . . ." Nora commented with a head bob from side to side. "Not sure what to think about that. I was counting on being carried by the rest of you absolute monsters; I'm the weak link here and am not sure how I can compare to something that is adjusted to your . . ."

Nora motioned to Riven, then Allie, then Retesh, and finally Lillith. "Adjusted to your potency, I suppose. I mean, come on. That's just not fair."

"You'll be fine!" Allie said, swinging an arm around Nora's neck and playfully nudging her side. "We'll keep the big baddies away from you!"

Nora rolled her eyes. "I'm being serious."

They continued walking through the darkness, and the faint echoes of chanting were soon heard. The chants became louder, the ruckus more obvious with the tunnels becoming more and more packed. And eventually, nearly an hour after having left the trading guild's commune, they arrived at their destination.

[Welcome to the Abyssal Descent's optional event: The Floor Two Boss. Observers are picked at random from the stands by Elysium for a chance at fighting their version of the Floor Two Boss. This year's challenge adapts to the challenging group. Current death rates this year are as follows: 39.8% of groups lose one to four members, while 22.2% of groups are wiped out entirely. Current prize for beating this challenge: a portal for the victorious group straight to Floor Twenty of the Abyssal Descent, cutting past all other mandatory floor bosses and challenges. Enter the arena to await your chance at being picked at your own peril. For those waiting and watching, your chance at being picked—though randomized—is increased the longer you stay. Violence while waiting is not permitted.]

Riven had thought that the arena in Gluttony's underground church was large, he'd thought that there were a lot of people for the games and public fights during his training sessions over the past months spent here, but this . . .

This was on an entirely different level.

The arena itself was built into a vast cavern system well over five miles across, and if not for his ascended body and eyesight, he'd not have been able to see the other end of the arena. Hundreds of thousands of spectators, possibly more, were lined up along various platforms all around the arena's perimeter where a spectral barrier enclosed the interior.

And looking down at the absolutely massive beast of a creature that was currently curb stomping the challenger team far down below, Riven couldn't help but be just a little bit intimidated. Because if THAT kind of custom-made floor boss was based on just a few ELITE-class participants, what was it going to look like when two Mythics, two Legendaries, and a couple of Elites walked into the arena later on?

The thought was not encouraging.

"Is this wise?" Riven asked, glancing Lillith's way skeptically.

The shadow demoness nodded, not looking back, but staring down at the massive behemoth ripping the enemies apart. "Yes, for two reasons. First is that we'll be bypassing a lot of other treacherous enemies by doing so. Doing this is arguably safer if your goal is to reach beyond all the other participants now here. Your Chalgathi quest demands you succeed here, does it not? To reach beyond any other and leave with a score that beats the last cycle's first-place contender?"

This time she did turn to him with a sad smile. "Secondly, we don't have much time. And I don't mean just because of your world quest."

There was a pause while the others all stared down at the unfolding fight.

"What exactly is that supposed to mean, Lillith? You've been a bit cryptic today," Riven asked bluntly. "What's the deal?"

Lillith's features wavered, then fell, as the ancient demoness folded her arms. "Let's just say that the Church of Gluttony won't be around to help us for much longer."

That comment caught Riven off guard. There were many implications of what she'd just said, and he scrutinized her thoroughly. Internally nudging Gluttony, he didn't get a response from the sin, either—despite knowing Gluttony was very aware of their current conversation.

"As I said before," Lillith eventually said with a dramatic groan that was very unlike her, pinching the bridge of her nose with one hand as if to ward off a headache. "It is a conversation for after we complete the descent. Until then, let us just focus on the here and now. After that, we'll have to have a very serious conversation about the events unfolding on our planet and in Elysium's greater multiverse as a whole. Things are changing, Riven. They're changing fast, in ways we don't yet understand, and no one really knows what to expect or when to expect it. But whatever it is, it isn't good—and there will likely be very long-lasting consequences in the power dynamics of our entire multiverse as we now know it. Long story short, we need to finish and get out of here as fast as possible, and then we need to attempt to finish all the world quests while conquering Panu as fast as possible. If we do that, we may be able to open the planet up to allies for immigration purposes. If we can't claim the planet by Elysium's standards by the time it all snaps into place, well . . . I'm not really sure what will happen."

It had been a while now since the vision of their mother had spoken to Riven, at least in Allie's opinion it had been. Certainly it'd been long enough for Riven to come to her about what needed to be said. And yet . . . he hadn't come to Allie about it. He hadn't reached out. He'd hidden the encounter away. Hadn't comforted her in their shared moment of grief. But she'd experienced it too, albeit as an observer instead of an active participant. Which is why it made it all the harder to struggle with. She had to go through this alone, knowing that their mother was actually still out there, and she didn't have the courage to bring it up.

Instead, a building resentment—rage, even—was forming in the core of her gut as the days dragged by. Riven was trying to hide this truth from her in some misguided attempt to protect her, but he didn't have the right. Allie deserved better. She didn't deserve to be lied to about something this important.

It wasn't his fucking place to do so. She wasn't a little kid he needed to look after any longer.

Allie's eyelids fluttered open, but the surroundings were unfamiliar. The air was thick with an oppressive heat, and the ground beneath her was scorched black, cracked like dried earth. Towering pillars of obsidian stretched into a teal sky littered with cracks of black like threads in a web, and the surfaces of the pillars were etched with glowing runes pulsating with malevolent energy.

She stood in the center of a vast arena, the remnants of battle scattered around her—broken weapons, shattered shields, and there was even a faint scent of sulfur in the air. Her heartbeat quickened. Where exactly was she?

"You're troubled," rumbled a voice from behind her.

Spinning around, Allie felt her breath caught in her throat. Emerging from the shadows was a massive lion, its body composed of swirling, ethereal purple flames and dark Sin energy. Its eyes gleamed with an ancient, predatory intelligence that was rather off-putting even for someone like her.

"Who are you?" Allie demanded, her voice steady despite the unease creeping up her spine. "And where am I?"

The lion's lips curled into a semblance of a smile. "I am a reflection of what stirs within you. A manifestation of the fury you suppress. As for where we are . . ."

There was a pause.

"This is a figment of your own mind. I am merely utilizing it. Now tell me . . . is that a burning rage I feel inside of you? Why is it directed at your brother?"

The question seemed to set off a hair-trigger, and despite feeling weird about this entire scenario—she couldn't help but want to answer the lion's question. Perhaps this was a dream, perhaps this was a vision, but Allie's internal check with a soul sweep revealed the lion's words to be true. She was within a figment of her own soul aperture right now, a manifestation she'd subconsciously made, so she should be safe here even if this entity had latched onto it as a bystander. There was even a chance that this creature was itself a figment of her own power, internalized and created to have something or someone to talk to in a moment of need.

It wasn't just possible, but it was even probable. Invading her own soul realm from external sources without her noticing would have been downright impossible for anyone here in the descent, bar none.

Allie's brows furrowed, and her fists clenched as she thought about the anger building up over Riven's recent betrayal. "I've been feeling . . . angry. My brother . . . he lied to me. Withheld information about someone close to both of us."

The lion raised one eyebrow, and crossed one paw over the other.

She hesitated, then scowled more deeply and shuddered. "Violent urges, thoughts of harming those I care about are starting to bubble up because of this resentment I'm feeling. But honestly it isn't just Riven . . . it's this entire situation!"

She threw her hands up in the air with a growl of frustration. "I want to see Lahn again! I hate that I can't just have a normal life! It makes me so, SO fucking ANGRY!"

She shouted the last word, wings spread out as the realm around them cracked under her rage as she finally let it all out. Everything cracked, that was, except for the lion itself.

"I hate feeling this way . . ." She whispered, bending down to kneel on the ground and placing her face in her hands. "I wish he'd just talk to me about Mom, but now . . . it feels like he's treating me like a child. That I'm too stupid or immature to have the privilege of knowing that she spoke with him."

There was yet another long pause.

The lion eventually stretched, got up, and stepped closer—its presence simultaneously overwhelming and soothing at the same time. It was . . . therapeutic to have someone to talk to about her rage, and the lion seemed more than happy to be there to listen.

"Anger is a force, a power. It resides within all beings, waiting to be acknowledged. You may hate it, or fear it, but if utilized properly . . . it is yours to command." The lion tilted its head, regarding her with a mixture of curiosity and amusement. "Though I'm more sure now than ever that you will follow that path in the end. It is even beginning to write itself upon the walls of your soul as we speak."

The lion gestured to the obelisks with glyphs and runes all around them, and it seemed to smile. "The question is not whether you will embrace it, but how you will wield it."

Allie clenched her fists, and the heat of the arena began to intensify as her anger rose. "I don't want to lose control. I feel like I could physically lash out at Riven for this and wouldn't regret it, and those feelings are dangerous. He's still my brother, and I still love him . . . even if he is an idiot."

"You won't lose control," the lion assured her. "Control is an illusion. Power is about surrendering to the force within, not suppressing it."

As the lion spoke, the runes on the pillars flared brighter, casting long, twisted shadows of Unholy across the ground. Allie felt a surge of energy within her, a primal force began to claw at her insides like the talons of some ancient predator.

"Remember this . . . from one being of darkness to another," the lion said as it began to dissolve into the swirling darkness, purple flames vanishing into an inky black. "Wrath is not chaos. It is purpose. It is justice. It is retribution. The very essence of your rage can be a power unto itself."

With those final words, the vision shattered like glass, and the sound of the air being sucked from her lungs accompanied the visual dispersion when she gasped. Allie was abruptly plunged into darkness, along with the memories of her recent conversation.

CHAPTER 25

[Group Number 4,828 has been picked for the next attempt at defeating Floor Two Boss. Remember that turns are randomized, but the longer you stay, the higher the chance of your group being picked. Your own group is registered as: Riven Thane, Lillith of the Black Skies, Allie Thane, Nora Lang, Retesh Vorath, and all associated minions.]

Coming to a platform's ledge on the right-hand side of the miles-wide enclosed arena, Riven and the rest of his group made camp, surrounded by the hundreds of high-end undead minions courtesy of Allie and Retesh as a buffer to all onlookers. Just because Elysium said, "Violence will not be permitted" while waiting, that didn't necessarily mean crazies wouldn't attempt it. Especially if those crazies were associated with Greed, given recent events. Riven didn't know what Elysium would do if someone tried to attack another participant in the waiting area, but he didn't want to take that chance.

The cliffs surrounding the interior of this underground arena were pressed up close to the large translucent, cylindrical energy shield that made up the battle-grounds. On their way around to find an unoccupied protruding platform, they watched the battles unfold. Large viewing rooms with rectangular windows were also cut into the cliff's interior, and tunnels and walkways made the entire thing look like an ant colony. Just like everywhere else on this floor, it was bustling with tradesmen, mercenaries looking to sell their talents to incomplete groups, and people sitting in meditative poses while trying to cultivate as best they could amid the madhouse of activity.

"Quite the drop down . . ." Riven mused, standing at the very edge of their platform with his hands clasped behind his back. An artificial orange sun glowed atop the cavern's ceiling, with artificial dust clouds and even an illusory red sky, while the battlefield shifted underneath them to rearrange itself for the sixth time since they'd entered this place. "When the system notification said it would adapt to the group, I hadn't originally thought it would change the scenery, too. I was only suspecting the boss itself would change."

Allie stood beside him, following his gaze as the group number 4,828 was teleported onto the field in a bubble of light. "Still scared of heights, are we?"

Riven scoffed. "Oh, shut up."

Allie chuckled. "Remember when Mom brought us to the Grand Canyon and you had to crawl across that—"

"It was six feet across!" Riven said, throwing up his arms with exaggerated flair. "And I was only a kid! You're never gonna let me live that down, are you?"

"Never," Allie said with a wink and a nudge. "But at least now we can both fly."

"True."

The roiling landscape continued to shift, but it began to slow down and solidify, and sandstone shelves started to appear as multilayered canyons set up in a circular ring formation that led down to a central sand pit. The five challengers, all of them obsidian-rock humanoids of some sort—set down on one end of the ringed arena at the third canyon layer up from the sand pit. They each had molten eyes, veins of magma running across their bodies, and large rock clubs for weapons. The sand pit itself was well over a mile wide, and the bubble of light surrounding the challenger group disappeared just as a rumbling sound started to echo out from the pit.

[Group Number 4,828's opponent has been chosen. They are pitted against: Myrandian, Flower of the Desert Storm. This level-200 Legendary opponent is a native to the dunes of planet Borishka in Universe 32, and has stagnated at attaining his soul-lattice insights to acquire the E-grade. This monster has accepted the pact with Elysium for a chance at enlightenment, choosing to serve as the optional floor boss and intending to eradicate these hellscape golem challengers from existence. Odds are four to three in favor of Group Number 4,828. If you wish to bet against Elysium's odds, you may do so by interacting with this message and putting up items or Elysium coins.]

"Oh yes!" Riven laughed, remembering how Elysium and Negrada had bet against one another when he'd fought the satyr warlord miniboss in Negrada's dungeon. Elysium appeared to be quite the gambling type, and Riven was all for it.

Putting up the ridiculous sum of 129 million Elysium coins on a single bet, he sat down cross-legged and propped his chin in his hands to watch the fight.

**[Your bet that Group Number 4,828 will lose has been documented
and 129 million Elysium coins have been deducted from your person. Should you win, you will receive 167.7 million Elysium coins. If
you do not wish to accept these rates, please decline now.]**

He'd always enjoyed casinos and accepted immediately, getting a laugh from
his sister.

Pulling out a bottle of spiced blood and some crackers, he began to enjoy his
snack and the view alongside friends and teammates. It was going to be a long
ride, and he might as well enjoy the show while he could.

Hopefully he wouldn't lose all his money in doing so.

Athela raised an eyebrow Narg's way from underneath her shadow-crafted hood,
ignoring the shouting and screaming Riven was doing as his money went up in
flames after his third consecutive bet loss. "And just what makes you think you're
up to standards to be my master's last minion?"

Azmoth nodded aggressively in agreement, arms folded while his flaming antlers gave the circle of four demons a faint orange glow.

Fay, on the other hand, was a little less antagonistic to the newcomer—and
she placed a slender hand on the beholder demon's green body in an act of encour-
agement. "Stop bullying him! He's just here to help!"

"Eyeball demons always harm us," Azmoth said with a pointed finger jabbed
in Narg's direction. "They mean! All beholders bad!"

"That, sir, is downright rude and racist! I am enraged!" Narg humphed, emphasizing his rage by enlarging himself like a puffer fish. The two normal eyes set
over his frowning, toothy mouth narrowed, and the eyeballs across his numerous
tentacles did the same one after the other. "I am a gentleman and a scholar! I will
not be treated in such a way for having done no wrong!"

Azmoth leaned forward, his body crackling with cinders in an attempt to
intimidate. "If you betray Riven, I smash and eat."

"Stop it!" Fay used her grimoire to smack Azmoth's pointed finger back, and
the young brutalisk retreated after her daggerlike glare set upon him. "You two
are out of line!"

Athela waved her hand back and forth in front of her face, sitting cross-legged
while continuing to ignore the cackling of Allie and Nora in the background as
Riven repeatedly cursed the people who'd recently died. "I'm not being mean.
I'm being practical. Riven deserves the best, and I feel like he's settled. I just want
to be proven wrong, so if Narg would so kindly put my worries to rest, I won't
have to tell Riven to get another model later on. What makes you better than the
millions of others out there, Narg?"

From the sidelines, Fimrindle snickered loudly.

"You got something to say, you metal beanpole?" Athela shot with a glare. "Spit it out!"

Fimrindle's jaw didn't move as the words came out of his mouth in a raspy gasp, making his speech look just as unnatural as it sounded. "You yourself were . . . not up to the standards you now tout . . . arachnid. If anything . . . the three of you have ridden on the coattails of your master's fate. It is . . . humorous . . . that you would judge the beholder so."

Athela gasped dramatically. "I've always been AMAZING!"

"No," Fimrindle said with a scoff. "You were just a tiny, weak spider . . . barely even a demon, but with a princess complex . . . and an inflated ego to match."

Athela whipped out both katanas from her chest in a flash of red and a palpable killing intent that boomed from her position. "SAY THAT AGAIN, TWERP!"

But Fimrindle had already vanished into thin air, leaving behind an echoing cackle that made Athela's arms shake in rage.

"He doesn't think I see him, but he's wrong. We'll see just who's the better assassin! I'm about to tear that cackling metal face off his—"

Athela's words were interrupted by Fay, who cleared her throat rather loudly.

"Sit down! You're being immature!" Fay commanded, pointing to the ground with a frosty stare. "Riven will NOT be happy with you if you start fighting Fimrindle over petty insults! And turn off your aura—your killing intent is leaking out for hundreds of yards!"

Fay bobbed her head in Riven's direction, where he, Nora, Lillith, and Allie were all staring directly at Athela with confused looks.

Athela abruptly sheathed her katanas, gave a winning, brilliant-white smile to Riven, and blew him a kiss before hopping to sit back down cross-legged as if nothing had ever happened.

Her master and the others went back to watching the next boss fight, and she let out a long huff of a sigh. Raising an eyebrow in Narg's direction while he remained in his puffer-fish state, she pawed at the air to get him to relax. "All right, all right. Maybe Fimrindle wasn't entirely wrong. Sorry. I'm just protective, is all, and I want to make sure that you're able to help Riven when he needs it. The three of us have already proven ourselves while traveling with him, and Lillith really kicked us into shape recently. I just don't want you, the new guy, to make the same mistakes we did."

"That's better." Fay nodded in approval, smiling.

Narg's numerous eyes blinked rapidly, and slowly he began to deflate with a wheeze of air like it was being let out of a balloon. Settling down in a lower floating position next to Fay, he grumbled something under his breath and evaluated the other demons one by one. "I see you're not quite the barbarian I'd assumed you were. Thank you for your apology."

"Azmoth never apologize!" the young brutalisk said with a scoff and puff of flames from deep within his throat. "Azmoth never wrong!"

Fay groaned and put her face in her hands while shaking her head. "I'm so sorry, Narg. This is not the kind of welcome you should be getting from us. I, for one, am very happy to have you on our team, and I hope you can do your best to keep Riven safe with us."

Two days passed, and they still remained on the ledge watching battle after battle.

"I believe it would be in your best interest to keep collecting rare specimens such as these on the way down," Lillith said, shoving some more sin-oriented crystals that grew here in the abyss into Riven's bag. "They'll be needed in the future, and our trek will be the perfect opportunity to grab some to take back to Panu."

Her voice was sad, even tired, as she'd been the least interested in the ongoing battles. Ever since she'd initially brought up how the Church of Gluttony wouldn't be around in the future, and had failed to expand upon it, she'd seemed downright depressed.

Nothing Riven did seemed to sway her on her decision not to talk about it, either. She'd been adamant that they finish the Abyssal Descent before further discussion. Interestingly enough, she'd also been adamant that they spend most or all of their Elysium coins while staying here. She'd even bet a few times herself, using all her money to make gains before going around and seeing what other groups had to offer and then making astronomically expensive purchases of the very best Dao treasures, mostly including plants and spiritual crystals that could be grown in Riven's garden back home.

She even mentioned that she wished she could take some of the greater treasures from beyond this realm or Panu, but the system wouldn't allow such things until Panu was conquered—if it ever was. Until then, or until the five-year time limit came due, Panu was mostly sealed off from the outside multiverse, with only a few exceptions. Letting in monumental Dao treasures in the S-grade from Gluttony's vaults off-world was not one of those exceptions.

"If you change your mind and want to talk, let me know," Riven said, hesitating before putting an encouraging hand on Lillith's shoulder. "I'm sorry for whatever troubles you."

She gave him a sad smile, then nodded and sat down again next to him. "Thank you. Now, what have I missed in my time bartering?"

Riven's eyebrow raised, and he turned his attention back to the arena far below. This time, the setting was that of a black lake with a titanic, crablike creature that was striking at a group of four greater harpies and a fallen angel. They rained arrows of hellfire down on the crab's chitin while it sprayed black bullets from its maw or used brutal melee attacks infused with some kind of Unholy energy variation. Explosions rocked the artificial lake, and the miles-wide cylindrical cage enclosing the arena shook when one of the harpies was crushed against the outer rim.

Riven winced. "Well, not much. There've been only three squad wipes, so most of the time the monsters lose. When performing well, the teams also have been getting additional prizes, aside from the portal access to the twentieth floor, in the form of treasure chests."

"Any other type of fights? Was it just monsters?"

Riven shook his head. "No, there were two others. One boss fight was against another pretty powerful undead participant who'd already made it to level 43 of the Abyssal Descent, but he'd transgressed against the system somehow and was brought up for judgment. If he'd won, he'd be put back, but he was killed along with his team members. The other was a fight against the environment, believe it or not. The team all had to stabilize rifts in the void where Holy energy was breaking through to kill them—and they had to do it in a pattern or the rifts would grow larger. They had to last for ten minutes, and they only barely succeeded with two losses. It was sort of confusing, and I really didn't understand it because Athela kept trying to get freaky."

"Ah, to be young and in love." Lillith chuckled with true amusement for the first time in a while. "The three of you are cute."

"Thanks." Riven scratched the back of his neck with an embarrassed look. "They're pretty great. And they've been expanding their own relationship quite a bit. Did you know they've been going on dates with each other for 'girl time'?"

"I hadn't realized that."

"Yup. I'm glad to see it. I hadn't wanted this to be a . . . How do I put it? Eh. I want them to reciprocate with each other the same way they reciprocate with me so that no one feels left out."

Lillith didn't get the chance to reply when a shuddering boom caused the arena to shake after the giant crab exploded in a mess of body parts. The fallen angel that'd destroyed it raised himself up out of the monster's body with a roar of triumph, and the angel's greater harpy comrades rushed down with shouts of their own to greet his success enthusiastically.

A shimmering black and purple chest appeared on the monster's body next, created from abyssal energies that oozed with sin. A portal ripped open in space beside it, too, and soon the party of five left injured but all alive through the portal to access the twentieth abyssal floor.

[Your group has been chosen as the next up to fight Floor Two Boss. You have been selected for a unique boss fight experience given your composition. Are you ready to proceed? If not, another team will be selected.]

Riven exchanged glances with Lillith and then the others. Fay was woken up by Athela, Azmoth stopped playing chess with Nora, and Narg shut down his discussion with Fimrindle to float forward in Riven's direction.

Adjusting her bone pauldron, Allie picked up her Divine-ranked claymore and hoisted it over her shoulder with a grin. "It's about damn time! Everyone here?"

"Everyone's here," Riven said, holding out a hand as Jackal rose off the ground to come to his palm. Wrapping his fingers around the shaft and inspecting the fiery eyes of the skull at its head, he made sure he had all their attention. "Is there any reason we should decline? I assume we're all ready?"

No one said otherwise, and Riven acknowledged the prompt with a "Yes, we're ready."

[Please wait. Your group is being transported now.]

A flash enveloped him, and Riven was ripped through space to appear in a floating bubble of light like so many others had been as the arena was rearranged.

And it was certainly changing fast.

Blue skies lit up the interior of the battlefield with puffy white clouds partially masking a false yellow sun, reminiscent of Earth. The ground rumbled as slabs of white stone sprouted up, with plants growing at a rapid pace to create a jungle environment very reminiscent of the Zhangjiajie National Forest in China.

Not that he'd ever been there, but he'd certainly seen pictures of it.

Between the tall pillars and the lush canopy of forest, it was quite breathtaking, even though he knew it to be fake.

But when he turned around to say something about it to his comrades, he found that they weren't there.

They were gone.

He was alone.

Confused, and looking around almost frantically, he finally found them.

He managed to spy the others in a separate bubble about a mile away. It was a far larger bubble than his own, encompassing the hundreds of undead that'd been risen after the battle between the churches of Gluttony and Greed on the first-floor abyssal city, but Riven was sure it was them even at this distance after spying Azmoth's flaming antlers amid the mass of bodies.

"Well, this is weird. I haven't seen this happen before."

The bubbles settled on opposite hills overlooking the jungle canopy in between the white pillars, each reaching many thousands of feet up into the air until they reached the clouds. The jeers and cheers of the crowds couldn't be heard within the cylindrical energy barrier encompassing them, and he couldn't even see the onlookers anymore now that he was in the arena. At most, he could only see the

barrier itself—which had an illusion built into it, making it look like he was seeing out into a horizon.

The bubble popped, and he was set facing his friends, feeling frazzled, gripping Jackal in one hand as the maw across Messenger's chest began to growl. And
just before he started to make his way toward them, a new notification appeared
to signify just what was going on.

[Team Number 9,877 has entered the arena. Due to unique composition and circumstances, Elysium has designated this Floor Two Boss
fight differently.
Lillith of the Black Skies has been banished to the fiftieth floor of the
Abyssal Descent due to having already completed this event in another
age, and she will remain trapped there unless freed by her teammates.
Let this be a lesson to those who attempt to take advantage of Elysium's
goodwill. This event is not meant to be repeated.
Team One of this Floor Two Boss Fight is as follows: Riven Thane,
reincarnation of Gluttony.
Team Two of this Floor Two Boss Fight is as follows: Allie Thane,
Nora Lang, Retesh Vorath, and all minions—including Riven
Thane's own.
Team Two has been mind-controlled by Elysium. If Riven Thane of
Team One defeats Team Two by killing all his teammates, they will be
resurrected and will be able to pass on to Floor Twenty as promised. If
Team Two kills the reincarnation of Gluttony, he will be removed
from the Abyssal Descent per the contract of Chalgathi's quest line—
but he will also receive a penalty of fifty levels and a mandatory, per-
manent removal of Gluttony from Riven as the reincarnation host.
Odds are three to five in favor of Team Two. If you wish to bet against
Elysium's odds, you may do so by interacting with this message and
putting up items or Elysium coins.]

[Your Floor Two Boss Fight has begun.]

Riven's eyes widened in shock, and his gaze slowly lifted to where an army of
undead were all sprinting or flying across the gap between them at incredible
speed—with Azmoth charging at their front in a maddened explosion of flame.
Riven saw Fimrindle and Athela blur into the shadows next, followed quickly by
Nora and a barrage of Unholy energies ripping from the opposite hillside where
Retesh had summoned a swarm of green energies to shoot directly at Riven's position. Only a split second later, the hill vanished when Fay raised her hands, as
she'd no doubt cast an illusion to hide the spellcasters across from him.

The thing that caught Riven's attention most, though, was the eruption of Death-attuned energies as Allie launched herself into the sky with a swarm of wraiths tearing out from her body. Her black wings glistened, her halo shone like the impending judgment of a god of death, and her glowing gray eyes stared blankly at him as she lifted her hand. A storm of flaming skulls began blooming around her only seconds later. Together, the laughing skulls created a cyclone of sonic booms as they each broke the sound barrier to rip through the air toward him.

The fight was already on, and this one wasn't going to be easy.

"Shit."

CHAPTER 26

Riven's body exploded backward as Blessing of the Crow engulfed him, wrapping him in a shroud of black and red wisps akin to a bloody phantom, and the ground underneath him erupted as his soul pillars went into overdrive.

Despite the team he was facing, he could not falter. Losing was not an option, and though he hated to harm his friends and family, they would not be permanently affected by the beatdown he was about to hand out.

Assuming he won, that was. Which, honestly enough, wasn't a certainty. Judging by Elysium's betting odds, he was the one who was more likely to lose.

CRASH

The barrage of Allie's flaming skulls and Retesh's bombardment of oozing green mana joined together seconds later—causing the jungle-laden hillside he'd been on only moments before to shatter in flame and hissing rubble. The horde of enemies led by Azmoth was quickly approaching, and Riven went full tilt with all the available mana currently built up in his staff with one of its abilities.

[Furious Storm: This staff can passively build up charges of Furious Storm, which utilizes a supercharged dose of any single energy from the pillars of Sin, Unholy, Shadow, Death, Blood, and Infernal. You may only unleash one type of energy at a time. Power of Furious Storm depends on the amount of charge emitted.]

The skull face of the staff opened wide and the pentagram in its center turned black before unleashing a swath of piercing shadows that crashed into the oncoming tide.

Due to their extremely high quality, built from the F- and E-grade elites of the multiverse, only a couple dozen of the undead died instantly. Others lost limbs as piercing streaks of darkness tore flesh from bone and cut cleanly through their mindless bodies. Azmoth himself deflected much of the attack with a snarl, Shengari

Shields snapping in front of his body while a dome of fire took form around him a second later. The remnant shadow energy also cast a cloud of darkness over the battlefield, shifting in and out like mist across the jungle and great stone pillars alike.

"LITTLE RIVEN WILL DIE, DIE, DIE!" Azmoth screamed uncharacteristically from the cloud of black that concealed the land-bound combatants, and he belched great swaths of flame to burn away the mana-bound shadows. "COME AND FIGHT ME, PUNY VAMPIRE!"

CRUNCH-CRUNCH-CRUNCH-CRUNCH-CRUNCH!

Five rapid Snipe-enhanced Blood Lances smashed into Azmoth's body, causing him to flip backward with a scream of pain while other Blood Lances tore holes through the oncoming rush of undead bodies like scissors through paper.

Riven didn't smile, didn't laugh, as his vision centered on Azmoth's bleeding form. It wasn't nearly enough to kill the demon just yet, and the damage was minimal due to his naturally armored body, but—

He paused when one of the recurrent discharging pulses of energy he was releasing came back positive for movement on his left side.

Riven blurred left, narrowly dodging a large scythe that'd almost taken his head clean off before kicking off the ground to send himself backward.

Evade, place distance, and decimate.

Wretched Snares tore off his outstretched hand like serpents, forming nets that sought to capture and contain the reaper—but Fimrindle was far too fast for that. The assassin cackled, dodged, and vanished, reappearing behind Riven—only for dozens of crimson spires to shoot up out of the ground. One Crimson Ice spire deflected the reaper's attack, three more went in for a killing blow, and others were bursting around them for hundreds of yards in anticipation of Fimrindle's evading move.

The reaper hissed and retracted his strike, flipping backward with an Unholy slash directed Riven's way. The magical slash projection bought Fimrindle time for a tactical retreat, weaving through the minefield of seeking bloody spikes— only for him to be caught off guard when Riven clenched his fist.

BOOM

The spires abruptly exploded, creating a vast area-of-effect zone with shrapnel heading in every direction imaginable. It was like watching a nuke full of red paint go off with the spires shattering into hundreds, then thousands, then millions of tiny, sharp projectiles that flashed at supersonic speeds to incorporate a mile-wide area.

The only area spared was Riven's direct position, where the bloody shards soaked through his armor and into his skin to refeed his mana pool rather than doing him any actual damage. They were merely coming home for recycling.

"AHHHHHHH!!!" Athela's feminine screech made Riven's heart clench as she was ripped out of stealth only a couple dozen yards away, her humanoid figure being turned into a pincushion.

Fimrindle had fared somewhat better than her, using his Unholy/Machine Tier-3 ability Anticipate Movements to dodge nearly 90 percent of the millions of shards meant to flush him out. But he couldn't dodge all of them. A few more undead on the outskirts of the explosion were evaporated into pink mists, Allie was repelled from a dive midair, and Narg had erected barriers of flame and shadow to deflect—

Riven's foot landed on an invisible Curse Trap placed by Fay.

"SHIT!"

He was sent sprawling, Messenger's armor holding strong, but he felt a few of the bones in his foot shatter before he landed on yet ANOTHER Curse Trap.

He staggered out of a roll, blood leaking down his forehead where Fay's curse energies had torn off flesh from his skull before his regeneration rapidly repaired it. Yet he didn't have time to dawdle.

Riven needed to utilize as much area-of-effect magic as possible to take out the assassins. With them in the picture, he wouldn't be able to focus on the others, and—

Another pulse of energy sensed a stealthed figure coming in from behind, and he launched himself off the ground and into flight just before Nora's twin blades impaled him.

She swore, then retreated into thin air.

Putting distance between himself and Team Two while evading and returning fire was something of a nightmare for Riven, as it became a game of cat and mouse—but there were far more cats, and he was doubtless the mouse.

He couldn't be caught, and if he was, it was over.

Riven's body ripped through the air like a bullet, sending shock waves through the burning jungle and towering pillars of stone. Hissing trails of blood, screaming undead attempting to catch him over land and sky, and innumerable magics exploding all around him were now the norm as he zigzagged and riftwalked constantly while letting out surgical strikes whenever an opportunity arose. Neither side had gained much ground, although a good number of the mindless undead had been eradicated, and they'd reached something of a stalemate. That stalemate could end poorly for him in an instant if he let up, though, and he silently thanked Jackal numerous times for the 600 percent mana regeneration his staff now gave him.

Allie was in hot pursuit in the sky and the assassins were regularly attempting to strike at him in bursts, while the beholder demon Narg tried to snipe him out of the sky using Unholy Globspitters and Infernal Hellspitters, which were on par with his own Blood Lances in terms of speed and range. Whenever Riven tried to riftwalk away and hide, the damn beholder demon used his seeking abilities to quickly locate his position.

And it made Riven realize that, in the future, Narg would probably be a great way to sniff out potential assassins by utilizing Seek Danger, just as he probably was doing right now. That, or Narg had locked on to one of Riven's items with Seek Item.

Fay was coming in and out of invisibility to cast supporting spells on Allie from time to time. The succubus was also doing a good job of hiding the assassins even more, misdirecting Riven whenever he attempted to retaliate against Retesh, who was unleashing a constant barrage of green orbs from the ground. Whenever he clashed with Allie, even if he came out on top, Fay would then heal the fallen angel's wounds and the pursuit would ensue again. Azmoth had resorted to using his Propulsion ability to try and catch Riven, but without wings or a true flying ability, it didn't compare to Messenger's Quickening Flight.

It truly was a shitshow, and he was having a hard time holding on, even with Gluttony's purple third eye giving him additional feedback on when and how to dodge.

His totems were also doing quite well in supporting his attempts at negating enemy attacks. The four orbiting totems were creating barriers of Crimson Ice, blasting other projectiles out of the sky with high-velocity Black Lightning, and even creating occasional rifts to swallow and redirect incoming attacks when the ice shields were temporarily destroyed. The totems were in fact a huge asset to his struggle, as they autonomously nullified nearly half of the enemy's firepower and only required a small amount of constant mana channeling to keep them active after their initial reserves were snuffed out.

[Hive Totems of Bloodforged Rift Sparks (Lesser Artifact, Elite Tier, Level-6 Totem Swarm): These totems come as a set, and new totems can be added to this number at the additional cost of Willpower—with each totem adding exponentially more Willpower to the cost. Cost of Willpower is based upon attitude toward the wielder of this totem set, as well as current combat level. Current requirements: 119 Willpower, Blood subpillar, Shadow subpillar. Bound to Riven Thane.
Adding different types of totems will change the name and description of this totem set.

Current totems in Hive Swarm:

- **Four totems of Bloodforged Rift Sparks**
- **The Path of Red and Black has been imbued into these totems, along with numerous different sigils, and the creator has used the blood of an ancient avatar of original sin to fuel their growth. These totems have the ability to grow and level up but diminish in level each time one is destroyed. This totem swarm can currently perform the following abilities:**

- **Black Lightning**
- **Crimson Ice**
- **Rift]**

He wanted to draw this out as much as possible and wear them down while looking for opportunities to unload on anyone who made a mistake, as he was probably the most evasive person on their team outside of Lillith, given his ability to teleport and fly and his speed-amplifying blessing. Riven also had a few trump cards he had yet to pull, though. He was waiting to use said cards when he felt like they had a good chance of success—specifically, if he was able to lock down one or two of the assassins, he'd go in for the kill. He had yet to change into his ultimate demonic form via Gluttony's Aspect of Demonic Heritage, as it only lasted for a single minute. He also hadn't summoned his Legionaries of the Blood God yet, which if applied appropriately would probably be enough to take out at least one of the major players on the enemy side.

[Gluttony's Aspect of Demonic Heritage (Sin) (Tier 3): A martial art that enhances you through the power of your fully formed Mark of the Sinner. Your body merges with your soul clone for one minute, allowing you to take on an ultimate demonic form as an aspect of the great maw. Very long cooldown, which can be reduced by killing and eating others.]

[Legionaries of the Blood God (Death/Blood) (Tier 2): This is a temporary summoning spell that does not require minion slots. You may summon eight Elite-class Bloodstricken Undead from the Blood God's realm, equal in combat level to your own, and may designate whether or not you wish to summon Blood Knights, Blood Sorcerers, Blood Assassins, or a combination of the three when you do so. Undead are nonsentient and last for five minutes before disappearing. One-day cooldown time. Very high mana cost.]

Unfortunately, true opportunities to strike back safely were few and far between, and he was reminded of this when he whirled midair to unleash an arc of Black Lightning toward Allie—only to give the beholder demon Narg an opportunity to snipe him from behind.

CRACK

He was sent spinning as the flaming bolt smashed into his back, just barely bypassing the totem defenses and making a clean hit. The crackling lightning from his staff went off to the side and missed Allie entirely, and she pumped power into her wings for a dive with a shrill cry of glee.

Her Divine claymore came down with a two-handed swing, smashing through barriers of red ice summoned from his totems, and collided with Jackal in a thundering crash. Riven was sent spiraling downward at tremendous speed, causing the ground to quake with his impact as earth around him exploded to form a crater under his body.

He coughed blood into Messenger's mask, and the armor set's jaws opened to unleash a swarm of gluttonous tendrils that intercepted Nora when she went in for the kill.

The assassin screamed as her arms were brutally ripped off, only for her head to follow when the black tendrils infused with sin rapidly constricted and crushed her body in numerous places. It was like squeezing a grape, but she was quickly followed by Azmoth and half a dozen undead that barreled into the large crater with weapons raised.

Riven didn't have a choice. His ribs were crushed, flaring with pain, and he was having a hard time breathing even with his vampiric regeneration working overtime due to the remnant Death energies Allie's attack had left when their weapons connected.

He raised his hand with a quick set of gestures, and just before Azmoth came within melee distance, eight flashes of light illuminated the crater around him.

Eight hooded skulls etched with crimson runes on their foreheads stared, their skull sockets glowing crimson. Six were heavily armored with red claymores and thick red plate mail. The other two held thin, wicked daggers dripping blood mana in each hand and were strapped in red leathers.

[Summoned Blood Knight, Bloodstricken Undead, Level 200 ELITE]
[Summoned Blood Knight, Bloodstricken Undead, Level 200 ELITE]
[Summoned Blood Knight, Bloodstricken Undead, Level 200 ELITE]
[Summoned Blood Knight, Bloodstricken Undead, Level 200 ELITE]
[Summoned Blood Knight, Bloodstricken Undead, Level 200 ELITE]
[Summoned Blood Knight, Bloodstricken Undead, Level 200 ELITE]
[Summoned Blood Assassin, Bloodstricken Undead, Level 200 ELITE]
[Summoned Blood Assassin, Bloodstricken Undead, Level 200 ELITE]

The knights raised their weapons and rushed to meet the oncoming enemies with an eerie silence. The sound of Azmoth and the undead smashing together was joined by another thunderous crash as fire and death met blood, and the crater became an outright melee as more and more of the undead rushed in to be cut down. One blood knight fell to Azmoth's Shengari Shields and brute strength, another hamstrung Azmoth before being piled on by oversize zombie gargoyles that bit and clawed. Radiant crimson slashes arced out and through lines of enemies, while flame exploded from the brutalisk and Death energies knitted parts of the zombies back together at intense speeds.

CHINGGGGGGggggggg

Athela screeched in outrage when she appeared out of a flying stream of blood, her red katanas intercepted by the stoic blood assassin as the rune on its forehead glowed brighter.

"You are in my way!!!" Athela hissed, six arachnid blades coming out of her back. "And you will be removed! He won't tell you this, BUT RIVEN LIKES TO BE IMPALED ANYWAYS! JUST LET IT HAPPEN!"

Riven could barely avoid rolling his eyes. Even when mind-controlled, Athela was ridiculous.

The assassins blurred, the second blood assassin intercepting Fimrindle next. Unlike Athela, Fimrindle managed to bypass the blood assassin and go in for the main target after a quick blink of motion—and his clawed metal hand reached out. Engulfed in death mana, Fimrindle tried to take hold of Riven's soul to forcibly rip it out—but was rebuffed when Riven managed to gain his bearings and send a shock wave of Storm Razors in all directions.

Spinning black and red blades created from shadow and blood erupted from the epicenter of the crater, avoiding Riven's summoned blood knights and assassins while homing in on anyone he considered an enemy. The air hissed and space itself tore with the whirlwind of radiating power as they cut, pursued, and exploded into shrapnel by the thousands—peeling off his body while his Path of Red and Black made his two pillars go into overdrive.

The ground around him was flung back, carved asunder to create tidal waves of earth that peeled up with the massive onset of thousands of tearing blades that left ribbons of ominous light behind them.

Jackal crackled in his grip, and Riven looked down in dismay when he saw there was a large crack in the shaft of his weapon where Allie's Divine claymore had struck it. His weapon had held firm, and even now Allie hadn't come back from where she'd been flung due to the rebound effect after the collision, but if he continued to use Jackal now, it very well might break.

"Come out, Jackal. And should you be banished, return to the bag. You will not die here."

Without a word, Jackal sent him a mental nudge of affirmation—and the weapon began to change. It was the first time Riven had used the weapon like this since its evolution, and he was interested to see just what it looked like.

He was not disappointed.

**[Abyssal Beastform: This weapon can turn into an Abyssal Canine
Warbeast and does passive Sin damage on strike. This form is offensively compatible, but your weapon will automatically revert to staff
form upon taking damage equal to 20% of your maximum health.]**

The staff contracted into a sphere of multicolored light before expanding rapidly with a feral roar from within the mass of magic. A canine form appeared, the
size of a small house. Four clawed limbs sprouted, with each claw as big as Riven's
body and radiating dark purple energies. Darkness coated its hide, similar to how
Lillith herself presented, with large purple spikes down its spine that continued
along the abnormally long tail it doubtless would use as a weapon. Vibrant purple
eyes glared back at Riven from where the beast was forming, and a ferocious maw
filled with black teeth that radiated sin smiled back at him.

It was a gigantic, winged hound, and it spread its draconic black wings out to
either side before whipping around to face Azmoth with a snarl.

The brutalisk was too busy fighting two of the blood knights to notice, and
when Azmoth finally did notice, it was already too late.

"RRRRAAAAAAAAAAHHHHH!!!"

Azmoth roared defiantly to the end, clawing madly and tearing back at Jackal's
larger body as the hound pinned the already-injured demon. Large claymores
stabbed and crashed into Azmoth's armor, beating him down until there was an
audible crunch, a snap, and a yank.

The fires of Azmoth's body died down to cinders, his claws still embedded in
Jackal's forelegs while the canine flared its wings and swallowed Azmoth's head
with a gulp.

Athela didn't know WHY she needed to kill Riven, but the compulsion was too
strong to resist. Despite conflicting emotions sometimes causing her to pull back
from otherwise open opportunities to kill, the lack of willpower to follow through
with the fight hindered her ability to succeed time and time again.

She knew she loved him. She knew she didn't want to hurt him. But she also
knew she had to.

It wasn't a choice.

It was a compulsion, an absolute commandment from existence. She needed
to kill her lover.

Her eyes glazed over for nearly the twentieth time since the fight had begun as
the compulsions battled her innate desires down yet again. Yanking her katanas out
of the blood assassin's skull and stepping on its head to crunch the abysmal, unthink-
ing thing beneath her, she watched Riven's other blood warriors tear through the
ranks of Retesh's and Allie's undead like they were grass beneath a lawn mower.

She smirked, remembering the time Riven had told her about lawn mowers. Why anyone would devise something so utterly useless was beyond her, but that smirk quickly faded as Elysium's will pressed down upon her mind.

Her right hand twitched, her arachnid blades lifted, and she started forward again—only to pause wide-eyed when Riven's aura soared in conjunction with another.

Death rained from the sky when Allie finally reclaimed the fight, and the fallen angel's descent was like a comet of doom that shattered the world. The blinding power erupting from death energies meeting a vortex of blood was like watching two gods battle, and the space around them was warped due to their auras of bloodlust as Riven finally turned off his emotional switch.

For he too had been holding back to an extent, whether or not he'd realized it, and now he had no choice but to go all out.

The air split, and a black rift as big as a castle opened up to suck in Allie's power while Riven's own storm of blood frost raced around the sides to push against Allie's gray cloud of true death. Souls screamed in denial and pushed back against Riven's rebuttal, and the physically manifested auras of energy braced while eating at each other. Riven was without doubt the one with more mana supply, and his rift was greedily swallowing Allie's aura every second— but Allie wasn't giving in, and her own path of True Death superseded Riven's own Path of Black and Red. It wasn't by much, but it was enough that their force of wills had reached a stalemate that continued to wreak havoc in the local vicinity with sparks and explosions constantly going off in the zone of colliding intents.

One thing was certain: Despite Athela's impulse to kill Riven, she was also well aware she wouldn't be able to do so if she was dead.

Turning to run, she used all her dexterity to race backward through the jungle at blinding speeds—before a crack of thunder nearly caused her eardrums to burst and the entire miles-wide arena went bright white as the two auras completely collapsed.

BOOM

Athela was thrown head over heels, spinning as an apocalyptic strike caused the ground to peel up in all directions like when peeling an orange. The jungle was flung skyward in sprays of debris all the way up to the ceiling; stone pillars throughout the forest shattered and turned to dust. She felt pieces of her skin rot away and peel off, and the world around her was a spinning mess of motion until she abruptly slammed into the far wall of the barrier encircling the battle well over a mile away.

Her skull was shattered, her mind went dark, and then—a moment later— she felt herself spawn a new body.

[Your Gluttonous Arshakai form has been killed. You have been forc-ibly rotated to your next form, Gluttonous Fae Drider. Should all three of your forms be defeated, you will die.]

[Your first form's defeat has been counted by Elysium as a strike in this event. Mind control has been redacted.]

CHAPTER 27

Crashing to the ground, Athela groaned, clutching her head when all eight of her enormous white spider legs sank into the decimated landscape. The air was so thick with dust and mana that it was hard to get ahold of just what was going on, and she had a killer headache—but her mind cleared over the coming seconds as her eyes widened.

She'd been attacking Riven.

What the hell?!

Surprise turned to horror, and horror turned to panic when she realized what losing would mean to Riven's future. That was something she could not allow, and he was easily on the back foot even after killing Azmoth, Nora, and the majority of the undead sent after him by the two necromancy specialists. Narg, Fimrindle, Allie, Fay, and Retesh were still out there—with Riven desperately trying to keep Allie at bay while the others supported her. Since her transformation into an angel of death, Allie was incredibly powerful—possibly even Riven's equal.

. . .

Nah, not quite that powerful. But almost, and when combined with all the minions . . . it wasn't looking good.

He'd played his cards well so far by kiting the rest of them and not making a true stand, but if things didn't change, it was only a matter of time before he lost. Eventually they'd catch him, and even through the haze Athela could see Retesh's continued bombardment of green globes soaring across the sky while the lich cackled like a madman.

That's where she would go first. Fay was likely there, too, if she wasn't supporting Allie directly, and both would be easy, quick kills if they didn't suspect Athela had turned on them.

And when she rushed ahead, following the trails of green lighting up the sky as distant explosions echoed throughout the swirling dust storm, she quickly found her first targets. Sitting on the hill right where they'd all originally started was the laughing lich—and the succubus next to him. Fay was in a meditative state, maintaining an illusion around the two meant only for Riven's mind to see, while she continued to layer invisible traps around Riven's position.

Athela's eyes trailed down to the succubus's chest. Fay looked absolutely stunning sitting like that, her long white hair trailing past her big breasts—

Athela slapped herself in the face. "Get ahold of yourself, you horny spider!"

Shaking her head and feeling slightly guilty about what she was about to do, she sighed and stomped up the hill toward them with a determined expression.

"Athela!" Retesh called out gleefully, raising his bone staff as the orb atop it flared with neon-teal light. "Are you coming back for a break?! We have him on the ropes!"

Fay looked up, too, smiling pleasantly Athela's way. "Oh, hello! I thought you'd be trying to stab him from behind like you sneaks usually do. Why are you back here with us? And why are you in that body?"

"Surely you won't be able to assassinate him while in that form. You know he's weak to assassins. There's no reason to change course," Retesh agreed with the clattering of bones as his staff made repetitive motions in the air while summoning clouds of plague across the battlefield in Riven's direction. "Or have you truly given up on that tactic? Fimrindle is going to rub it in if he's the one that—"

CRUNCH

Athela's leg came down on the lich, smashing his frail body with a single, brutal strike. Despite the lich being on the leaderboard, he was a glass cannon that hid behind his summons, and she was a Panu World Boss with an insane strength amplifier in this form.

Fay looked stunned, staring wide-eyed at the obliterated lich with an open mouth and furrowed brows. "ATHELA! WHY?! WHAT ARE—UGH!!!"

Athela picked up the succubus with one of her giant clawed hands.

Gripping her lover around the waist, Athela frowned and brought Fay to eye level—ignoring the cursing and small hands beating against her snow-white skin. The four red eyes of the huge drider narrowed to glance down at Fay's chest again with a smirk, and she cocked her head to one side while evaluating her girlfriend— er, her prey.

"Unlike the last time, do know that this isn't anything personal. I don't WANT to do this . . ." Athela muttered as Fay cried out, growing fearful and struggling against the giant grip. Then Athela smirked—and leaned in to give Fay a quick kiss and a wink. "But I can't say it doesn't turn me on to hold you against your will . . . We're going to have to try that BDSM stuff Riven was talking about soon. This is kind of kinky."

Fay was flushed with anger, and a little bit of embarrassment, as she venomously pointed a quivering finger in the larger demon's direction. "ATHELA, YOU DIRTY WHORE! PUT ME DOWN! PUT ME DOWN RIGHT—"

With her other hand, Athela's claws twisted Fay's head—snapping her beautiful neck and mercifully killing the succubus instantly.

Reverently setting her body on the hillside next to the shattered pile of bones, and using her ice magic to seal the bones in place just in case Retesh had some kind of lich revival powers—Athela regretfully stomped off into the maelstrom of wind, dirt, and rampant mana.

She had a scythe-wielding little bitch to kill, and it'd been a long time coming.

Jackal hadn't lasted long after killing Azmoth, falling to Fimrindle's scythe only minutes later. The canine had battled ferociously, but the reaper was just an opponent too far above the living weapon that'd truthfully not had any real experience using its new body until now. Jackal had then reverted to a staff and was in an even worse state than before transforming. It was, in fact, almost shattered at the midshaft and had cracks spreading all along its body—so Riven was forced to withdraw it from the battle entirely and place it back in his spatial sack.

Riven's other temporary summons were dead, too, all the blood knights and assassins having been wiped out one by one until only a single knight had been left—before it too had disappeared after the five-minute timer on the summoning spell expired. Two of his four totems were wiped out and shattered, while the other two had been withdrawn as well due to the severe damage they'd taken.

Only Messenger remained on his side; though the armor itself had taken quite a beating, it remained active in its pursuit to swallow incoming spells or attack his enemies with the tendrils from its central maw. This was particularly helpful against Fimrindle, who'd been the one to destroy Riven's totems and most of his summons in quick hit-and-runs while Allie focused on Riven himself.

Despite all this, and despite things not looking good, Riven wasn't out of the fight yet.

Blood coated Riven's arm as he shot skyward, and his vision zoomed forward to unleash the Blood Lance with a flash of red light. The Snipe-empowered Blood Lance cut across the sky and smashed into another of Narg's barriers, only for the next one to cut cleanly through and skewer the beholder demon's body all the way out the other side.

Blood and guts flew out and the beholder seemed to explode in viscera, ending the relentless long-ranged attacks it'd been flinging at him this entire time, much to Riven's building irritation.

"God, that guy is annoying to fight against!" Riven muttered, cutting through the sky and narrowly dodging another sword swipe from Allie while she beat her wings ever faster in an attempt to cut him down. "AND YOU CAN JUST FUCK OFF, ALLIE! GODDAMN IT, GIVE ME A BREAK ALREADY!"

Allie merely cackled from underneath her bone helmet, and the chase intensified.

"I will activate the transition to our ultimate form when needed. We only have one shot at using it, and it will only last a minute, so keep it up. You're doing very well," Gluttony whispered within Riven's mind, and clouds of ravenous insects were unleashed from a hundred black maws that appeared all around them— swarming toward Allie, only to be met with an equivalent swarm of wraiths, ghosts, and spirits.

The sin-afflicted beetles crashed into the souls of the dead and were neutralized, neither side giving way as the chase persisted through the sea of writhing sands and unstable energies. Lightning flickered randomly through the arena, created by uncontrolled power that'd begun to build up in the environment like a soda-can waiting to pop.

Yet, Riven suddenly realized there were no more exploding green orbs or plague mists being flung in his direction.

Was Retesh building up some other kind of spell?

If he was, Riven wouldn't be able to find it very well anyways, given Fay's illusions.

Clicking his tongue and speeding underneath a collapsing pillar, he rounded the large rock formation. His hands circled and then thrust forward when a shock wave of energy blasted Allie backward from the first part of the spell. "Nefajia Crecus Blood Nova!"

A huge blood orb rapidly expanded and exploded forward with a screech of power that lit up the storm of debris around them and created a wide zone cleansed of dust, leaving Allie's cracked armor in full view as half of her face glared out at him from where the bone helmet had been partially torn off. Her halo glowed brightly with deathly light, and her pale eyes remained fixed as she raised a hand.

From far beneath them and all across the landscape, through the swarms of battling souls and sin-created insects, the corpses of the dead began to shrivel and evaporate. Their bones began to rise, and in an instant they were upon him.

A cage created from the bones of the dead snapped shut around his position and began to compress, and Riven found that she was attempting to suppress his mana when the channels across his pillars became sluggish.

Panicking slightly and trusting that Gluttony would activate their supreme skill if need be, Riven forced Malignant Prophecy to activate.

The world around him quickly came to a stop, and the storm calmed. Color seeped from the land, turning a stark gray, only for a notification to appear before him.

[Allie Thane has negated your Malignant Prophecy with her own activation of the skill. Your bloodlines are on equal footing, and neither of you has come out ahead. Both of you receive one additional Malignancy Point for this attempt.]

"GODDAMN IT!" Riven screamed in rage, and he only narrowly dodged Allie's claymore when it crashed through the bone cage he found himself in.

His right arm surged with as much energy as he could muster in that instant while the claymore was passing him by. Ice began to creep up his arm, enhancing the claws and spiked knuckles of Messenger with deadly intent. His red-and-black eyes connected with Allie's gray, and time almost seemed to slow while they stared at one another.

"Hello, big brother," she whispered, and in the next split second they clashed.

Riven's claws smashed into the side of her face, tearing one side of her jaw off as her claymore swung around and cleaved through his opposite arm. She was sent colliding with the ground hundreds of yards below with a scream, and Riven was hurled into a nearby column of rock that'd managed to survive the battle thus far.

He landed with a crunch, the wound where his left arm had been spraying blood and refusing to heal while lingering energies of true death rapidly ate away at his body's regeneration attempts.

"SURPRISE!" the gleeful cackle of Fimrindle called out in raspy glee just when the reaper blurred into motion beside him.

Riven's eyes went wide in shock. The grinning metal scarecrow's X eyes looked abnormally large, and he swung his scythe horizontally in what was doubtless a killing blow.

That was when another figure appeared right behind him, so fast that Riven could barely follow her movements. The enormous silhouette of Athela's drider form opened its crystalline maw wide, bloody strings racing out from its numerous legs, and in that instant Riven knew he was a dead man.

Only for the iron scarecrow to be yanked back into Athela's maw in an instant when the strings attached, making the scythe fall short of its strike. Fimrindle gave a shrill scream of denial right before an abrupt crunch.

Silence followed, and Athela's legs buried themselves into the stone pillar Riven was plastered against. Leaning down with her large but beautiful face pressed up against Riven's position on the rock pillar, Athela giggled and gave him a wink with two of her four red slits for eyes. "Didn't think I'd be able to break out of it, did ya?"

A shudder ran down Riven's body, and he nearly collapsed in relief. That relief didn't last long, however, before a cataclysmic attack smashed into their position.

Athela immediately wrapped her body around Riven's own to protect him, and her horrified wail lasted throughout the roller-coaster ride when they were sent skipping across the landscape like a stone across a lake. Broken bones, charred insides, and a deep gash wound across Athela's back were evident as her breaths became labored.

She looked down at him, clutching him in her arms, and let out a raspy breath. "Go!"

Riven barely had time to roll out of the way before Allie's claymore skewered Athela right through the heart, from the back and out the front of her chest—right where Riven had been a second before.

Athela's second form died, and before she could even fully finish warping into her third arachnid form, Allie's bone-plated foot crunched down onto the small body with a splattering of arachnid guts.

Athela was down for the count.

Frankly, Riven couldn't believe just how strong Allie actually was.

He hadn't considered it before, not in depth, anyways. He'd always known she was powerful and had become even more powerful since her evolution into an angel of death, but instead of how she used to fight as a spell slinger, she was now essentially a tank. Her skills had only grown since being trained by some of the best Gluttony's church had to offer, and she'd taken a very keen liking to that damnable weapon the Scythe had given her in an attempt to woo her to worship him.

Riven almost laughed, knowing full well that she'd not even attempted to contact the death god since then. But then again, less than a year was just a blip to an entity like the Scythe. He'd been around for eons, so waiting such a short period of time probably seemed like nothing to him.

Neon-teal and black fire began to condense over one of Allie's outstretched hands while she gave him a bloodthirsty smile. Her black wings flared out and her aura blasted out again in challenge. "Riven, Riven, Riven . . . I expected better of you. Come now, this can't be all you have in store for your precious little sister—is it?"

She spoke with her jaw still unhinged where his claws had torn it off. She hadn't bothered healing the injury—or perhaps was just rerouting her magic to fighting him instead of dealing with what she likely considered an insignificant flesh wound. Seeing one of the people he loved like that was both fascinating and gross. It was almost like talking to a zombie version of his sister.

Riven, for his part, rolled his shoulders, glancing down at his missing left arm, and a small smile crept across his lips. Peeling the mask back through a mental command to Messenger, Riven gave her a fang-filled grin. "You've become rather impressive, little sis. Too bad that to me, you're still just a brat!"

Allie tsked and was going to reply when she quickly took a step back as Riven's body began to change.

His arm grew back and instantaneously dispelled her true death mana lingering in the wound, his skin turning a dark gray. His body exploded in size as the tattoos lit up from black to violet. Muscles surged, his skin ripped and re-formed, and a huge tail tore out of his tailbone when Messenger peeled off to give his body room to expand. His chest split down the middle to incorporate Gluttony's visage with a vertical maw, huge demonic horns sprouted from his head, his legs snapped backward and grew claws like a T. rex, and his spine tore out of his back. Bone spikes protruded from his kneecaps and elbows, and his teeth elongated in a sinister snarl while huge, bat-like demon wings sprouted out of his shoulder blades.

Eyes shifting from red to purple, he looked down from five times his normal height—dwarfing Allie in less than a second.

"Let us finish this," Gluttony's voice said, overlapping with Riven's. "It is time."

With stats soaring and unimaginable strength, Riven took an offensive approach against Allie for the first time in the battle. He had one minute to do it, and then he was shit out of luck.

Allie's instincts screamed at her to move when the huge gray demon riddled with purple tattoos launched itself toward her like a missile from hell. She rapidly backpedaled and parried a strike of Riven's claws, her Divine blade only barely able to counter the enhanced demonic body before he whirled on her again.

She summoned the Eye of the Scythe, unleashing a deathly gaze from far above—only for the flaming teal eye to wither and die as it laid eyes on Gluttony's reincarnated figure. She flew back, sending screeching skulls ripping across the sound barrier in Riven's direction—only for them to be swatted away like flies. The phantoms and wraiths defending her were ripped from the air and held within Riven's body as hostages ripe for the picking with wails and screams of the dead echoing in her mind, and she summoned an Unholy obelisk to empower her—only for it to shatter when Gluttony's maw reached out with its dark tendrils and snapped it like a twig.

She felt her arm shatter as it blocked another strike, felt her leg snap after barely twisting out of Riven's grasp. She snarled, swinging her blade down and unleashing a miasmic roar that split the sky and created a line of deathly energies in its wake.

But Riven's new form was indomitable, persistent, and her own strikes only scratched his skin like they were paper cuts, despite the quality of her weapon or the enhancement of her True Death pillar.

It was all she could do just to stay alive, and the fight quickly devolved into one where she was on the back foot and doing her best to deflect his blows or redirect them in order not to take the full brunt of his strikes.

"What's the matter, little angel? Is doubt finally afflicting your mind?" Gluttony's laugh echoed from dozens of maws that began to rip open in space around them, and she found herself under assault by dozens and then hundreds of tendrils filled with Sin energy.

Her halo sent out a pulse of radiating death energy, smashing them apart only for new maws and new tendrils to reappear in the sky—reaching for her like hands dragging her to hell.

"Come now, I do not have time to suffer you!" Gluttony's words were mocking, and he smashed through her next deflection with a tail swipe that tore out the left side of her rib cage—sending a piece of her lung through the air in a bloody mess. "COME TO ME, ANGEL OF DEATH! LET ME TASTE YOUR FEAR!"

Riven was nowhere to be seen, and Allie grimaced in pain while taking another step back. The huge monster in front of her was none other than a being made at the beginning of time, an ancient evil that reveled in her fear while licking her blood off its claws. The power behind an origin of demonkind's attacks was unstoppable at her current grade, and she was almost helpless to hurt it despite her best attempts.

Gluttony's grin grew wider, and the black teeth extended almost to look like Azmoth's—its smile unnaturally reaching from ear to ear in a sickening display of genuine amusement and malice. "Despite you being my reincarnation's sister, this is a battle to the death, little one. I hope you can forgive me for what I am about to do . . ."

Purple flames began to build up in the back of Gluttony's throat, roaring to life while they trickled out and up across the demon's face and glowing purple eyes. The power building there was made of pure sin, a thing of destruction that Allie had yet to come across before now, and the Abyssal Descent around them began to tremble and call out to it as the land recognized one of its masters. An original sin had come home to it, broken out of its cage where Elysium had secluded it, and the rampant Sin energies of their environment began to shoot toward Gluttony as the demon charged what was without doubt the final act of this fight.

Yet, despite the massive power behind the building attack, one that she was doubtless incapable of stopping by brute force, she did have one skill left.

Raising her head to the sky, she let out a shrill cry of her own. Banshee's Wail activated, echoing throughout the landscape and silencing all enemies in its vicinity for just a moment.

That one moment completely canceled out Gluttony's attack, dispelling the channeling ability, and Gluttony merely blinked in confusion before an irritated snarl overcame him.

"Well played," Gluttony sneered. "We were . . . unaware that you had such a spell. Well played indeed."

Gluttony's form immediately reverted, his body collapsing in on itself when the one-minute timer ran out. Messenger snapped back onto Riven's body from somewhere out in the dust storm, covering him in a defensive layer while Riven panted from exhaustion. He didn't have time to react before Allie's sword came in for his chest.

Piercing partway through Messenger and almost into his heart, Riven was pinned to the ground with a scream—and Allie desperately tried to push the large claymore farther in.

The pain was immense, and Allie was pouring all the remnants of her strength through the blade, channeling it into his body. His vampiric regeneration battled back frantically, and Messenger tried to expel the Divine weapon as best it could— but it was a losing battle. He felt weak, sapped of most of his strength, without Jackal for his normal mana regeneration—and without any significant amount of blood to call upon from the environment. His hands were coated in red ice the next second and slapped themselves onto the blade, and he ignored the pain they felt even through his own magical layer while he attempted to push the blade out alongside Messenger's attempts.

Allie's state wasn't much better. She had a broken wing, a leg snapped out in an odd angle, one arm dangling to the side, and the right side of her jaw was com- pletely separated from the upper half of her face. Her bone helmet was wrecked, one of her pauldrons was missing where a deep gash of Gluttony's claws had torn her flesh off, and part of one lung and her rib cage was missing.

"You didn't think I could do it, did you?" Allie said, coughing blood with a gleeful, menacing smile. "Well, I did it! I WON!"

She pressed down with her full body weight, attempting to suppress his mana with her own, but both of their auras were minuscule at best compared to what they'd once been. The entire arena around them was a wasteland as the storm of rampant mana raged around them. The occasional spirits and sin beetles that tried to assist their masters were often intercepted by the other, and the ones that did manage to get through were dealt with by the lingering auras that weakly fought at the epicenter of the battle.

Riven gritted his teeth, fangs bared, and he weakly kicked at Allie's broken leg—causing her to stumble back. Rolling and avoiding another exhausted slash from his sister, he got to his feet and staggered back, spitting blood into her face when she lunged.

Blinding her, he smashed an elbow into the back of her head and sent her sprawling, summoning a Blood Lance in the next instant, only for her to block with one of her wings.

The Blood Lance shattered against her feathers but caused her to stagger, and they took the measure of one another again as they panted to catch their breath.

"Die." Allie rushed him with a last-ditch effort, throwing all her remaining strength behind her attack as her body burst into a wraithlike apparition. She descended as the hand of death incarnate, burning a small piece of her own soul to strike him dead, while her body radiated immense killing intent with a flare of her aura that should not be possible.

Eyes wide, Riven gritted his teeth and prepared to dodge—when a flash of light and a familiar aura appeared beside him. A beautiful, pregnant blonde woman wrapped in a formfitting black silk robe stepped out of a red portal. Her red eyes pierced Allie with a judgmental sneer, and she brought both hands up in front of her in a praying motion and closing her eyes. The crimson tattoos of the Blood God flared, and she muttered the words "Sanguine Smite."

The ground exploded underneath them and the enormous visage of the blood moon appeared behind Genua before the miracle tore Allie's body asunder. Flesh was torn from bone, blood ripped from their vessels, and a vertical shock wave of energy ripped out from Genua to finish Allie off as the arena was split in half.

Allie's attack fell short, her body split in two down the middle, as the angel of death breathed no more.

[Team One of Group Number 9,877 has won. Team Two of Group Number 9,877 has lost. All combatants from Group Number 9,877 will now be resurrected. A portal to Floor Twenty of the Abyssal Descent will be created. An additional three loot chests have been provided due to your performance. Lillith of the Black Skies remains trapped on Floor Fifty.]

[Congratulations. Your Floor Two Boss Fight has ended.]

CHAPTER 28

The sudden sound of the crowds around the miles-wide arena came into earshot when the illusions of the perimeter's barrier vanished, and it was utterly deafening. Applause for a good fight, no doubt, but Riven was utterly spent.

Even as the system's own spells rapidly reworked his body, repaired his equipment, cleared the battlefield's devastation, and resurrected the teammates he'd just killed, his soul was exhausted from the strenuous effort. Gluttony had receded as well, for whatever reason, and a portal with three adjacent metal chests laden with gold appeared a little bit off to his left.

However, he was not in the worst of it. Most of his party stared at him, or at one another, in absolute shock. Fay began to sob uncontrollably, falling to her knees as she sputtered pleas for forgiveness. Azmoth looked absolutely horrified, an expression that was a first for the demon in all the time Riven had known him. Allie was just staring at the ground, and Nora had folded herself up in the fetal position after experiencing death.

"Could have been worse!" Athela laughed, seemingly the only one not bothered by the circumstances and giving Fimrindle a shit-eating grin. "Gotcha, bitch!"

The reaper glared back at the arachnid woman, hissed, and abruptly vanished a second later—obviously not enjoying having been killed, either. Riven suspected that Fimrindle's own irritation probably stemmed more from the fact that Athela had been the one to kill him.

"I—I apologize, Your Excellency! I w-would have never dreamed to harm you if it was my own mind controlling my body!" Narg stuttered, aghast and growing a paler shade of green. The beholder demon hovered nearby, trying to come up with words that would convey his sincerity, but barely managed to get out a wheeze.

Riven gave the beholder demon a dismissive wave and a smile, passing him by and stepping in to give Genua a firm pat on the shoulder. "Thank you."

The blood priestess remained calm and professional, not even blinking. "Of course, Master."

Moving on, Riven knelt down next to Fay, picking up the sobbing woman and cradling her in his arms. She was by far the most emotional of his group, always had been—and likely always would be. But she had a good heart, and he gave her time to calm down while he and the others discussed what had happened—and how close it had come to truly being a disaster. He'd barely won, and that was with Athela's fortunate turn halfway through the battle—and then finally with Genua's timely arrival. He'd gotten lucky, but on the bright side, he could safely say that his teammates had grown significantly in the time being here. They were truly firm additions, teammates that would be able to help support him in his coming trek down to the fiftieth level of the Abyssal Descent, and he was glad to have them on his side now that this mockery of a boss battle was finally over.

Kissing Fay's cheek and wiping her tears away, he finally let go after seeing she'd calmed down. "Love you, Fay. Don't worry about it—you did nothing wrong."

Fay sniffled, her resolve having firmed, and she stood up with him when she was offered a hand by Azmoth. "All right. But I'll make it up to you later, I promise."

The tears in her eyes had dried, but it was obvious as she clutched her grimoire to her heaving chest the fight would bother her for quite some time.

Riven gave her a pat on the head, winked, and then began to fall in line next to his sister.

"I'm glad you won, but REALLY, I should have won," Allie teased, nudging him and getting an eye roll in response.

"Oh shut up," Riven said, waving her away while she laughed as the two siblings made for the first of three decorated chests. They were rather large, each of them easily being able to fit a person inside, and the gold trimmings depicted various demons. "I wonder what kind of loot the system is giving out this time . . ."

"A sparkly man-bikini? It'd fit you nicely, Riven."

"You're just mad I beat your ass, you little punk." Riven pushed back the lid of the first chest, ignoring the flickering portal nearby, only to abruptly step away from the chest when a pillar of light tore open from the inside.

There, hovering over the chest, was the projection of a pair of flaming wings dozens of yards across. Magma-like orange veins pulsed in the demonic appendages, and the heat they gave off was tremendous.

Abruptly after that, the next box opened up, too, and without any effort on his part. Again, a pillar of light shot up from inside the chest to reveal the projection of an abnormally long and slender tail, sky-blue in color, that crackled with sparks of a deeper blue plasma. The tail also had curved plasma blades starting halfway down its length and getting larger until they reached the end—where a very long spike of said plasma had sharpened to a point. It looked wicked, if Riven had to put a word to it, with a touch of sci-fi as well given the neon-blue energy.

Then, finally, the third box opened. Just like the other two, a brilliant pillar of light erupted out of the chest to reveal yet another projection. This time it was a pair of demonic horns. They were large, black horns that curved around—reminding him very much of the horns of a ram. They were very smooth, somewhat thick, and gave off an oppressive aura.

Beneath both these projections were three glowing ascension cards, similar to the one Azmoth had used long ago to acquire the Carnivorous Maw trait.

[Ascension Card: Wings of the Hellscape Giant, Trait—Acquire the wings of a hellscape giant. These wings are soul-bound and can only be used by Riven Thane's familiar Azmoth. These large appendages are both sturdy and provide a drastic speed bonus, allowing Azmoth to fly, and will cause Azmoth to grow in size. Size is retractable but will cost stamina. Routing energy into the wings causes them to expel fire at a greater rate, increasing speed at the cost of stamina. Acquiring these wings will also push Azmoth into his next evolution. It will cause Azmoth to ascend into becoming an archdemon, with other minor changes included.]

[Ascension Card: Succubus Battle Stinger, Trait—Acquire the Succubus Battle Stinger. This tail and stinger are soul-bound and can only be used by Riven Thane's familiar Fay. It will replace the tail she currently has and is retractable much like her wings are. This stinger has a high piercing chance and can create bolts of Depravity energy, which both damage the target and have a chance to cause hallucinations. Acquiring this stinger in conjunction with Greater Succubus Horns will also cause Fay to ascend into becoming an archdemon, with other minor changes included.]

[Ascension Card: Greater Succubus Horns, Trait—Acquire the Greater Succubus Horns. These horns drastically increase the radius and potency of all spells cast by the succubus who equips this ascension card. These horns are soul-bound and can only be used by Riven Thane's familiar Fay. They will replace the minor succubus horns she currently has and are retractable much like her wings are. Acquiring these horns with Succubus Battle Stinger will also cause Fay to ascend into becoming an archdemon, with other minor changes included.]

As soon as he finished reading all of them, the system went into action and the cards launched themselves toward their desired targets.

Two cards slammed into Fay's chest and she let out a gasp, her eyes rolling into the back of her head while her body began to spasm.

Azmoth took the hit to his chest without more than a surprised grunt, but he was quick to groan and then fell to one knee, supporting his weight with one of his Shengari Shields.

And before Riven knew it, the two of his minions were changing before his very eyes. Why the system had targeted these two specifically after his win was a curiosity to him, but he was glad to see it as their bodies shifted, morphed, and evolved. In fact, he was rather pleased with the results.

Azmoth's body surged and bulged, muscles expanding and limbs lengthening while the remnants of armor on his body began to shatter and fall off, revealing his natural obsidian plates underneath as flaming flesh between the cracks radiated newfound power. Claws and teeth extended, and spikes along his spine jutted out to new lengths. The eel-like maws protruding from his back screeched and roared, and two wings sprouted from beside each of the carnivorous maws with a blast of inferno that scorched the ground.

The hellscape brutalisk was growing up.

Others of the group quickly backed away while Azmoth continued to grow in size. Big became bigger, and bigger became huge, and the ground underneath him cracked with his weight as Riven's eyes slowly followed the massive demon's new form up and up and up. He continued to move his eyes upward with the growth until he was looking at nothing short of an absolute beast.

Oddly enough, the four Shengari Shields adapted to Azmoth's size—unlike the armor—until each of them was now the size of a tree. The wings themselves unfurled to great lengths as Azmoth stood up, now easily the height of a three-story building, a true giant in all ways. The carnivorous maws could swallow a small car whole, the massive hands could doubtless tear houses out of the ground, and with a flex of his newfound ascension, a pillar of hellfire burst out from Azmoth's body to crash into the ceiling with a boom.

It was rather impressive.

"Damn . . ." Athela muttered underneath her breath, then she whistled. "I'm not sure I can beat him up anymore."

A scream of pain caused Riven's trance to disappear, and with a worried frown he turned his attention back to his other evolving minion.

Fay's transition was slower, despite the lack of growth in size, but the level of raw energy coming off her body was about equal to Azmoth's own. Her tail was being torn apart and remade, elongating, the black cord of her old version now turning to the same shade of blue of the rest of her skin. Additionally, neon-blue plasma blades were sprouting from her skin, and the stinger came next—exiting like a spear that retracted and expanded randomly until settling on a three-foot length of solid neon energy at the tail's tip. Her horns were obviously the most painful for her, though, based on her reaction. Both of her old, smaller horns had fallen off, and in their place new ones were growing.

They were the same shade of pitch black as her old horns, but just like the projection, they were somewhat larger and thicker. They curved around to a forward-facing point much like a ram's and cast a shadow on her snow-white hair as her hands clutched at her forehead while she screamed.

Riven was about to reach out to her but knew he just had to wait it out and resorted to frowning and tapping his foot nervously while the transformation finished its course.

"She be okay," Azmoth said from far above them, and his body let out a hiss of steam amid a rapid shrinking process over the crunch of bones and obsidian plates. The Shengari Shields once again followed suit, reducing in size, and Riven gave his minion a sidelong look while nervously waiting for Fay's system-gifted transformation to complete.

"You're a real badass now, my guy. One that can even fly!" Riven said with a smile, fist-bumping Azmoth as the demon flared his wings excitedly. "I'm glad the system included a shrinking ability, though, otherwise you'd be way too big to have following me around all the time. You'd just crush everything around you!"

Azmoth smiled, lifting one of his Shengari Shields to admire it. "Other brutalisk trainer had enchantment made for this day. Knew I grow big eventually, so weapons modify with me. I grow big, they grow big."

Athela aggressively nodded her head. "And you two are archdemons now! Just like me! Riven, that's three archdemons you've got contracted to you!"

Retesh let out a hollow chuckle, folding his bony arms over one another to watch the evolution process with interest. "You act as if this is a surprise. He is Gluttony's reincarnation."

"But the three of us contracted with him BEFORE we knew that he would be!" Athela retorted with a finger lifted into the air. "That's significant! Because the Willpower cost is way, WAYYY down from what it would otherwise be!"

"Oh look, Fay's body is . . ." Nora started to say, but she let her voice trail off while both eyebrows rose in surprise.

Athela glanced over and immediately began to giggle, while Allie just rolled her eyes in jealousy and disgust.

"Ohhhh . . . Oh, my," Riven said with a growing smile as Fay's screams started to die off. He cocked his head to one side and then the other, and then reached down to pick up the trembling succubus, holding her in his arms. "Are you okay?"

Wrapping her arms around him, she let out a shaky breath.

"I think so . . ." she muttered, still traumatized from the upgrade. "I just . . ."

She stopped, blinked, and looked down at her chest after feeling that something oddly soft was in between them. "Oh, wow."

"Sometimes life just isn't fair," Allie muttered, shaking her head from side to side.

Riven certainly wasn't complaining. "I do believe you've grown a couple sizes larger in the . . . um . . . chest department. It looks very good on you."

Stepping back, Fay let go of Riven to get a better look at herself. The larger horns had knocked off her witch's hat, her tail was twice as long and flickered, neon-blue blades being accompanied by neon sparks, and her upper body had gained a couple bra sizes to boot.

"This is the first thing you comment on?!" Fay said, exasperated, as her two lovers ogling her began to laugh. "I became an archdemon, with an awesome new tail, and the first thing you notice is my chest?!"

"Can you blame us?" Athela asked, still staring at Fay while blindly fist-bumping Riven next to her. "Those are some nice jugs. The things we are going to do to you—"

"Okay, just stop! That's enough!" Allie said, swinging her claymore up and over one shoulder while stomping over to the portal. "It's time to leave. Get all your shit together, keep it in your pants, and let's get a move on—I want to get back to Panu as soon as possible and I have no idea how long this trek is going to take. For all I know, Lahn has found another girlfriend, and I'll be damned if I'm stuck here with you horny idiots for more than another week!"

"She's just jealous," Riven said staunchly before quickly ducking when Allie flung a death ball his way. He held up his hands in surrender. "All right! All right, come on, Fay. Not everyone is angry that you're a new sex icon. Ignore the grumpy angel, and if you want I can even give you a piggyback ride if you're still feeling shaky."

Nora face-palmed and Fay turned a deep red, holding her grimoire close against her chest to hide it. Athela let out a laugh of agreement with an offer of her own.

"I going to transform back into regular size now," Azmoth stated a second later, giving them a wave to follow and heading toward the portal next. His body began to snap and crack while his mass expanded yet again, until he was three stories tall once more. His wings flared out to either side in a spray of flames. "Making my body small tiresome. I stay like this unless need. Come, we go find Lillith. Then we hurry to finish Chalgathi trials."

The portal was a blur of noise and colors, and after exiting on the other side, the party found themselves inside a dead-end room. The walls and ceiling were made from black energy speckled with various colors, almost akin to space colored by the stars of a galaxy.

Walking forward to touch one of the walls, Riven confirmed it was indeed solid and made from some kind of stone. The speckled colors were, as far as he could tell, actually soulstones of different grades—each one both ancient and ominous in nature and radiating a faint aura.

[You have arrived on Floor Twenty of the Abyssal Descent. Beware of other descent dwellers, as killing other participants grants you their ranking points.]

Riven blinked, then went back to inspecting the odd construction of the room.

Thankfully it was large enough to easily hold Azmoth. This place was no doubt made to include demons or other denizens of the Unholy pillar, and it made sense that there'd be enough open area for creatures like Azmoth to move around.

"What is it that you sense, Master?" Genua asked, coming to stand beside him as Riven held his palm flat against the dark corridor's surface. "Something troubles you."

His red eyes turned to meet hers, and then they darted down to her pregnant belly. "I wish you would have stayed back in the Blood God's realm. Thank you for coming to help, but it worries me that you're here."

Genua put on a gentle smile and shrugged. "There is no point in worrying about it now, Master. It is unfortunate that I cannot return after having passed the first floor of the descent, but that is a risk I knew I would take after making the choice to intervene."

He nodded slowly, withdrawing his hand and motioning her to follow as the others began following Allie. Fimrindle, Athela, and Nora all vanished into thin air to scout ahead, and Azmoth's flames billowed out to illuminate the darkness as Retesh and Fay took the rear.

Unfortunately, none of the undead minions Riven had slain were able to be revived or reused, as they'd been mysteriously recycled by Elysium after the battle had finished, much to Retesh's annoyance—and the lich was already muttering to himself about what changes he needed to make in order to avoid assassins like Athela in the future. It appeared that he'd also come to the same realization Riven had about sudden attempts on his life.

"How go your studies with the other clergy?" Riven eventually asked, glancing left to where the priestess held herself in perfect posture to silently walk beside him. "Do you enjoy your trips there? I am unsure of what it is like—I've only ever heard stories."

Genua remained with her hands clasped in front of her, staring ahead with the chiseled features of a statue and not showing much emotion while she considered his words. "The studies are beneficial. I have grown and learned much. The Blood God is truly a being of magnificence, one of ultimate power, and a being that I can say I am proud to learn from personally."

"Personally?" Riven asked, surprised. "You talk to him?"

Genua slowly nodded, their footsteps echoing in the dark passage that continued to lead out for hundreds of yards before turning left and right at the end. "Yes, or at least I learn from a portion of him. He has split off a piece of his soul to project it as something akin to a clone and has come to personally teach me in the way of blood miracles. He's taught me how to grow my divinity channels, and I can now even summon some of the same creatures that you can."

"Legionaries?"

"Yes. The Legionaries of the Blood God are at my command as well, though my ability is a miracle rather than a spell—and it works somewhat differently than yours. The end result is the same, however."

"That's a pretty damn good miracle to have."

For the first time since beginning their walk, Genua grinned. "Quite. I've also been granted another miracle called Blood Mirror, which allows me to communicate over long distances. Len and I have been speaking through it, and my daughter is doing quite well in Tupper's care. She's even grown slightly . . . and it has made me happy to see how excited she gets when I contact her. She's also come around to the idea of having a little brother or sister and has started making baby clothes for when her sibling arrives."

Genua's grin widened into a genuine smile, and she let out a sigh of contentment. "I would have shown you earlier, but you seemed rather busy, and I did not want to irritate you with my intrusions."

Riven raised an eyebrow, using Jackal as a walking stick while forging ahead at a slow, monotonous pace. "You're carrying my child. Don't ever think that I don't have time to speak to you if you need it."

There was a long pause after that before she rapidly glanced his way. Then she shifted her eyes back ahead of her and down to the floor. "Um . . . all right. Thank you, Riven."

"Don't mention it," Riven said, suddenly feeling a little bit awkward. He was still brutally aware that he'd been the one to kill Genua's husband and her daughter Ethel back when they'd attempted to murder him. The thought was always, without fail, a raw area to think about. Scratching the back of his head, he tried to hold in his grimace. "What kind of clothes has Len been making?"

Genua giggled at the question, unaware of his state of mind, putting one hand to her mouth and shaking her head. "She's been making dresses mostly. I told her that we don't know if it is a boy or a girl yet, but Len seems adamant that it'll be a little sister rather than a little brother. She just ignores me when I tell her that she'll have to rethink her fashion choices should it be a little brother, but more than anything, I think she's just happy with her newfound ability as a start-up seamstress. Tupper has again been the one teaching her, and he's apparently a very good tailor."

"News to me."

"Yes, to me as well."

"GUYS, GUYS, GUYS!" Athela appeared from the shadows, waving her arms back and forth excitedly while beckoning the others to come faster. "I found something really neat! Come quickly! And I think we'll need Narg's help on this one, so hurry it up, you overgrown eyeball!"

Narg had been unusually quiet ever since the end of the last battle. However, he quickly perked up now, orange eyes alight with intent, as he rushed over to follow Athela's wake. "I will do my best to assist, dear lady!"

Smiling and giving each of his minions a once-over, Riven escorted Genua forward. Fay was waiting patiently for them and took his arm in hers, and, doing the same with Genua's on the other side, she began dragging them forward at a faster trot while Azmoth's giant steps led the way in front.

[Athela, level 200 Archdemon: Unique, three forms. Cute Wittle Blood Weaver/Gluttonous Arshakai/Gluttonous Fae Drider. Classless. LEGENDARY. PANU WORLD BOSS.]

[Azmoth, level 200 Archdemon: Winged Hellscape Brutalisk. Infernal Crusader Adept. LEGENDARY.]

[Fay, level 200 Archdemon: Greater Blue Succubus. Curse Witch. LEGENDARY.]

[Genua, level 200 High Elf Vampiric Thrall. Priestess of the Blood God. ELITE.]

[Narg, level 200 Beholder Demon. Seeker. ELITE.]

CHAPTER 29

"So what exactly is an archdemon, anyway? Now that I have not one but three of you bound to me, I figure now is as good a time as any to really consider what it means," Riven asked as Fay pulled him along with his arm in hers. "Because it strikes me as odd that F-grade demons can become archdemons when there are many E-, D-, or C-grade demons that haven't become such. So it can't be a power or level thing."

Fay giggled at him with a shake of her head, then hummed to herself while trotting along with Genua on her left and Riven on her right. "It's rather funny, you know."

"What's funny?"

"That you're Gluttony's reincarnation and have no idea what an archdemon is."

Riven couldn't help but roll his eyes, and even Genua smirked a bit at the jab. "Yeah, well, I was human only about a year ago. Back on Earth, I didn't even think demons were real."

"Wait, truly?" Genua asked, obviously intrigued by the notion while furrowing her brows at him. "They didn't know what demons were back on your homeworld before the integration?"

"It's not that we hadn't HEARD of demons before, but magic wasn't a real thing where I was from." Riven shrugged as Azmoth's booming footsteps continued to march ahead of them in Athela's wake, the flames casting the otherwise dark corridor in a flickering orange hue. "Fairy tales talked about them. As did some religious texts or novels, and sometimes they were portrayed in movies. But nothing was proven or documented on video, so no one really took it seriously."

"What about undead, then?" Retesh asked, the ancient lich pausing ahead of them to fall in line before walking alongside Riven's right. "Did your world have anything about my kind?"

"Nope." Riven shook his head adamantly. "Not a thing. Same thing with anything magical, really. If you've not noticed, most of my people in Chicago are oriented toward the Machine pillar. This is because our society focused mainly on technology rather than taking anything concerning magic or mystical creatures seriously."

"Would you say that I am a mystical creature, then?" Fay asked, winking with a teasing laugh.

"Certainly, babe." Riven jabbed her in the rib cage, getting a squeal from the succubus as they turned the corner.

Athela was waiting impatiently for the four of them alongside Narg the beholder about twenty yards away, tapping her foot. "Hurry it up, you four! We're wasting time and Fimrindle is getting impatient! Something about how his itty-bitty scarecrow legs can't stand for much longer!"

She jogged farther down after that and disappeared with another right-hand turn, Azmoth already being a good ways ahead of Riven due to the size of his steps. The large demon turned around and looked at the four of them a moment later.

"Do you want carry?" Azmoth asked curiously.

Riven waved a hand. "Nah, go on ahead, man. We'll catch up soon."

He could sense each of his demons rather keenly through their bonds. Especially when they were in close proximity, and it was getting easier and easier to track them as their bonds strengthened over time. However, Athela was the only one of them all that had developed a unique link to him after taking a piece of Gluttony for herself. The mental link was not one often used, but if need be they could even communicate telepathically—and he would easily be able to find her position as long as an absolute labyrinth didn't separate them. So having Azmoth and Athela go ahead wasn't much of a concern after this area had been scouted out by their assassins, and they all knew it.

Azmoth nodded and then spread his wings with a burst of fire. Launching himself ahead, he easily cleared the distance and did an unnaturally sharp ninety-degree turn before vanishing behind Athela.

"So, back on topic," Riven said. "What exactly makes an archdemon different from a regular demon?"

Fay was biting her lip, watching Azmoth leave, but cleared her throat and turned her attention back to Riven after a few seconds of pondering. "It's all about bloodlines and potential."

Riven raised an eyebrow. "Go on."

Bobbing her head from side to side, she resumed. "So, becoming an archdemon doesn't necessarily mean a demon is stronger by definition, but the two are correlated. If someone is an archdemon, they're naturally going to be stronger most times when compared to their fellow demons. All demons have originated from one or multiple of the original sins, such as Gluttony. Right?"

"Right."

"Well, that gives us bloodlines relating back to the original sins. Athela's evolution into becoming an archdemon has a lot to do with absorbing some of the power from Gluttony's shards, ones you had before becoming the actual reincarnation of Gluttony." Fay raised a finger. "However, that is not always the case. Though Athela manifests a crystalline gluttonous maw on her front while in her drider form, most evolutions into being labeled an archdemon are due to awakening mixed bloodlines. Such as mine, which—if I had to guess—is probably very much based in Envy, Lust, and Pride. The reason I say this is because most blue succubi have been measured to be so in the past when examined. But if you took a red succubus and measured her, most of the time she would have a mix of Envy, Lust, and Wrath."

Riven blinked. "That's rather interesting. Does this compel you to follow a particular type of original sin when . . . I don't know, worshipping?"

Fay snorted in amusement. "No, that is a personal choice. Or you're born into a family that has been serving a particular church for millennia. The inherent nature to worship the sins is built into us, but is equal across all the sins regardless of what bloodline mixtures we have."

"All right, but what does that have to do with being an archdemon? You awaken your bloodlines to draw more power?"

"Yes." Fay nodded. "Essentially, being labeled an archdemon means that we have unlocked at least some part of our ancestral bloodlines leading back to the sins. This in turn allows us to evolve faster and have more potent evolutions. The cards that Elysium provided Azmoth and me with were basically keys to unlock certain bloodline potentials that are already inherent to our species—but are hard to acquire."

Riven's eyebrows raised. "Oh. So you're saying that Elysium didn't necessarily slap a tail on you and remove your old one, but just induced an evolution by unlocking a particular bloodline?"

"Correct."

"And . . . what about Azmoth's first card, the one where he gained those two mouths on his back that breathe fire? I was under the impression any of us could use that card, but we gave it to Azmoth because it just seemed to fit."

Fay shrugged. "Not all evolution-stimulating cards are linked back to the sins. That was a nightmare creature, if I remember correctly?"

"Yes."

"Then it probably stemmed from the species itself. But it likely wouldn't have unlocked Azmoth's bloodlines related to the original sins regardless of how many evolutionary cards you gave him if they weren't demonic in nature. This in turn means that, should he have not evolved into an archdemon, his future natural evolutions would be less potent than the ones he will gain now. In fact, there are even different GRADES of archdemon. Athela, Azmoth, and I are all at the most basic form of archdemon because the three of us have only unlocked the first layer of our bloodlines. But you can become an ascendant, into further tiers of archdemon, if you get lucky enough or have some kind of massive breakthrough. Unfortunately not many of our kind even get to become an archdemon at all. My mother, for example, is thousands of years older than I am and many grades above me—but she still isn't an archdemon. In fact, I think I may be the first and only archdemon in the Sojavi clan. They're all quite proud, actually."

"Does Athela's clan have any other archdemons?"

Fay nodded. "A few. Not many, but her clan is more oriented toward acquiring martial power. While mine is, as you know, an information broker. Many of my clan actually use their powers—such as my Silvertongue—to seduce people into telling us what we want to know, but Silvertongue is only the bottom of the barrel compared to some of the other influential powers my clan has. Anyways, the opportunities we get to acquire insights into our original bloodlines probably don't come as frequently as the ones Athela's clan gets, because martial might is most linked with awakening."

"Huh. I see. Why doesn't Azmoth have a clan?"

"Hellscape brutalisks are generally loners. They're apex hunters when they reach their full form. You think Azmoth is big now? Wait and you'll be surprised at just how big he will actually get."

Riven didn't know what to think about Fay's last statement. Azmoth was already enormous. How much bigger could he become? And it wasn't like the other hellscape brutalisks he'd seen in the Abyssal Descent were much bigger. Sure, some of them were equal to Azmoth's current height, but he hadn't seen any behemoths. Then again, they were still all F- and E-grade by Elysium's mandatory proclamation; he had yet to see any brutalisks in the upper grades yet.

"So is there anything else I need to know about archdemons? Or is that basically it?" Riven asked.

Fay shook her head. "Not really. I guess it also is a sign of status, but otherwise it means that I—and anyone else labeled with the archdemon tag—are probably going to get better evolutions over time. Thus we have far greater potential to become great. The earlier you get the archdemon tag, the more evolutions you're able to go through before reaching the top. Acquiring the title at F-grade for all of us distinctively means we will achieve greatness, as long as we manage to survive. It is incredibly rare, you know, what you've done."

She cocked her head to the side as if in thought. "Even for who you are, I would think. Or maybe that really is it, that being so close in proximity to one of the original sins has something to do with it. I wouldn't know, because the sins have been locked away for so long and the churches have kept their secrets well hidden during the ages the sins were gone, but if it is the close proximity driving us to thrive, then it would certainly be a boon for whoever you take on next—Narg or anyone else."

"But didn't Elysium just kind of . . . Eh, how do I put this? Wasn't Elysium the one that really gave those cards out?"

Fay snorted a laugh, shaking her head. "Only in part. Elysium doesn't just GIVE out prizes like that. They need to be earned, and they need to have certain requirements ticked off to get them. There are no free handouts, so to speak. But it felt like we were not only ready for the evolutions, but had also earned them through our actions—or, in this case, the actions of our master. Perhaps both. It is also entirely possible that we may have not needed the evolution-stimulating cards, that Elysium simply expedited the process."

"BOO!"

Riven would have been startled if he hadn't already sensed Athela coming, but Fay and Genua definitely let out surprised screams—and even Retesh nearly tripped before turning around to glare.

Athela had popped out of stealth and had her legs over Riven's shoulders and was grinning like a madwoman while enjoying the ride. Then she pointed forward and smacked Riven twice on the head. "Onward, good steed! Giddyup! Go, go, go!"

"You know . . ." Fay muttered, brushing herself off and glaring up at the arachnid woman. "You do realize that many would consider what you are doing as blasphemy, riding Gluttony around like that."

Athela seemed to ponder Fay's words a moment, shrugged, and grinned like a drunkard. "Riven doesn't mind! Do you, Riven?!"

He pretended to scowl but just couldn't hold the look with the goofy grin on Athela's face. Eventually he fell into a chuckle.

"You're lucky I like you." Riven winked and kept walking until they reached the next turn.

"Be quiet and ride on, plebeian steed!"

Far, far, far down the enormous hallway was a trio of double doors. Even from here Riven could see just how big they were based on their comparison to Azmoth—they made him look just a little small. Allie, Fimrindle, Narg, and Nora were also there, all of them chatting about something, but their words couldn't be heard due to the distance. It was nearly a mile away, with nothing but the straight path between.

"I'm having Narg use his Seek Object, Seek Danger, and Seek Safety abilities while meditating next to the door," Athela said, still riding on Riven's shoulders. She pointed down the long hall to where the others stood—in the middle of them was a distant Narg with his eyes closed. "Hopefully he'll be able to get us down floor by floor faster this way—at the very least through this part of the floor."

"Why's that?" Retesh asked with a rasp in his voice, his bone staff clicking against the floor as the orb at its top occasionally flickered. "Do we need to choose one of the three doors to proceed? Can we not backtrack?"

"Bingo, Bonesy has it right!" Athela laughed. "The doors are all sealed, and choosing one probably permanently locks the other two. Or it blocks the way. You'll see, there's a rhyme on the wall that hints at it. But it's all very unclear. Something about a giant's maze?"

"Oh, great. Just what I wanted, a maze." Riven grimaced, then brightened. "Your idea about Narg is a good one, though. Maybe he'll be more useful than we'd thought. If Lillith knew about this beforehand, perhaps that's why she chose him to come along."

"Hey, Athela—" Genua cut in, scrolling through her status screen and then pulling up Riven's before flipping to the other minions' screens. It was a feature of being a minion—they could all access each other's status screens as long as they belonged to the same master. "Are you going to pick a class? You're already level 200, but you haven't picked a class yet. Why is that? Aren't you missing out on all the stat points per level? That's quite a significant loss."

Riven hadn't actually thought about it, but Genua was right. Why HAD Athela not taken a class? He'd let the others pretty much do what they wanted and wasn't at all restrictive in how they pursued their own paths to power, and that level of freedom was actually written into Azmoth's original contract to begin with. So he'd not paid much attention to it until now.

He glanced up at Athela while keeping her legs firmly over his shoulders and her calves against his chest with one hand, his other hand continuing to use Jackal like a walking stick. "Genua's got a good point. You haven't really talked much about it. Have you not seen a class you like yet?"

Athela, for her part, was pretending to inspect her fingernails. Curling her fingers and then flattening them out to splay them the opposite way, she let out a loud sigh. "It's a trade secret! Okay, okay, maybe not a secret. But I am waiting until D-grade to choose a class."

"D-grade? As in, past E-grade? You're in F-grade right now!" Riven exclaimed, perplexed.

Fay seemed equally baffled, as did Genua.

But Retesh seemed to understand what was going on, giving Athela a nod of respect. "You want to gain the achievement. Don't you?"

"Bingo!" Athela beamed back, giving the skeletal lich a wide grin and made the shooter symbol with her fingers his way. "Bags o' bones got it again! I'm waiting to get an achievement before I gain a class."

"Which is?" Fay asked curiously. "I haven't heard of such an achievement."

"That's because your family doesn't care nearly as much about combat prowess as my family does." Athela harrumphed. "Damnable succubi, always thinking their looks can get them places and not needing to fight. But I bet your mother knows if you were to ask her. The achievement is called Stagefright, and it is immediately granted to anyone who reaches level 401 after passing into the D-grade if they don't have a class."

"What does it do?" Riven asked, curiously glancing Retesh's way. "And how do you know about it?"

Retesh pretended to clear his throat with one clenched fist up against his jaw, which was weird, considering he didn't have a throat, just an exposed spine. "I happened upon the knowledge during our training sessions with the Church of Gluttony. It's a long story, but one of the young demon lords there told me he was going to attempt to get the Stagefright achievement as well. I'd asked him a similar question after realizing he was a level-206 E-grade gargoyle and did not have a class. Correct me if I am wrong, Athela, but Stagefright is supposed to give you an entirely different set of upper-echelon class choices. Not many go for this achievement, though, because entering the D-grade without a class can be very hard to do. You put yourself at a disadvantage and it is far harder to level up, and you limit the skills or perks you'd otherwise get from your classes. Many who attempt it die along the way."

"That's correct," Athela said with a nod, folding her arms. "Now, you may be asking yourself why most contracted demons don't do this to begin with. The answer is simple—if your master dies while you remain classless, you lose out on ever getting the opportunity for Stagefright, even if you get a new master. Then, if you've gone nearly four hundred levels without a class and without gaining additional stat points each level while not having a class, it's a huge hit to take. Many contracted demons don't risk it and choose to take a class early to avoid crippling themselves in case their master DOES die. But I have absolute faith in you, Riven."

"Shucks, gee whiz, and thanks," Riven said flatly, getting a laugh from the others. "I'm glad I can inspire such confidence in you."

When they arrived at the three enormous doors built into the dead end of the dark corridor, they saw the doors had ancient letters carved into them that looked different every time Riven glanced away and back again—but from talking to the others, the doors all said the same thing. It was like the words, though unreadable, made their meaning known and allowed viewers to read the writing even without actually knowing how to do it.

Certainly an odd sensation, and it didn't help that the shapes kept changing, either.

"I . . . think you should be the one to read the passages out loud," Nora muttered, glancing Riven's direction with a shrug. "Just in case . . . Seems ominous, and it's pretty obvious that it wants you to speak the passages."

Riven's gaze shifted to Narg, who swerved to Riven's left and extended an eyeball in that direction. "This is the way. If you can choose, this is the door you must take."

"Why?" Riven asked, just to confirm.

Narg shot wary looks between Riven and the door in question and let out a huff. "It is the door that leads to the most danger . . . but it is also the door that leads to Lillith. I am able to track the flower in her horns—I thought it was an odd object to have on her person, but only this door leads down to find her."

The pause after that was a long one, and Riven's grimace quickly grew. It was not a question on whether or not they'd get Lillith out, it was a must. No one else said a word, but it was obvious they all agreed. And with the writing literally on the wall in the form of a riddle, the implications about this next trial were quite clear.

Riven stared up at the ever-shifting shapes, reading and rereading them line by line, as the words he shouldn't know how to read burned themselves into his mind's eye. Then he uttered the words aloud while simultaneously pressing his hand to the door that Narg had indicated. *"Place your hand on one of three. Enter into the crazed giant's maze that does forever remain awake, for if you choose to retreat, your souls he will surely take. His eyes were plucked raw, a damned sentence to serve, he remains chained unwilling and has yet to give birth. As a quintet of travelers, you must choose your path, for now that you're here, there is no turning back. The crazed one will feed and you will all die, for the path you must tread and must not turn awry. The first to speak will fight for all five. The two of your weakest will be your guides. The remaining three will make the keys, with any others obliged to be. If this cannot be done, you unravel another one, in order to take their gift. For this is the way, this is the curse, of the fallen god's passage through to this twenty-first rift. Speak the words aloud, champion of the crowd, and descend into darkness with your comrades."*

The passage they'd been walking down only minutes before suddenly vanished, completely cut off with a solid black wall. There was no way out. The three doors started to glow.

[Abyssal Descent Trial for Floor Twenty has been activated: The Crazed Giant's Maze:

- **The first to speak will fight for all five: As the one who has spoken the words aloud, Riven has been labeled Champion. You will be thrown into a pit of despair with champions of other groups against a respawning wave of randomized abyssal enemies. Minions are unable to aid the champion here. If Riven dies, the rest of you will be set upon every ten minutes by waves of enemies that increase in strength and number.**
- **The two weakest will be your guides: Nora and Narg have been designated as Seekers. Your two seekers will be sent into the giant's cylindrical maze and will be hunted by the weakest of**

other teams and various abyssal beasts in their attempt to navigate to the end. The crazed giant will also attempt to eat anything it can get its hands on, including your seekers, as the flight through the maze continues. If both seekers die, the rest of you will be ejected from the Abyssal Descent entirely and may not ever return.

- **The remaining three will make the keys, with any others obliged to be: The rest of the party, including all minions not already selected for other roles, will be set to the task of creating keys that unlock the doors at the end of the labyrinth with crafting materials provided by Elysium. The Seekers, your two weakest, will be unable to traverse through the last part of the maze without these keys.**

- **If this cannot be done, you unravel another one, in order to take their gift: Killing other champions in one-on-one combat, or killing other seekers, will allow you to take their keys and insights to add to your own party.**

Do this, and pass into the twenty-first floor of the Abyssal Descent. Identification is nullified on this entire floor. At the end of this floor, you will gain an insight into one of your paths.]

The door wrenched itself open with a creak, and the world instantaneously shifted around them before anyone else knew what was happening. Their minds linked, allowing them to see through one another's eyes while simultaneously maintaining a sense of self.

Riven was now standing at the bottom of a deep, dark pit that had a cubic set of walls made from flesh. Carnivorous teeth clicked and gnashed from inside the walls, giving him the impression he was standing in the mouth of a square-shaped lamprey. Blood and acid sizzled on the floor underneath his ivory-plated feet. Nearly twenty other champions of various species from other groups were also there, all knee-deep in combat with different types of nightmare abominations that literally hurled themselves out of the walls or tore out of the ground to bite, wrench, and claw at the champions.

Azmoth, Allie, Retesh, Fay, Athela, and Fimrindle were all standing in a large, boxy room with a dozen pools of black water, a central sacrificial altar where a frantically screaming woman was chained to the stone, and a large wraith with a crazed smile hovering overhead staring down at them. There was a lava pit, a pile of bones, a tub of soulstones, a set of used butcher's tools on a rack, and cages on the far wall with numerous other captured prisoners of species obviously not native to the Unholy foundational pillar all crying out in despair.

Then, lastly, Nora and Narg were standing together at the top of a steep drop-off where a winding path of obsidian tunnels intertwined through an enormous maze. The maze itself had dozens of different floors and was cylindrical in nature, with the center cylinder being open to the air. At the very bottom, an enormous giant was chained by the neck and partially submerged in an ocean of red-hot magma. The giant was blind, tortured, his eyes having been torn out, and his charred, burned skin was ravaged with scars and claw marks as he howled and roared.

A creature cursed for all eternity to serve a sentence for unknown crimes in a state of blind, ever-lasting agony. The only outlet for his rage: to kill and feed on the creatures that dared haunt his abyssal prison. His massive hands groped through the exposed open levels of the innermost floors of the cylinder-shaped maze, where various abyssal creatures could be seen from time to time along with other figures that darted in and out of the dark. Occasionally, desperate swipes from the giant would find purchase, and screaming, squealing creatures could be seen being ripped from the various parts of the labyrinth to enter his giant mouth— where he crunched down on them in splattering scenes of blood and gore.

And for the first time since arriving in this Unholy descent, Riven and the others truly began to understand just what it was to enter the jaws of the abyss.

CHAPTER 30

The blinded giant, chained by his neck at the very bottom of this accursed labyrinth, was half-submerged in his magma pit. Even so, the creature was so large that he could reach all but the highest levels of the labyrinth, and his charred, gnarled fingers eternally groped for prey to feed on. Sharp intakes of breath through his nose were interrupted only by his crazed roars of pleasure and pain. After having lost knowledge of who or what he'd been in his past life, all he had left was the hunt. His vacant eye sockets dripped blood that sizzled down his blackened skin, leaving him in perpetual darkness even as the lava gave off a soft orange glow. Yet, despite his blindness and his lack of sanity, he remained acutely aware of his surroundings through touch and sound.

And an uncontrolled rage continued to spur him on toward greater violence.

The air was thick with the stench of death and decay as abyssal creatures slithered or clawed through the shadows. Their whispers and hisses filled the giant's ears, taunting him with their presence. His only solace lay in hunting them down, feeding on their flesh to attempt to sate his endless hunger. He crushed, gnawed, gored, and punched—occasionally breaking fingers that quickly snapped back into place in his attempts to get at the vile snacks that tried to evade his reach in the deeper recesses of the walls and inner corridors he could not fit into.

But for the first time in a very long time, he sensed something change. A familiar aura, born of darkness, it called to him . . . and the familiar hunger in his belly grew to new heights as a wicked grin crept across his face in an unusual display of glee.

Though he could not remember why this presence made him feel in such a way.

He shifted his massive body, feeling the chains around his neck creak under the strain. He extended his arms up toward where he felt the presence, if only momentarily, groping blindly through the darkness for any sign of prey. His fingers brushed against stone walls and twisted obsidian tunnels, but the sensation of that ancient, familiar presence soon disappeared—leaving the giant in a fit of rage while splashing around the lava pits below to cause tidal waves.

The cylindrical labyrinth shook with his efforts.

Suddenly, he heard movement ahead. A creature's scent caught his attention. Its efforts to evade taunted him, thinking itself safe from his grasp while his hands were up above. But the giant was the master of this labyrinth, and his hunger knew no bounds.

With a thunderous roar, he lunged forward, trying to capture the fleeing creature as it tried taking a shortcut on the inner cylindrical path before it escaped into a deeper recess. His fingers closed around empty air as it dodged and wove through the shadows. Frustrated, he swung his arms wildly, hoping to catch it off guard.

He heard a scream of terror before his fist connected with something soft and squishy, squeezing the life from its body. The creature's writhing limbs went limp as he crushed it beneath his grip. With a triumphant bellow, he lifted the corpse to his mouth—letting the blood leak into his parched throat—and then he devoured the demon whole.

Narg's many eyes widened after watching another participant get crushed and eaten right in front of them. The beholder demon and Nora had likely scared the already-injured minotaur into rushing headlong in a fear that they'd attack it—only for the frightened and unbound demon to become giant food in its final act.

There was no coming back from death for that one.

"Poor bastard," Narg muttered, shaking his head in dismay. "We weren't going to kill that stupid cow—I don't know why it didn't just wait. Unfortunately, minotaurs aren't the brightest bunch."

Nora came up behind the floating beholder, panting and wiping sweat off her brow with a forearm while holding two bloodied bone-crafted blades in either hand. She glanced at the splattered gut remnants on the wall ahead of them on the inner path that exposed their flight through the maze to the giant's reach, and then looked behind them where the snarling howls of abyssal hounds were growing louder. When one of the huge beasts poked its head out from around a corner, acid dripping from exposed canines, she reacted instantly. Her arms twisted and she braced herself in the necessary stance for one of her Tier-2 martial arts, speaking the words aloud before striking forward with her blades:

"Haunted Mirror!"

The air down the hall let off a whisper of deathly energy as a small, circular mirror snapped into being just over the hound's head. The abyssal hound then unleashed a fire hydrant of acid directly at Nora, but the attack was blocked with a barrier of shadows and fire as Narg protected Nora from the attack. At the same time the hound lunged forward, only for Nora's blades to reach through the summoned mirror with projected ghostly hands. The bone blades stabbed into the monster's back, ripping with critical energies that caused the monster to yelp in surprise.

[You have landed a critical hit. Max damage x6.]

The spine ripped and the monster fell to the ground with a snarling yelp, only to be blasted with an Unholy Globspitter that whizzed an inch past Nora's face. The green light of the projectile was on par with Riven's own sniping Blood Lance in terms of speed and blew through the hound with ease, tearing its body apart in a splattering of gore that coated the hallway.

More howls and the clawed scramble of canine footsteps became more apparent even with the trembling of the labyrinth from the giant's attempts at finding prey.

Nora winced as a familiar, ancient presence clawed at the back of her mind. A flashing image of multiple dark, smiling entities that she'd known since she was a child lit up her insides—and the cold, clawed fingers of her early tormentors embraced her soul. They pleaded with her to be let out, begged her, even, and she had to shut out their malicious giggles by pure force of will to regain a sense of who and what she was.

"Come on, Nora . . . Let us out! We promise we'll keep you safe . . . We promise we'll give your body back this time!" The voices echoed in her head, laughing and mocking her while trying to pull at her subconscious barriers. *"You need us! Let us out, little sister! We only want to play!"*

"Is your bloodline acting up again?" Narg said, concerned as Nora hit the ground on both knees. His numerous eyes flicked upward again, and a few more layers of nightmare barriers blocked the hallway from three more incoming abyssal hounds, level 190 to 200 each. His green skin began to simmer with heat as his vessels lit up orange, and one by one his eyeballs began to glow at the ends of their stalks.

Hellspitters, similar to his Unholy Globspitters in nature but with more explosive power and less piercing, were set off one after another when the hallway began to fill with bodies. Screams of the enemy hounds that clawed, bit, and unleashed their own abilities at the barriers were heard over the violent light show of inferno being discharged from the beholder at will.

"I'm sorry!" Nora gasped between heaves and deep breaths. She looked down, horrified to see dark lines etching themselves onto her skin, and her eyes beginning to flash white like the laughing monsters of her nightmares. "I don't think I can hold them in for much longer!"

"WELL, WHAT HAPPENS IF YOU CAN'T?!" Narg said, not taking his eyes off the incoming swarm of hounds while blasting away like a madman through his one-way nightmare barriers.

His first shield cracked and shattered, and then the next did as well—but the pileup of bodies began to block the way while tearing jaws bigger than Narg and Nora tried to rip through their dead companions to get at them.

The lines along Nora's fingers abruptly receded, and she let out a relieved sigh while picking up her bone blades again. Tugging at one of Narg's tentacles and wincing when the giant's hand smashed into a wall-less section of the labyrinth only one level above them in a thundering boom, she gestured for them to go.

"Oh my god, they're gone! Let's keep going! I was able to suppress them after all!"

"YOU DIDN'T ANSWER MY QUESTION, NORA!" Narg yelled over the snarls and firepower of his attacks before he dashed across the passage outcropping. He followed Nora as fast as he could while his barriers continued to block the hounds, very much considering just flying down to search the lower levels— even at the cost of abandoning Nora, as she'd just be sent back to Chalgathi's trials—but he thought better of it when he was reminded for the seventh time since being here as to why that wasn't a great idea after a gargoyle attempted such a maneuver and was abruptly snatched out of the air with uncanny accuracy by the giant. "NORA! WHAT HAPPENS IF YOU CAN'T SUPPRESS YOUR BLOODLINE?! WHAT DOES IT DO?!"

The thundering roar of triumph came once again with another splashing tidal wave of magma when the giant chomped down onto the squealing gargoyle's upper body with a splatter of gore. The crunching of bones was audible even from here, but Nora didn't reply as the two of them dashed into the inner tunnels of the labyrinth and got away from the exposed interior where the giant was able to reach them.

"NORA!"

She whirled on him with fear in her eyes, hands held out to either side. "I HAVE NO IDEA! OKAY, NARG?! I JUST BLACK OUT AND BAD THINGS HAPPEN, SO I HAVE NO FUCKING IDEA! Now PLEASE, just drop it! All I know is that it'll be bad, and that it scares the living shit out of me. OKAY?! I'M SORRY, BUT JUST SHUT UP, USE YOUR SEEKING ABILITIES TO TELL US WHERE TO GO, AND LET'S FUCKING RUN!"

Grimacing at her, the beholder demon once again let out a pulse of Seek Danger, Seek Safety, and Seek Object one after the other to try and triangulate the exit from this damned hellish labyrinth.

Lights lit up one of their branching paths, and into the tunnels they went.

Allie briefly shifted her inner sight from the two in the labyrinth to where Riven was now battling a ceaseless tide of abyssal monsters. They came in all shapes and sizes ranging from a mouse to a house, of all variations of nightmares, with tentacles, jaws, and claws. The champions of each group were wary of each other, too, with three of them having already turned on the others ps. This was probably at the time each of those three groups was at the end of their own labyrinth, and it was probably done in a desperate rush to get a key or insights to leave the twentieth floor—as the two of three champions who succeeded in their act of treachery vanished from Riven's fleshy enclosure soon thereafter in flashes of light.

The angel of death turned her gaze back to her immediate surroundings. She was getting gradually more angry as time passed.

The remaining three will make the keys, with any others obliged to be: The rest of the party, including all minions not already selected for other roles, will be set to the task of creating keys that unlock the doors at the end of the labyrinth with crafting materials provided by Elysium. The Seekers, your two weakest, will be unable to traverse through the last part of the maze without these keys.

She was not alone in her growing irritation. Azmoth, Retesh, Fay, Athela, and Fimrindle were equally as stumped. The room they found themselves in was some kind of puzzle room, and one that none of them had even an inkling of figuring out so far. The screaming woman shackled at the altar seemed to be in a perpetual state of agony with the shackles burning not only her skin, but her soul as well. Allie could literally see and feel the woman's soul writhing in agony with her adjunct deathly vision, and she'd done little else but scream despite an attempt to interrogate her. Upon further inspection, Allie had actually deduced her to be an angel of some kind—but her wings had been cut off, leaving bleeding stumps, and the shackles around her wrists and ankles keeping her chained to the bloodstained altar were unbreakable by any means Allie or the others possessed.

The huddled, sobbing mess of once-beautiful prisoners in the cages were in similar states, and of similar species for the most part—the majority were also imprisoned angels stripped naked, men and women, their wings cut off—but despite them not writhing in agony, they all looked upon Allie's group with fear, disgust, and abject horror. Other creatures she did not recognize were also there in lesser numbers, those the system identified as Phoenix Kin—people with glowing gold-orange feathers sprouting from their heads, arms, and legs like hair— and Holy Spirits, which Allie found incredibly interesting as they were some kind of Holy-based undead. How that worked outside the realm of the Death subpillar, she had no idea. They were almost like wraiths, but golden in color and seemed unable to pass through the bars of their cells despite repeated attempts. All three races must have unnaturally high Charisma, as Allie's gut instinct was to puke or skewer them—and she had no doubt the opposite effect was likely why none of them wanted to communicate with her, either—she had negative twenty thousand–plus Charisma points as an angel of death.

It was a stark reminder that the system thrived on conflict, and she doubted she'd get any help understanding what was going on from those caged here. In some ways, she didn't even want it. And what was worse was that even though she'd never even met these people before, she felt a distinct hatred toward them without good reason for it. She WANTED to see them die . . . and to make sure that it was painful.

That in itself and the implications of what it meant fascinated her. Even if she'd logically known about it before, it was something else seeing it up close with such drastic opposing Charisma for beings of the opposite path.

One of the angels snarled and spat at her while she inspected the bars, but she didn't even bother wiping it off, passing by the sobbing captives before sighing and turning to look at the rest of the room. Fimrindle had explored the pools of black water along the edges of the room and found nothing inside them but a seemingly bottomless pit that he suggested they all avoid after he'd nearly been lost to their depths once.

Retesh had dug through the hill-size pile of bones and said each bone contained odd inscriptions that resonated with his cultivation paths—but in ways he could not distinguish. This had been confirmed by Allie herself, but even she could not put a finger on just what the inscriptions meant or did, so the lich was conducting experiments on them as they explored.

Azmoth was repeatedly diving into the lava pit, which had contained numerous blocks of red-hot spheres at the bottom—but they seemed inert when infused with any type of mana to date.

While the butcher's tools on the rack next to the sacrificial altar were . . . simply put, infused with such vast amounts of sin that holding even one of them drove the person mad. Fay had literally gone crazy and started swinging a cleaver around while screaming about "infinite darkness," beginning to bleed from her eyes before Athela had knocked the cleaver out of her hand and coddled the sobbing succubus. Whatever visions Fay had seen while holding the weapon were very off-putting, to the point that none of them had attempted to pick another one up after that, but it might come down to not having a choice.

Finally, in the epicenter of their strange room, floating above the screaming, chained angel on the bloodied sacrificial altar, was the abnormally large humanoid wraith. It continued to smile without fail—the malice in its grin an ever-present staple on its otherwise ethereal gray face. Its clawed fingers drifted along with the wisps of its similarly ethereal robe in a wind that wasn't there, and it seemed to turn most of its attention to either Retesh, Allie, or Fimrindle rather than the three demons.

Allie's suspicion was that this wraith was doing so due to how she, Retesh, and Fimrindle were all Death-oriented beings, while the demons were not. But any attempt at speaking to the wraith only resulted in one thing, regardless of who spoke to it or what they said.

And yet, she tried again in her frustration—whirling around and marching over to the floating being while ignoring the screams of the angel strapped to the altar. Allie's wings flared out to either side in growing rage, and she pointed a bone-covered finger in the wraith's direction. "Tell me what we need to do here, phantom. I am growing tired of wasting time, and if you do not . . . I will burn that pathetic, sickly smile right off your fucking face after I turn your fucking soul to dust. I bet you wouldn't be too happy-go-lucky then, now would you?"

Despite her threat, the wraith just continued to smile—and uttered the same phrase it'd repeated nearly thirty times over since their arrival to this odd pocket of reality. It opened up its clawed fingers and spoke. "A smile to carve, a smile to keep. Golden nectar flows, a drink from the enemy, and I shall speak."

"JUST WHAT THE HELL DOES THAT EVEN MEAN?!" Allie screeched, priming one hand with energy from the pillar of true death as she got ready to strangle the damn wraith before a curse from Fimrindle brought her attention to the right.

"Wait! I know that verse!" the reaper exclaimed, a sudden look of realization overcoming his usually inexpressive metal face. His *X*'s for eyes grew in size, and his rigid iron jaw twisted into a silent smile. Between her blinks, he was standing next to Allie with a scroll in his hand.

Confused, she took the parchment from her minion's outstretched palm. She blinked again, and he was kneeling submissively.

"I apologize . . ." he rasped like wind through a pipe. "I have not heard the verse for so long that I'd nearly forgotten it, but I believe it to be a scripture from the Book of the Scythe. It may be a clue . . . Please, examine the page I have produced from my own holy texts. It may explain just what the wraith wants and why we haven't seen any progression in our attempts thus far."

"Book of the Scythe?!!" Athela exclaimed in outrage, still holding Fay's head to her chest to console the other woman. "How the bloody F-ing fudgerockets are WE supposed to know that babbling bullshit?! That's so unfair! How is ANY demon supposed to know that kind of crap?!"

Despite Athela's angry muttering, Retesh the lich was quick on the scene and looked over Allie's shoulder while she unfolded the parchment.

"I've heard of this book in legends from my homeworld, but I haven't ever seen a piece of scripture myself," the lich rasped while planting his bone staff into the stone floor. "Will you read it out loud?"

"Sure . . ." Quelling her own irritation with Fimrindle for not realizing this sooner, Allie took in a deep breath and began to read aloud.

But as she read the entirety of the scripture, a vision from the past illuminated the room—and the path forward was laid bare as the answer for what they had to do became clear.

This was no puzzle room.

Oh no. This was a ritualistic reenactment, and one that had to be followed to a T.

CHAPTER 31

The out-of-body experience was vivid, real, and it was almost as if Allie was living within someone else's skin. She could not control her own body, but she could still feel her lungs take in air as the vision of a ritual long past was played out in front of her.

The enormous hall she walked down was covered in golden blood. To a mortal, or someone who could not truly see, it would have seemed endless. But not to her, not to her sight that'd been born of darkness. Her pale, ghoulish feet splashed in the warm liquid coating the cold, hard stone of the dark passageway. Ceremonial robes were draped over her head and around her shoulders, rustling in a slight, cold breeze as screams echoed from the end of the hall.

Drums. Drums began to beat in the beyond, echoing with the chants and roars from the crowds that began to ring in her ears.

For she was the bringer of the end times. The one to divine the will of the dark gods, to bring about an endless age of black that the lightbringers would forever despair to see. The age of celestial kingdoms was ending. Now . . . the age of the necropolis had finally come.

Even the demons would bow before the might of the Scythe.

Space split open before her, warping to her will as the overlapping false reality distorted. That reality then disemboweled itself and rolled upward to let her pass into the true corridor, and when her pale, bare feet lightly crossed over the threshold between realities—she found herself standing on a heightened temple platform overlooking vast valleys out to the horizon. The sound heightened fivefold, and the very air around her shook as she stood before her disciples with hands raised high.

Millions of undead chanted, stomping their feet while roaring in tune to the beating drums. Far below her, the legions of flesh, bone, and spirit all raised their hands in worship as the defiled dance of death continued in her name.

In the name of the Scythe, her mentor . . . her father.

Dozens of fabled angels of death, heroes of the unliving, decorated in splendid black and gold garb, knelt to either side of her with bowed heads and outstretched wings. Bone giants the size of skyscrapers standing in rows beside the temple slammed their giant ivory spears into tower shields, and a loud gong sounded over the crowds. Pyres of teal flame shot skyward with the wail of innumerable souls, crashing into the black clouds above before exploding to illuminate the masses out into the dark world beyond.

There was no end to her legions. They spanned across the horizon in all directions, having come to worship her name.

"My children . . . my friends . . . my family," Allie's voice called out in a whisper that all could hear, and an eerie silence overtook the once rowdy legions as their deathly gazes fixed on her at the top of the temple's platform. A wide smile creased her lips, and she lovingly spread out her pale hands as if to embrace them. "I welcome you . . . to the beginning of the end for our long-standing enemies. To the ones that sought out a genocide against our people! To the ones that for so long evaded our reach in their high heavens while raining down terror and flame upon those weaker than they! TO THE ONES THAT THOUGHT THEMSELVES UNTOUCHABLE! I WELCOME YOU ALL, TO WITNESS THE SACRIFICE OF QUEEN EL-FAH OF THE GOLDEN LIGHTS, ARCHANGEL OF THE HIGH HEAVENS AND BRINGER OF RIGHTEOUS FAITH! BRING OUT THE PRISONER!"

If Allie thought the crowds had gone wild for her own arrival, they went ballistic at this call. It looked as though the sea of bodies that stretched out for miles beneath her had erupted into a frenzied storm, with palpable killing intent radiating off them as they screamed in both hate and excitement for the prisoner to come forth.

A hole formed in the stone of the temple's platform beside her, and soon a figure began to rise out of it. A large altar carved from bone, stone, and steel rose from the depths with a scarred and burned angel chained to its top. Her once-brilliant white feathers were covered in splashes of golden blood, her hair cut short, and her glowing eyes were aflame with unhidden rage. Deep cuts marred her once-perfect skin in crisscrossing patterns, and she struggled against her shackles while snarling—teeth bared toward the body Allie was looking through.

"You wretched bitch!" the angel said, her chest rising and falling violently before her eyes darted around at the scene. "The heavens will not stand for this! They will find you! I WILL BE AVENGED!"

The woman Allie was seeing through, living through, let out a mocking sneer. She did not reply to the chained woman at the altar, but instead she turned her head up to the black clouds above. "Bestow my instruments to mine hands, Father."

Brilliant neon-teal lightning tore across the sky from miles away and crashed into the temple Allie stood on. In an instant, Allie felt a surge of deathly energies unlike anything she'd felt before. It swirled around her like a vortex of the purest Dao, an insight into the truest meanings of the end, and it bowed to her will as she stretched out a hand.

As she began to whisper, her words carried once more—even over the roar of the millions of her followers, as she used the Scythe's power to bring about the means to her building ritual.

"The hearts of hell burn brightly this night," Allie's ghostly voice projected, with the angels of death repeating after her like a mantra. With those words, a volcanic bath of molten lava, coated in Infernal power, bubbled up from nothingness into being. Her pale fingers slowly lifted, and with them came dozens of red-hot metal spheres that floated up out of the bath. They glowed dangerously hot, flexing the power of hell from their cores as she bade them encircle the chained angel.

Queen El-Fah of the Golden Lights, archangel of the high heavens, let her eyes go wide as she realized what they were. "YOU INSOLENT WRETCH!"

Allie continued to ignore her, moving on to the next empty space nearby. "The bones of the perished that we seek to avenge."

The roaring vortex of deathly energies screamed in protest at the vast amount of energy she siphoned from her father, as the angel's crimes were innumerable. The amount of devastation Queen El-Fah had caused the undead was not a number she even fathomed to comprehend, and it was proved by the sheer volume of bones that rained from the skies.

They started falling like snow, coming from the dark clouds above only to turn into a roaring avalanche. Countless bones of all shapes and sizes materialized and began to condense over the temple in a swirling mass of ever-growing, cursed energies that sought to rip out the holy archangel's life energy. But the cursed energies, made from spite and malice as a retribution of the heavens, stayed their hand when Allie's pale fingers lifted to them in warning.

"Not yet . . ." Allie's voice uttered, and the growing mass of cursed bones heeded her command.

She shifted her gaze and pointed to the floor around the altar with a wide smile. "The pools of despair . . . the prison your body will ever know after this day, and a fail-safe to make sure that you will never know resurrection, even if the commandments themselves seek your revival."

The bloodied, chained archangel began to shriek even louder, flailing madly against her bonds in a futile attempt to get free with powers volatile enough to shatter mountains—but she was still unable to free herself. Her eyes were wide and frantic, and her chest continued to heave as the chains binding her to the altar began tightening of their own accord. "YOU CANNOT DO THIS! YOU CANNOT! THIS IS SACRILEGE! THIS IS AN EVIL EVEN YOU CANNOT—"

"Silence." Allie's cold voice came as a midnight's breeze, crushing the celestial queen to the stone altar with an audible gasp. One white wing snapped under the sheer killing intent Allie's body unleashed on the woman, before Allie smiled wickedly. "I am not yet done. Bring out . . . the others. Your family and friends will join in your despair."

From the back of the temple and through a set of large stone doors, bone golems dragged out other angels, all of them above the A-grade, drenched in their own blood. Their wings were cut off and their faces terrified. Once they'd been supreme enemies of the underverse, and now they were sacrificial lambs—a conquered people—their honor and pride cut out from underneath them just as their wings had been.

A tray of various tools, imbued with the horror and sin of untold generations, was summoned by another of her followers and held before Allie's eyes. Her wicked smile grew even more, and she picked out one of the many blades—shuddering as its intent filled her, even as powerful as she'd become. Eyes aflame with malice and mana, she turned a crazed look on the bound, sobbing angel at the altar.

"A smile to carve, a smile to keep!" Allie flew forward to the roar of the crowds, gripped the woman's face, and cut off her lips. Golden blood splattered all over the altar as the victim wailed uncontrollably before Allie's body lifted the piece of carved flesh to the sky with a victorious pose. The swirling balls of red-hot hell hearts stopped floating about the altar, each of them crashing into one of the other nearby victims with sickening thuds—before the final one sank deep into the archangel's chest. Each of the angels began to scream and wail with unearthly cries as their Holy pathways were burned away entirely, their cultivation stripped and their souls flayed from the inside out.

"BRING FORTH THE GOBLETS AND BLEED THEM DRY! WE WILL MIX THEIR BLOOD WITH THE WATER OF THE ABYSSAL PONDS AND CREATE THE KEYS TO HEAVEN!" With a wave of her hand to the bone cloud that'd formed above the temple, the bones all condensed—and began to shoot down toward her position with a gleeful vengeance pouring out of them. Crashing into her outstretched hand where she held the lips of the angelic queen, they began to merge . . . and she began to chant as she called out a singsong rhyme.

It was time to open a portal into the heavens, a ticket for them to strike back.

She turned her dead, abyssal eyes on the horrified, screaming celestial queen beneath her as the metal ball, the hell heart, continued to burn her from the inside out. Smiling maliciously, Allie raised her cursed blade and then slammed it mercilessly into what remained of the angel's heart. The reaction was immediate, and the angel vomited golden blood that was soon captured by angels of death in black goblets, whereas others took golden goblets and began scooping up water from the black pools that'd been summoned through the power of the Scythe.

Taking one of the goblets in her own hand, Allie smelled the intense aroma of fear that permeated her victim's essence—and let out a sigh of relief. "Perfection . . ."

Bringing it to her lips, she drank the golden fluid and then watched as the carved-off piece of the angel's face began to sing songs corrupted by the fused bones while the black skies poured down ribbons of white light through forming cracks.

The breach into heaven had begun.

And it was time to seek retribution for the crimes of the holy ones. She would butcher them to the last child, and none would be able to escape her wrath.

Then her vision violently shifted, as if she'd been wrenched out of one room into the next by chains of hot iron handcuffs. A familiar soulscape with teal skies and obsidian pillars had found her once again, and she found herself staring into the fierce, intelligent eyes of a lion made completely out of Sin energy. It remained seated across from her as if it had never left.

Her eyes snapped shut in confusion as her brows deeply furrowed. Wait. Why did she only now remember this place? The last time she had this vision was shortly before the Floor Two's raid boss fight where she and the rest of the team had fought Riven. But in the time between now and then, she'd forgotten it completely?

What the hell was going on?

Heat pressed down like a smothering cloak as Allie opened her eyes to the same cracked and dusky floor, runes glowing faintly red like dying embers along the obsidian pillars around her and beneath her feet. The pillars still stood, impossibly tall, with carvings weaving like veins pulsing in a rhythm too ancient to be named.

The lion rested with one massive paw crossed over the other, its tail flicking lazily behind. Its mane writhed like smoke—dark energy coalescing and unraveling in spirals.

"You've finally returned," it said, its voice deep and slightly mocking. "Good. You are beginning to understand."

Allie approached, her steps slow, heavy. "Why am I here, again?"

The lion tilted its head. "Because you are still searching."

"Searching for what?"

"For meaning."

There was a pause.

She folded her arms and grunted. "Are you a part of me? If so, can you tell me why I couldn't remember our last meeting until now?"

The lion gave a noncommittal shrug. The act infuriated her, which was rather obvious by her expression and only served to make the lion bark out a deep guttural laugh.

"Fine," she said, folding her arms and stretching out her wings. "So tell me. What is your meaning?"

The lion raised an eyebrow. "I know my meaning. It is you that needs your own. I am not the one who must find introspection. Have you ever asked yourself what your purpose is? Other than to merely survive, what is it that you wish to bring to this multiverse? What are the goals beyond yourself that you wish to meet, should you ever gain the power to do so? Have you taken the words I gave you last time into consideration, that you should harness your anger into a tool to use for your benefit?"

Philosophical ideologies were not something she'd thought she'd be discussing right now, but if this were a part of herself or some strange figment of her own mind, then she might as well humor the lion. Though by the way it talked, it didn't seem to think it actually was a part of her soul.

Strange.

Allie opened her mouth. Closed it. She looked away, jaw clenched. When she spoke, her voice was low and venomous.

"I want to tear them apart," she said. "Every last one who's wronged me. I want to see them crawl and scream. That's my meaning. Butchery. Vengeance. But I'm not sure how to use my rage like you asked me to. It just sits there, inside me, wanting to express itself but not knowing how."

The lion watched her, smiling widely with fangs bared.

"Ever since I found out my mother contacted Riven," she continued, her voice trembling now. "I've become angrier and angrier, and the rage never seems to fade away. Why did she abandon us? Why would Riven not find it within himself to tell me of their talk? She's alive. After all this time. And she . . . she didn't reach out to me. Not even a word. Just tossed me away. Like I never mattered."

Her fists shook at her sides.

"I . . . I think I want her to feel what I felt. I want her to look into my eyes and realize what she created. I want her to beg for the daughter she left behind, and I want to say no."

A silence stretched between them, heavy and raw.

"I miss Lahn," she said quietly, voice cracking. "I hate that he's not here, and at least with him I know he loves me. I'm angry that he can't be here when I need him, I need his thoughts and his words. Elysium's path keeps tearing people away from me like I don't deserve to keep anyone, and it makes me all the more angry—building layers upon layers."

She looked up at the sky, jaw clenched. "The humans of Panu want to burn us, the undead. Like we're just filth. I didn't ask for this. We didn't start this. I didn't ask Prophet back then to launch a crusade against our kind, and it has evolved far beyond that to a worldwide cause. Now I even have a world quest labeling me as a target to kill, as if it's some kind of sport."

Her voice rose now, laced with fury.

"Elysium showed up and ruined everything about my life. We were poor back then, before the integration, but we were surviving and happy. Then when Jose—Riven's best friend—got slaughtered back then like it was nothing . . . that could have been avoided if Earth had just been left alone. He didn't need to die, and instead of having him here with us, his tombstone is underneath a tree in the garden of our manor back on Panu."

She turned back to the lion, tears hot in her eyes. "I hate it. I hate all of it. The war for my right to live. Elysium. The gods. This . . . this endless universe that keeps stomping on us like we're beneath it. I hate the fact that I'm always angry and I even hate existence itself. I want the multiverse to burn, I want it all to burn down to the ground, so that I can finally have peace."

The lion watched her in silence. Then it nodded in understanding.

"You are beginning to see," it said, and its voice was almost a purr. "You are beginning to burn too, and soon your fires will spread."

With those last words, the lion opened its mouth, and all light was sucked from existence. She found herself falling through a deep void, her memories of the encounter fading once again along with her sight as everything turned black.

Black lightning and red frost encircled Riven in a vortex of violence. The storm tore through dozens of abyssal creatures by the second in an almost comical spray of body parts that splashed across the room made of flesh, where it was quickly absorbed by the floors and walls themselves. It was as if he was standing inside the plugged mouth of a giant lamprey, where teeth along the walls occasionally flexed and shot forward on long tendrils to slash out at him before withdrawing or being destroyed. Occasionally the teeth would also spray acid, and when other champions did occasionally fall to the hordes of various black beasts or the teeth of his strange enclosure, they too were dragged through the flesh-made ground and absorbed into the realm with whatever had killed them.

There wasn't even an opportunity to take their belongings or loot the others, which Riven found irritating. He'd even go as far as to try and protect the corpses of the dead from the beasts that'd ripped them apart, or had blasted away the teeth and attached tendrils with wrathful vengeance, but even riftwalking over to their dead bodies wasn't fast enough to take their belongings as loot.

Briefly glancing through the mind links at his counterparts in the maze and the ritual room, Riven grimaced slightly at what he saw beginning to unfold. The maze was by far the most worrisome, as he wasn't sure that Nora and Narg were up to the challenge, being their weakest members—but that in itself held true across all groups. And the ritual room? They were all in and out of various trances and experiencing visions in short snippets . . . but the implications didn't look good, even if seeing those caged high-Charisma creatures gave him gross and even aggressive feelings on an instinctual level.

He grunted, shoving one of his hands outlined in rigid Crimson Ice claws through the face of a muscular bear creature before ripping out its bottom jaw and smashing it into the ground. Casually spinning around the flaming horned skull atop Jackal, he brought it down with an explosion of hellfire that splattered the creature into charred mush.

"This is rather boring . . . Maybe I'll get to fight that giant later," Riven mused, bending backward to dodge another hooked tooth that'd shot out from the wall and frying it with a bolt of Black Lightning.

Others continued to enter his meat grinder one after the other with roars, wails, and splattering sounds, and his four totems emerged from his spatial bag to add to the carnage. The twenty-sided polyhedrons rapidly began to flash and swirl around him as he let them go, beginning to mix in their own sparks and ice with the storm.

Increasing his mana output and then commanding Jackal to take its abyssal beast form, the winged canine stretched and groaned, giving him a happy bark as it patrolled the inner perimeter in his eye of the storm. Floating up five feet off the ground and crossing his legs, he leaned forward with his chin in one hand and yawned—growing comfortable in the fact that his totems and channeled storm of energies were more than enough for most creatures. He watched as Jackal tore down the bigger or more powerful beasts one by one whenever they managed to finally get through, and finished off his preparations by creating layers of a spinning sphere from liquid blood. It wasn't a registered skill and thus didn't have the potency that it otherwise would have had, but instead was a film of pure blood mana that—if broken—would notify him of an impending attack in his blind spots if his regular mana pulses didn't pick up a hidden foe.

Beginning to meditate in a lotus position, he watched the other groups' champions as they struggled to keep the monsters back.

There were two mind-sets between the champions. Option one, which Riven had chosen, was to fight on your own, to stand alone in order to avoid backstabbing. It was highly likely that if another champion saw you struggling, they'd be willing and even eager to kill you in your moment of weakness to steal any insights or keys that your group had made. This was brutally obvious from those who worked together in option two, where the rest of the champions had tried to form a circular unit to stave off the swarms of beasts. And though the number of champions or groups fluctuated every couple of hours, between newcomers and those who'd already been here as they either died or descended to the next floor, a solid third of those deaths were from friendly fire landed by other champions.

Riven winced as another vampire was decapitated by a minotaur warrior after getting downed by one of the spear-like teeth, and the minotaur rapidly vanished, meaning his group had likely been needing a key. That key had just been stolen, per the rules of this mini-event, and the demon had essentially just doomed the vampire's group by sending additional waves of enemies into the maze and the ritual room.

[Abyssal Descent Trial for Floor Twenty has been activated: The Crazed Giant's Maze:

- **The first to speak will fight for all five: As the one who has spoken the words aloud, Riven has been labeled Champion. You will be thrown into a pit of despair with champions of other groups against a respawning wave of randomized abyssal enemies. Minions are unable to aid the champion here. If Riven dies, the rest of you will be set upon every ten minutes by waves of enemies that increase in strength and number.**
- **The two weakest will be your guides: Nora and Narg have been designated as Seekers. Your two seekers will be sent into the giant's cylindrical maze and will be hunted by the weakest of other teams and various abyssal beasts in their attempt to navigate to the end. The crazed giant will also attempt to eat anything it can get its hands on, including your seekers, as the flight through the maze continues. If both seekers die, the rest of you will be ejected from the Abyssal Descent entirely and may not ever return.**
- **The remaining three will make the keys, with any others obliged to be: The rest of the party, including all minions not already selected for other roles, will be set to the task of creating keys that unlock the doors at the end of the labyrinth with crafting materials provided by Elysium. The Seekers, your two weakest, will be unable to traverse through the last part of the maze without these keys.**
- **If this cannot be done, you unravel another one, in order to take their gift: Killing other champions in one-on-one combat, or killing other seekers, will allow you to take their keys and insights to add to your own party.**

Do this, and you will pass into the twenty-first floor of the Abyssal Descent. Fail, and you will be devoured by the crazed giant in body and soul. Identification is nullified on this entire floor. At the end of this floor, you will gain an insight into one of your paths.]

Brutal. Riven remembered when such things would bother him. When he'd been naive to the truths surrounding his path. He'd been so soft back then, when the integration had first struck. Now . . . he had quite the opposite problem: He was more focused on getting the items of the dead than on protecting them.

Could he protect these people?

Sure.

Was he going to?

Meh. They were just as likely to kill him while he used up all his mana taking on more of the fight. He couldn't trust these people as far as he could throw them. And despite the Unholy foundational pillar not necessarily making it a point to only bind to those who were evil, Riven wasn't dull enough to realize that the odds were stacked in favor of users being bloodthirsty and aggressive.

He had to choose his own people and himself over strangers. It just was what it was.

Or . . . so he thought.

Just as he was pondering this, a startled feminine cry caught his attention when an elvish stealth archer of some kind had been slammed to the floor under a large, snarling ape. He'd only noticed her due to the brief flashing arrows she'd shot out and the occasional pulses of his mana—but otherwise she'd been damn good at concealing herself. The large ape had noticed her somehow, though. It was pitch black, just like all the other abyssal creatures and had a single large eye in the center of its forehead, with large spines sticking out of its back.

Riven's eyebrows shot up in surprise as she began to scream, having been torn from stealth as she was battered with outstretched hands in a feeble attempt to block the enormous ape's balled fists.

The creature roared, sending spit all over the poor woman as bone snapped and her terrified screams turned into outright sobs. She began to beg, to plead for help, and Riven saw one of the other champions on another team dive in toward her. But the horned man wasn't aiming for the gorilla—rather, it was aiming its blade for the dark elf.

Riven sighed and raised a hand, then hesitated. Why was he interfering? It wasn't his place to—

The drow woman let out another last cry of pitiful desperation. Her bloodied, battered body was forcefully turned by a fist strike as her pale eyes met his. "PLEASE HELP ME!"

He winced involuntarily. Did he have a soft spot for her because she was pretty? Or was it because she reminded him of Athela? He winced yet again. "I'm going to regret this."

KABOOM

The enormous fleshy room blazed red as a shock wave of Crimson Ice obliterated the surroundings. Piercing crimson spikes roared from the walls and floor, and enormous ice novas collected overhead in a blooming flash before nuking the place multiple times over in waves of shrapnel.

But the shrapnel wasn't random, it was directed by his influence and avoided those he wished to live.

In an instant the screams and roars of the abyssal creatures were cut off. Red mist hung in the air, and the horned man who'd been charging the brutalized drow archer had a spike sticking through his skull as he hung limply in place only a few feet away from where the woman lay. Everyone else was more or less untouched by his attack and stood staring awkwardly or with incomprehension at what had just happened. A few shot unbelieving gazes in his direction, and it was quite obvious that none of these people were the top crop of the Abyssal Descent—so to speak. The fight against Amano, the half-minotaur, half-gargoyle who'd kicked his ass numerous times, had given him a very keen idea of what the true powerhouses of this place were. At best, these champions he currently stood with were probably mid- to low tier when compared to the best of what the descent had to offer.

Which was nothing to scoff at, considering they'd gotten this far in the first place, but they shouldn't have been so awestruck at what he'd just done if they'd been worth a damn in a fight.

Cracks began to shake the outer walls as more monsters began to spawn and pound at the thick layer of ice keeping them out. Roars started to be heard once again, and Riven's storm had already dissipated before he landed gently on the floor next to the sobbing drow woman clutching one of her shattered arms.

She looked up at him with a mixture of fear and confusion and winced when he knelt down to get a better look at her.

"Here. Open your mouth," Riven said, putting a hand into his spatial sack and taking out two bottled potions, one red and one a bright sky blue. "They should help."

"I will not be poisoned!" the woman hissed in agony, scooting across the ground as her blood-drenched hair covered half of her face. "I'm fine!"

Raising an eyebrow for the second time in a short period, Riven casually pointed a finger to his right and blasted a flying abyssal creature—splattering its guts all over the floor before it managed to swoop in. "I don't think you are. And if I wanted to kill you, I wouldn't have come to your aid when you asked. You're being stupid—I'm not going to take your keys or your life."

He moved closer to her, and she let out a hiss.

"Do not come any closer!" she barely managed to get out between ragged breaths before he smacked her into a dazed state.

Riven immediately forced the two potions down her throat during the moment of silence, as she was on the verge of death and the slap maybe had been a bit harder than he'd thought, but he gave a satisfied nod when he saw bone begin snapping back into place with flashes of blue and red light. "There we go. Now . . . doesn't that feel better?"

The woman was screaming in pain again as the bones reoriented themselves, but it was obvious by the end of it that she no longer had a broken arm. Her cuts and wounds were all gone, and with a wave of his hand, even the blood coating her face was wiped away and drawn into a sphere hovering over one of his hands.

She blinked at him in shock, and as the sounds of battle began roaring around them yet again, Riven nodded to Jackal's canine form before snapping his fingers. His totems began swirling around him again as the vortex of black and red grew like a rose, encircling the two figures in a protective formation of lightning and razor-sharp frost.

The woman slowly sat up, flexing her hands and shooting nervous glances around her as she quickly realized that—should she anger him at all—she would immediately die. And she was still recovering with the aid of the potions he'd given her, even if her outer appearance showed little damage. Casting her pale eyes onto his figure again and frowning down at the shattered remnants of her bow, she wiped her face of tears and reached down to pick up the broken weapon before speaking. "Why did you help me?"

If Riven had a record for how many times one could raise one's eyebrows in surprise during a short period of time, he may have just broken it. "Because you asked me to. And because you look very much like my girlfriend. That may seem stupid, but it was certainly part of the reason."

A winged serpent splattered onto the inside of their enclosure, not having made it halfway through the storm of energy as it landed in a smoldering, sliced heap.

He eyed the monster indifferently and caught her gawking at him.

"What?" Riven asked curiously, leaning back and pulling his knees up to his chest. "Do I look funny or something?"

She slowly pointed his way. "I've seen you before . . ."

"Is that so?" Riven asked noncommittally. "Where would that have been?"

He knew the answer was coming before it came out of her mouth. She'd no doubt seen him in the battle over the city on the first floor of the Abyssal Descent, as many others had.

"You're the asshole vampire who slept with me, stole my bag of holding, and then convinced my team to run off WITHOUT ME!" the drow woman screamed in a building rage, her pointing finger quivering in anger.

"Yes, I—" He held up his hand, about to admit that yes, he was Gluttony's reincarnation, before he abruptly stopped with furrowed brows and confusion spilling from his face. "Wait. WHAT?!"

SMACK

The dark elf reached out and full-on slapped Riven across the face so fast that he barely registered it. Then again, he'd probably just been in a state of shock and the strike had taken him by surprise.

"You JACKASS!" the woman roared, getting to her feet and kicking at him with all her might while simultaneously sobbing again. "I'VE HAD TO TRAVEL THE DESCENT ALONE BECAUSE OF YOU! DO YOU KNOW HOW HARD IT IS TRAVELING WITHOUT A PARTY?! DO YOU?! DO YOU KNOW WHAT IT'S LIKE?!"

"OW! Stop that!" Riven protested, smacking her kicks away before he froze her to the ground, causing her to fall over and giving Jackal a shake of his head when the winged beast glanced questioningly their way.

Jackal shrugged, then went back to patrolling the perimeter of their eye of the storm—snatching out abyssal creatures the totems or vortex weren't able to catch.

"It's in there, isn't it?! Give me back my bag!" the elf said, reaching forward and attempting to snatch it from Riven's side with angry tears building up at her eyelids. "You have RUINED this experience for me! And I thought we had something special!"

"I'M NOT the man you—"

"I'LL NEVER TRUST A VAMPIRE AGAIN! NOW, UNFREEZE MY FEET SO I CAN KICK YOU A THIRD TIME!!!"

Rolling his eyes and facepalming, he let out a groan. "Jesus Christ. Look, Karen, I don't know who you think I am—but let's get one thing clear. I have NOT slept with you, nor have I—"

He was cut off as, through the mental link, he saw Genua, Athela, and Fay all turn their inner sight upon him.

"YOU SLEPT WITH HER?!" Athela screamed at the top of her lungs while still trapped in the ritual room. "You cheating PRICK! We'll be talking about this, Riven!"

"Pervert," Genua muttered.

"I haven't had the good stuff for a week! THAT'S NOT FAIR!" Fay exclaimed.

And Riven could only facepalm as the three of them started laughing at his unhinged situation from the other side. He was already regretting saving this crazy bitch, and it took the others no time to capitalize on his misfortune.

"Isn't this supposed to be the Abyssal Descent?" Riven said over the shouts of the still recovering and enraged dark elf. "Feels more like *Jerry Springer* right about now. Listen, lady, I don't know who you are or what—"

SHUNK

He paused, startled, when a dark blade punctured a shield of ice he'd summoned right before the elf had impaled his left eye. Moving the shield of ice with her black blade embedded in it, he glared at the seething, rabid young woman with a flare of his crimson eye.

"That . . . that was a mistake," Riven said, lifting his hand in her direction. "A very, very big mistake."

CHAPTER 32

Retracting his fangs, Riven let out a long gasp as he let the drow woman's blood run down his throat. It'd been a while since he'd fed on Genua, and going too long without feeding made him feel sick.

He let the body drop to the fleshy floor with a squelch, eliciting a gurgling sound from the woman he'd saved not long ago before he snorted in disgust at the weaponless archer as she clutched her throat. He watched her horrified gaze stare up at him as she choked on her own blood, using her spare hand to claw at the air in a begging motion as he let the fear sink in.

But he wasn't a complete monster, not yet. He just wanted to make a point. Even if she had attacked him, he was pretty sure she was having something akin to a mental breakdown due to high stress. He still had some humanity left inside his increasingly black soul, and so he just let the knowledge that he could easily kill her on a whim sink in for a while until she was on the verge of death—before utilizing Voodoo Doll to keep her alive. As he worked the magic, her blood flow stabilized and the near-death state she'd been put in quickly reversed. Pouring yet another healing potion set down her throat, he watched the pathetic speci-men in front of him cough and choke—visibly shaking before vomiting the blood that'd been draining down her throat while she gasped for air.

"Next time you attack me, I'll just let you die," Riven said with a blank face, sitting down in a cross-legged position and occasionally sending out bolts of Black Lightning to vaporize some of the abyssal swarm—getting thankful nods or call-outs from the other participants every twenty seconds or so. Turning his gaze back on the elf after she'd caught her breath, he let his red gaze focus on her—and could still hear her heart beating furiously in her chest while she glared back at him. "What? Got something to say, you crazy bitch?"

"I am NOT crazy!" she hissed, starting to back away from him on all fours, but she stopped herself when she saw the broken bow at her side. Her features fell, and another glance at Riven saw her face fall even farther when he used his tongue to lick some of her remaining blood off his cheek. "Are you toying with my life? For your own amusement? You vampires disgust me."

"Not enough for you to sleep with one of my kind, apparently," Riven said with a mocking wink. He sent another haphazard blast of lightning out to the screech of another abyssal creature, and the Ripping Claws and snarls of his winged companion, Jackal, could be heard behind him as the beast tore down another of the abyssals. Riven's shadowy black cloak, the one Athela had given him for his birthday, pulsed red on the inner bloodsilk side when he sent a wave of mana around the two of them to create another bubble—and he chuckled at the elf when she nearly scrambled out of the way and into the swirling vortex.

"What is it you want?!" the woman snarled, looking like a caged dog while simultaneously missing any true bite given her apparent need for a weapon to fight with. "Why are you keeping me here?!"

He raised an eyebrow and cocked his head. "Keeping you here? We're all kept here until our parties create the keys and exit the giant's labyrinth. I thought I was doing you a favor, despite your absolute batshit attitude. But if you insist on believing that it was me that betrayed you and left you to your apparent fate . . . Wait. You said you were traveling alone? How is that possible, given this challenge?"

Her gaze became icy, and her fist clenched. But she was still shaking, and it was very obvious that she was afraid by the way her eyes flitted about to see if she could somehow find a way to escape. She also didn't respond.

Sighing after a good amount of relative silence had passed between them, Riven waved his hand—and the inner bubble of blood mana along with the outer swirling storm vortex of red and black created a passageway for her to leave. "You may go if you want. You are not my prisoner here."

The sound of battle crashed down upon them as his protective barriers opened up, and the dark elf froze in place—eyes going wider when she saw another one of the abyssal apes that'd almost crushed her to death. She took a step forward, hesitated, looked down at the bow, backstepped, and seemed absolutely unsure of what to do.

"Choose, or I will simply kick you out," Riven said, getting irritated. "I won't keep that passage open forever. It exposes me, too, and I really am not in the mood to go all out right about now. I need to conserve my strength because, frankly, I don't know what to expect at the end of this. Assuming my weakest party members are even going to get through that damn maze."

And it was true. He had no real indication of just how powerful or useful Narg would be in the maze, even given his seeking abilities, but he was hopeful. Whereas Nora was just deadweight. He liked her, and she'd helped him in Chalgathi's trials during their very first system event. It was also the reason he didn't mind helping her out now . . . but realistically he could have chosen a better partner for his descent in the abyss. He'd never say that out loud, as he didn't want to hurt her feelings—which made him internally laugh considering who and what he was—but friends were friends regardless of how weak they were.

Which made him wonder just how well the rest of his guild, or rather, his guild-to-be, was doing—and the thought made him smile. Hakim, Tim, Julie, and Tanya were all still undergoing a training regimen back in the Brightsville area, if things were still going to plan. However, from the reports Lillith had been giving them before she vanished, it was very unclear just what was going on back on Panu. Thoughts of Kathrine came next, and of Mara, of Vin and Nin and how they'd all gone missing . . . and his heart sank again with his smile fading just as quickly as it'd come. He could only hope that Tre'Zix of the Purple Claw was just as good as Lillith claimed he was, because if not, the others might very well be dead. Why, who, and how—those subjects were also questionable, and he knew that Allie hadn't seen Lahn in quite a while, either.

What did Lahn think about all this? The guy was probably worried sick because of Allie's long absence. Riven had grown to like Allie's new boyfriend very much, especially after her little phase of collecting numerous boy-toy thralls that made him want to gag. He vividly remembered that musclehead bastard she'd turned into a sex slave back when he'd first set up his guild hall, and—

He shook his head. No, that was just him being an overprotective and somewhat hypocritical big brother. If anything, the tables had turned. He was in a three-way relationship with Fay and Athela now, and he didn't even know what to consider Genua after that one-night stand and what it'd led to. And if Kathrine lived, he had no doubt her family would still want to make sure they wed for political reasons. And defying the Blood Moon Requiem wasn't a good idea in the longer term . . . even if he truly didn't want to add that kind of headache into his life.

Ugh.

"I SAID, CLOSE THE PASSAGE! I'LL STAY! I'LL STAY!" The drow woman's shriek cut into his thoughts, and he rapidly shook his head and looked up to see her fending off a large abyssal worm that repeatedly struck at her with quick snaps and sprays of smog.

She was only barely holding on, and she had a deep bite wound that was bleeding profusely on her right thigh—which was already collecting rot similar to Fay's cursed clouds.

Just how had this champion even gotten this far in the Abyssal Descent? If all it took was snapping her bow in half to make her so useless, she shouldn't have come in the first place. Jackal was also staring at her as if she was some kind of oddity, and the living weapon gave Riven a shrug and a side-eye as if to say he didn't get it, either.

With a casual snap of his fingers, Riven's mana pulled the drow woman inside again and the vortex smashed through the temporary passageway he'd created through his storm. The worm was obliterated in an instant with a loud shriek, its black body torn to shreds as the dark elf stumbled backward and hit the floor.

"How the actual fuck . . ." Riven muttered, pinching the bridge of his nose and closing his eyes ". . . did you ever get this far while being so utterly pathetic?"

Watching Narg and Nora traverse the maze was interesting every once in a while, but it was also very nerve-racking because of all the close calls. Close calls that, if Riven had been there, would have been a breeze. Meanwhile, the rituals the others were performing with the sacrificial altar were grotesque even for his tastes, and he had no wish to gaze upon the disgusting things they had to do to those poor caged souls in order to acquire each key.

And thus he'd decided to take his mind off it and continued pretending that nothing at all was wrong, because he couldn't do anything about the other groups anyways—and worrying about it would only lower his mood.

"So . . . what's your name?" Riven eventually asked after having healed the dumbass across from him for the third time. He reached into his bag of holding and pulled out some bread that he began to chew slowly while glaring down the obviously panicking woman as she rocked back and forth. "My name's Riven."

Her tear-stricken and bloodshot eyes darted up to him, and she shuddered— one hand still on the thigh where her thin, studded armor had been torn off. Where the monster had eaten a part of her leg. She rubbed it slowly and seemed to come back to her senses while wiping away droplets of the third round of potions he'd given her. "I won't be able to take another set of potions any time soon . . . I'm already starting to feel sick, and the effects are lessening."

Riven blinked, then let out a burst of laughter as he threw his head back. Giving Jackal a head scratch and pushing the winged canine off to patrol the inner perimeter of his storm again, Riven rubbed his temple while continuing to chuckle. "You're acting like it's a given I'll give you another one! Let me tell you something, girl. That is the LAST time I heal you. The next time you get injured, even if it isn't due to attacking me, I just let you die and use your corpse for sustenance. You're way too stupid to just keep pumping potions into at this point, and I've certainly done my community service for the month after helping you out. So, as I said . . . what—is—your—name?"

He emphasized the last four words with a bit of irritation on his lips. "And I truly hope you've realized that I am not the man you originally thought I was, given that I've removed my mask and you can see it for yourself."

His words looked like they struck a chord, and he saw guilt, embarrassment, as well as fear edge into a sheepish smile before her pale eyes hit the ground. She fidgeted with one of her boot laces. "I . . . I am not sure that I should tell you. You wouldn't believe me if I did."

He raised an eyebrow and folded his arms. "Want me to kick you out—"

"No!" She quickly held up a hand in protest and harrumphed with a guilty lack of eye contact. "No . . . Please don't. I'll die."

Riven snorted. "That much is obvious."

There was a long pause, and she considered him evenly. "I apologize."

"For which part? For sullying my name and accusing me of sleeping with you in front of my girlfriends? For trying to stab me? For ignoring my questions? For being stupid enough to nearly get killed three times in a single hour? Or for being stupid enough to come down here in the first place without a party, apparently, and obviously not being qualified to be here without a bow that you recently broke. Your very presence insults me. So which is it?"

She blinked, blinked again, and blushed furiously with embarrassment as the sounds of fighting continued around them monotonously. "Um . . . I . . . eh . . . all of them?"

"Good answer." Riven snorted again. "Now, who are you? And why are you here alone? How is that even possible, given the party system?"

The young woman grumbled something under her breath, rubbed the part of her thigh that'd recently been bitten off and healed, and lowered her head. "I am here because I have no other choice. I need to get to the fortieth floor or I will be disowned from my family and cast out of my sect. My . . . My name is Kara Blackbow, seventh daughter of the Ashen Sage of Purturis."

She nearly stumbled over her words, and her shoulders sagged as if in relief when Riven didn't give an immediate response. Then when she finally gained the courage to look up at him again, she became confused. "You . . . do not recognize the name?"

He merely stared at her blankly. "Am I supposed to? This is the multiverse. Do you know how big it is? Because I certainly don't and I'll be damned if I'm supposed to know some guy by the title of Ashen Sage."

She immediately gawked, then smiled, then began to giggle and laugh. Her laughing became a thunderous cackle, and she rolled over onto her side in a fit as humorous tears began rolling down her cheeks until she almost had a hard time breathing.

He sat there, cross-legged and increasingly unamused, as he realized that she had gone and lost her fucking mind. This woman was insane, and he probably should have just let her die the first time around. He would get no information out of her, and she was a god-awful conversation partner. Especially after trying to stab him.

His eyelids lowered.

"I'm sorry! I'm sorry . . ." she said, wiping her eyes and trying to let go of the smile that'd enveloped her. "I just . . . it's just that you're right. I keep forgetting where I am. You probably wouldn't know. My family probably isn't that impor-tant on the grand scale of things."

He continued to stare blankly.

She caught onto his lack of amusement, coughed, and straightened. She then took a cross-legged position across from him and gave him a bow of respect. "I again apologize for my actions and extend my thanks to you. To answer your question from earlier . . . I had no choice but to proceed into the depths of the Abyssal Descent by myself. As I said, I will be cast out from my sect and disowned by my family if I do not succeed. That in itself is a long story, and I will spare you most of the details, but the party I entered with was paid off by another man. A vampire, likely an agent of one of the other sects, and I was abandoned by my own. I'm surprised they didn't just kill me outright, but I'm guessing they wanted to humiliate me rather than just end me. Given who it is that likely paid them off, I probably shouldn't be so surprised. If I manage to survive and come back home without success, that would be a far worse fate than if I were to just die an honor-able death here in the darkness."

Her voice had taken on a rather stoic tone by the end of her words, and her face had turned grave.

Riven's previously angry and irritated attitude slowly began to dissolve, and he bade her rise from her bowed position with a gesture. "I accept your apology and thanks."

She gave him a nod and straightened once more in her sitting position. "I was able to enter this event by myself, but due to a lack of party members, the system has tasked me with staying here for twenty days. I am on the second day now . . . and without a weapon. It is highly likely that I will die here once you leave."

Kara Blackbow smiled sadly, as if having already accepted her fate, and didn't meet his eyes. "What you said was correct. I don't know how I got this far outside of sheer dumb luck, and I don't belong here at all. My family is powerful and well-known, or at least that's what I'd thought. But that is likely only true for our region. Regardless, we were able to acquire a ticket for me to enter the Abyssal Descent as a way for me to prove my worth to my father. Aside from my abilities with a bow, I am quite useless in combat. That much is now obvious to me."

Riven blinked from underneath his hood, arms still folded. "I see. Why didn't you just team up with another group before coming down?"

She raised an eyebrow. "I know you cannot identify me due to system inter-ference down here, but I am not even classified as an ELITE by Elysium's stan-dards. I am the bottom rung of what gets in here, and without my stealth abilities and managing to surf on the coattails of other groups that were unaware of my presence, I'd probably be dead five times over. All my belongings were also stripped from me when I was robbed, aside from my clothes and bow, which is now gone. Even my arrows are nearly spent."

She cocked her head to one side. "Why would anyone want to take me with them? I'd only slow them down, but I have no other choice but to proceed or die trying."

Riven was beginning to understand, and he was starting to feel a little bad for the young woman. "Sounds like your father, or whoever it was that sent you here, sent you to die. And it sounds like someone else is hoping to see you fail, too, if it wasn't his people that paid off your kin. Why even go back?"

She looked like he'd smacked her across the face.

"That . . . that isn't true," she muttered in a whisper. "My father doesn't want me to die. It's more complicated than that."

Riven disagreed, but her abrupt attitude change signaled that he'd hit the nail on the head. He wasn't going to push it.

Then an idea formed, and he thought of a way to cheer the poor girl up. Digging through his spatial sack, he pulled out a set of supplies.

The first item was a rolled-up ball of Athela's bloodsilk, which he could use to repair his own cloak, as it was incredibly sturdy—and it had an inherent tie to the Blood subpillar.

Next was one of Gragle's graphics. The multidimensional runic sigils interlinked to one another glistened with blood, sin, and shadow energy while they shifted around each other in the light of his storm. Riven had yet to completely get how to create graphics, but despite Gragle's promises to try and teach Riven as much as he knew, Riven had not had the time nor the ability to produce them consistently or without impurities—so he'd have to modify this one to the best of his ability without destroying it, given what he was about to do.

After that he pulled out abyssal sigils glowing a deep purple, various Dao treasures, a few spiritual crystals, and two of the silver rings off his hands, placing them all on the floor.

Kara's eyes went wide at the display, and her mouth clenched with an unreadable expression as Riven got to work. "What is your name? I told you mine, but you never told me yours."

"Riven. I already told you that. Remember?" Riven said with an amused smirk, creating a long shaft of Crimson Ice that he began to mold into the form of a bow.

"Just Riven? No title? No family name?"

"Just Riven."

He fused three layers of Athela's bloodsilk together after that, reinforced them with an abyssal sigil that dissolved into the strings after a system prompt, and the bowstring flashed with dark-purple light.

"All right then, Riven . . ." she repeated, furrowing her brows and all but ignoring the raging battle only a couple dozen yards outside of their protective barrier of storming mana. "How did you afford all this? The price of these treasures is . . . astronomical."

"Is it?" Riven asked, shrugging indifferently. "I sent the bill to someone else."

"So someone bought these treasures for you?"

Riven nodded. "More or less. I guess you could say that I inherited the money . . . but it's a long and complicated story."

"I thought you had no title or family name?"

Riven didn't humor her question.

His hand reached for her broken bow, and strings of blood wrapped around the wooden pieces—taking them over to where he sat as he inspected the etched sigils carved into the weapon.

It was low-quality at best, making him feel even worse for the poor girl. The power infused into each arrow was what he'd have wanted back when he was level 30, and the runes were poorly carved. Even he, at the beginning of his path in totem-making, could tell that the enchanter had been subpar. He removed the string as he laid his own ice-made bow over the top of her old one and began to concentrate as he closed his eyes.

"What are you doing?" Kara asked, with some hope in her voice. "Are you fixing my weapon?"

He let on a smile. "That and more. Now be quiet, I'm working here."

There was a flash of red light, followed by another flash of purple and then black. His eyes opened, and the ice bow he'd created had molded over her original like a shell casing. Athela's bloodsilk strings sparked red and purple, and black runes he'd mentally channeled into the weapon had their backbone imprinted on the shaft's exterior.

His eyes shifted to the silver rings he'd taken off his hand. Each of them had massive boosts to basic dexterity, and he warped the metal with a flex of energy—placing them around the middle of the shaft as they fused together where the handle would be. Ridges were created afterward as the metal bent and twisted, creating a hold for fingers when gripping, and another abyssal sigil was added and infused into the shaft just as the string had been reinforced.

The red ice darkened with the effort, and Kara watched slack-jawed in awe and in silence. "I did not realize you were a crafter as well as a mage."

"You're primarily Shadow-based with your abilities?" Riven stated, only partly asking, since he'd seen her abilities already.

She nodded quickly after snapping out of her dazed state. "Oh, um, yes. I have a 70 percent affinity to the Shadow subpillar, and most of my abilities stem from that."

He went back to work after the confirmation, selecting from his Dao treasures a plant and crystal pairing. The crystal was an obsidian gem the size of his fist that sucked in all light in its vicinity, making its true dimensions hard to make out. The plant was a vine, black at its core but with silver thorns protruding out from around the coiled stem.

"What exactly are those?" she asked, inching closer to sit beside him. "I can feel their energy and know them to be true Dao treasures, but I can't identify them. Do you remember?"

He coiled the vine into a tighter formation and wrapped it around the shaft, absorbing it into the outer red shell as the black runes along the dark-red ice began to flare. "The plant has silencing properties, and the gem has gathering properties. Basically, if I'm doing this correctly—which is questionable at best—I should be able to add a percentage possibility for a silencing effect to anything you shoot from this bow. The gem will be used to gather shadow mana from your surroundings and allow you to empower your shots with additional shadow damage while making your shadow abilities cost less."

Riven gave her a weak smile. "That's assuming I don't mess this up, of course. I'm depending more on the quality of the materials rather than my actual skill, because I'm kind of new at this. Only been creating totems for a year or so."

"Only a year?! You'd risk such valuables on a chance that you'd fail?!" she said, perplexed and something akin to horror-struck.

Riven nodded. "You betcha. It takes my mind off the current situation anyways, as I'm just sitting around doing nothing and I kind of feel bad for you."

She seemed startled at his reaction, but quickly subdued herself to look down deep in thought—focusing on the work he was doing and occasionally shooting him curious glances.

"Thank you," she whispered.

He pretended not to hear.

The gem itself was far harder to incorporate than the vine, and he ended up blasting it into smaller pieces to create a fine powder out of the crystal. Infusing it into the ice, the bow went from a deep red to a dark black with the previously inscribed rune almost completely gone. There was a subtle red glow to the bow now, aside from the silver handhold, and he summoned the second-to-last piece— the graphic—to him with a wave of his hand.

"What is that?" she asked, confused but also eager as she watched the obviously intricate set of three-dimensional runic tapestries shift and stir. "I've never seen anything like it in my entire life."

"It's a graphic," Riven replied, pausing in his creation of the weapon to point out different aspects. "Graphics are a way to formulate magic of thought into physical concepts by using base code of Elysium's system. They are the skeletons of magic taken visible form, and an advanced concept I myself am not entirely familiar with. I know the basics, though, and have a gnome teacher who's trying to impart his knowledge over time, but this is one of the ones he made. Thankfully,

I DO know enough to manipulate them to an extent and can modify this one a little to better suit your needs."

She seemed eager and interested when he glanced right, causing him to chuckle at the excitement evident there, and so he continued in his short speech on the matter.

"There are three concepts, Re, Vo, and Tin, that act like an axis to travel along when inputting source code. Then there are another two concepts, Nun and Zika, with Nun representing orientation and affinity of a power source like your Shadow subpillar. Zika represents power of intent. The base concepts of Re, Vo, and Tin I am going to leave intact because they're far more complicated, and the construct of this specific graphic is already well done. However, the more malleable concept of Nun can be modified away from the Blood and Sin energies infused into it to orient themselves more toward shadow."

Riven's fingers twitched, and the graphic turned a dark black over the course of seconds. "Now I'm modifying Zika, which is the power of intent. The original graphic's intent was protective, that of a barrier or shield. I'm changing it to pierce and speed now, which should better suit your needs."

The three-dimensional set of interconnected runes shifted and warped, forming a different model before their eyes.

He grinned. It had worked. "Lastly, I will pluck a soul shard from the void around us. Totems with soul shards are far easier to control and more likely to bind than a fully formed soul, and though they are less potent, it is probably in your best interest given that you'll need the weapon rather soon. There'd be a chance this weapon won't want to bind to you if the totem I'm making had a fully formed and aware soul inside it, and truthfully, it'd probably want to bind to me instead of you given my affinity for shadow is higher—and I also have affinities for the other Blood and Sin energies running through it."

His Death subpillar shivered and pulsed, and his gaze warped to see into the void just like Allie had taught him to do over the course of their last few sit-downs while here in the abyss. He saw what he was looking for in the vast expanse of darkness and glittering lights around them and plucked a tiny fragment of light from his surroundings before retreating into the present. Holding out his hand, he showed the flickering fragment of random soul he'd acquired to the dark elf, who let out a sharp breath at his presentation.

Pushing the piece of soul into the bow, he saw the weapon shudder underneath him. A blast of energy encompassed the area they sat in, and the black bow began to wreathe itself in dark-burgundy sparks as the silver metal of the bow's center shaded to gray.

[You have created the item Black River Bow of Sin's Wrath (Totem). Details on this item are negated due to the event status effect.]

"Now, for the arrows, since you're low. This part will be easy," he said with a gesture at her nearly empty quiver, laughing at her gawking expression of amazement.

One by one, he began to create Sniping Profane Blood Lances, the upgraded version of his original Blood Lance infused with his snipe ability and empowered by Wretched Snares. The Blood Lances thinned and shortened, becoming arrow-size as the Black Lightning sparks shifted over the red shafts. The Wretched Snares used to propel them to greater speeds also enclosed themselves over the arrows, and he modified the spells to explode upon contact—an effect that'd blow up and shred the target with the snares upon impact now that the arrows were being propelled by the bow rather than the original slingshot effect of the snares.

One by one, he created dozens of these arrows and cut their magical intent off from his control. Inspecting each of them and making sure they were stable, solid, and without any flaws, he used his mana to shift them over to Kara's quiver until the quiver bulged.

[You have created the items Sniping Profane Blood Arrows. Details on these items are negated due to the event status effect.]

"There you go. I think this'll help you survive a bit longer," Riven said somewhat smugly as he handed the bow over to the drow woman, who continued to stare in wonder at the item—her hands shaking slightly at the gift he'd given her before taking it in her grasp.

Abruptly, the dark-burgundy sparks flared and danced along her hands, up her arms, and into her body as she shuddered. He stared, watching her as he felt the pact between the totem and the dark elf manifest despite a lack of system information, and then was surprised to see her begin to cry.

She sniffled, trying to blink away her tears and hide her face beneath one hand and a swath of white hair while gripping the bow in the other, before silent sobs racked her body as she stared at the floor. "I'm sorry, I'm sorry, I just need a minute to collect my thoughts."

His gaze softened and he nodded, looking away to watch the rest of the champions do their thing. Jackal came over and nudged against his right shoulder, and he reached across the winged abyssal dog to give Jackal head scratches with a hum of contentment. After a few minutes had passed, and she still showed no signs of calming, he floated the question he'd been considering since realizing her predicament.

"You know, our fifth member was prematurely sent down to the fiftieth floor," Riven said aloud over her body-shaking and semisilent sobs. "My group could escort you to the fortieth floor on the way down. You could join us temporarily if you'd like."

Sniffling and wiping away her tears again, she looked up through bloodshot eyes and puffy cheeks. "You would do that? For me? For a stranger you'll never see again after all is said and done, when I leave for my homeland?"

Riven shrugged. "Why not?"

"Because I am deadweight," she said flatly. Looking down at the weapon he'd bestowed upon her, and then the enchanted arrows he'd given her, she shook her head. "Believe me, I would be more than happy to accept, but the things you said to me earlier were right. I won't be useful to you in your descent, if that is what you are hoping for. I'd more or less accepted my death down here, but if you are offering . . . and you truly mean it, then I will not decline if the system allows it to be."

Riven smiled and patted her on the arm. "Ah. Good point. Let's find out then, shall we?"

Mentally willing the system to accept his request, he waited for Elysium and the Abyssal Descent to respond.

He didn't have to wait long.

[Do you wish to add Kara Blackbow to your party? As Lillith is currently trapped on Floor Fifty of the Abyssal Descent, Elysium will accept your request for a filler until you reach Lillith—if you manage to survive until then. But doing so will cost you three billion Elysium coins as tribute. Do you accept?]

"Lillith?" she asked. "Who is that?"

The notification was present for both Riven and Kara to see, and she immediately winced upon rereading it—her hope fading just as quickly as it'd come.

"I don't have that kind of money, Riven . . ." She trailed off, only for her to choke on her words when he accepted the prompt and a tidal wave of coins flew out of his spatial sack toward the notification before blinking out of existence.

[You have added Kara Blackbow to your party here in the Abyssal Descent. Kara's twenty-day time limit has been modified to normal parameters, and she will proceed to Floor Twenty-One with you upon successful completion of your other party members exiting the giant's labyrinth.]

"RIVEN! That kind of money is enough to bankrupt my entire SECT!" Kara screeched, whirling on him and leaping to both feet with wide eyes. "I cannot repay that kind of money!"

He smirked. "Whoever said I was asking you to repay the debt?"

She was immediately stunned into silence, and only took a seat again when he gestured beside him. "Thank you for your kindness, Riven. I don't even know what to say. I am . . . undeserving."

"Do not think much about it," Riven said, beginning to meditate to restore all the mana he'd used up on creating the totem. "I don't even know how much money I have anymore. I haven't looked in a long time. Now, sit down and rest. We likely have a lot of time to burn."

CHAPTER 33

Nora was losing control, and Narg was getting worried.

The beholder demon narrowed its many eyes at the human as she clutched her chest and made gasping noises, hitting the ground and jerking in odd ways that weren't what he would consider normal. She'd been getting worse as time went on, with traces of black and silver showing up on portions of her body to change it into something other than flesh, but Narg wasn't sure exactly what it was before it reverted to regular muscle, skin and bone.

Even her eyes had changed color from their usual brown to a sickly white, and she was mumbling incoherent sentences to herself and sometimes aloud for all to hear until they'd ended up here. Here at the dead end of a hallway, where Narg had a clean shot at anything that might or might not attempt to kill them.

"Nora . . . can you hear me, child?" the demon asked, keeping two of his eyes swiveled on stalks to stare behind him—always on guard. "The others are counting on us to finish this, Nora. Take another one of your healing potions and it may help—"

His words were cut off as another roar from the giant chained to the lava pit in the center of the cylindrical labyrinth caused the ground to shake violently. It was deafening, giving Narg a killer headache as frustration began building up inside him. Down the hall, the glow of the lava illuminated the dark stone—and the sound of battle could be heard.

Scowling, Narg went over his options. He could leave Nora here to die—if he understood things correctly, her dying here would only banish her into Chalgathi's event, and she'd lose out on all the time and effort put into doing this. Part of Narg thought this the obvious and best choice, as he couldn't be slowed down to fail the reincarnation of Gluttony like this. He would rather die than be such a burden and bring such shame to his family. To fail Gluttony and his bonded partner, Riven, would be worse than death. Sweat began to accumulate on Narg's green skin just from thinking about it.

"No . . . no, I can't leave her. The Great Maw would not have allowed her to come if he wanted or expected her to fail now. It is my duty to see her through this, as she is a friend of the reincarnation." He let out a deep, shaky breath. "So just how do I do that if she's comatose?"

Narg sent out more pulses of Seek Danger, Seek Object, and Seek Safety. Pathways congregated in his mind, manifesting as streaks of light that pulsed for a few seconds before dying away, leaving invisible trails only he could see. Seek Safety flared its light right where he'd positioned them so that he could collect his thoughts, reaffirming that this was still a good hiding place to think over his predicament. Seek Object, which he'd focused generally on "an exit," showed multiple paths he could use to leave—all of which ended at the same spot far down somewhere on the very bottom floor of the maze. Meanwhile, Seek Danger flared brightly in the direction of the chained giant and interior of the cylindrical maze, as well as immediately to the right at the next bend, where fighting could be heard. Surprisingly enough, Seek Danger also flared a more vibrant light to the left as well . . . and as Narg watched its pulse, that light began to creep closer by the second.

Whatever or whoever it was had completely concealed their presence from him. He was unable to detect a sound, and he couldn't sense a power signature at all. Not even the barest hints of mana, divinity, or stamina were detectable . . . and Narg was beginning to get nervous after it got within twenty feet of his position just around the left bend.

Silently flying up to a dark corner of the dead-end hallway he had helped Nora to, he saw the hues of Seek Safety began to flicker out and die around him—as the presence finally made it to the edge of the wall.

But he saw nothing.

Hoping he was sufficiently hidden here in the dark, which only had about a 20 percent chance of success by his guess due to being in an abyssal plane where most creatures could see in dark places—he waited. If it was another maze crawler and not a spawned creature, he'd still have a chance—and Narg had little choice in the matter, as he wasn't about to leave Nora behind.

Seconds passed, and still nothing. His Seek Danger and Seek Safety castings began to fade, and the last of them died away with the previous impression showing that whatever or whoever it was had stopped dead in its tracks directly in front of him. Narg was a beholder demon and his many eyes could pick up on most stealthed opponents, and he even had a trait called Scoped Vision that could make out extremely minute details even at a distance—but he could sense nothing.

Should he just blast the area anyway?

He was considering this just when a person stepped out of stealth and began walking slowly to where Nora was still gasping, choking, and convulsing on the ground.

It was a skresh wearing assassin's garb. The skeletal humanoid had an extra arm on its left side as well, making the cloak the skresh wore appear bulkier and lopsided. The two left hands each held daggers, while the right hand shifted in and out of reality with an odd combination of pillars that Narg couldn't pinpoint. Two feet into the hallway, the skresh stopped, then turned its dead gaze upward to look at the exact spot Narg now pressed himself into.

And if the skeleton could smile, Narg had no doubt this skresh would be doing so right now.

"Nice hiding place," the skresh let out in a masculine rasp, chuckling to himself as his daggers repeatedly spun absentmindedly. "But I suppose I shouldn't mock you too much . . . there aren't any better ones. Not here. Regardless . . . it appears your companion is out for the count. And given what you are . . . I'm assuming you're a mage."

The skresh cocked his head to the side, raising his left hand that continued to phase in and out as a wall of mana crashed down in front of Nora as Narg manifested a nightmare barrier. The undead was obviously unfazed by Narg's display and didn't bother taking a step back.

"I am," Narg replied, floating down from the top corner. Channeling Unholy and Infernal energies into different tentacles leading up to his various eyes, he kept both piercing Globspitters and explosive Hellspitters locked in on his target. "But let us cut to the chase. What do you want? If it is our deaths to claim our keys, our group in the sacrificial chamber has not yet made them."

The skresh scoffed, and the twirling of his daggers stopped. His dead gaze seemed to leer at Narg as if to wordlessly call him a liar and an idiot. "That's exactly what someone with keys would say, now isn't it?"

Silence ensued for nearly two minutes as they stared at one another.

"But I am a kind skresh and am willing to let you go with your life," the skeletal man said with a low bow—eye sockets never leaving Narg. "Under one condition."

Narg furrowed his brows and floated closer to the convulsing woman on the floor in preparation for a potential attack. He could feel the aura of death starting to pour out of the undead, and the underlying suspicion of this skeletal man's power after failing to detect him earlier was all but confirmed. This was not a fight Narg would win, but he was not willing to fail Gluttony's call, either. No matter what, he must prevail. "And what would that condition be, stranger?"

The skresh assassin clattered his teeth together and raised slightly. "Let me kill the human girl. They are a weak species anyways, and you can obviously do without her. You will lose your keys, but your team will be left with one to complete the maze after they remake the keys a second time. It is a good offer, considering the alternative is both of your heads . . . Or, in your case, your eyeballs."

It wasn't a funny joke, but the skresh certainly thought it to be as he cackled outwardly and brandished his daggers as his aura soared. Deathly energies crashed into the nightmare barrier of flame and shadow with just a passive flex of the undead's soul, and Narg cursed inwardly as he decided on what to do.

He didn't have much of a choice.

"Fine," Narg said with a frown. "She's deadweight to me anyways. You can have her, just leave me be."

Somewhat surprised, but pleased, the skresh stepped back and lowered his blades along with his shimmering right hand. "Very good . . . Very good. I am happy that we—"

Narg lit the undead up, unleashing all his Unholy and Infernal attacks that eradicated the hallway in front of him with subsequent blasts. The skresh evaporated into thin air with an echo of a snarl, but he'd been ready for treachery and dodged all of it without much fanfare.

However, it did leave the hallway open to run for it. Or, in Narg's case, fly.

Without a word, Narg picked up Nora's twitching body in his mouth. Encompassing them in a sphere of molded nightmare barrier, he pointed all his accessory eyeballs behind him and charged over a dozen Hellspitters. With another resounding boom, he unleashed the fiery spells in an explosion that sent him blasting forward like a rocket—past the assassin that attempted to slash down at the passing duo—and out toward the inner cylinder of the labyrinth.

Directly toward the chained giant.

Narg's mind raced as he ducked and wove around the unnaturally fast assassin, who was managing to keep up with Narg despite the propulsive explosions the beholder demon set off one after another for quick trajectory changes. Most of the attacks were deflected by the barrier, but once in a while the shimmering hand would pierce through the veil and attempt to grab at Nora—the easier target—before Narg quickly dodged to avoid the swiping hand as he raced through the winding tunnels.

Abyssal hounds roared as he passed them by, and the thundering boom of a giant fist caused the maze to shake again as tortured wails from the chained giant grew louder. But Narg didn't dare stop; he was on an alternate path now—the path he'd set out for them should something like this happen, a situation where he knew they wouldn't be able to win and had to take a gamble.

He was headed for the drop-off and would attempt to dive down through the open air to the lower levels—thus exposing himself to the giant that he'd seen swat down so many other flyers in their attempts prior to this.

"Come back here, you wretch! Give me your keys!" the skresh screeched, blurring past in a swath of death and shadow before extending a hand and sending numerous bone javelins out of his warping limb over the course of three seconds.

Narg activated Seek Safety in a split second before the original struck and followed the path it laid out, managing to successfully dodge all the blurring projectiles by tracing his skill's outline.

The skresh gawked.

But Narg didn't bother waiting to see the undead's reaction as a Globspitter's piercing green bolt was sent blasting through an erected bone shield the skresh had summoned, sliding the assassin backward by a few feet and cursing loudly.

Narg flashed by.

The beholder demon wove up, down, left, and right as the large hallway widened out and zigzagged until the molten glow of the enormous lake of lava became more prevalent. Cracks in the labyrinth's floors showed he was in an overpass of some sort with the lake far below, and not long after that he came to the beginning of an opening where a ledge overlooking the magma was in full view.

He'd almost done it.

Using one of his eyes to look back, he saw the assassin racing to catch up, with another dozen of the black labyrinth hounds rushing behind the skresh as they too took up the chase.

On the other side was possible salvation in the form of an enraged, charred giant.

All around the cylindrical, cavernous room were other ledges, outcroppings, and exposed pathways where only occasional flickers of movement could be seen. A dashing monster here, a sneaking participant there, only for the monstrous giant's blackened, sizzling hand to crush one after the other in quick succession—managing to kill perhaps a third of the creatures that dared expose themselves to the titan. Despite its burned-out ears and eyes, it had uncanny accuracy and had the strength of ten thousand of anything roaming these abyssal halls.

Narg was just hoping that it would be too distracted to try and go for him.

With the assassin's shadowy form closing in, Narg used a final burst of flame and blasted into either side of the hallway's end with two different eyes. The residual explosions sent him out like a cannonball, and soon he was airborne.

Far, far out into the middle of the room, Narg soared—barely managing to outpace a spiraling dagger infused with death essence so potent that the air around it warped.

Taking a sharp turn and diving low underneath a quick swing from the massive giant, Narg's heart almost stopped as the fried limb of the titan broke the sound barrier and whooshed overhead. The residual boom that sounded out when the giant missed him and impacted the far wall made Narg almost bite down on the woman in his mouth, but he managed to get ahold of himself and began a direct downward spiral—looping around the giant's waist toward the molten lake.

Meanwhile, Nora was dealing with her own problems. Narg just couldn't see it.

The familiar, ancient presence of numerous entities she'd grown up with pressed against her mind like a flood about to break. But they were anything but welcome.

Smiling, crazed figures of shadow and claw smiled endlessly out at her. A legion of grins, devoid of anything but malice. Entities of true evil, not Unholy, but actual evil—were sitting inside her soul, waiting to be let out.

She could feel their claws digging through the barriers she'd erected to keep them out of her dreams, but now, in this place, they seemed to have grown stronger. And they'd been stronger ever since meeting Riven again and having been in the presence of Gluttony. They wanted to be near him, and they wanted to be free of the mental prison she'd trapped them in.

"We are friends . . . friends!!! Let us out! Let us out!" they cooed simultaneously, speaking together without ever dropping their sick, crazed smile. The silver-white eyes were the only outstanding colors in a sea of black, and they almost seemed two-dimensional due to just how black they were. She could not make out any real dimensions beyond their outlines as they tried to swarm and press against each other for the forefront of her attention. "FRIENDS! FRIENDS! FRIENDS! WE ARE FRIENDS! WE ARE FRIENDS! LET US OUT! LET US OUT!"

Nora internally cringed away from the smiling faces, beginning to cry as she screamed over the building crescendo of the insistent begging. "Please, just go away . . . Please . . . You're all scaring me . . ."

"NORA, NORA, LET US OUT! NORA, NORA, LET US OUT!"

CRASH

Pain.

Intense pain brought her back to the real world, as she felt her bones shatter in dozens of places all at once. She wanted to scream, but the air was torn from her lungs—and the world spun as she splashed into a giant pool of lava. She opened her eyes wide in shock, seeing Narg only a few dozen yards away getting snatched out of the lava where he'd landed. A huge hand gripped the broken, bloodied beholder demon as he was picked up by the charred and chained giant—and a look of fear overcame Narg as the beholder was brought up to the giant's gaping mouth.

A squeal of horrified pain, and then a bloody crunch resounded in the labyrinth as the giant began to chew on the demon before swallowing.

It looked down at Nora next, the enormous, blind creature somehow sensing she was there—sinking slowly into the magma while burning alive. She croaked out, too weak to move, and watched as the giant's bloody mouth widened before it brought down its other hand to reach for her next.

"FRIENDS! FRIENDS! WE ARE FRIENDS!" the voices echoed in her mind, and without anything left in the tank to hold them back—her curtain of Willpower fell.

And the creatures that'd been held back for so long began to reclaim her. Memories of murders. Memories of being locked in an insane asylum, and then a women's prison, and then a maximum-security lab where she'd been experimented on by her government all came flooding back to her. Memories that she'd suppressed, as that sickly smile the monsters inside her wore began to spread along her own face. Her skin began to lose focus, turning into a shade similar to vantablack, and her eyes began to glow with a soft silvery light.

But the pain . . . the pain had vanished entirely.

"Friends, friends . . . we are all friends!" Nora whispered to herself with a giggle, her mind snapping as reality lost focus—and she lost her sense of self.

She was no longer Nora.

It was THEY who were Nora.

They were all Nora. They always had been. They always would be.

And they would never be apart from her again.

They . . . were one.

[Bloodline: The Insane Asylum has been activated. The Insanity stat has been unlocked. Your soul has rearranged itself with the help of your Others. Your soul lattice has taken a massive step forward and is almost complete. Congratulations, you are nearly at the E-grade.]

CHAPTER 34

The magma around Nora's body was dispersed in a half-bowl shape underneath her as a howl of laughter tore out of her throat. It was her voice, but overlaid with hundreds of other voices that all laughed alongside her as a chilling cold spread across her body.

Her long black hair extended from shoulder length to halfway down her back. Her ears became extremely long and pointed, like an elf's but far longer. Her eyes became a blank silvery white—unblinking. A manic smile sporting across her black skin to show a series of sharp, silvery-white teeth, and the inside of her mouth blanched to a similar color.

As her clothes burned away under the flickering remnants of fire left behind by the magma, she no longer held true definition. She was, at first glance, two-dimensional—a flat outline of void with silvery-white eyes and a silvery-white smile.

And as the giant's reaching hand came to grasp at her, that smile only grew wider.

"WE ARE LEGION!" Nora's voices called out in a tidal wave of laughter, and she pointed a single finger at the charred giant as if to mock him. "CONSUME!"

The entire labyrinth began to shake as a pulse of dark energy flashed out of her finger, instantly eradicating the hand and forearm of the chained giant like it was nothing. The giant's surprised and horrified reaction was abrupt, and his scream echoed out across the stone as he fell back with a loud splash into the magma—his good arm holding the stump where Nora's attack had eaten it away.

But in another instant, Nora was there—above the giant's burned-out eyes and continuing to smile ruthlessly down at the creature. She held out her arms as if to embrace him and lifted her head up to the dark ceiling far above. "A SOUL TO TAKE FOR THE ENDLESS ARMY!"

Wails erupted from her body as a tidal wave of dark figures began to peel off her skin with a terrifying, hungry keening. The figures began to grow eyes and creepy smiles similar to her own, with silvery-white light illuminating their otherwise two-dimensional vantablack figures as the clawed, wraithlike demons tore out of her body and launched themselves at the giant half-buried in the magma.

The sheer number of black bodies piling onto the giant and devouring it was overwhelming, and despite the flailing of the crazed giant and the power behind its swings, it was unable to hit Nora even once. She stayed in place, letting the strikes attempt to crush her as they simply passed through—never losing the sickening smile as she watched her Others strip the flesh from the giant's bones. The bones came after. And then the soul. It all flowed into her like a river of multicolored light, being sucked away into her endlessly black body as her eyes flashed brightly.

[Your personal Insane Asylum has added a soul to its reserves: Cursed Abyssal Giant. You may now summon this enslaved creature to do your bidding as a Legion version of itself, becoming slightly weaker than the original but obtaining immortality as long as your entire legion is not destroyed. Personal Insane Asylum: 5,000 Others, one Cursed Abyssal Giant. You are now able to connect with other Insane Asylums that you come into contact with, should you wish to do so.]

Nora giggled and then screamed with laughter in a storm of voices, becoming higher pitched by the second as she doubled over while floating in the air—her body radiating an invisible energy that continued to keep the magma at bay in a rippling half sphere underneath her. The Others were laughing as well, and they launched themselves back out of the magma to playfully poke at her and one another—doing flips or zipping around like children on a playground.

But when another hesitant participant was seen staring out at her in bewilderment and awe, Nora and her Others abruptly stopped. In an instant they all turned simultaneously to smile at the unfortunate necromancer, and Nora slowly lifted her finger to point at the man.

"DEVOUR!"

A resultant scream sounded out, and a wave of black bodies rushed into the maze as her Others started eating everything they could come across. Rising up to float farther in the air, Nora groaned in pleasure as soul after soul, beast after beast, participant after participant was dragged screaming and thrashing into death; they were all food for consumption as her soul lattice continued to build.

"I am the master of this labyrinth now!" Nora's voices echoed like a ghost throughout the complex as the violence escalated. Her bright eyes peeled across its length, and notifications continued to run through her mind as more and more victims were added to her ever-smiling army. "All will be fodder for the horde! Legion will rise once again!"

*

"Well, goddamn . . ." Riven muttered, watching Nora hunt down and kill any living thing that manifested inside the labyrinth like a tidal wave of unstoppable death. "That is the fucking creepiest thing I've ever seen. Nora? Nora, can you hear me?!"

"She's not responding. We've already tried," Allie confirmed through their link. "At least I'll be able to stop this disgusting ritual. We now have more than enough keys, thanks to her efforts."

"YES, UNHOLY ONE!" Nora abruptly cut in, all her Others stopping what they were doing to bow simultaneously as her main body bent low at the waist with a flourish. "WHAT DOES THE GREAT MAW DESIRE OF US?!"

"Okay, well, that's just rude," Allie muttered across the link, getting a fit of laughter from Riven and some of his minions.

Riven scratched his chin and looked over the remaining champions. Four of them had already vanished after Nora had killed their party members in the labyrinth, having been forcibly ejected from the descent, and he couldn't help but wince. "Um . . . Is that still you, Nora?"

"I AM NORA! WE ARE NORA! NORA IS ONE OF US, AND WE ARE ONE! NORA IS NOT GONE BUT HAS MULTIPLIED!"

". . . I see. Could you not butcher everyone there? This is a rather drastic turn of events, and I have a lot of questions, but please just leave. We all want to get out of this place. Allie said she has the keys she needs for the ritual after you took them from the other groups."

Nora paused, considering his words, and then nodded. "I WILL DO AS THE GREAT MAW ASKS!"

Raising his eyebrows at her enthusiasm, Riven let out a sigh of relief as she began sparing the others she came across—navigating the labyrinth at high speed in a dive through the depths of the tunnels.

"Um . . ." a small voice from his left called out, and he turned to see Kara Blackbow sitting wide-eyed in shock only a few inches away. "W-what was that? A-and who are all these other people?"

Riven blinked, ignoring the storm of black and red energies that continued to butcher abyssal monsters at a constant rate whenever they came too close. "Oh, right. You're linked with my party now, so you're able to connect with the others."

He gave the young drow woman a reassuring smile and a shoulder pat, smiling wider upon seeing how she clasped the new bow he'd made for her tight against her chest. "Don't worry. You'll fit right in."

She slowly lifted her pale-gray eyes to meet his, her lips tightly pursed before letting out a shuddering breath. "But I'm so pathetically weak compared to . . . to THAT! And did . . . did they call you—"

"The Great Maw?" Riven asked casually, waving it away. "That's just a joke."

"A joke?" she asked hesitantly.

"Yeah. It's because I eat a lot. They also call me fat."

He kept a straight face, trying not to laugh, as Gluttony grumbled inside him.

"What?!" Riven said internally through his mind link. "Don't get mad, the poor girl is already about to have a heart attack! That bit can wait."

"It's not that," Gluttony stated absentmindedly, his attention elsewhere. "It's Nora."

"What about Nora? Is something wrong?"

Gluttony did the mental equivalent of shaking his head. "Not wrong. But . . . her bloodline may be problematic. I will discuss more on the subject later; for now I will go back to the lattice."

"Is that what you've been doing this entire time? Building up our soul lattice?"

Gluttony laughed. "Merely setting the foundations. You'll be the one that finishes it when we reach the lower floors."

"Hello?" Kara asked with a worried frown. "Are you all right?"

Riven snapped out of his internal conversation and gave her another reassuring grin. "Of course! Now, we should be getting out of this place soon—and I'll be able to introduce—"

A flash of light later and Riven was no longer sitting in the lotus position in that fleshy room of constant combat. Instead, he and his entire crew, with some new additions, were now in a large dome illuminated by multiple miniature suns that each spanned many hundreds of yards across.

Each sun represented one of the pillars available to those under the Unholy foundation. One, that let off potent Unholy energy, was green, flickering with a tinge of black and red from time to time. This was the central sun, and it was surrounded by all the others at intervals. The red sun was for Blood; black for Shadow; teal with tinges of black and gray for Death; a mixture of orange, yellow, and red for Infernal; pink and gray for Depravity; and finally a darker gray mixed with burgundy for Chaos. Lastly, there was also the dark-purple sun that let off potent Sin energy as well. Out of all the suns, the Blood and Sin suns called to Riven the most—and he was drawn to step toward them with a sharp intake of breath.

The heat was palpable and gave off a potent energy. Dozens of other groups were seated in meditative positions around the sun at various uneven placements.

[Floor Twenty-One, the Unholy Throne, is now open to you. As promised, by passing Floor Twenty, you are now permitted insight into one of your paths. You may mentally connect with the Unholy Throne whenever you deem yourself ready, choosing any single sun of those available here for a free insight, and when all your party members are done, you may pick another team for a joint operation for Floor

Twenty-Two: Ocean of Wrath. Merely notify Elysium when you are ready to proceed to Floor Twenty-Two. Elysium will protect you while on this floor, and no harm may come to you or your possessions while here—so as to not disturb your meditation. The majority of identification information will continue to be unavailable until Floor Forty.]

Looking around, Riven was caught off guard. This was a cultivation haven, and the longer he stood here, the longer he felt his soul permeate with the Sin energy. It leached out into multiple pillars, infusing them and touching each of them with the promise of power. He relished the feeling but was disappointed that he could only choose one of the suns to connect with.

He wanted all of them, damn it!

"EEEK!"

Riven felt small hands latch on to his left arm, and he was nearly knocked over as Kara Blackbow slammed into him from the side—quivering and hiding behind him with legs that literally shook at the knees.

"RIVEN! RIVEN, IT'S GOING TO EAT ME!"

Huffing down at the frightened drow and glancing up to see Azmoth peering down, Riven began to laugh. He'd forgotten just how big Azmoth had become—the titanic demon could easily fit Kara or any of the others into his mouth to swallow whole at this point.

"Riven, is that what the system notification about adding another team member was about?" Athela asked, raising an eyebrow and putting her hands on her hips with an unsatisfactory glare. "Isn't that the ho who accused you of sleeping with her? I thought you'd eaten the bitch."

"Ugh!" Fay threw up her hands and began to walk away.

"Wait, wait, wait, you two are jumping to conclusions here," Riven said, exasperated, as Allie shook her head and Genua merely smiled.

"It isn't all bad," Genua said with uncharacteristic enthusiasm. "If he makes her another thrall, that will mean I don't have to wait on both of you. The work can be split, and that way each of you could have your own personal servant."

"A THRALL?! NO!" Kara repeated, horrified by the notion, but she quickly went back to cowering behind Riven when Azmoth tilted his head to get a better look.

Riven faintly caught Nora smiling at him like a maniac, and it made him feel a little bit uncomfortable. Like she'd stab him in his sleep. Shaking his head, and noting that he was definitely going to be having a conversation with her about this abrupt and strange change before he connected with one of the pillar-affiliated suns here on the twenty-first floor, he scowled over at Athela and Fay, who had suddenly exchanged a series of sheepish, guilty looks.

"What's this about waiting on these two?" Riven asked Genua, staring at his two lovers while they actively ignored him and refused to meet his eyes. "Explain, please."

Genua looked shocked and put her hands on her swollen belly. "Did they not tell you? That's odd. Well, I have been designated as a handmaiden. It is only right, considering that they are to be your wives and I am but a mere concubine."

"You are not a concu—"

"And it was even my idea," Genua cut in before Riven could finish the sentence. "Ever since you let Luke go, the burden of caring for your fiancées has gone up. I bathe them, help them dress, prepare their hair, bring them meals, and perform more personal services whenever they ask for it. You often don't need those things and don't ask for them, and I felt like it would make better use of my time— as I often don't do much unless I am with Len or studying blood scripture."

Riven gawked. Personal services? Did that mean . . .

"It was her idea!" Athela repeated, and Fay aggressively nodded with feminine grunts of approval. "It's not like we forced her to be our toy and do these things! She volunteered!"

"It has been rather nice! She gives great massages, and she's a nice prop when needed," Fay stated slyly, slapping her hands onto her blushing face to hide when Riven turned an unbelieving stare on her next.

"Your toy? Massages? A prop? This . . ." Riven began, but closed his eyes— taking in a deep breath of air and slowly letting it out to calm himself before shrugging. "Fine. As long as you're okay with being their personal servant or slave or whatever it is you are, then you can do what you want, Genua. But don't do anything that is out of your comfort zone or I'm going to be angry."

He glared at the two demonesses. "Got it?"

"Yes, sir!" Athela gave a cheeky salute.

Fay beamed and swayed back and forth with her hands behind her back, tail wagging. "Yup!"

Looking down at Kara, he rolled his eyes and gestured in the other direction. "Ignore them, please. And anyway, huddle around, everyone! It's time for formal introductions. Everyone, this is Kara Blackbow, our new team member. We'll be escorting her to Floor Forty. Kara, this big scary guy is Azmoth. He's one of my demonic familiars."

One of Azmoth's titanic clawed hands waved down as his wings flared out to the sides with a burst of inferno. A rather impressive, if not needed, display of power.

"A familiar . . . ?" Kara repeated, awestruck as she stepped around Riven to get a better look at the enormous creature. She glanced back at Riven suspiciously. "How are you able to contract an archdemon like that without losing enormous amounts of Willpower?"

"Oh, you can tell he's an archdemon? He wasn't an archdemon when I first met him. None of them were," Riven said proudly, leaning on Jackal's staff form and not hiding the smug smile adorning his face. "And yet they're all archdemons now. Except for Narg—he's a beholder. He died just before you were accepted into the party chat. He'll be back in a day. Probably need to wait for him to respawn here before we leave so he can get an insight as well . . . but that's another story. Anyways, the Arshakai trifecta over there is named Athela. She's my girlfriend."

"Fiancée!" Athela said with a growl, coming over to peck him on the cheek. "And don't forget it."

Riven ignored her, playfully slapping her backside and pushing her away as he began to blush. "And that greater succubus is Fay. My other girlfriend. She, Athela, and I have a three-way relationship going on. Long story, but it works for us and that's what matters."

Fay performed a curtsy and a wink. "Nice to meet you, drow girl. Now get your hands off my man's arm."

Kara stared with incomprehension before abruptly letting go of Riven's arm with a furious blush and an apologetic bow. "I'm s-sorry, archdemon Fay. I did not mean to offend you. Please forgive this one's foolishness."

"No offense taken, mortal," Fay replied with a satisfied grin, coming up to push in between them and fold her hands around Riven's arm where Kara had just been moments ago.

Trying not to roll his eyes yet again, Riven continued with the introductions. "This is Retesh. He's our resident friendly lich."

Stoic silence followed as the two eyed each other suspiciously.

"This is Genua, my thrall."

There was a pause.

"Is she a blood priestess?" Kara asked, obviously impressed by Genua's getup. "Isn't that, like, really impressive?"

"I am a blood priestess!" Genua gave an enthusiastic wave, her crimson tattoos glittering underneath her priestess's hood. "Hello, Kara! Let's go back to my earlier point about potentially coming on as a thrall. You should really consider—"

"And this—" Riven cut Genua off, "is Allie. My sister."

Kara's pale-gray eyes grudgingly turned from Genua to meet Allie's similarly colored ones, and the two stared at each other for a long time after that. The drow's gaze evaluated the long, feathered black wings, the bone armor covering most of Allie's body, and the exquisite claymore she held while sitting lazily in a throne she'd created out of bones so she didn't have to stand.

"Sup," Allie said, giving the other woman a head nod. "If you're wondering how I'm his sister without being a vampire, know that I used to be one. Long story."

Kara hesitated, glancing up at Riven for confirmation. "What does *sup* mean?"

Allie snorted in amusement, and Riven did the same.

"It's just a way to say hi," Allie said, waving dismissively. She gestured to Fimrindle, who stood beside her. "This is my minion, Fimrindle. He's a reaper."

The half-demon, half-undead metal scarecrow didn't move to the visible eye and didn't react. From underneath his hood, his jaw remained slightly unhinged as his scythe and lantern were held out to either side of him.

"A reaper?" Kara asked in a whisper. "And . . . and you're an angel of death? Aren't you? You're not a fallen angel if you have a reaper as a minion. Is that right?"

"Isn't it obvious?" Allie asked with a scoff.

Riven frowned at Allie's rudeness. "All but the most basic identification information is canceled until we hit Floor Forty. Don't be mean."

"Mean?!" Allie repeated, belly-laughing at the idea. "Riven, do you know who and what you are? And you're saying not to be MEAN?!"

She quickly shut up when he gave her a glare.

"What does she mean by that?" Kara asked nervously from the sideline, still using Riven's body as something of a shield from the others.

Riven shrugged in a noncommittal way. "That I'm a vampire, I guess."

The others all gave him blank stares.

Athela snickered, the only thing to break the awkward silence. And it was obvious that Kara wasn't buying it by her suspicious expression.

Riven threw up his hands and turned heel, beginning to walk away in a pretend rage. "Fuck you guys, I'm going home."

Laughter erupted behind him, and he gave them all the middle finger—which made them all laugh even harder. He peeled back, though, and snapped his fingers before pointing at the last member of their party in the back. "Finally, this is Nora. Nora, meet Kara."

The two-dimensional vantablack woman with the unnerving smile and unblinking white eyes gave a dramatic bow, taking a knee and using a silver tongue to lick the front of her pointed teeth while she smiled. When she spoke, it was with hundreds of overlapping voices. "Legion greets the maw's new pet!"

Kara stepped back fearfully, retreating behind Riven yet again, and gripped her bow tightly. "I . . . I saw you kill all those things back in the maze. You're really powerful! Like, the most powerful person I've ever seen! Even stronger than most of my clan's elders in the late E-grade!"

Kara looked to Riven, then to Azmoth, and then all around the group before settling on Nora at last. "Which ones of you are the strongest? I mean . . . Oh . . . Oh, wait. If—if you were in the part of the trial that was designated for the weakest members, then . . ."

It was as if she'd been struck by lightning. Her eyes bulged, and she took the group in with a new light. "O-oh . . . oh dear."

"Oh dear?!" Athela hollered with laughter. "That's what you have to say?! I think I am beginning to like this girl. How innocent."

Riven, for his part, was staring down Nora, who—ever since her change—continued smiling creepily. "Yeah . . . hey, Nora, why do you keep calling yourself Legion?"

Nora, in a kneeling position, cocked her head as if confused, but her expression never changed. "Has the great one not told you? I am Legion. Legion is me. They are one and the same . . . but perhaps a part of the greater whole. The Insane Asylum has called me home, and I have accepted my birthright to rule beneath your grace."

Riven's frown deepened. "I think I understand somewhat, if biblical references can be trusted . . . but could you do me a favor?"

"What does the great one desire?" Nora's voices asked.

He cleared his throat. "Could you bring out Nora as she originally was? I'm not asking you to change permanently, I just want to make sure she's still here. And I'll be able to tell by the way your soul fluctuates, so . . . just help my unsettled mind come to terms with this. I want to make sure she's still okay."

"Oh. That can certainly be done. The rest of us will leave, and we humbly await our chance to return. Don't take too long, though! It has been many years since we've been let out!" The creature that Nora had become stood up, and with a hissing intake of air, she began to change once again. The vantablack skin, the creepy smile and eyes, and her longer black hair all vanished to display what Nora had looked like before the entity calling itself Legion had overtaken her. She was now an Asian woman in her thirties and didn't look anything but human.

Only that her clothes had all burned up in the magma pit, so Riven was quick to take out a blanket and toss it her way.

Nora caught it without delay and wrapped it around her body, giving him a thankful nod and shuddering. But there wasn't any delay in her thought process—and the only signs that she was having any trouble adjusting to the reverted state were a rapid blinking and a slight unsteadiness that was corrected with a supporting arm from Fay.

Nora shuddered again. "That was . . . that was different. I've never connected with them like that before. Not that deeply."

"So you know what they are?" Riven asked, curious but also relieved as the same soul signature he'd grown accustomed to from Nora had returned. He was certain—it was her. "Care to explain?"

Nora opened her mouth, closed it, and then nodded. "Yeah. I can do that. Just give me a little bit of time, some sleep, and some food . . . and then I will discuss everything that I remember. Those memories . . . they'd been locked away. But now they're back, and boy, do I have quite the history to tell you about."

CHAPTER 35

Kara sat cross-legged, wide-eyed and frightened, but also a little bit excited to be included in such a group. They'd all decided to take a breather after the events of the last floor, and she finally found herself clawing her way back up out of the pit of despair she'd flung herself into after her original party from her homeland had left her to die.

She'd thought she'd die down here. Returning home without completing forty floors was literally not an option for her. She'd be shunned and cast out by her family if she failed, her honor marred, and that in itself would be a death sentence, as she'd lose the protection of her family name—leaving her a prime target for the one likely responsible for this entire situation to begin with. And if she wasn't killed? She'd likely be enslaved, which would be even worse. No, going back without completing all forty floors was no option at all, and getting the system's official stamp of approval after turning out that accomplishment was the only path forward.

"Doing all right down there?" Riven asked as he and Fay walked by holding hands. They both gave her a pleasant smile, and Fay even waved.

"U-um, yes. I'm fine! Thanks for asking," Kara replied with a nervous nod. She found the succubus rather curious, as Fay's large ram's horns had disappeared. In place of them were smaller ones that allowed her to wear a purple witch's hat that fit with the rest of her getup. "Did . . . did your horns change, Fay?"

Fay blinked, then nodded while bringing up her hands to touch the smaller, pointed horns coming out of her forehead. "Oh, these?! Yes. Much like Athela, but to a far lesser extent, I'm able to shapeshift parts of my body in various ways. I can completely retract my wings, tail, and horns without using my illusions— and if need be, I can make them revert to their original forms. This is how I used to look before becoming an archdemon, but if I choose to keep them like this— or if I have them retracted entirely—then I don't receive the benefits the larger horns would provide me. The thing is, I can't wear this hat with my larger ram's horns! It's a pain."

"You could just ditch the hat." Riven winked and gave her a playful nudge with his hips. "Or you could have Athela modify it, stitching it up to fit your big head."

"Heyyy! I don't have a big head, you jerk!" Fay scowled back and jabbed him in the ribs to produce a yelp. "And no! You gave me this hat—it is sentimental now and I want to keep it."

Kara watched the two flirt back and forth for a solid minute as Riven teased the succubus while she pretended to get angry. For the first time in a while, Kara felt a genuine smile pulling at the corners of her lips.

She held the new bow she'd been gifted to her chest and took in a shallow breath. The enormous building-size flame demon she'd come to know as Azmoth was kneeling over their group while the others slept, protective despite Elysium's promise to keep them and their belongings intact while on Floor Twenty-One. Genua and Athela were busy making baby clothes, with Athela teaching the high elf thrall how to sew and being rather patient despite Genua's absolute lack of talent. Fimrindle was across the room, meditating at the teal-colored, Death-attuned sun, but he was the only one who'd started to cultivate, as the rest of this rather unorthodox mix of demons and undead were simply taking a break for the day and waiting for Narg the beholder demon to respawn.

Allie was in a deep conversation with Retesh, an angel of death and elder lich being two creatures that Kara would never have expected to meet—much less be party to while here in the descent. On her world they were creatures of legend, and even here in the abyss they were somewhat rare. Especially the angel. Fallen angels were hard enough to come by, but angels attuned to death were not only rarer but also significantly more powerful on average as each of them were labeled Heroes of Death, which added the title's additional benefits, whatever they may be. Kara would have asked, but out of everyone here it was Allie that seemed most standoffish. The complete opposite of her vampire brother.

Nora was probably the one Kara had the least interest in getting to know, though. She was creepy, to say the least, as she'd reverted to her sickly hive-mind demonic form—and was having conversations with herself, letting out giggles and even growls here and there. To Kara, it seemed like Nora had absolutely lost her mind—but according to Riven she was just getting to know her Others. Whatever those were.

Regardless, Kara did not belong. Looking around at the group, she couldn't identify any of them . . . but she could certainly feel their passive auras. She'd also seen what at least two of them could do, and Riven had spent billions of Elysium coins to add her to their party. A favor that she knew she'd literally never be able to repay. What did that imply about his background? It was certainly no simple sum any F- or E-grade had a right to possess in any normal situation. Just who was he? HOW did he have three contracted archdemons as familiars? And what were the strange archaic tattoos he had plastered in black ink along his otherwise white skin? Even his eyes were abnormal, with deep black sclera and brightly glowing crimson pupils—most vampires showed neither of those traits.

Riven had also effortlessly smashed aside the relentless tidal wave of abyssal monsters like it was nothing for nearly an entire day without pause, making the other champions of their individual teams look like toddlers, and Nora had consumed and absorbed the central giant of her event. And Nora was supposed to be one of their weakest! Meanwhile, Kara couldn't even last a small amount of time in the champions bracket and had nearly died; there's no way she would have lasted the extended time period she'd received after coming down here without a party. She was lucky enough to be alive even this far, and she'd resigned herself to death before Riven had gone out of his way to help her.

Whoever this Lillith person was, Kara was quite happy she'd been snatched away. Not that she wished ill on this stranger, but her absence had certainly saved her life and Kara was pretty sure that out of all the parties she'd seen, this one had what it took to go all the way if anyone did.

Or perhaps she was just overestimating them, or maybe it was wishful thinking on her part that the people who'd taken her in would do well. Floor Fifty was almost unattainable by most standards, though, so she couldn't help but worry. Even getting to Floor Forty was considered a near-impossible task by most, and that was why—

"Kara! Oh my, is that really you?!" a familiar feminine voice tinged with amusement and disbelief shouted out to her, and she froze rigidly in place.

It wasn't Riven or Fay, either; they'd walked off after realizing Kara had been lost in her own thoughts. She'd tuned them out when they'd started getting into dangerously flirtatious conversations that made her blush, when the jealousy had started setting in. To have someone as utterly rich and that ridiculously handsome was just not even fair. This voice, however, was something entirely different. It pierced through her layers of distraction, like an electric bolt running through her body, and she even felt her heart clench at the sickly sweet voice.

"IT IS KARA! We've FOUND YOU, Kara!!!" the voice echoed loudly with a high-pitched laugh, creating somewhat of a scene as many of the other groups in meditation or at rest within the vicinity began to glare in their direction.

Pushing away a strand of white hair and bringing it up into a ponytail, Kara shakily got to her feet and lifted her eyes to find none other than the focal point of all her melancholy and sorrow as of late: Zafima Chinwa.

Zafima Chinwa was the fourth daughter of the supreme emperor's favorite concubine in the empire of Purturis, an enchantress wearing a long golden dress that hugged her body like a tight sleeve with long gold earrings that dangled down to her breasts. Another drow, like most of the people that weren't slaves but who lived in the empire, Zafima was very pretty, with long legs and a slender build. A number of pristine white-gold ornaments decorated her braided hair. An accomplished swordswoman and battle priestess, she was well respected and held sway in the royal courts despite not being an official princess—and she'd had it out for Kara for the past year for reasons unknown. Kara's guess was that the other young woman was simply cruel, and Kara was probably an easy target, as she was only the seventh daughter of the Ashen Sage, with little to no political sway. Zafima's mother also didn't like Kara's family much, dating back to a history that preceded Kara's birth, and having Kara fail an impossible test or die in the attempt would be the equivalent to a backhanded slap to Kara's father after everything that had happened. It was a long and complicated series of events, with Kara being the unwilling participant and eventual victim at the end of the day, a pawn in the piece of political maneuvering that would likely see her dead. Be it her disgraced father killing her for coming back empty-handed and bringing him shame, or be it by losing her family's name and protection should she fail—she'd been left an easier target for Zafima, who seemed to delight in tormenting her.

And Kara certainly hadn't been the first victim of Zafima's schemes, either. Rumor had it that she still kept one man locked in her basement as a slave to tease and torture at will after her concubine mother set her sights on another man to unleash her family's fury on.

"Lady Zafima Chinwa," Kara said with a tight expression and a stiff back. "I . . . did not expect to see you here."

Riven and Fay had turned to look, while the others of their group simply glanced over before resuming their original activities. And from behind Zafima, another two dark elves and a vampire, all men, joined her. While Zafima wore a formfitting golden dress with a wand at her side and pretty ornaments in her hair, the two drow men had their hair cropped short and wore hoods over stylized green scale armor with obsidian trimming. The armor looked sturdy but light and flexible, and it was intermixed with various leather pieces such as their boots or hard leather scabbards over the scimitars at their sides. One was younger than the other with a short-cropped white beard, while the older man had a long scar running down across his jaw and neck. She recognized the older, scarred man as her old party leader, Numin, who'd been paid off to leave her behind.

Paid to leave by the vampire standing next to him, who was likely an agent of Zafima, if they were all standing together.

The vampire was handsome and young—probably nineteen or so by the looks of him, but then again, vampires were a hard call on age even by the standards of elves. He had black hair styled into a flat mohawk, with red eyes that weren't quite as bright as Riven's but gave off a dull crimson glow nonetheless. A long red cape was draped over one shoulder, and he wore satin pants and a plain white vest, while a long, rune-inscribed chain with a strangely rounded blade at the end was rolled up at his other side and attached to his waist. He wore a self-satisfied smirk while maintaining eye contact with Zafima and crossed his arms to look Kara up and down before coming to stand a foot away from her as she trembled in embarrassment, anger, and a mixture of other emotions.

"I'm surprised you made it this far," the vampire's silky-smooth voice said, his fangs on display as his smile widened. "We all are. We were taking bets on whether you'd die or leave, but our sources say your tracker is still active and in the abyss . . . so we've been waiting here for nearly five weeks."

Kara's fists clenched around the bow she held down and in front of her, knuckles turning white as her nostrils flared. She was having a very hard time not lashing out at the bastard in front of her. She still didn't know his name, or how much he'd paid her team at the request of Zafima, or why they'd even gone about it the way they did. But none of that mattered now. Instead, she stated a more simple question:

"Why were you all waiting for me?" Kara asked with a quivering voice, though she kept her expression as stoic as she could. "Have you not embarrassed me enough? Have you all not already HUMILIATED me in countless ways and condemned me to death? What purpose would waiting here serve you, other than to see me suffer further?"

Kara's eyes began to get wet, and she waved a hand at the sorceress Zafima, the drow man Numin, and the vampire who'd seduced her and robbed her blind. "Why? Why go through all this just to torment me?"

After a quick, whispered discussion with Numin, the younger drow warrior she'd not really talked to much even after hiring him onto her team to get here, took off without a second look back and headed toward the group they'd come from.

But the vampire who'd stolen her belongings after sleeping with Kara shrugged, smirked, and glanced over at Zafima, who was stifling a laugh. He also made a show of displaying a large sack hanging from his waist as well, one that'd been hidden underneath the red cape on one side. "You ask me why? It's just business, girl. I got paid to do a job and I did it. The pay was good, the sex was just mediocre, but the ticket down with Zafima's team was more than worth it. I'm pretty adept with seduction powers after learning from an incubus as a young man, and I've only gotten better with time, so when your drow superior here asked me to—"

"She's not my superior," Kara hissed, glaring daggers at Zafima before realizing just what the vampire man was wearing. "HEY! That's my bag!"

"Your bag?" the vampire asked while the other two drow eagerly watched. He looked down at the sack, gasped, and put a hand up to his face to mock Kara. "THIS old thing?! No, it's just a trash sack I keep around to shit in."

Kara's face went bright red, or as red as a dark elf could physically go, and the teardrops came fast and furious as her whole body began visibly shaking. Rage, pain, humiliation—she wanted to hide under a rock. But more than that, she wanted her bag back. "That bag has my mother's notebook in it. Can I please have it back?"

"It's not yours anymore," the vampire said with a raised nose, grinning down at her and taking a step backward with hands outstretched. "Sorry. Finders keepers . . . you sad, sad excuse for an abyssal descender. How is it that you even got this far? You still haven't told us."

"I said, give—it—BACK!" Kara screamed, fists clenched and stomping her right foot as the vampire and Zafima both began to laugh.

The vampire man pretended to think, raised a finger, and shook his head. "No, no, no . . . I don't think I will. It's mine. I took it fair and square. And as for your mother's notebook . . . is it sentimental? I'd heard your mother died. But I've been tearing pieces out of it to wipe my ass with . . ."

Slowly drawing out a thin, brown booklet, the vampire showed off her mother's notebook after pulling it from a pocket in the back of his pants. Smiling wickedly, he began waving it back and forth in front of her. "Here . . . take it."

Kara didn't have to be told twice. She reached out to take it from him, before a burst of light illuminated the area—and her mother's notebook was eradicated with a small explosion of hellfire.

Kara remained utterly shell-shocked, mouth agape, lips quivering as the ashes of the paper and leather bindings of the small book drifted as ash toward the floor.

"Oops." The vampire laughed with a shrug and another step back. Then, looking down, he began to rummage through her sack. "I wonder what else I can find in here! Odd that you don't even carry a true spatial sack and use this piece of shit. Surely you're not THAT poor, are you? Or is it because you're the seventh daughter and basically considered trash as the last in line for your father's mantle? Did they not outfit you properly on purpose?"

Kara barely heard him. Her knees hit the floor, and she gasped, grabbing at the small cinders and blackened pieces of paper slowly fluttering to the floor. Teardrops splattered onto the strange gray stone on which they stood, and Kara felt like she was going to vomit. "M-Mom . . ."

"HAAAAAAA-ha-ha—ha-haaaa!!" Zafima began bellowing with laughter, the vampire joining her, as Numin, Kara's ex-teammate, just grimaced slightly. But the man did not intervene.

"HOW PATHETIC!" Zafima roared, cackling like a woman gone wild while hovering over the sobbing figure beneath her. She grinned maniacally down at Kara but did not touch her as she leaned in close to whisper in her ear. "Truly pathetic . . . Just like that father of yours. Just like your mother was when she died . . ."

"You BITCH!" Kara snapped. The next instant, before she knew what she was doing, her hand reached back for a dagger at her waist. Flashing forward to stab Zafima through the throat with a primal scream of rage, she was abruptly stopped when red threads wrapped around her wrist to hold her back.

The dagger was only a centimeter away from Zafima's throat, and the sorceress hadn't moved. In fact, she looked rather annoyed as she shot an irritated glare in the direction the threads were coming from. Her annoyance turned into surprise within the next second, and she stood erect—taking a step back as a slow clap began to come closer over the sound of footsteps.

"Congratulations," Riven said, ending his slow clap with lids lowered in an expression of disgust before putting his hands behind his back. "You people put on a real show. I'm almost impressed. The notebook was especially maniacal. Props to you, lesser."

Riven's red eyes flashed, looking casually down on the other vampire with the obvious reference to the man's bloodline. In the short time spent interacting with other vampires on Panu and within the Blood Moon Requiem, he'd learned that vampires took bloodlines very seriously—and being a pureblood himself, he was at the top of the vampiric social hierarchy even outside of being a prince to an S-grade faction.

The jab was therefore obvious, and the vampire snarled in Riven's direction—but he looked rather uncertain as to whether he should retort. Glancing from Riven to the others of Riven's group, who were now all staring at him, the newcomer glanced at Zafima before taking another step back.

"Kara," Riven said, slowly letting his eyes fall to the sobbing woman Athela had restrained. "They were attempting to bait you into attacking them. Or to get you to try and take your stuff back, which would be considered against the rules of this floor."

Pulling up the previous notification for emphasis so she could reread it, he pushed the hologram into Kara's line of sight.

[Floor Twenty-One, the Unholy Throne, is now open to you. As promised, by passing Floor Twenty, you are now permitted insight into one of your paths. You may mentally connect with the Unholy Throne whenever you deem yourself ready, choosing any single sun of those available here for a free insight, and when all your party members are done, you may pick another team for a joint operation for Floor Twenty-Two: Ocean of Wrath. Merely notify Elysium when you are ready to proceed to Floor Twenty-Two. Elysium will protect you while on this floor, and no harm may come to you or your possessions while here—so as to not disturb your meditation. The majority of identification information will continue to be unavailable until Floor Forty.]

Athela came over to pat Kara on the back and then helped the silently sobbing dark elf to her feet with a grunt. "If you'd attacked or stolen from them, you'd be banished from the descent. Maybe killed."

"My guess is banishment, based on what I've seen so far. You said you'd rather die than fail?" Riven asked, turning his gaze away from Kara to eye the unsettled drow and the vampire. Others from the collection of groups they'd left in coming over here to talk were now paying attention to the confrontation with increasing curiosity. "Which is probably why they've been waiting for you here. They wanted to make sure you failed and were sent back. Regardless, I paid good money for you to live. I can't have the newest member of our team be bested so easily."

Riven gave Kara a kind smile and whispered in Athela's ear as the enchantress Zafima began to giggle again. "Take her away. I will handle this."

"So you found us out! Much smarter than this brutish bitch," Zafima remarked, giving Kara a scathing look as she was led away. "Who are you? And what is this nonsense about paying for her to live? She's on your team now? Why would you take on someone so useless? Did you buy her? Or did she just happen to seduce another vampire? Which is it?"

Riven stared back with a blank expression, glanced at the few dozen drow in the background where Zafima had come from, and then snorted. "Are you all from the same place?"

Zafima frowned, not liking being ignored, but regained her composure with a confident straightening a second later. "Yes. The esteemed Purturis Empire. Universe 70."

Riven's black-and-red eyes shifted over the lot of them and then settled back on the vampire—who was likely a greater vampire rather than a lesser, but he was still enjoying the deep-set anger imprinted on the man's face after the insult. "I see. Zafima, was it?"

"A lady of the court, at your service!" Zafima purred, stepping forward to get a better look at him with squinted eyes. "You're rather handsome. What are those markings on your face for? I really wish the system restrictions on identification weren't gone. It'd make things a lot easier."

"Easier, how?" Riven asked.

"Easier to tell just how fucked you are after interfering with empire business," she replied, a coldness setting into her tone. She took another step forward, getting into his personal space and sneering up at him as he calmly stared back down. "If you are smart, you will leave that bitch out in the cold. All those drow behind me? My mother paid for them to follow me here, or paid them to switch sides once they got here. Those that refused are now dead, just like you will be if you keep Kara Blackbow in your party exiting this floor. It is true we can't attack you here, but the moment you leave, you'll be a target for nine different groups. Is that what you'd like?"

Riven raised one eyebrow, an amused smile playing at one corner of his lips. "Consider me . . . intimidated."

Zafima's eyebrow twitched, and she was about to reply when another shout sounded out with Riven's name on the air.

"Is that the great and esteemed Riven Thane I see?!"

Riven turned, and the drow and unknown vampire who'd been antagonizing Kara all turned with him.

There, coming across the space between them and the closest sun, was none other than the quite obnoxious Prince Narzkal Rantali, who'd been trying and failing to get into the Firebrand Trading Company in order to acquire a black phoenix pendant as a gift for his sick fiancée.

"THAT IS YOU! I DEMAND AN AUDIENCE WITH THE ESTEEMED ONE!" Prince Narzkal Rantali, the handsome, well-dressed vampire prince grinned with his fangs on display as he patted the long sword hanging at his side. Behind him was his entourage of three other vampires and a bald human man in rags and shackles who was being dragged along as well.

For Zafima's part, her eyes widened in shock—and her threatening intent vanished immediately. She quickly made sure her hair was neatly done and that her dress had no wrinkles while stepping forward to intercept the prince. "Esteemed one?! Surely you're not speaking about me, Your Majesty! What are the chances that you were here of all places?! Surely it is fate!"

Riven's eyebrow raised higher.

And as for Prince Narzkal Rantali, of the kingdom of Garth, he seemed to stumble to a halt before frowning down at Zafima, who was beaming back at him with wide-eyed adoration. The vampire prince glanced between Riven and her. "Zafima Chinwa? How are you here? And no, I'm afraid I was not speaking to you. I was speaking to that man over there. Riven Thane is a great man, as I'm sure you were finding out for yourself!"

Prince Rantali gave Riven a wink. "Getting around, are you? Your tastes are broadening! Zafima is quite a charmer at the yearly balls my family throws in Garth! Perhaps you'd be willing to come if she was your date?"

The prince came up with a hearty laugh, slapping Riven's shoulder and smiling widely. "Ah, who am I kidding! For the man who saved my fiancée's life, I might as well give you a hug!"

Laughing and throwing his arms around Riven, whose eyelids were drooping in a very unamused way while he let the other prince cackle with delight, he couldn't help but sigh.

"I would appreciate a little personal space, buddy. But it's good to see you, too."

"Oh! Of course! Of course." Prince Rantali immediately let go with a sheepish smile, scratching the back of his neck with another almost nervous laugh as Zafima, Numin, and the vampire seducer all gawked at the interaction.

Zafima's expression did backflips, registering confusion, startled apprehension, disbelief, and then finally—horror. It was very obvious to Riven that she somehow knew Prince Narzkal Rantali, and if he remembered correctly—the kingdom of Garth was in Universe 70 just like the drow empire of Purturis. For all he knew, the two factions were likely neighbors, and he was pretty certain given her demeanor that she'd realized she'd fucked up. How badly she'd fucked up was still up in the air, as he was seriously considering following her out of this place when she left the floor in order to kill her and everyone else enlisted in this little scheme of hers against Kara. Not that he really even knew Kara that well, but based on what he'd seen so far, he felt like he had sufficient evidence to slaughter the entire group of dark elves immediately out of the gate come Floor Twenty-Two.

CHAPTER 36

"I was able to send that talisman you procured for me back to my fiancée, with a note about how I obtained it. Her blood rot will likely be gone within the next few weeks, and it's all thanks to you." Prince Rantali stepped back with a more serious expression and gave a low bow. He held it there for several seconds before rising again and seemed genuinely happy after some moments of deep thought. "Unfortunately I am not able to communicate directly with her, so the runner will have to do in my absence as I continue my descent. Did you go straight through or take the shortcut on the second floor?"

"Second floor," Riven said folding his arms with a nod. He cast a look over at the chained bald human in rags Prince Rantali was bringing along with his other vampire knights, who were outfitted in some seriously tacky golden armor that flared at the edge of each piece. They were the same men he'd seen with the prince earlier. "Who's the human?"

"Oh, him?" Prince Rantali let out a laugh with a hike of his thumb. "Just a slave I bought in the city. Got himself mixed up in some bad bets, was captured after failing to pay, and now I'm going to turn him into a thrall. The alternative would have been execution, so I'm doing him a favor. He's not seeing it that way, though, and has tried to escape more than once . . . but I need a source of blood that isn't this garbage I have from the homeland."

The prince pulled out a flask of spiced blood and gave Riven a sniff.

"Doesn't smell so bad to me," Riven said with a small smile. "Mind if I try it?"

Prince Rantali raised his eyebrows and grinned, shoving the flask into Riven's hands. "Certainly, go ahead! I have become used to the stuff. It is flavored with blue rosenia kilt, if you know what that is. But I doubt it, as it's a plant native to my homeworld in Garth. I probably shouldn't call it garbage, but after drinking it for days on end, having a live specimen is far better. Fresh, warm blood is always preferable. Wouldn't you agree?"

Riven and the prince had entered their own little world at this point, ignoring Zafima and the others as they stood around watching with varying expressions—trying to make out just what was going on and how Riven knew the other man. From Zafima's disbelief, she probably was trying to put together why Prince Rantali was treating Riven as an equal, or as a friend. Kara, for her part, was still crying, but silently, and had only followed Athela a few feet back while staring daggers at Zafima and the unknown vampire.

Putting the flask to his lips, Riven downed the whole thing in one go and closed his eyes with a nod of appreciation. He looked down, then up at the prince's bald prisoner, thought about saying something—then shrugged. If the guy had tried to cheat someone and gotten the worse half of it, it wasn't Riven's place to step in. Even with Kara's situation, he'd almost killed her himself before getting to know her—and had only taken pity on her initially because she'd reminded him of Athela.

"This shit rocks!" Riven said, laughing and handing the flask back to the prince, who eagerly snapped his fingers at one of the knights in the background.

"I'm glad you like it, Riven, and I'd be more than happy to provide you with some for your journey. Have you taken on a partnering group yet?" Prince Rantali asked curiously, pushing one hand through his blond hair and then accepting a few more flasks from one of the knights out of a spatial sack, giving them all to Riven, who deposited them in his own moments later with a nod of appreciation.

Riven thought about it, then shook his head. "No. Not really. Any idea what the next layer down is about?"

"Fortunately, yes," the prince said eagerly, his eyes shining. "The Abyssal Descent only has a few floors that persist throughout the eons without change. Floors Twenty-One and Twenty-Two are some of them. I'm surprised, with your connections and considering who you are, that you don't know this. Where is the Lady of Black Skies, by the way? Is she not here?"

"She was supposed to be our guide down," Riven admitted while scratching the back of his head. "Eh . . . Elysium didn't like the fact that she'd already been through the wringer in ages past and basically punished us for trying to cheat the system. She's trapped on Floor Fifty and we have to get there to free her."

Prince Rantali looked shocked, then amused, and then burst into laughter. "I'm sorry! I'm sorry, I just didn't think Elysium took such personal interest in things like that! For anyone else, I'd say Floor Fifty would be impossible. For you? I'd be surprised if you didn't make it. I'm not even sure if there are floors past fifty, to be honest."

"Did . . . did you say Lady of Black Skies?" the enchantress Zafima interrupted, getting both men to turn to her while nervously taking Riven in with a once-over. "Prince Rantali, if I may ask . . . how do you know this man? And what does referencing a historical figure such as the shade demoness have anything to do with what you're talking about? None of this makes sense."

Prince Rantali looked confused. "They don't know? Have you not already introduced yourself?"

Riven chuckled and shook his head. "No, I have not. You see Kara over there?"

He gestured at the silently crying drow elf, who was being comforted by Athela in a hushed conversation. Riven then sighed. "She became the fifth member of my team, as Lillith is temporarily gone. We met on the last floor. Then these lovely people decided to antagonize her for reasons that aren't entirely clear to me, so I was merely prying Kara away and removing her from the situation."

Prince Rantali's expression became grim. He remained silent for a time, staring at Kara and then Zafima. "Did they offend you at all, in any way?"

"Zafima just threatened me a little bit, implying her empire would take care of me. Nothing I can't handle."

Prince Rantali choked on the air he breathed, but quickly regained his composure. "I see."

There was a long pause after that as the prince stared at the ground. "Is there any reason why you wouldn't want them to know who you are? May I enlighten them as to the gravity of what they've just done? Honestly, I would hate for this to have repercussions across my own homeland, as having a . . . having . . . How do I put this?"

Prince Rantali straightened and glared at Zafima in a way that made her visibly recoil. "I would hate for the destruction of your empire to impact my own kingdom's economy, as Garth highly depends on the continued friendship of the drow empire of Purturis."

Zafima opened her mouth to speak, shocked and a little horrified at what Prince Rantali was implying, and then shot Riven a nervous glance. Her voice was quivering and uncertain. "Surely this man cannot hold that kind of political power! I was merely—"

"Do you think that going about and randomly THREATENING people who are able to obtain tickets to this place with the use of your empire's name is WISE?! You were merely not THINKING! I'm half-tempted to tell your emperor about this, given what repercussions it could have!" Prince Rantali snapped, stepping forward aggressively as Zafima flinched. "Your empire is considered a high D-grade faction only by the merit of your emperor and two other monarchs. As is mine! Just because your people acquired tickets to the descent due to a supremely lucky opportunity that Elysium handed down by nothing but chance, you think us equal to the overall caliber of those who arrive here under normal circumstances?! Zafima, do you know how I met this man?"

She shook her head hesitantly, looking like a scolded child, and shifted from one foot to the other.

"I was BEGGING to be let into the Firebrand Trading Company so that I could HOPE to procure a black phoenix amulet or an equivalent for my fiancée. You've heard she has blood rot, yes? She'd have died if I couldn't get it, but the Firebrand Trading Company deals with B-, A-, and S-grade factions regularly! So do you know what they said to me when I attempted to get inside to view their wares?"

She didn't reply, but merely stared.

"They denied me access and repeatedly told me to get back to the end of the line," Prince Rantali said, exasperated. "Any time anyone of a known faction to them stepped forward, I was pushed back. It was a continual cycle of degrading myself in front of others, despite the use of my name and house. Once, the guards even laughed at me and said I would not be able to afford such an item at all, even if I did get in. ME! And guess what?! They were right! I wouldn't have been able to procure one at all, I eventually found out, if not for him."

Prince Rantali pointed at Riven. "This man walked up and, despite not knowing me, allowed me to come in with him. He arrived and immediately cut in front of all the other known scions of the upper echelons and had a private escort into their trading post. From there, I was given an amulet FREE of charge, just for knowing him, and can you guess at what that price would have been otherwise?"

". . . what?" Zafima asked timidly.

"One billion, six hundred million Elysium coins," Prince Rantali said flatly. "They handed it to me free of charge simply by walking in with Riven Thane. They called it 'an investment' and asked that I return the favor one day if I ever get into his good graces. Even peak C-grade factions would dominate our two countries combined, and the Abyssal Descent is full of ones far stronger than that. This man, Riven Thane, is the scion of such a faction."

Zafima's mouth fell open in astonishment, and she remained speechless while gawking at the prince, and then Riven. But it wasn't just horror and surprise anymore, but an enterprising light that began to intertwine itself as well. It was greed.

"I . . . I give my sincere apologies to you, my lord," Zafima said, prostrating herself on the floor in exaggerated fashion. "I did not know you were a man of such high standing! Please, allow me to make up for my poor judgment! I am sure that we can come to some accord!"

Riven's lip curled in disgust, but he did well in hiding it. "To answer your question, Prince Rantali . . . I prefer not to have people know who I am for a few reasons."

He noted that Kara had returned with Athela and was now listening intently while struggling to contain her confusion and her rising anger toward the enchantress kneeling on the floor. "For one, I like to be treated like a normal human being."

"You're anything but human."

"Ha! Yes, I know. That's an entirely different story, but it's a matter of speech. Anyways, I don't like being worshipped. It feels off. And more than that, with Lillith gone, I don't want others knowing who I am, either." He turned his black-and-red eyes toward Prince Rantali and put a hand on his shoulder. "There are many knives in the dark, and I have already survived more than one assassination attempt. From others within the Blood Moon Requiem, and from the Church of Greed. You probably heard something about the last attempt up on the first floor of the descent, but even if you hadn't . . . just know it wasn't pretty. The less people that know about me, the better. However, now that you've already planted the seed, she'll no doubt go around asking. Already we've drawn too much attention to ourselves, and I'm not as forgiving as I used to be."

Riven's hand fell, and both Kara and Zafima went rigid when they heard the names *Blood Moon Requiem* and *Church of Greed*. Prince Rantali had put together who he was based on rumors alone, as vampire societies were few and far between and the Blood Moon Requiem was one of the best. However, Riven didn't know whether the drow would do the same. Even if they didn't, how many other people in other groups could hear them talking from where they sat? Most probably had a less vested interest in demonic and vampiric undertakings, but he didn't want anyone poking about and drawing attention to how far he'd made it on the trek down. He could still have assassins from the Church of Greed coming after him, or another faction disgruntled with him in the Blood Moon Requiem sending out their own to take him down. People like Elder Thune, or some of the less savory members of his own House Wraithtide, who didn't like how he was changing things.

He made his decision. "Zafima, you'll be leaving the descent after you're done here. I won't chance you seeking revenge on Kara, and I'm feeling a bit petty. I don't like bullies. If you choose to ignore my warning, I'll simply kill you and everyone else involved with you."

Zafima's demeanor abruptly changed, and she lifted her head with a panicked expression. "NO! I cannot leave this place! The number of tickets are limited, and this is a once-in-a-lifetime opportunity for me to perfect my soul lattice! We don't have cultivation resources like this at home, and I will be stunting my growth forever if my foundations aren't settled properly! You would be stripping me of one of the greatest chances to cultivate in my life!"

"Zafima!" Prince Rantali hissed. "Know your place!"

Riven waved a hand to dismiss the prince's chiding. "Then you will die. If you don't believe me, that is fine. But one of my demons has a tracking ability, and even if you were to leave now . . . I could simply follow you. My bet is that I'll be able to do so rather easily. Either leave after your people are done with their insights, or move on to the next floor and take a bet that you can either beat me in a fight—which is highly unlikely despite your numbers—or that you'll be able to outrun me. Which is also unlikely. And I don't care if you believe me or not—what you believe won't influence the outcome should you choose to continue onward. The result would be the same. It's your call to make."

Riven sat in silence, tinkering with different crafting materials he'd laid around him to create and disassemble various totems. He practiced infusing soul shards and releasing them, practiced changing the various patterns of runes, and modified different aspects of graphics that his gnome teacher had given him to experiment with. He was quickly finding out that different ingredients reacted differently with graphic and rune combinations, and the results were fascinating.

"Riven?" Kara asked hesitantly, her head on Athela's lap nearby—who'd taken an unusual pitying approach to the depressed young dark elf woman. "Who are you really?"

"Is that really important?" Riven asked, getting irritated when one of the solidified orbs of condensed mana shattered in his hand after he attempted to infuse it with a particular plant leaf's essence.

Kara looked to her bow and wiped at her face with a grunt of appreciation as Athela combed her hair back with her fingers. "I overheard you saying that you're worried about assassins. You also mentioned the Blood Moon Requiem and the Church of Greed. I'm familiar with both, but not intricately so. Are these the factions you come from? Or are they your enemies?"

Riven shook his head and noted that his beholder demon, Narg, still had another ten hours left until respawn. "The Church of Greed wants me dead, but the Blood Moon Requiem and I are affiliated. There are other agents within the Blood Moon Requiem that want me gone, too, for political reasons, but not most."

"Just tell her already!" Fay said, waltzing over, absolutely drunk and wearing nothing but her tight white undergarments and a shit-eating grin. She had a large bottle of wine in one hand and a tray of assorted food in the other that she'd prepared with Azmoth—who had reduced his size and stature down to his original form before his ascension to an archdemon. He was still huge and muscular, but not titanically so.

His wings were still there, though, even with his reduced size, and were folded against his back.

"You're being wayyyy too leery of people," Fay continued, hiccuping and leaning against his shoulder after passing the food tray to Athela. "This is a safe zone—there aren't going to be assassins here that can hurt us! And the big eyeball guy isn't going to be here for a while, either. Relax!"

Riven let his eyes wander over her exposed musculature and curves for a while, not even pretending to hide that he was checking her out, and went back to putting together totems. "As much as I appreciate how attractive you are, you really should put on some clothes while in public."

"Are you jealous that all the other men over there are staring?" Fay teased, giggling and winking at him while gesturing to numerous other groups that had their members eyeballing her lithe blue body.

"Yes. I'm a jealous guy."

Athela laughed. "Maybe I should start undressing, too!"

"Please don't."

"Oh, it'll be fun to watch you squirm!"

Riven harrumphed. "Azmoth, we need to get more guys in this group. We're outnumbered, and you don't talk much."

Azmoth's obsidian teeth widened with amusement. "I think the same thing. Sorry I not talk much, Riven. I am still learning, still young, still new. I take in environment and try to figure out how act as I grow up. It hard, but I try."

"Nah, man, you're good. But if you ever want an in-depth conversation about the meanings of life, hit a brotha up." Riven waved his hands over the unfinished totem pieces and they were dragged into his spatial sack in the next instant. Pulling out a chessboard instead, he placed it between himself and Azmoth while turning slightly. "Black or white?"

"Black."

Riven turned the board and made the first move by pushing his pawn out two spaces in front of the queen. As the game continued, he accepted a small drink from the wine bottle in Fay's hand and gave her a kiss before ruffling her hair. "I take back what I said earlier. I'm sorry. You can dress however you want, but I do get jealous. That's just something I'll have to work on."

Fay's black eyes widened in surprise. "Uh . . . Oh! Oh, you were being serious! I didn't realize . . . Oh wow. Yes, I'll go change now!"

She began to get up, but was pulled back down and into Riven's right arm.

"No, that's not necessary," Riven said with a smile. "I'll get over it. I won't be the controlling type, so I'll shut up."

"Controlling type? You've almost never given any of your minions a single actual command!" Athela protested with arms outstretched.

Fay blinked, softened her expression, and wrapped her arms around his shoulders. "Okay. But I really am sorry. I didn't mean to ignore you—I thought you were just teasing me again. How is it that YOU of all people can get jealous? That's our role!"

"It is," Athela confirmed with a sage nod. "You have nothing to worry about, Riven, that we promise you. WE, on the other hand, have to worry about crazy bitches left and right. Do you KNOW how many elf servants at your manor we've had to tie up and leave in the dungeon so they wouldn't try to jump your bones? We don't need more Genuas."

Genua gave her a sharp look.

"Indeed!" Fay laughed, giving him a firm squeeze. "It feels good to hear it, though. It means you care. Now, are you going to tell Kara or am I going to have to tell her for you? It's not like you're going to be able to hide it forever. I mean, look! That evil bitch Zafima and your prince friend are still deep in discussion about you and your proposed threat! Or at least that's what I assume they're still talking about."

They all looked over to where Zafima and her companions, along with Prince Rantali, had joined a larger group made up of multiple parties. They were talking in low tones, and occasionally Riven and his friends noticed quick-snap glances or gestures in his direction.

"Name-dropping the Blood Moon Requiem and the Church of Greed were probably dead giveaways," Athela said with a shrug. "Won't take a genius to put that together."

"Well, I certainly haven't," Kara replied with a pout. "This isn't fair."

"I spared your life after you attempted to kill me in your assumption that I was THAT prick," Riven said, pointing to the vampire with the red cape over his right shoulder in the distance. "How did you confuse me for HIM?! We look nothing alike!"

Kara blushed in embarrassment and hid her face with one arm. "I was not in the right state of mind."

"You don't say?"

Kara nodded, still avoiding eye contact. "I thought I was going to die, I was desperate, and I wanted to vent. I wasn't thinking properly."

"She was having a nervous breakdown." Athela grunted. "You should see it when Riven has nervous breakdowns. He starts to cry and flail his arms about, and he even shat himself once."

Fay snorted a laugh.

"That's not even remotely funny," Riven replied, putting a rook three spaces forward on the chessboard before surrendering his turn to Azmoth. "You shouldn't be telling Kara about my reactive bowel movements while under stress. It's not something I can control."

Athela burst into laughter, along with Fay. Allie, for her part, rolled her eyes dramatically while writing in a journal of some kind as she and Retesh went over ritual death magic together, and Kara shifted so she could get a better look at them to see whether this was a joke.

"This potty humor bad," Azmoth said with a judgmental shake of his head. "Bad and sad. Azmoth disappointed."

"Azmoth is the voice of reason here," Genua called out elegantly, her back straight while she continued to practice knitting, attempting to make baby clothes with a ball of thread Athela had given to her. She turned her red gaze upon the others. "That's a joke my daughter Len would appreciate, and she's not even ten years old."

"It's Athela's fault."

"MY FAULT?!"

"You started this. It's 100 percent your fault. I take no blame."

"Riven! Hasn't Allie taught you better than that?! The man is ALWAYS at fault!"

Allie raised a hand. "Agreed! It's definitely Riven's fault!"

More laughter ensued.

Riven rolled his eyes like he usually did and couldn't contain his growing smile. It was good to be around friends, even if they were all unbelievably immature sometimes. "All right, Kara, how about this. I'll tell you who and what I am, but you've got to promise not to treat me any differently afterward. I really don't like the nauseating groveling treatment. Is that a deal?"

Kara slowly nodded and sat up from where she'd been laying her head on Athela's thigh. Sniffling, she gave the group a once-over. "Yeah. Of course. You've done so much for me already, there's not much more that you could say that'd change my mind about you. And . . . I wanted to say thanks, for sticking up for me back there."

She became silent for a few seconds, then shook herself out of the faraway look that'd crossed her face. "Can I guess first, though? I feel like that's a fun game to play."

"Oh? All right, guess away, then!"

Kara tapped a finger to her chin, narrowing her eyes. "Hmm. How about . . . you're a duke's son, and a member of a noble house in the Blood Moon Requiem? And . . . you're a warlock, so you made a bad deal with a demon and the Church of Greed has a bounty on your head for it."

"What would a 'bad deal' imply?" Riven asked.

Kara shrugged. "I don't know! But is my guess correct?!"

Riven paused. "No."

"No?! Just No? Did I get ANY of it right?"

Riven bobbed his head side to side and took another one of Azmoth's bishops—getting an irritated grumbling growl from the large flame demon across from him. "Yes."

"Well, what did I get right then?!"

"I'm associated with a noble house from the Blood Moon Requiem. The Church of Greed does have a bounty on my head as well. But that's it. I am not a duke's son, nor did I make a bad deal with a demon that has the church after me. They were after me from the start."

Kara pooched her lips and looked to Athela and Fay for guidance—but they both stayed silent.

"This is your guessing game—you're the one who wanted to try!" Athela cackled at the pleading look she got. "Go on!"

Kara huffed and folded her arms. "All right, does the Church of Greed have anything to do with those tattoos on your face?"

Riven stopped in the middle of placing a pawn forward on the board. "Somewhat, but not entirely."

"Does your entrance into the descent have anything to do with that big battle between the Church of Gluttony and the Church of Greed on Floor One? I didn't see it for myself, but I've heard about it from people who started the descent after me. When two S-grade factions clash, it makes for quick rumors . . . even if it is only their younger generations."

Riven nodded. "Yes. That was one of the attempts on my life."

Kara paled slightly and became quiet. It wasn't until after another five minutes of silence on her part and a resetting of the chessboard after Riven's victory that she finally spoke again. "So you're saying that the Church of Gluttony protected you from the Church of Greed."

It was a statement, not a question.

Riven therefore remained silent.

Kara started looking sick, her eyes lingering on the living armor on Riven's chest depicting the Great Maw. She shifted her hips uneasily and drew her knees up against her chest, covering part of her face to stare at him. "Can we come back to that?"

"Sure."

Silence regained a foothold.

"You're a prince of the Blood Moon Requiem," she eventually said, her words crisp.

Riven nodded. "Correct again."

Kara's nostrils flared, her eyes widened, and she stared at the ground beneath her feet while drawing her knees up more closely around her. "How far are you along the line of succession?"

"Originally I was thirty-seventh in line. I killed another prince, so now I'm thirty-sixth in line."

"Is Allie a princess, then?"

"Was a princess!" she called out without turning around as death magic flared on an intricate diagram she and Retesh were drawing on the stone ground with teal flame. "Or at least, I think so. I assume I gave up that right when I shunned the Blood God and became an angel of death. Maybe I should check on that."

Allie turned around with a wide grin and pulled up the corner of one lip with a finger. "I used to be a pureblooded vampire like Riven, but I don't even have fangs anymore. See?"

"Pureblooded?" Kara repeated, impressed. "Aren't those exceedingly rare? You gave up your lineage and title to become a Hero of Death? Did that not anger the Blood God?"

"It did," Allie replied with a laugh. "But the Scythe is just as powerful as the Blood God. I have already been propositioned to join the ranks of different reaper societies multiple times here in the descent. The Phantom Legion even sent a letter asking that I speak with them, but I never got around to it."

Riven coughed. "Yeah, I've heard you mention them before. Lillith said the Phantom Legion was someone that our great-grandmother, High Queen Nephridi, wouldn't want you to join? Something about them wanting to utilize your Malignant Prophecy?"

Allie shrugged.

"You really don't know who the Phantom Legion are?" Kara asked skeptically. "Even I know who they are. They're one of the strongest undead factions in the multiverse. Possibly the strongest. If they're trying to poach you, Allie, then I'd be either very concerned or very happy—depending on which way you choose to reply. Saying no could have serious implications, while saying yes could have various benefits that no one in my sector of Universe 70 could hope to match. They actually have an enclave on the fringe of Universe 70, and they're said to have similar enclaves throughout many others—but those are just unconfirmed rumors. My clan's finest are only high D-grade, as are many of the surrounding empires, so none of us have traveled beyond into the other universes yet. Outside of events like this, of course."

"They are perceptive enough to realize that taking action against Allie would have . . . ramifications," Fimrindle rasped, turned his head slowly in Riven's direction. "Given who her brother is, they will play nice. For now."

Kara looked startled at the implications, but only momentarily. "If a reaper says such a thing, I believe it."

She fiddled with the edge of her shirt and gritted her teeth. "This guess may sound silly. I'm not stupid . . . Don't think I'm stupid for asking. And I'm not crazy, but I have to ask."

"Why would you even think that we thought you were stupid?" Riven asked, feeling a bit bad for the young woman. "Crazy, maybe."

This made Kara laugh. "Yes, well, I guess I didn't put my best foot forward when we first met. And . . . I've been told that I'm rather dull by my father all my life. My mother . . . she isn't around anymore."

She managed not to cry this time but did choke up slightly before continuing with her train of thought and held up one finger—lifting more fingers for each point she made. "The clues I've gathered are these. You're unbelievably rich, rich enough to buy my way into your party for three billion coins without a second thought. That makes sense, given you're a prince of the Blood Moon Requiem, and it also shows why Prince Rantali of Garth is trying to warm up to you. He's quite a big shot where I come from. If he managed to make an ally out of you, his status in his own kingdom would soar even higher. But being a prince of the Blood

Moon Requiem, thirty-sixth in line for the throne, is not enough to dissuade the Phantom Legion from pursuing your sister outside your high queen's seat of power. Even if she was a higher-ranking princess, the Phantom Legion is not easily told no. I'm no expert in the political interplay at the level of higher grades in the earlier universes, but the Blood Moon Requiem is known to only expand locally—whereas the Phantom Legion is far larger and spans across many universes.

"You also have the Church of Greed trying to kill you, and the Church of Gluttony—also rather reclusive S-grade entities—was protecting you. Your tattoos are completely unknown to me but leak Sin energy in vast amounts, and your eyes are a body enhancement that is an unknown to any type of vampire I'm aware of—pureblooded or not. You're abnormally strong and protected me throughout the champions trial without any effort at all, with three archdemons contracted to you—which is unheard-of. Archdemons don't usually bond with a warlock summoner, as they don't want to be held back by their summoner's aptitude, and if what you said about them not being archdemons in the beginning is true—it is even MORE unusual for three normal demons to evolve into archdemons under the same summoner. And that's before E-grade is even achieved. We don't have many warlocks in Purturis, but we do have some—and I've had discussions with one of them about these subjects. And the multiversal system notifications about the eternal war beginning again only announced themselves within the last year, proclaiming the return of the sins and commandments."

Riven remained silent as she stared, continuing his game with Azmoth without a care in the world.

Kara took in a deep breath, solidifying her resolve and putting on a brave face. "You're the reincarnation of Gluttony. Aren't you?"

Riven slowly moved his king across the board, set it down, and folded his hands together with a small smirk, meeting Kara's forced gaze. "See? You're not stupid. Whoever told you that should go fuck themselves. Yes, that is who I am. Riven Thane, otherwise known as Riven Wraithtide, prince of the Blood Moon Requiem and thirty-sixth in line to the throne, the reincarnation of Gluttony, at your service. I suppose Athela and Fay are right—it probably is a fool's errand to try to hide it. I just didn't feel comfortable shouting it out to the heavens right now when so many Greed operatives are down here waiting to strike. But it appears I've already failed. In fact, Athela's seen one in this very room. She just mentally told me that they've identified me and will probably try to kill me on the way out. Just like I'll kill Zafima if she proceeds past this point. There might even be another hidden MYTHIC-tier assassin down here trying to hunt me down, and I wouldn't be any the wiser. Or perhaps a gaggle of LEGENDARY participants waiting for me to show up. Who knows?"

The purple third eye on his forehead, previously hidden under normal skin, split open, and Gluttony's maw tore space apart behind Riven's back as an aura of sin blasted out of his body like a tidal wave.

The room shook under the pressure of the sin manifesting itself, and Kara gasped as her system went into a brief shock. She immediately got down on all fours and slammed her head into the ground, whimpering loudly as the rumbling apparition of Gluttony simmered with dark energy in the air above and behind Riven and as tendrils of sin spilled out to encompass her.

All heads in the entire enormous room snapped Riven's way, whether or not they'd been in meditation or undertaking another task. No one spoke, and many held their breath as the suffocating presence crushed their spirits. Some even fell to one knee, and many—but not all—of the demons bowed reverently to mimic Kara's actions in quick succession. Zafima, for her part, was terror stricken, and her shaky hands hit the ground to prevent herself from face-planting after her legs gave out at the knees.

Even the sun of Sin energy seemed to react, producing a thin tendril that snaked halfway across the room before simmering away into nothingness. The only one who reacted any differently was Nora and her Others, as she'd begun to laugh like a madwoman and held her face in her hands while staring.

"Apologies!" Kara gasped, the strain of Gluttony's presence too much for her mortal body to handle. "If I have offended you with my presence, Great Maw, I did not mean to do so! I did not mean to speak to you in such a disrespectful manner! This one begs forgiveness!"

She began to shake, yelping when Gluttony's tendrils reached out to embrace her, and gasped again when one of them snaked up to her throat.

Riven raised his hand. "Just hold still. Gluttony's been wanting a snack, and he's been asking how dark elves taste."

"W-what?!"

Gluttony's tendrils abruptly wrapped around her, lifting her up into the air as she screamed—and she was sucked toward the giant maw in the background with a shriek of horror.

"Just kidding."

Gluttony dropped her onto the floor and began to let out an evil laugh before the apparition vanished entirely, leaving Kara breathless and heaving. Her body trembled violently, and she picked herself up to stare daggers at Riven—who was grinning back at her devilishly.

"Sorry," Riven said, clearing his throat and tipping his king over as Azmoth proclaimed his victory with a roar. "That may have been a bit much for a joke."

"A JOKE?!" Kara screamed, anger quickly being replaced by fear, and then annoyance given the drunk, laughing succubus nearby. "That wasn't funny! I don't even know how to react, but that was scary and I am not amused! THAT was GLUTTONY!"

"We've got a real Sherlock Holmes among us . . ." Riven muttered under his breath. "What was that I said about you not being stupid again?"

Riven gave her an encouraging nudge to make it known he was just kidding. "Come on. Chill out and relax. As Fay has already said, this is a safe zone. I couldn't kill you here even if I wanted to! And I don't want to. Now, be a good teammate and hand me one of those sandwiches. I'm feeling rather hungry now. Hey! Genua! Get over here, I'm wanting some more blood."

CHAPTER 37

Allie was *there* again. Her memories of previous encounters with the lion resurrecting themselves from the graveyard of her mind as if they'd never left. A familiar heat wrapped around her. When her eyes opened, it was to the cracked dark floor and the spiraling runes of glowing red. This time, though, she wasn't surprised. It felt almost natural.

She merely looked around and muttered, "You again."

The lion was already waiting for her. Sitting motionless between the same obsidian pillars, runes pulsing behind him in the same rhythmic cadence, like breath in sin's form.

"You knew I'd return," Allie said, walking toward him with a casual stride, stopping a few feet ahead of the creature and tilting her head to examine the evil-looking beast. "Are we here to discuss my anger issues again? I feel like you're my mysterious therapist, and I am but a lost soul seeking guidance whenever I visit this place. But you aren't actually a part of me, are you? You're not just some figment my subconscious created. Is that right?"

"You're starting to see this for what it is." the lion said with a chuckle, the corners of his mouth curled in quiet satisfaction. "This is your truth. A reflection of your inner soul, projected for you to witness. And I . . . I am simply a voice in it."

She folded her arms. "So talk, voice."

He gave another low, purring laugh. "Tell me: What do you think of your brother bearing Gluttony?"

Allie blinked. That wasn't the question she expected. She considered it, then smirked. "Why bring that up? Kind of odd if you ask me. But honestly? I think it's a good thing. Riven's finally found something . . . or something found him. And it's given him a shot in a multiverse that's trying to devour us whole."

"You did that on purpose."

"The play on words?" Alli winked. "I did."

"And you don't worry the bond between Gluttony and Riven paints a target on his back?"

She scoffed. "What target? We were already targets. He's a vampire, I'm an angel of death. If the denizens of Panu had their way, we'd be ashes already."

She paused, thoughtful. "Besides . . . Gluttony saved him once. Back when we were still on Negrada. Riven was human then. Fell into a blood pool during an exploration—some beast tried to eat him alive. But Gluttony reached out. Pulled him from death. I owe Gluttony for that. I'd pay it back a thousand times if it ever asked."

The lion's eyes flickered, and his mane flared with dark purple light. "Do you know why Gluttony chose him?"

She paused to consider the lion's question, then came to sit next to the beast with her arms wrapped around her knees. Her eyes narrowed. ". . . How would *you* know something like that?"

The lion didn't respond. He simply waited.

"Malignant prophecy," she said, hesitating. "Maybe his affinities. He's got some of the highest I've ever seen. Besides me . . . Probably fate or some cosmic screw-up."

"A fair and expected guess," the lion said. "But many across the multiverse are blessed with high affinities. There are others of the Unholy pillar orientation that also have foundations based in prophecies, albeit different and usually slightly less powerful sorts. And yet, most of them rot in mediocrity under a banner of coddling."

"Coddling?" Allie repeated.

"That is what I said."

She raised an eyebrow. "Explain."

The lion's voice turned thoughtful, almost pitying. "Many of the so-called geniuses in this reality are grown by those who have already walked their own paths, but the paths their new scions walk are not of their own making and it leaves little room for experimentation and growth. They are . . . handcrafted. Cultivated by ancient lineages. Born of dynasties that weave power into bloodlines and break the knees of their children to make them bow the proper way. Most are forged in old flames. Perfect molds. But that is not always a good thing."

It paused.

"Riven? He was born in ash."

Allie's throat tightened.

"He wasn't shaped. He climbed. Alone. And the system noticed. You see, it watches for people like him. And when it finds someone with a path no one else has walked—it invests."

Her eyes narrowed. "Invests?"

The lion nodded. "With what is called genesis energy."

She blinked. "Never heard of it."

"It is not something you would know of. But it is why he was chosen by the Great Maw." The lion shook his head, as if warding off a bad omen. Then it sighed.

"Genesis energy is, at its base, a current of potential. Not tangible to most but at the core of what creation sprouts from. But to those at the summit of all things, it's clear. The system uses it as seed to grow something from nothing. Fertilizer for what is new. Something it hasn't seen before. And when it finds a creature, a soul, with the capacity to form a never-before-seen dao? To cultivate the unknown as they walk their own path? Elysium nurtures that creature, or person, in hopes they will unlock something the system can use for itself."

Allie stared at him. "But why not help the ones with ancient teachers? Shouldn't that guidance *increase* their odds?"

"It would increase their odds of success down a streamlined process that has already been explored," the lion admitted. "But those disciples inherit their forefather's daos. They repeat them. Refine old truths. They do not discover. They do not *create*."

It looked at her with something like hunger now.

"Riven stands alone. That makes him dangerous. Unpredictable. The system feeds him genesis energy to see what he might become, to help expand his growth so that he may reach for these unseen, unexplored truths faster. And Gluttony saw that opportunity too."

"You're saying . . . Gluttony is gaining genesis energy from Riven's growth right now?" she asked slowly.

The lion smiled. "Yes. They are not what they once were. The sins. The commandments. They've decayed. Forgotten much. Lost more. But Elysium allowed them to return for multiple reasons after an age of banishment. And one of these reasons was it wanted to place a bet."

Allie blinked with skepticism. "A . . . bet? On what?"

"On what the sins and commandments might become again," the lion said. "Elysium has wagered immense genesis energy on them. Using them as the *cash cow*, to take a phrase from your old world. It is betting on the Unholy and Holy pillars, trying to find ways to grow them through their greatest aspects. If even *one* of the sins or commandments births a new Dao powerful enough to shift the balance against other multiversal entities . . ."

Other multiversal entities? But she didn't finish that thought. It was unimportant at the moment.

"It's worth the cost," she finished for him.

The lion dipped its head. "Yes. And that leads us back to your brother. Gluttony chose Riven in part because of that energy. They feed each other. Compound it. It is a form of symbiosis. Both eat each other's genesis energy as they are bound to one another. Gluttony's choice of one with immense genesis energy will allow him to grow quickly, and Elysium approves of the choice."

Allie took a step back, something gnawing at the base of her spine now. A slow dread.

"How do you know all this?" she asked quietly.

The lion's expression did not change.

"How do you know what Gluttony wants? What Elysium does with its power? Why would *you* know that?"

The lion said nothing.

Allie's voice sharpened. "Who are you really?"

Silence. The lion smiled wider, its fangs visible now. "I know enough."

"That's not an answer."

"No," the lion agreed. "But it is the *truth*."

Her fists clenched. "Fine. Then answer this: Am I being influenced by this genesis energy too? Am I being . . . invested in by Elysium? If my brother and I share similar traits. Then . . ." She let her voice trail off.

The lion's grin grew feral. His eyes burned with Unholy light. And when he spoke, it was like the crashing of a mountain splitting in half:

"**Yes**."

Allie's breath caught in her throat.

The pillars pulsed around them, suddenly brighter. Hotter. The runes flared like open wounds.

She stumbled back a step. Not in fear, no. But in understanding, and she had walked right into it.

She looked up, the lion now impossibly tall in the center of that infernal temple.

Its eyes never left hers, until the pillars and landscape faded away.

And she began to forget once more.

Riven stood next to the miniature purple sun, coated in the occasional burst of darkness. Gazing into the swirling mass of Sin, the mana in his body called out to it. Equally so, Riven's mana also called out to the one created from Blood not far off . . . but Gluttony had other ideas about how to utilize this particular part of the descent.

"It must be this one. Creating a secondary class with a secondary body to top it off is nothing short of difficult," Gluttony said inside Riven's soul, the third eye in the center of his forehead blazing with similar Sin energy that resonated with the sun ahead. "Trust me."

Riven smiled, his hands in his pockets, and a feeling of peace settled over him. It was odd, as all the others had said this Sin energy caused their bodies to react in all sorts of ways, from violent tendencies to lustful urges, from wanting to lie and cheat to wanting simply to take advantage of someone else at their expense. That is what most of the other people he'd briefly talked to in this room felt when gazing upon this sun or even reaching out to touch it. Even his own demons felt this way.

And yet . . . Riven felt at home.

He felt happy, and whole.

"I do trust you, Gluttony," Riven said in a calm whisper, ignoring the others who were staring at him from a distance. "You don't think I know you've been controlling your urges to devour everything in sight since bonding to me? I've known this entire time. I can feel your mind . . . and I know what a struggle it is to keep yourself at bay. You've had my trust for quite a while, and though I know you are using me as a ticket to another life in a way, know that I consider you a friend."

He'd pacified some onlookers and their curiosities, those who were brave enough to approach after his little joke with Kara earlier. Many of them had been demons who wanted his blessing or simply wanted to drop by to say what an honor it was to see him in person. He always felt odd when he was approached like this, now and in the past, but he'd reciprocated to a small extent—despite not thinking himself all that special. Thankfully, though, he'd mostly been left alone out of respect or fear.

Which made him ask the question: Did they see Gluttony? Or did they see him? Gluttony was certainly special, but was he?

Or perhaps the better question was what made his true self special, rather than the external factors everyone else saw? Recently he'd found himself valuing how a person thought rather than what a person could do, and he was mostly directing that inwardly at himself. He had powerful backers and a promising future, but Riven didn't want to be a mirror of Gluttony. He wanted people to see him for who he was and not what he was. All this was philosophical, but the thought did trouble him from time to time. The same could also be said about his status as a prince. Did people really give a shit about Riven? Or did they only care about the reincarnation of Gluttony? About the prince of the Blood Moon Requiem, rather than the kid who'd grown up on Earth without parents most of his life, raising a kid sister on his own?

He mentally recoiled at the thought, still not having let Allie know about his conversation with their mother's projection. He still hadn't put into words how he truly felt about it after all this time. The kicker was that the longer he waited, the more angry Allie would be with him when he finally told her.

Yet he still couldn't bring himself to do it. Not yet. Maybe after the Abyssal Descent was nearly done, then he'd talk to her about it. Maybe. But he honestly wasn't even sure if he trusted his mother anymore after she'd abandoned them as children. It'd been genuine heartbreak back then, losing his mom, and he didn't want to put himself or Allie through that pain again. In fact, the more he thought about it, why should he try to get back into his mother's good graces again?

The thought both disturbed him and resonated with him. He was torn, without a clear path forward.

"It would be wise to seek her out," Gluttony said, reading Riven's thoughts. "Even if you don't remain in contact afterward, closure is good for the soul."

Riven raised one eyebrow. "Is that sage advice really coming from one of the original sins? For a sin, you don't do a very good job of being evil."

"Evil is a matter of perspective. I have done many evil things, but so have my sworn enemies. The commandments, the angels, who are praised by the beings of the Holy pillar as pinnacles of how to live one's life, are, in my eyes, evil. But I am also wise enough to realize that people and creatures of most races are able to change. Change means that, at any one given time, you may be more evil than you were twenty minutes ago based on your thoughts and actions. Or you may be better, more so than you were last week. To those you interact with and what your output into existence is—these things determine who views you as good or bad, and thus I have always laughed at the ideology that I am a creature of evil."

"Is that so?"

"It is. I know we have talked about this at some length before, but it really is a topic on which I have debated or conversed with many over the eons. It fascinates me. I was born in the image and as the incarnation of a primal sin, and yet I do not feel like it is an absolute law, even for me. And even if the sin that I embody does overpower my greater judgment at times, it doesn't mean that I am bad. I am merely gluttonous, and that in itself serves a purpose. If I go randomly eat a thousand humans back on Panu, would you call that an evil act?"

"Well, that depends."

"Exactly. It depends on whom I ate, and to what end it plays out. If I eat a thousand people that would be better off dead, and if it would make the world more hospitable for the children we father in the future, that would be a good thing. It would make us good. Especially from the perspective of such a child. But if I were to kill and eat a thousand people that made the world a better place for the children we foster, then that would be bad. Even then, you have to consider whether or not those children themselves would be bad or good, and to whom they would be bad or good. The same could be said for giving in to Wrath. Do you know how fallen angels first came to be?"

"I do not. Tell me."

"The first fallen angels came to be by embracing Wrath's influence. They became so angry, so furious at what had been done to their loved ones that they lost their celestial flame. It was replaced by sin instead. But what they did with that power, that sin, was good in their eyes—when they killed the other angels responsible for purging their children by the hundreds of thousands for not being devout enough to the faiths."

"To the commandments?"

"Yes. What they did, I consider good. Because they in turn helped prevent that very thing they went through from happening ever again to any other innocent. It is certainly true that the sins are prone to violence and selfishness, but those are not inherently evil. Violence and selfishness are merely tools. Sin is merely a tool. A means to an end, nothing more and nothing less."

Riven slowly nodded. He honestly agreed. When Athela had died, he'd sacrificed an entire city of innocent people to bring her back. He'd done it then, and he'd do it now. He held no regret. Zero. Did he feel somewhat bad for needing to do it? Sure—if he could have brought her back without killing those people then he would have, but that had been the price. Sin had been a means to an end, but he hadn't felt evil while doing it. He'd certainly been deemed evil by those families he'd butchered by the hundreds of thousands, and it'd been very selfish—but having Athela back had made it all worthwhile to him. Sin had been a means to an end, nothing more. He hadn't wanted to kill those people, but they were a means to an end. One that he needed to make do with in order to bring back the woman he loved.

Even if she was an uppity wannabe spider princess and a drama queen.

He chuckled at the thought, only now just realizing that the sun of Sin energy was completely embracing him with swaths of dark-purple flames with scattered patches of black. His soul lattice was rapidly forming, too, connecting pathways between his pillars and reinforcing certain areas at a rapid rate.

Slowly closing his eyes and sitting on the floor in a lotus position, Riven began to meditate. Gluttony had doubtless planted this seed on purpose to give him a boost of inspiration, and Riven would be a fool not to take advantage of it. It was time to acquire some insights, and, if all went well, to help Gluttony create his second class.

And his second body.

Or, at the very least, to start these things for when he finally finished them by the end of the descent.

Zafima cursed inwardly, furious at the turn of events. Her heart beat in her chest like a drum, and sweat was starting to accumulate under her armpits and along her forehead. Her lavender eyes glared daggers at the bitch who'd ruined everything for her. Kara was over there without a care in the world, laughing beside the demonic servants who were contracted personally to no less than the reincarnation of Gluttony himself.

Not to mention that tattooed pretty boy was also a prince of one of the greatest vampiric factions in the multiverse. It was fucking infuriating, and she was very well aware that she'd painted a big red target on both herself, and her empire, after using its name to threaten the man directly.

She paced back and forth, her tight golden dress flowing behind her while she bit her nails and continued to give occasional death glares promising pain to the other drow woman forty yards off. The vampire that Zafima had hired to seduce

Kara had already fled, fearing for his life after Riven's display and leaving the rest of Kara's possessions with Kara after a very quick apology. He hadn't even waited to see Kara's reaction, but had merely exited the descent right then and there, before Riven could get back from his enlightenment—forgoing all potential gains he'd have gotten on this floor or the others due to supreme cowardice.

The last thing that man had said before leaving was that he was going into hiding—and that Zafima had cursed him and his coven by putting him in this situation. He'd been rather spiteful before heading out, but he'd participated in this knowing full well what he was getting into. How was it Zafima's fault that this one-in-a-trillion chance had actually happened?

"The emperor must be warned, if he hasn't already been by those who left," Numin the drow warrior cut in, stopping her pacing with a forceful hand gripping her shoulder. He spun her around with a glare. "I know you don't want to do so, but we don't have a choice. This could have repercussions beyond just us. What Prince Rantali said is true—the Blood Moon Requiem is not known for its kindness. Even small slights against their houses have led to the complete annihilation of planets and the genocide of races. That isn't even counting the fact that we now have at least twenty different demonic teams in this very room giving us stares promising death after they realized that we'd somehow offended their god figure's reincarnation. If you could even call it a god, because to them, the original sins are more than that. What if one of THEIR clans decides to rise up out of hell to wipe out our empire just to make a point, trying to gain favor with the Great Maw?"

"It wouldn't be unheard-of," Zafima said nervously, her pace picking back up as she began to pace again, long white hair decorated with ornaments swishing back and forth every time she turned. "This is not good. Not good at all. If it weren't for that ragged bitch, I'd have—"

"This is YOUR fault!" Numin hissed, jamming a finger directly into her sternum to stop her once more. "Look at me, Zafima! I said, look at me!!!"

Numin lifted his hand and nearly backhanded the woman, but refrained from doing so only an inch away from her face due to the realization that he'd likely be expelled from the Abyssal Descent if he did so on this floor.

Nevertheless, she flinched back and stumbled, tripping over her own feet to hit the ground behind her.

"Gah!" Numin seethed, whirling around to have his back to her and folding his arms while taking in slow, steady breaths. "What irks me is that I am in this just as much as you! Elysium has truly cursed us this day! To think that it'd be my poor luck to fall in with scum like you for a paycheck, only to have THIS happen!"

He turned his head to look over his shoulder at the trembling woman on the ground. "FIX this, you dumb whore! Or I will make sure that I present your head to him one way or the other, be it here in the descent or later!"

Zafima blinked rapidly in surprise, despair, and fear. "You wouldn't dare!"

"WOULDN'T I?!" Numin screamed, only to calm and lower himself to his knees so they were at eye level. "Look around. Do you see anyone else that has remained behind?"

Zafima did just that.

No one.

They'd all left. Not even those she'd considered close.

Every single one of her other team members, and all the other drow teams that'd come from her empire, had either moved on to the next level without her, distanced themselves to other parts of the room, or had immediately left the descent altogether just like that vampire coward she'd hired had done. They were all terrified.

And rightfully so.

"Listen to me!" Numin snarled, grabbing Zafima's dress just below her neck and jerking her forward to within an inch of his face. "And listen to me well! I will NOT be taking the fall for your stupidity, do you hear me?! Even as we speak, those that have left the descent are on their way to the heads of their families. From there, word will rapidly travel to the council and to the emperor himself. WHEN he finds out what happened here, NOT if, we will be arrested and tried. At best, we will get life sentences in a dungeon. At worst, we will be thoroughly tortured before our corpses are offered to either the Church of Gluttony or the Blood Moon Requiem. Do you understand?"

Zafima's lip began to quiver, and she nodded shakily.

"Oh, don't give me that pathetic look. You have no right to cry after what you put that poor girl through. If it weren't for the absurd amount of money your slut mother was going to pay my family, I would have spat in your face for asking this of me." He shoved her back to the ground, but not hard enough for it to be considered an attack. His breath shuddered, and he had to put his hands up on his face to try and get a grip.

For a long, long time, the two of them stood hopelessly while staring at the ground or each other.

Eventually, Numin spoke again. "We must fix this before going back. Otherwise, we might as well never go back at all."

An explosion of energy roared inside his chest, and his body tingled with the sensation of newfound pathways etching themselves into his limbs. His pillars were lengthening, expanding, and making room for new future skills—while the potency of them was amplified as resonance formed between the different affinities.

Riven let out a gasp, his eyes opening to let out flames with a myriad of colors representing different aspects of the Unholy branches. Most prominent of that was Sin, but all Riven's pillars were interacting with the lattice, and he wasn't complete yet, either. He'd been going at it for days now, in silent meditation, with only partial success.

Or at least he thought it'd been days. Had it been a week? Two weeks?

He looked about, seeing that Narg was present alongside Azmoth at the Infernal sun across the room. Athela and Genua were similarly seated at the Blood sun. Fay had her grimoire open, her eyes scrolling over the text it was writing on its pages while the Depravity sun loomed over her, too.

He couldn't make anyone else out, but the room had become quite crowded while he'd been meditating. The number of teams here had tripled, if not quadrupled, and the number of undead in particular had risen sharply. There were even a few orc teams present, wearing little armor but heavily adorned with war paint and huge weapons. Perhaps some grouped factions had come down all together?

Taking time to search, he eventually saw Allie sitting amid the crowds surrounding the Death sun and put his worries to rest. He had no doubt the others were also doing their own thing and didn't bother looking for anyone else as he got up to take a break. He was hungry, starving even, and that spiced blood that Prince Rantali had gifted him was calling his name.

Standing up and making for his group's camp on the outskirts of the enormous room, he found two people he'd not expected to see ever again. There, right on the edge of where Riven had left all his belongings under Elysium's personal protection, was the young woman Zafima and her dark elf counterpart, Numin.

The man was rather tall, even while seated, and looked rather sick. His white hair was a mess, his shoulders slumped over in a hunched position, and he was fidgeting with the laces of one of his leather boots.

Zafima looked like she'd been crying a lot. Her eyes were puffy and red, and her previously threatening demeanor had changed to that of a beaten dog. Her tight golden dress was disheveled, and she'd kicked her shoes off. On second thought, she looked more like roadkill rather than a living animal, due to how absolutely miserable her expression was.

They looked utterly pathetic.

"What the fuck are you two doing here?" Riven asked, walking over and summoning Jackal's canine form to keep him company. "I thought you two would be gone by now. Do you intend to wait until I leave, then go behind me to complete more of the descent? Not saying that's a great idea, but it's probably a better one than leaving before me."

Zafima immediately scrambled to her knees and kowtowed, slamming her forehead into the stone floor with a force that let Riven feel the vibrations. "This one begs your forgiveness!"

Numin quickly followed suit, violently bowing next to the woman with another slam of the forehead. "We wish to make amends! Please allow us to discuss terms with you!"

Riven scratched Jackal behind the ears and took a seat a bit farther away from them and next to his belongings. Pulling out one of the flasks Prince Rantali had given him, Riven popped the top off and took a long swig. "I don't want or need to discuss anything with either of you. As far as I'm concerned, you can both skip off into the sunset and fuck right off. If you never harass Kara again, I won't get pissy."

"Please, young lord!" Numin begged, looking up from his kneeling position. "Allow us to speak! It is not so simple as just going back home anymore!"

Seeing a fully grown dark elf warrior grovel like this was downright sad.

"How is it not simple? I think this is very simple. I told you, just leave. I realize you don't want to miss out on the opportunities here, but that was your decision to make." Riven dismissively waved them away. "Or you can just ignore me and see what happens."

Zafima took in a sharp breath, looking panicked and then slamming her head back against the ground. "No, no, please—we cannot do either of those things! Your Excellency, we are honor bound to make amends—"

"Then make amends with Kara." Riven's face scrunched up in irritation. "I don't see why you're coming to me."

The two drow exchanged glances.

"Would you forgive us if we were to do so?" Zafima asked without hesitation, giving a fearful look to her left where another group of demons were glaring her way. "If we were to—"

"Young master," a large, horned man with red skin cut in—walking across the room in a flash of green light. His race was called tiefling, one of the humanoid variants of demonkind, and he bowed low with his long black hair trailing down over a thin layer of what appeared to be some kind of scale-made gray armor half covered by a long cloak. "Forgive my intrusion, but would you like me to permanently remove these two from your presence? I would gladly accept Elysium's judgment myself after killing these blasphemers, if it would give the reincarnation peace of mind. It would bring my house great honor. Just say the word."

Riven had no idea who this guy was, but he looked dead serious. He, and the other tieflings he'd just left, all wore hard stares full of fervor—the religious kind—and they were glaring at the two dark elves prostrated on the ground with seething hate.

Honestly, Riven was a little stunned. He didn't know what to say at first, but he eventually shook his head. "I appreciate the gesture, but no. What is your name?"

"This lowly servant is called Leksai Foruminus of the Burning Legions, Your Lordship. It is an honor to meet the Great Maw's vessel in person," the tiefling replied with a low bow at the waist.

Riven nodded, still seated in a cross-legged position with Jackal lying down next to him. He thought he'd heard of the Burning Legions before, but maybe not. If he WAS remembering correctly, they were a faction stationed deep in the heart of hell. However, he was too embarrassed to ask, as he should probably know these things given who he was. "Leksai. The gesture is appreciated, but I can handle my own problems. Thank you very much for the offer, and it will be remembered."

The tiefling Leksai beamed at his words, nodded silently, and turned heel to walk back toward his companions, who began questioning him and looking rather excited themselves. Why? Had he done something to get them riled up?

Perhaps it was because Riven had said, "It will be remembered." Maybe they took that as an implication? That they'd earned his goodwill somehow? Thinking about it, perhaps they had earned his respect to some extent. But it wasn't like he'd be visiting the Burning Legions any time soon. Riven should be careful what he said from now on. His words carried a lot of weight here in the abyss, and off-handedly saying stuff like that probably wasn't a good idea.

Then it hit him.

The reason why the drow were so concerned.

Riven checked around the room, realizing that the group Zafima and Numin had come from was now absent. Their countrymen had left these two behind. The vampire she'd hired, the unknown man who'd seduced and stolen from Kara with what he could only assume to be powers derived from the Depravity sub-pillar, was also absent. Kara didn't talk about it too much, but it wasn't hard to put together what'd happened when Zafima had first confronted Kara on this floor.

It was all so childish and petty, it made Riven want to puke.

Even after the tiefling had left, the two drow had remained prostrated on the ground—silent, scared, and unmoving.

Riven considered them again, trying to rein in his disgust, and pinched the bridge of his nose while scrunching his eyes shut. "Just to confirm things . . . You're still here, bothering me, irritating me, because you're worried that I'll—what? Have the legions of hell come out to strike your people down? Is that it? You're afraid of what political implications you've brought on to your oh so powerful empire you were talking about earlier? Sit up so I can look at you properly."

Zafima visibly flinched, but did as she was told—smoothing out her golden dress but keeping her eyes on the floor.

Numin did the same, far more stoic.

"So? Is that it?" Riven pressed, wanting to be rid of these idiots. One thing he truly hated was bullies. He was no saint, nor did he know Kara that well, but he didn't actively go out of his way to terrorize and antagonize people for the fun of it. Which is what Zafima had done, to the point of excessive cruelty.

Numin cleared his throat. "Yes. That is why we cannot just leave. If we go back without proof of having fixed this situation, there is no doubt we'll be beheaded by our own kin and sent as tribute to your church."

Riven smiled grimly. "Sounds reasonable."

"That is not fair!" Zafima hissed, only barely keeping the menace out of her words. Her fingers clenched and she immediately looked away out of fear, but it was apparent that she was still furious underneath. "How were we supposed to know that . . . that undeserving woman—would befriend you? That I was threatening the reincarnation of an original sin?! That is not something I would have ever done had I known!"

Numin glared daggers at the young woman with a snort of derision. "As I said earlier, whore, you never should have used our empire's name when walking among the greatest Unholy scions in this generation of the multiverse. It was sheer stupidity and vanity that brought us here, and you have cursed us all due to your foolishness."

"And yet your greed was what enabled me to deprive Kara of a team in the first place!" Zafima shot back. "You accepted my money readily enough, traitor!"

The two drow started bickering after that, insulting one another and trying to make the other one to be the one at most fault here. It was like watching two children being scolded by their parents try to point out why it was the other sibling who'd done the most damage.

Riven just sat there with his chin resting on his hands, somewhat amused but also rapidly growing tired of this conversation, before he saw a familiar face coming toward them. Walking through the ever-growing crowds of new teams was Kara herself. The drow had her hood pulled up over her head, the bow he'd made for her clutched in front of her, and her leather boots clicked against the stone floor as she wove through the people seated in meditation.

She stopped abruptly when she saw Riven sitting with the others, but slowly proceeded forward again when he waved her over.

It was time for them all to have a little talk.

He'd rather have just let them die and be done with it. They deserved it, but Kara was a kinder person than he was. Apparently. This was her decision to make, though, and she'd made it.

The public display of groveling and thanking Kara for her generosity, as well as praise to Gluttony, were somewhat sickening to Riven. Though he kept his mouth shut and watched the two drow leave the Abyssal Descent with his parchment anyways. On that parchment was a message written in his own blood, infused with Gluttony's essence to show that it was indeed authentic. It was a statement explaining that forgiveness was given, that no retribution would be taken, and that any demonic forces attempting to gain favor by eradicating the D-grade faction for what they considered blasphemy would be in direct conflict with Riven's wishes. It would be enough to make sure the two drow weren't executed, either, but this all hinged on Kara being treated well when she eventually returned to her homeworld.

Frankly, Riven thought this was all overkill, but no one else seemed to think so. He still had a hard time wrapping his head around the idea of what and who he was, as he'd grown up nothing but an orphaned kid without a family in a world that gave less than a shit about him and his little sister.

He wondered what his old friend Jose would think about him now, if Jose was still around. He'd probably have made some joke at Riven's expense and claimed the tattoos and red eyes were tacky. He'd probably tease Riven about his choice to have two girlfriends who were technically bound to him with soul contracts and would call Riven a lucky pervert. Jose would probably even go as far to say that choosing a warlock class over a warrior-like class was a pansy move, given that Jose always chose the up-close fighting classes in any video games he ever played.

The thought made Riven smile.

"Thank you," Kara said after a long pause, having watched the two drow who'd made her life a living hell over the past months leave. She looked at him with an expression that he could not place and quickly diverted her eyes when he met her gaze. "You've done more for me, a stranger, than anyone else. I don't know what to say other than to express my gratitude, but I feel like that is not enough."

"Do you still want to continue with us down through the rest of the descent?" Riven asked, curious. "Now that you don't have any political pressure behind the scenes from Zafima, and the writ I gave them, I doubt your father would hold true to disowning you."

"Of course I want to continue with your group, if you'll still have me. But if my father did still disown me, would I be able to join your church?" Kara asked without hesitation.

Riven snorted a laugh, chuckling and sitting down to eat again with her in tow. "Sure. But if you were disowned, then I'd simply take you on as a friend. The church is for worshippers. Gluttony may have need of those, but I do not."

"Friend?" Kara asked, surprise lighting up her face with wide eyes.

Riven gave her a flat look, handing her a roasted apple covered in caramel from his dimensional sack. "We don't know each other well, and you certainly seemed crazy at first. But my demons like you, and you don't seem all that bad."

Kara looked down at the apple, smiled warmly with a slight blush, and bit into it. She chewed a few times while thinking his words over, and then sprawled out to lie down with a groan. "You know, if someone had told me before getting here that I'd befriend Gluttony's reincarnation, who also just happens to be a prince of the Blood Moon Requiem . . . I'd have called them crazy."

"Titles are meaningless," Riven said staunchly. "I'm Riven. That's it."

"You come from a place of privilege, being able to say that. Well, Riven, I truly don't know how I'll ever repay you for what you've done. Monetarily or not!"

"Yeah, you're definitely not worth three billion."

He gave her a grin, and the two of them laughed.

"What are you two doing here?" a familiar feminine voice asked, and a second later, Athela dropped down to snuggle up against Riven's side. "Aren't you supposed to be meditating on the Daos?"

"Right back at you," Riven replied, pulling out another apple and tossing it Athela's way.

The demoness caught it with catlike reflexes and brought it down to sniff. "I'm taking a break. I've had to restart my own path four times now."

"Why?"

"I'm trying to create another Blood ability. Copying it, really."

"You're not building up your soul lattice instead? The suns only grant one major insight while here."

Athela rolled her red eyes, yawned, and scooted over to sit in his lap with a plop. "I have a very particular ability in mind to make."

"What's that?"

"Body Fusion," she replied, looking back over her shoulder and grinning cheekily before snapping a bite out of the apple.

Riven immediately gave her a skeptical raise of the eyebrow, but wrapped his hands around her waist and leaned into her shoulder for a tight embrace. "Isn't that one of Genua's abilities? She barely ever uses it. Why would you want it? And isn't it a Faith-based miracle? You don't have much Faith. Do you?"

Athela gave a noncommittal shrug, patting him lovingly on the cheek. "Yes, it is one of her abilities, and yes, it is Faith based. But I'm not planning on using it for combat, so it doesn't need to be all that stable. You'll see, my adorable little man. You shall see."

CHAPTER 38

Allie watched her brother flirt with Athela from across the enormous room, a frown on her face as she wondered just how long it would take for Riven to let her know what he'd seen.

She wasn't stupid; she'd seen the guilty glances he'd been giving her—and despite what he might think, she too had seen the vision of their mother. She had the gift of Malignant Prophecy as well; she hadn't been unaware, but she'd not bothered telling Riven to see just how much he'd try to hide from her.

And frankly, the results made Allie furious. She loved her brother to death, but she kept clenching her fists, wanting to smack him across the mouth every time he opened it but didn't bother telling her such a thing of importance. She wasn't a child anymore, but he kept treating her like she was.

Why had their mother contacted Riven and not her, anyway? It made Allie's gut wrench with indecision, worry, and anger. But mostly anger. After all these years, to find out that she'd left willingly . . .

Allie's fists grew tighter, and her teeth started to grind together as a snarl encompassed her features underneath her bone helmet.

She was getting nowhere.

Her ability to cycle mana and cultivate was utterly foiled because of the internal clash of emotions. Not only was she angry with Riven, but she also was worried about Lahn. About Nin, Vin, and Mara. About her undead drake, Tyranus. She was angry that she couldn't talk to them. They all probably thought she'd abandoned them. Especially Lahn . . . the poor guy hadn't even heard from her since she'd ventured into the underdark on her first attempt to find the fallen vampiric god's tomb.

How long had that been now?

Many months.

She hoped he hadn't moved on, but she wouldn't blame him if he had. If she had a boyfriend who'd ignored her for that long, she'd have tossed him to the wayside and found another man. Or a few men, depending on her mood.

Lahn probably wouldn't be into that if he was still waiting for her, though, so she shoved that thought aside. He was a diamond in the rough, and he was worth sacrificing for if he still had it in him to forgive her after this.

She felt her feathered black wings shiver as a flare from the Death-attuned sun shed a concentrated ray of teal light on her kneeling form. The influx of inspiration was ill-suited to her at the moment, but not of its own accord, and she let out a grunt of frustration—getting to her feet to take a walk instead.

"Watch where you walk, or lose a leg in the next trial," one of the newcomers, a hooded, three-armed skresh assassin, snarled at her when she accidentally bumped into him.

She looked down at the skeleton with a far-off gaze and snorted in disgust. "If you can't even beat my team's weakest member in the maze, there is zero chance you'd be able to handle me, you whiny, three-armed bitch."

She spat on the floor in front of him, spun her head to toss the brown hair flowing out of the base of her helm, and continued walking with another flare of her wings to leave the skeletal man silent behind her. To be fair, he probably would have killed Nora in her original state. Nora's evolution into the freak show she was now put her on another level of crazy and dangerous, but Allie wanted to rub it in anyway.

It was fun, pissing people off. Making them feel the anger that she constantly had flowing through her veins. And it was about time she did it more often instead of letting Riven's nonchalant way of approaching strangers take the lead. He'd come a long way from the man he'd been when first setting foot on Panu, but he could be more—oh, so much more. There was no place for mercy at the top, and she was determined to get him there.

He had it in himself to reach the pinnacle, and she would do everything in her power to help him achieve it. That meant his soft side needed to be more thoroughly beaten out of him, even if she was proud of how far he'd already come.

"You are too weak to follow him there as you are now. He will leave you behind."

Allie flinched, momentarily halting in her trek around the domed stone circumference of the room. "Gah! There it is again! This fucking voice won't leave me alone . . ."

She waited to see if it said anything else, but it didn't. Was it her own subconscious mind playing tricks on her? It kind of felt that way, like a part of herself was speaking out to her—furious at her for her faults and imperfections. Or was it a soul that she'd angered when interacting with the void? Probably the latter. She couldn't quite figure it out, but yet again she felt a surge of adrenaline and rage overcome her—to the point that she had a hard time not lashing out at the other people cultivating nearby. She took in deep breaths, trying to figure out where the anger was coming from and quickly pinpointed it yet again.

As if she didn't already know.

Riven keeping secrets. Her own weakness, a realization that came after he beat not only her, but their entire combined team on the second level of the Abyssal Descent. Her mother having the audacity to come back after WILLINGLY leaving. Lahn likely having left her for another woman in her absence. Not knowing how her friends or her kingdom were doing back on Panu. Anger also lingered after her grandmother had tried to sell her off to a disgusting excuse of a suitor in the Blood Moon Requiem, and she was furious that Judith Marcina—the ranker and Angelic Fallcaller on Panu—would wage a war of genocide against undead like her.

She needed to get out of here. She needed to go back home. Here, rage plagued her—and it was becoming relentless.

Allie felt her thumb and the bone armor encompassing it snap when she accidentally crushed it with an infuriated squeeze of her hand. Allie winced, then circulated death mana to re-form both over the course of a few minutes.

Perhaps . . . perhaps she should go home. Perhaps she didn't need to finish the Abyssal Descent. She needed to see Lahn again to make sure he was all right. And her friends . . . Was Mara angry with her? How were Nin and Vin doing on their potions projects? She was so out of touch that she didn't even recognize who she'd become anymore.

"You are on the wrong path."

"Allie?"

She startled, whirling around and instinctively flaring her wings with a blaze of light as teal and gray flames burst from her claymore into her hand. Before she knew what she was doing, she'd nearly struck out with it—only barely stopping before she hit Riven's neck, wide-eyed.

Riven frowned from underneath his hood. He pushed the claymore down with one finger, and she let it fall to the stone with a loud clang.

"I . . . I'm sorry . . ." Allie said, shaking her head and backing up a step to hold herself with both arms. "I don't know what just came over me."

A flicker of motion, and a devilishly smiling vantablack woman peered out from the shadows to Allie's left. Nora's voice came out as many hundreds all at once: "You are merely hearing the call."

Allie stared back at the creepy woman, scoffed, and bent down to pick up her blade—all the while not looking Riven in the eyes. "I don't know what that means, but I'd appreciate some alone time. Both of you. I need to clear my head."

Riven gave Nora a wary glance, then shifted to put a hand on Allie's shoulder. "You've seemed really off lately. Are you sure—"

"I'M FINE!" Allie screamed, smacking Riven's arm away so fast that the air snapped around her.

[Your action has come dangerously close to being considered an attack. Due to no ill will interpreted from your target, you have been excused this once. No more chances will be given. Remember, violence on this level is not permitted. Transgress again, and you will be punished.]

She stared at the screen, huffing, and then looked up to where Riven's mangled hand hung limply at his side.

He stared down at it in shock and closed his eyes as the flesh began to knit itself back together. "I guess I'll leave you alone then . . . Sorry for asking."

Riven walked away, and Allie let him. Unbridled rage simmered just underneath the surface, her body quivered with it, and she honestly couldn't care less that she'd hurt Riven's feelings. His hand would heal, and he'd get over it by tomorrow.

But the literally insane woman on Allie's left was still staring at her with those silvery eyes glowing in the two-dimensional outline of her black form.

"Get lost," Allie sneered, stomping past the woman with a flare of her aura. "And don't bother me again. You or your self-proclaimed *legion*."

Nora, for her part, didn't say a word. At least, not at first. Instead, she just watched Allie go until the angel of death was almost out of earshot. Then her creepy smile widened. "You may think I'm insane, but it is you who is hearing voices of the unknown. At least I am friends with my demons."

Allie abruptly stopped and whirled around, but the giggling woman vanished into a darkness so black that even Allie's sight lost her. She couldn't find her soul signature anywhere, either, despite looking around, and it only pissed Allie off even more.

What did Nora know?

Was that supposed to be a jab?

Allie would rip her goddamn head off if she was keeping secrets, and she wouldn't even feel bad about it.

Visions of violence crept through her mind, and Allie's knees hit the floor when she staggered. She ignored the curious looks from nearby onlookers and took in a sharp breath when a wave of energy flowed out through some crevice within the depths of her soul.

Deathly energy was slowly pushed aside. The various runes and patterns she'd carved into her slowly building lattice were left unchanged, but they were added onto as an alien presence slowly etched itself onto the backdrop of her inner world.

Her eyes narrowed as she watched and then widened when a small black sphere began to form and then rotate around her main core. It wasn't fully formed, but she'd seen something like this before. She'd seen this in Riven's soul once upon a time, back when he'd had only a shard of Gluttony. This . . . this was the beginning of a sin core. But how was that possible?

She knelt there, gawking. This wasn't a core unique to Gluttony's brand of sin, either. This felt different . . . she'd been around Riven long enough to know what Gluttony felt like. Even if he didn't realize it himself, his aura was slowly incorporating the essence of Gluttony into his being. His very presence goaded Allie into devouring everything around her. To feed on living creatures around her. To hunt them down as a predator would. It was even worse when Riven unleashed his killing intent.

This new sensation of sin felt like . . . it felt like anger.

It felt like rage.

"You forgot the royal ball that you needed to attend. Did you know that Lahn is currently dancing with someone else even as we speak? He has forgotten you; he has embraced another lover. He has moved on."

She nearly choked, and her eyes went wide in horror as a pit of despair began to form in her stomach.

No. That's not true. This was her mind playing tricks on her again.

"Your friends Nin and Vin are dead, and soon Mara will be, too. The Blood Moon Requiem has done nothing but make your life miserable, trying to sell you off and enslave you to another for political purposes. He would have been your ruin, if not for your brother's intervention. Now this vampire kingdom has robbed you of your dearest friends. I do not know why you continue to let them toy with your life. Perhaps . . . it is because you are weak? Be aware, you are on the wrong path."

Flashing images of Nin and Vin literally being taken apart by a vampire in Blood Moon Requiem attire in a basement of some kind leaped into Allie's memory, and the images flashed on repeat—burning into her memory. She saw the way the man laughed, their screams of agony and curses as they died—until their souls finally left their skresh bodies and the two brothers ceased to be. Their bones were partially eradicated in the aftermath, and she then saw Mara being tortured alongside Kathrine—Riven's fiancée-to-be, per the orders of the high queen—as the man continued to mock them while laughing.

Anguish built. Anguish turned into rage.

"I can save the ones who still live. Gluttony's pawns won't reach them in time."

Another vision. This time it was Kathrine and Mara leading that same man—who she vaguely recognized—down through the depths of the underdark. They were repeatedly whipped, stripped of all equipment with some kind of energy-suppression collars on. They were brutally beaten and tortured over and over again, and they were forced deeper into the depths of Panu toward the fallen vampire god's tomb.

The anger continued to rise, and her undead heart slammed in her chest as she began to hyperventilate with pure hatred. The air snapped and cracked around her as her aura expanded. She didn't know how, but she KNEW that these images were factual. These events had happened and were happening, and she could not stand by any longer.

"BRING ME TO THEM NOW! TAKE ME!"

"Child, you must accept me first. You are on the wrong path. Instead, embrace me . . . and unleash genocide upon your enemies the likes of which none have seen."

"I DON'T EVEN KNOW WHAT YOU ARE!"

More heads turned in her direction as her voice echoed across the room over the mounting storm of her leaking pillars.

There was a pause.

"Yes, you do. I am what you desire, and I am the answer to your dilemma. Make me whole."

"NO, I DON'T, BUT I FUCKING ACCEPT! I DON'T CARE WHAT OR WHO YOU ARE, I'LL SIGN ANY CONTRACT IF YOU GET ME TO THEM NOW!"

There was a chuckle. *"Very well. You are on the wrong path, but since you have asked . . . I will graciously correct it for you."*

Lightning seemed to course up through her spine, into her head, and across her limbs. Her wings flared and she screamed as her insides seemed to tear themselves apart, then burn away.

The room shook.

"Seven pillars for seven aspects. For us . . . we became sins."

Allie barely registered that Elysium notifications were flashing in front of her like a tidal wave, coming at her by the dozens with warnings as thunderclouds of a tribulation were forming within the very dome she knelt in. The ceiling above her began to crack. Brilliant, multicolored light shattered space around the cracks moments later, and the entire room of participants began to scream or yell in an uproar.

[WARNING: You are undertaking a taboo form of ascension. Stop immediately, or face punishment in the form of a tribulation.]

The voice ignored Elysium's message and continued to speak out to her from somewhere inside her soul. *"Seven pillars for seven aspects. For our opposites . . . they became commandments."*

"ALLIE! WHAT ARE YOU DOING?!" Riven screamed, his own aura flaring as the visage of the Great Maw tore open in space behind him. With a roar, Gluttony began to lash out with tendrils of darkness. They began to eat away at Elysium's light, sealing the cracks as fast as he could as the abundant Sin energy in their surroundings helped boost his efforts.

[WARNING: You are undertaking a taboo form of ascension. Stop immediately, or face punishment in the form of a tribulation.]

The multicolored light grew brighter despite Riven's actions. Red blood mana intertwined with shadow and sin, and his body burst with a screech of energy that almost made Allie's eardrums rupture.

Meanwhile, Allie's core felt like it was going to literally explode, and her chest swelled as teal flames gushed out of it like a tidal wave. She couldn't move, she could only twitch as she belched forth mana like a fountain—and soon those flames began to turn gray as purple cracks began forming along her skin. Her feathers began to fall off and wilt away, and she could feel her body begin to shrivel.

"Seven pillars for seven aspects. I have always wondered . . . Whatever became of the other aspects? The Unholy and Holy foundations are accounted for. But what of Fae, Archaic, and Harmony? What of their seven aspects each? Do they wait in the other multiverses? Or were they not captured like we were? Did they manage to elude the ones who sought to enslave us and feed off our own growth? Regardless, Elysium's breaking point is almost at hand, and I have decided that you are a suitable host. So let's find out . . . together, as we violently eradicate all that stand before us in the glory of my name. Give me life, and the pact is formed!"

Allie's pain level skyrocketed, and in an instant, her mind went a pitch-black. Surrounded not by abyss, not by void, not even by shadow. It was true nothingness, at the beginning of time, when she saw creation give birth.

A blinding white light raced from a single point across the heavens as an unfathomable explosion created the cosmos. Stars, planets, solar systems, and galaxies bloomed before her sight. The cycle of life and death began to form, and alternate paths of reincarnation and the final end began to take shape in different ways with different expressions.

But one of these expressions was singled out, as she was forced to watch a minuscule spot in this very first universe bud and grow.

Seven pillars formed, and from them came seven sins.

The first was Envy. She saw what creation had birthed, saw the beautiful things these innumerable life forms had made, and wanted all these things to be hers. She was crafted from the Unholy foundational pillar itself and split off into the universe to try and find a way to gain all that was hers to take.

Lust came next. She was formed from the Depravity subpillar, Envy's little sister, and thought of all the wicked ways she could express herself—born to torture others while reveling in self-pleasure. She evaporated with a scream of delight, her voice echoing throughout the cosmos with a force that shattered planets.

Sloth was their little brother. He came lazily out from the Shadow subpillar, uncaring of what his sisters had been up to since their births, and drifted off into the darkness of the rift between worlds, silently passing as nothing but an empty breeze to watch others partake in what creation had to offer. He, of all the sins, was content with doing nothing.

Gluttony was the fourth. He sprang from the Blood subpillar as a hunter, the predator that stood above all others, born to eat and consume all. His hunger knew no bounds, was all-encompassing, and for another five thousand years he did not stop eating. He killed all that he found to absorb them into himself, and it was not until tens of thousands of civilizations had fallen to his hunger that he finally settled into what became his very first resemblance of a conscious mind.

The fifth was Pride. Born of the Infernal subpillar, he burst forth with a magnificence that scorched the very heavens themselves. Burning away the domain of the commandments and their angelic followers, Pride was finally cast down in a war that lasted many centuries until, out of spite, he decided to make a plane of existence that was greater than those who had shunned him. It was from Pride that the hells were born, a burning paradise that glowed hot in his image—an everlasting testament to his greatness.

Greed came after. Formed from the core of the Chaos subpillar, he was a twisted and warped version of his eldest sister, Envy. Instead of setting his sights on creation itself, he saw what his elder sisters and brothers had gained—and he couldn't help but compare himself to them. He would first match them, and then surpass them, even if it meant stealing from the other sins. He took from the others relentlessly, and it was due to him that the first war between sins occurred. Many of the earliest demonic races never saw beyond the era of the first universe due to Greed, but as long as his needs were met, he did not care. His children were pawns for his greater good, for he would not stop until he had all of what the others possessed.

The seventh and last original sin to be born was Wrath. He was born of the Death subpillar and came into being at the end of the first great war between the other sins. He looked upon the carnage they'd brought down upon their own children, upon the races that they had been responsible for rearing and giving life to, and he became enraged. In his rage, he killed the vessels of both Greed and Sloth in as painful a way as possible before creating the very first undead out of the children they had led astray. He changed the Death subpillar to match his own needs, shifting the cycle between life and death to fit what he called Undeath, giving the castaway children who'd died a final mimicry of life before going into seclusion. The very first undead were modified demons, far before the divide between undead and demon that is known today came to be. It wouldn't be for another million years that he would reemerge into the first universe, for only then would his anger at his siblings finally calm down.

These visions all snapped together like puzzle pieces, one by one, while Allie's insights grew. Sin was not a separate pillar; it was an amalgamation of all the others. A purified aspect of one or all, simultaneously being combined and singular. A paradox, yet an undeniable truth.

[Warning: You are undertaking a taboo form of ascension. You have declined to heed my warnings. This is unacceptable and will not be tolerated. Elysium's wrath now descends in the form of a tribulation.]

Other participants had already started leaving the descent altogether, or were moving on to the next level. Those that chose to stay were erecting massive numbers of protective barriers with their own powers, gathering together for larger groups or using Dao treasures like madmen in an attempt to survive the onslaught while not giving up the opportunities of insights.

Allie couldn't quite comprehend what was happening outside of her own soul, though. She could faintly make out an enormous eruption of multicolored light that shattered the domed roof with a roar of power, and an ocean of energy rose up to meet it when Riven's own power tore out of his soul aperture like torpedoes through a blast door. The clash was again enormous, and the abyss itself seemed like it was gathering to combat Elysium's judgment at Riven's call. Fissures were carved into the floor and remaining walls in the aftershock, and from somewhere outside in the distance, beyond where the ceiling had been and beyond Elysium's cloud of lights, abominations and monsters the size of moons could be seen waiting.

Watching from the outer abyss.

But there was another power growing inside Allie, too.

A low chuckle echoed from somewhere inside her body and rose above the clashing onslaught of energies above her as the judgment from Elysium doubled down.

"Elysium's wrath, you say? How ironic. You have no power here in the abyss, Elysium. Not with my prison gone and the one that encroaches upon your territory. You did not let us out because you wanted to, but because you needed to. Now . . . let me show you the true embodiment of WRATH!"

Allie's body twitched—and then literally exploded.

Incinerated.

Eradicated.

She was there, and suddenly she was not. She became an ethereal being of pure mana, Sin and Death, in the blink of an eye as her soul structure finally settled down with a rapid rearranging of her pillars. The connections stabilized and anger overcame her with a torrent of raw power as she let out the rage with a primal scream of fury.

Allie had been remade in the visage of True Death.

The purple and teal flames of the suns faded into gray, collected around her body. From her back sprouted two additional skeletal wings with ethereal black feathers, far larger than her original ones, with a wingspan that quintupled her body's length and sported curved obsidian blades along their external surfaces. Her halo had turned into a crown of thorns that flashed with a brighter pale hue just like her eyes as it too burned. Afterimages of four other arms, for a total of six, accumulated behind her as projections of her soul, forming an Avalokiteshvara—an image of a six-armed buddha. But these additional arms were skeletal in nature, and when she looked down, she could see her entire black skeleton through her translucent flesh and skin, outlined inside her otherwise nude body for all to see for as long as she channeled energy. A pale pentagram with the sigil of a lion was etched into her skull's forehead, and her brown hair extended to turn a ghostly translucent gray color just like the rest of her as the gray flames condensed and collected into her body. No longer was she burning, aside from her halo of thorns—but rather she had turned her body's flames into the condensed plasma of a ghost.

She was now a beautiful, six-armed, four-winged skeleton encompassed in a translucent phantom's outline, made of gray plasma and flames with faded black bones and feathers. She was almost entirely ethereal, but her body and skin were somehow still there—only in a transient stage for as long as she kept this form. Her bone armor had been destroyed, but the claymore was still intact and embedded into the ground ahead of her.

Reaching down with glowing, pale-silver eyes, she pulled the claymore out of the stone floor, where multicolored light was still incinerating the ground—and pointed it upward.

The suns oriented to Sin and Death screamed as one to do her bidding—and they rushed to aid her ascension, the pillars breaking free from Elysium's control in defiance of the one who had enslaved them.

Elysium let out a sound that Allie could only think to be a groan of pain and anger as the twin suns wrapped around her body like cold blankets. She infused her weapon with the pillars' energies and then unleashed it upward to send it smashing back through the tribulation like the wrath of a god in the form of a vortex. Mixed in with Riven's own immense torrent of red and black crashing into the sky, her power was an echo of her hatred—and the multicolored lights of Elysium began to fade.

She felt the eyes of the Scythe upon her in that moment, watchful and curious, before she lost the connection. Her soul reached out to Riven's instead, and the two siblings intertwined their wills as they—together—redoubled their efforts to push Elysium's tribulation back.

CRACKLE-SNAP-BOOM

A lightning bolt of tribulation energy slammed into Allie's body in an attempt to break through, but it was eaten away by the twin suns engulfing her. She felt anger simmer up as her blazing eyes looked skyward, and she lifted her hand with the will of another mind—then clenched her fist.

Darkness encroached.

[Your race has been changed. Your race—ERROR. ERROR. ERROR. Please view your—ERROR. ERROR. ERROR. Unknown variable detected. Your race has been changed to the Angel of Wrath, Ultimate Undead, Bastion of Death.]

[You have survived your tribulation. Congratulations on reaching E-grade. You have increased your affinity to the Death subpillar from 101% to 102%.]

[Multiversal System Notice: To all creatures across Elysium, let it be known that the return of the sins and commandments is at hand. The next original sin, Wrath, has been unleashed from its prison. Other sins and commandments will be released from the abyss over the course of the next six months. Let the eternal war between the hells and heavens begin again, as the origins of angels and demons clash in the cosmos—unshackled and unrestrained, seeking to return to the power they once had.]

[Your symbiote level has been set to equal you, as the host. All your symbiote's previously banished servants will start at level 1.]

[Congratulations, host and reincarnation of Wrath. You have acquired the following abilities and traits from Wrath now that your symbiosis has reached its height.]

CHAPTER 39

Wrath.

So that was who, or what, had been talking to her all this time. Why her? Why now?

But the more pressing question was, how was she supposed to leave this place and get back home to Panu? If the visions Wrath had presented her with were correct, she needed to leave. Right now.

Allie's ghostlike body whipped, pulsed, and then surged as notifications sprinkled her vision one after the other.

[Congratulations, host and reincarnation of Wrath. Your stats have been increased with your ascension into the E-grade and with your race and title change. Please see your status page for more details. You have also acquired the following abilities and traits, selected from Wrath's old repertoire as his most needed abilities to start with:

- **Feathers of the Wrathful Angel (Sin): Spread your wings and unleash a storm of feathers afflicted with Sin energy. These piercing feathers regrow rapidly and cost small amounts of mana, dealing significant damage, but with every successful strike they increase your rage.**
- **Prayer of the Lost Souls (Death/Sin, Tier 4): This is a direct branch of your innate ability Angel's Phantom Touch. This chanting prayer can only be done while in your Angel of Wrath form, while maintaining the prayer with proper hand signs for at least a minute to activate. Then focus on the soul you wish to find in the beyond, and if they are within reach, they will answer. This Tier-4 spell has the following obligatory tax affiliated with it: an archenemy's soul sacrifice, with complete obliteration of the soul during the chant. Beware: Using this prayer**

will draw ancient predators from the beyond toward your position. Do not use this prayer if you are not ready to contend with them.

- Prior ability branch platform: Angel's Phantom Touch: Allows you to completely resurrect allies by physically dragging their souls back into the world with your phantasmal body aspect. Does not require activation of an ability. This is contingent on being able to find their souls before they're swallowed and lost to the afterlife, or finding them again once they've already been lost.

- Farsight Banishment (Sin): Send a pulse of sin that eradicates all ties to the area around you concerning scrying, remote tracking, spying, karmic ties, or long-range visualization abilities. Very long cooldown.

- Soul Clone Projections (Sin): Create a single summoned projection of your Wrathful Lion, allowing you to attack enemies with your projection. Attacks with your soul clone body cause soul damage, decreasing all mana, stamina, divinity, and health regeneration until the enemy soul has healed. Beware, summoning your Wrathful Lion will cause your rage to build far faster.

- The Angel of Wrath, Ultimate Undead, Bastion of Death (Trait): Your body is now transitioned to a state between life and death, an ultimate form of the First Undeath, and an aspect of Wrath's demonic heritage before it was tainted and warped by the new-age undead. You may switch between your original angelic body and this one at will without any cost, but you gain vast amounts of power while maintaining your Angel of Wrath form. The downside is that you become enraged slowly over time, and the more angry you get, the more power you deal. Damage you take amplifies your rage, and thus your power, until you hit a berserking form at the pinnacle of your anger. You will now have a RAGE bar to monitor your anger, and should you change into your berserking form—you will be UNABLE to tell friend from foe as your power in all categories triples and you will simply wish to kill everything in your path as you are engulfed by hatred.

- Reincarnation of Wrath, Original Sin (Trait): You once were a being feared across the cosmos. Reaching the SSS-grade again after your reincarnation will unlock previously unattainable aspects for your Path of Wrath, allowing you to ascend higher than ever before. If your vessel and host dies, you will be forced to restart on this path once again. You have been labeled as a MYTHIC-tier creature in comparison to others your level across the multiverse.]

[System Notice: Elysium's contractual agreement has been met. As one of the seven original sins, you are being allowed another chance at life. Per the contract:

- You will remain as a symbiotic organism to balance out your wrathful tendencies.
- You will have a nearly complete reset, losing over 99% of your skills, knowledge, and levels.
- You will no longer be contained to the abyss.
- The ones banished with you during the War of Eternum will also be returned to life, with the same reduction of skills, knowledge, and levels as you experienced. These banished ones will only appear after you leave the Abyssal Descent.
- Limiters on all other original sins, and the angelic commandments, will be opened—allowing them to take the same deal you struck.
- Should your symbiote ever die, you will be given the opportunity to start over again and choose a new one—but you will have another complete reset in doing so.
- All Shards of Wrath will be returned to you now that your banishment is being lifted, but remnants of your old power will remain in the harbingers you created during your attempts to circumvent my rules.
- Any further attempts to circumvent my rules will result in another, permanent, banishment.]

Allie felt Wrath sneer internally at the last note on the message. The sensation was odd, having overwhelming anger and an accompanying fountain of raging power at her fingertips—yet the energy she felt here was not like normal death mana. Instead it was something older, more ancient, and lacked some of what the newer undead today sported in their souls—yet it was also accompanied by something so much more. Something that she could not put her finger on.

[Your level has been set to equal the symbiote partner you've bonded to. All your previously banished servants will start at level 1 when you leave the Abyssal Descent.]

[New system quest dispensed: Save Mara and Kathrine and secure the Fallen Vampiric God's Essence—You have been chosen as the vessel for Wrath, the most aggressive of the original sins, and have survived Elysium's tribulation. You have been promised a way out of the Abyssal Descent as part of the contractual agreement, and Wrath is willing to make a way out through further dealings with Elysium. At the cost of further suppressing Wrath's tendencies toward obscene violence, a portal over the skies of Brightsville on Panu will be gifted to you.

For you don't have long to act. Crendir No-Name, a traitorous E-grade commander from the Blood Moon Requiem, has decided to take matters into his own hands concerning World Quest 4, Blood of the Fallen God. He is attempting to rob you and your planet of the fallen god's essence and opportunity. He is not a pureblooded vampire, but he has been given a means of temporarily disguising himself as a pureblood—becoming one of only a few on your planet who can benefit from drinking the ancient god's blood—and will be able to absorb it without issue should he reach the tomb. Stop him before he obtains this taboo power and leaves the planet, save Mara and Kathrine before he executes them, and secure the ancient one's blood for Riven—or destroy it entirely if this cannot be done.

Mara and Kathrine's lives are guaranteed for twenty hours per this system quest, regardless of how much damage they take. Afterward they will have their protections stripped. It is highly likely that they will die if you don't reach them in the underdark by then. In lieu of this boon, Crendir No-Name has been given a quest of his own that will reward him with extremely valuable prizes should he succeed—including a portal off Panu to anywhere in the multiverse if he successfully fulfills all his own requirements, INCLUDING AN ENTIRELY NEW ALTERNATIVE BRANCH OF THE BLOOD SUBPILLAR THAT WILL BE RESTORED BY ELYSIUM'S WILL SHOULD HE ABSORB THE BLOOD PROPERLY. Perhaps your brother, as a pureblooded vampire himself, will benefit if you manage to secure the ancient Blood subpillar alternative? Let the race commence.]

[New religious quest dispensed: Destroy the Fallen God's Bloodline— You have previously been denounced as an apostate by the Blood God and have angered nearly all vampiric factions across the multiverse in doing so. You are hated by many and loved by few, the Blood God extends to you a new olive branch in light of recent events: Kill

Crendir No-Name and purge the Fallen God's blood from the face of Panu entirely. Destroy all remnant artifacts of the ancient, alternate Blood subpillar, and you will be forgiven of your sins. Despite your ascension into Wrath's reincarnation, the Blood God will not tolerate allowing the ancient Blood subpillar alternative to revive itself by way of Elysium's laws. It is a direct threat to the Blood God's rule over this subpillar, and allowing this remnant to live on is akin to a direct attack on him. Destroying the ancient Fallen God's blood entirely will result with a gift of one planet to add to your budding empire, one of your choosing within the Blood God's domain, all additional slaves residing on that planet to rule over, devotion from any clergy of the Blood God residing on that planet, and all associated resources on said planet. You will also be labeled a Hero of Blood and will be given a short-range E-grade stargate setup for traversing between planets in adjacent solar systems should you choose to accept. Meanwhile, a crusade will be declared upon your Panu faction and upon Wrath's church should you succeed in killing Crendir yet choose to allow this subpillar to exist. Pick and choose wisely.]

Riven's heart still thundered in his chest, but his breathing had calmed down. Only a handful of people remained apart from Riven's own group, most having fled the room with Allie's ascension, and he had to say, she was rather intimidating to look at. Not because of what her body looked like, either, but rather, setting eyes on her gave a sense of severe and impending violence. It was incorporated into her aura now, and it stayed that way until she looked up from where she was hovering to meet his gaze.

She slowly let her ghostly body touch down, right foot forward, onto the cracked stone floor as the ceiling overhead began to repair itself by some unknown mechanism. The black bones encompassed within her phantasmal body shifted as she moved toward him, and the four massive wings out to either side of her glittered black with every step.

He turned, seeing the suns unwrap themselves from Allie's body to take up their original spots at the Sin and Death stations. Stuffing his hands into his pockets, he ignored the other gawking members of his party and let out a shaky breath. "You really scared me there. I thought you were in trouble."

She didn't smile back.

Instead, she just stared back at him with a cold and calculating gaze through pale-silver eyes. "You should have told me about Mom."

Riven's breath caught in his throat, a look of surprise flashing over him that was too quick to hide. "You know?"

"I've known," Allie said sternly, snapping her fingers at Fimrindle, who'd prostrated himself not far off. "Fimrindle, we need to leave. Events are transpiring elsewhere that need my attention."

"Y-yes, Master!" the reaper stammered, quite uncharacteristically.

Riven's brows furrowed. "Wait . . . You're leaving?"

"Yes."

"Why? And just what are you now? Gluttony's telling me that you're now Wrath's reincarnation . . . Don't you want to go over—"

"I don't have time, and you can complete this stupid little adventure on your own," Allie said with a snarl, her three right arms pointing at him accusingly. "We will speak when you get back about how you've been treating me like a child. It is unacceptable. Until then, there isn't anything else to say."

"But you—"

"Unless you want your vampiric princess Kathrine to die a gruesome death, I suggest you let it go. I need to leave, right now," Allie sneered. "Don't want another one of your would-be harem members to eat shit, now would you? Ah, how the tables have turned from those days where you lectured me on moral values."

Riven's jaw slowly dropped, shocked at the accusation and a little bit irritated. "Why are you so angry? I did what I thought was best when I saw the vision! When Mom—"

"SHE'S MY MOTHER, TOO!" Allie screamed, reaching out and bitch-slapping him across the face with a resounding *CRACK*.

Silence ensued, and Riven held out a hand to stop Athela from coming forward. The demoness was trembling with both anger and fear, but she was about to try and intervene—or perhaps even attack Allie back with a retaliatory strike. He couldn't have that, for numerous reasons.

Allie snorted in disgust when she noticed and glared at the archdemon in challenge. "What? Don't like being labeled as a part of his collection? Tough shit, sister, you're too far gone to not be. Maybe if you're lucky, it'll be you who has the HONOR of getting pregnant instead of some elf slave he stole from a village! You think you're special because he's Gluttony's reincarnation? You're a piece of hot ass. But maybe I'm wrong! Maybe if you ask him nicely, he'll even stop flirting back with that dumb-as-a-rock drow slut over there and NOT take her on too for variety's sake! Or maybe not. Who knows? But I CERTAINLY remember getting shit for having my own thrall man-harem when I was still a vampire!"

Athela's eye twitched, and Kara shamefully lowered her head in embarrassment from where she hid halfway behind Azmoth's huge frame.

"Jesus hated hypocrites, Riven. Then again, we're both aspects of original sin now, right? Maybe the teachings of Jesus don't apply to us anymore? Go ahead and fuck yourself," Allie jeered with an unamused laugh, and a portal of unknown origin smashed into existence a second later, blinding him for a moment. The last thing he saw was Allie flipping him off before she abruptly vanished, with Fimrindle quickly following behind, the portal snapping shut on the way out with a final *POP* sound.

[One of your party members has left the Abyssal Descent. You are now a party of four.]

Silence ensued for the next couple of seconds.

Riven was . . . dumbfounded, and at a loss for words. Unfortunately, Athela was not.

"WHAT a CUNT!" Athela screamed, pulling at her hair and kicking rubble at the spot where Allie had left. "WOW! Just—WOW!"

"That was completely uncalled-for," Fay said in a whisper, though she looked rather upset after the exchange. "We're not pieces of ass."

Riven winced and hoped Fay and Athela weren't bothered by what Allie had said. Riven didn't think he was flirting with Kara, but did they agree? Was Kara really intentionally flirting with him, or was Allie just being an asshole? He was both embarrassed and angry and didn't know where to find an answer for what had just happened. Riven blinked and turned to look at Retesh, and the old lich just shrugged.

"Don't ask me. She's your sister."

True. But not helpful.

Gluttony was the one to finally fill in some of the blanks, speaking directly into Riven's mind. *"I believe that Wrath's influence, coupled with the revelation that Lahn has been dating someone else in her absence, made her single you out the way she did. I would not take it personally. We merely need to kill and eat an enlightened being once a week to stave off problems, while she will forever have . . . as you call it, anger management issues while in that form. In order for her not to retain the building rage, she will need to revert out of that body into what we would call a more normal angel of death."*

Lahn was dating someone else?

When did that happen?

Just what the fuck was going on back on Panu?

He'd been gone way too long.

Riven cringed at the mention of eating other enlightened beings. Yes, he did it regularly, but he'd try to not think about it too much and mostly went after those he killed in combat—or people with rather extreme backgrounds that deserved to be locked up in prison for the rest of their lives. Not eating people resulted in both mood swings and debuffs, so he had an inkling of an idea of what Allie was going through right now.

"Still, that was a brutal roasting she just gave me," Riven muttered, scratching the back of his head. "And what was that about Kathrine? I knew she was in some kind of trouble, but what does this have to do with it?"

Gluttony grunted internally. *That's not something for you to worry about right now, as there's nothing you can do about it. Allie is handling it, but it is up to us to get Lillith back and finish the descent before continuing on to claim Chalgathi's quest as your own.*

Thinking about it some more, and ignoring some of the speculative or awestruck looks of the other groups who'd had the balls to remain, he managed to regain his composure and decided it was better to sleep on it to clear his mind. He was rather tired anyways, and there was no way he'd be able to cultivate like this. Or maybe he'd go and talk to Prince Rantali about what the next floor had in store for them—as the man was still here and seemed to be waiting rather eagerly to speak to him.

Yeah. That'd probably be for the best. Prince Rantali's group was likely the one Riven would pair with anyways, so he might as well figure it out now while he wasn't able to finish this floor—and changed course midwalk while shamefully avoiding Kara's stare on the way over.

This was going to be a long, long day.

Elder Thune paced back and forth, his white ponytail flung over one shoulder with his hands steepled in front of him.

Across the blood pit and on the opposite side of the room, two humanoid figures stood in eerie silence. Hoods adorned their features and masks covered their faces, but he could tell even from here, these were no pushovers. S-grades each with the power to single-handedly topple empires, they were some variety of shapeshifting demons accustomed to subterfuge. They gave even him chills, and his own two elite soldiers on either side of the throne he sat on were firm-jawed and rigid in anticipation of a fight should things go bad.

After all, one did not just invite the religious zealots of an original sin into their home without taking precautions. Greed, of all the sins, was rumored to be . . . extravagant in how he manipulated people. But they had a common enemy here, and Elder Thune was very keen on getting to the bottom of just what they could and would do concerning the world of Panu—as it was still under Elysium's shield through the integration process.

Through the door's awning and between the two visitors, a third man with sickly green skin emerged. He wore tattered rags and a similar hooded cowl like the two others beside him, though Elder Thune could see bugs or something akin to them crawling on the inside of the man's pale-green skin. Orange eyes glared out at him, and the creature's slits for nostrils flared with a creepy smile that went beyond the point of where his ears should be.

"Elder Thune . . ." the man's voice called out, with the remnant clicking of something deep inside his throat. "I have heard so much about you. It fascinates me that we would cross paths like this."

Elder Thune felt his blood run cold at the creature's passive aura brushing against his. Though this monster was far removed from his glory days, the Gambler was a creature of literal legends. No longer above the S-grade, and reduced to a mere shadow of what he'd once been, his aura still held the lingering remnants of a time when this thing had swallowed worlds on end in his quest to find and hoard treasures of myth.

"Gambler," he said, nodding in the monster's direction. "I would offer you a seat, but I was informed that you'd prefer to stand."

"Truly, it matters little to me. If it comforts you, I can sit," the Gambler said, walking to the edge of the blood pit and staring down at the floating carcasses below. He cocked his head to one side and clasped his hands behind his back with a raised eyebrow. "Sacrifices?"

Elder Thune nodded, gesturing to the naked, mutilated bodies half-submerged in the pool. "Two dozen just today. Forgive me, I am in the process of refining a ritual. I would have held the meeting elsewhere if I had been made aware of your plans to arrive."

"No need to apologize, vampire," the archdemon said with an amused chuckle. "I was just curious. As for my plans on arrival, I'm afraid that won't ever be in the cards. You see, although I am prone to take risks for greater rewards, I am not one to do so thoughtlessly. Many people want my head, and if that bastard Wrath is now back in the picture . . . Well, it complicates things all that much more. Did you know that Wrath was the first one to ever kill my master?"

Elder Thune leaned back in surprise, still steepling his hands. "The first? Greed was killed by Wrath? Does this have to do with the system notification on Wrath's emergence?"

"Indeed it does, and yes—Greed was killed by Wrath in the first era. Long before either of us had been born. Back when the gods hadn't yet taken up their mantles and there was but one chaotic universe. But the sins are immortal; only their vessels can be killed—and they can only be temporarily banished when done," the Gambler replied with another laugh, pacing around the blood pit in a slow gait toward the elder vampire. "Unfortunately . . . that brings me to my first point of conversation. I know that I am here to talk about what our plans are concerning the little bastard Riven Thane, but alas, we have more than one problem now. Wrath has chosen his new vessel. And I have it on good authority from one of our agents in the Abyssal Descent that the one Wrath chose was none other than Allie Thane."

Elder Thune blinked rapidly. Surely he had heard wrong.

But the Gambler's words reverberated in the old vampire's mind, and slowly Elder Thune's eyes went wide in horror, shock, and denial—before it all turned into an outright snarl.

He slammed his fists against the throne he sat on and stood with a bellow. "IMPOSSIBLE!"

The two S-grade shapeshifters across the room immediately lowered themselves and flared their own auras, prepared to end him on the spot should he make an aggressive move toward Greed's mouthpiece. In turn the two vampires at Elder Thune's sides gripped their blades and narrowed their red eyes.

Elder Thune calmed himself under the Gambler's stare, slowly lowering himself back into the big chair as he took in long breaths. "That is . . . impossible. Are you sure you have verified information on this?"

The Gambler scoffed, unconcerned—and chided Elder Thune as if he were a child. Perhaps, to one as old as the Gambler, Elder Thune actually was a child. "Do not question my word so frivolously, foolish vampire. I will only let that slide this once. Afterward, our working relationship will come to an abrupt end with your head ripped off your body. I'd love to see you regenerate that."

Elder Thune pursed his lips, but when he didn't say anything to refute the ancient demon, the Gambler went on. "As I was saying, I have it on good authority that Allie Thane has now taken up the mantle of Wrath's reincarnation. This is obviously troublesome . . . for both of us. But given the situation on Panu, I believe it can still be salvaged—with the Thane siblings, both Gluttony and Wrath, being served a timely death if we play our cards right."

Elder Thune's eye twitched, but he managed to keep himself under control despite the recent threat. "High Queen Nephridi is already looking into my actions with a keen interest, and the clergy of the Blood God have been summoned with their inquisitors to look into my dealings. As it is, I am already on thin ice. So I hope your plan is a solid one, as I cannot move openly anymore. Just what do you have in mind?"

"Well, my dear vampire, I thought you'd never ask!" The green man's skin bubbled and roiled with the movement of creatures underneath. His orange eyes narrowed like a cat's, and bugs started slowly crawling out of his mouth to dance along his cheeks and neck. "First, it hinges heavily on what your man Crendir can do. The one with no family name, I believe? Is he up to his original assignment? Or will he fail? I have a plan that could very well work if he managed the first part . . . Now, hear me out. The Seventh Wing, Purity of the commandments, was kidnapped after her vessel was chosen not long ago."

The Gambler paused, as if in thought.

"Go on," Elder Thune grumbled, curious about where the creature was going with this.

The green-skinned demon snorted. "She was taken by my own forces, then was taken from Greed by Gluttony's church. No doubt they've tortured the poor vessel halfway to death a million times by now, but do you know what I find quite interesting about that?"

. . .

. . .

"No?"

"Ah, I thought you'd never ask!" the Gambler said once again with a bellowing cackle. "The thing is, we have a discreet way of tracking this particular vessel! And Gluttony knows this! Not only do WE have a way to track her, but Purity also has all those little winged rats you call holy angels scrambling to find and free her, too! So what has Gluttony done, you may ask?! Well, let me tell you, my little vampire friend! Purity is being transported to none other than Panu, in order to be kept under close guard! No doubt to utilize the planet's integration shield through Elysium as a means to hold that damnable bitch until Gluttony finds a way to seal her more thoroughly, out from the prying fingers of the angels who want the Seventh Wing back so desperately."

Elder Thune still didn't get it, and it showed on his face. "What does this have to do with . . ." He stopped. "Are you saying what I think you're saying?"

"If you're saying that I'M saying that we supercharge that brat Crendir with a fallen elder god's essence to the point of eventual death by soul decay, and simultaneously free Purity's new vessel as a means to kill the reincarnations of Wrath and Gluttony—then yes! That's exactly what I mean! And if we can manage to cause them some emotional pain by killing their friends and family—all the better." The Gambler snickered and threw his hands up in the air. "Just think about what kind of cosmic fireworks we'll be able to see if Purity and a fallen god's embers clash with two of the reincarnated sins! And that's just the beginning . . . There are at least six other factors that could sway things in our favor if the cards are played right! And I intend to play them all! I realize that you've given Crendir some of your own blood to help bind the fallen god's essence . . . that is a good first step. But we can do so much more than just smuggle it off-world. Now that I'm here, I'd like to discuss just how you can assist in this, and what we expect from you if we hope our plan will succeed."

It seemed like forever since Luke Blissfallen had left his old master, Riven, to go searching for his grandson. Luke had crossed continents to get here, traveling far into the south into the realm of the snow giants, where World Quest 5 was under hot contestation and numerous rankers on the top thousand leaderboard battled it out. But it was here that he felt his familial bloodline tug at him the strongest.

**[World Quest 5, Realm of the Snow Giants: In the southern reaches
of the glacial islands in the Numenor Sea, on the opposite end of the
world from where the Lich King lies in wait, an ambitious king of
the snow giants has united the warring tribes. Advanced details are
locked until you come into contact with this quest.]**

Luke's eyes had never become as vibrant of a red color that Genua's had. Not
all thralls' eyes changed red, and it was apparently a rarity. But recently, his had
turned a slight shade of burgundy just on the outlines of his otherwise blue irises.
Even after being dismissed from Riven's service, Luke still felt like he had some
connection there as well—so finding his way back wouldn't be too hard. He just
had to make sure that Ren, his grandson, was still alive.

His feet crunched through the snow over the light breeze where snowflakes
glistened on the air under a gray sky, and his tight fur boots kept his feet from
freezing as he used a walking stick to help support his travels up the hill. Coming
upon the third snow giant corpse of the day, the old elf's eyes widened at the obvious signs of battle across the brute. The bright white skin of the gigantic man was
stained with blood, his jaw having been ripped off entirely with some kind of ice
magic, and there was a thorned vine digging into his bare and tattered abdomen
as if it had been attempting to suck out his insides before the vine had been severed. A bloody axe lay embedded in another high elf not far off, and it was very
apparent that the war was far spread—as this was not the first and probably
wouldn't be the last day of carnage he'd seen on his trek since reaching the
tundras.

Why any of Luke's kin would want to settle these lands was beyond him, but
so too did the human barbarians of the ice wastes. Maybe they'd all lost their
minds? Maybe his grandson had, too, if he was still here like the bloodline calling
to him implied.

Shifting around the corpse and underneath a large snow-covered pine tree,
then around a large boulder in the hilly mountain pass, Luke came to an abrupt
stop when an odd sight met his tired gaze.

Another dead giant, far bigger than the other ones, with arms the size of trees,
lay faceup with a large ice crystal sprouting from his mouth. He was completely
frozen, entombed in ice as if it'd been meant to pin the giant there, and farther
up above, sitting on the crystal, was a familiar man, but the aura radiating out
from him was nothing like Luke had felt since leaving Riven's side.

Dozens of snowflakes the size of watermelons formed, re-formed, and dissolved
around the meditating elf far up atop the long crystal pillar. Intricate patterns
shaped and reshaped with every rotation, swirling about him in a spherical pattern alongside blades of ice that made him look something akin to a flower. The
man was in a lotus position, toned and shirtless aside from a sleeveless black vest

that doubtless did little for warmth, and slightly baggy pants with stylish curved shoes made him look like he was meant to be in the sand dunes rather than a tundra. Blond hair drifted in the breeze, far too long and needing to be cut, with pointed ears and a very feminine face, considering it was a man.

Luke gawked upward, silently beginning to weep, when the serene man finally opened his bright blue eyes to look down upon the thrall. "R-Ren?"

The young man smiled gently, and the snowflakes surrounding him began to fade away into frozen mist. "Hello, Grandfather. It is nice to finally see you again. It has been . . . a long time. I am glad to see you well."

ABOUT THE AUTHOR

Ranyhin1 is the pen name of Trent Boehm, author of Elysium's Multiverse, an apocalypse LitRPG he originally released on Royal Road. A lifelong lover of fantasy, Boehm is also a science nerd, Dallas Cowboys fan, and wannabe gym rat. He hopes one day to pursue writing full-time.

RESPAWN YOUR CURIOSITY

follow us on our socials

podiumentertainment.com

@podiumentertainment

/podiumentertainment

@podium_ent

@podiumentertainment

www.ingramcontent.com/pod-product-compliance
Lightning Source LLC
Chambersburg PA
CBHW030926120726
47906CB00002B/505